ADRIFT

SWATI M.H.

Kismet Publishing

Copyright © 2022 by Swati M.H.

All rights reserved.

No part of this book may be reproduced in any form or by any electronic or mechanical means, including information storage and retrieval systems, without written permission from the author, except for the use of brief quotations in a book review.

This is a work of fiction. Names, characters, businesses, places, incidents, and events are either a product of the author's imagination or used fictitiously.

Cover: Cover Me Darling

Editing: Silvia's Reading Corner

Publicity: Give Me Books PR

ALSO BY SWATI M.H.

Feel the Beat Series

My Perfect Remix

(Single-dad, friends-to lovers romance)

My Beautiful Chaos

(Fake-relationship, second chance romance)

My Darling Neighbor

(Enemies to lovers, surprise pregnancy romance)

Fated Love Series

Kismet in the Sky

(Slightly forbidden, second chance romance)

Surrender to the Stars

(Enemies to lovers, hospital romance)

AUTHOR'S NOTE

Content warning: This book is intended for a mature audience. It deals with themes related to death of a spouse that may be triggering for some readers.

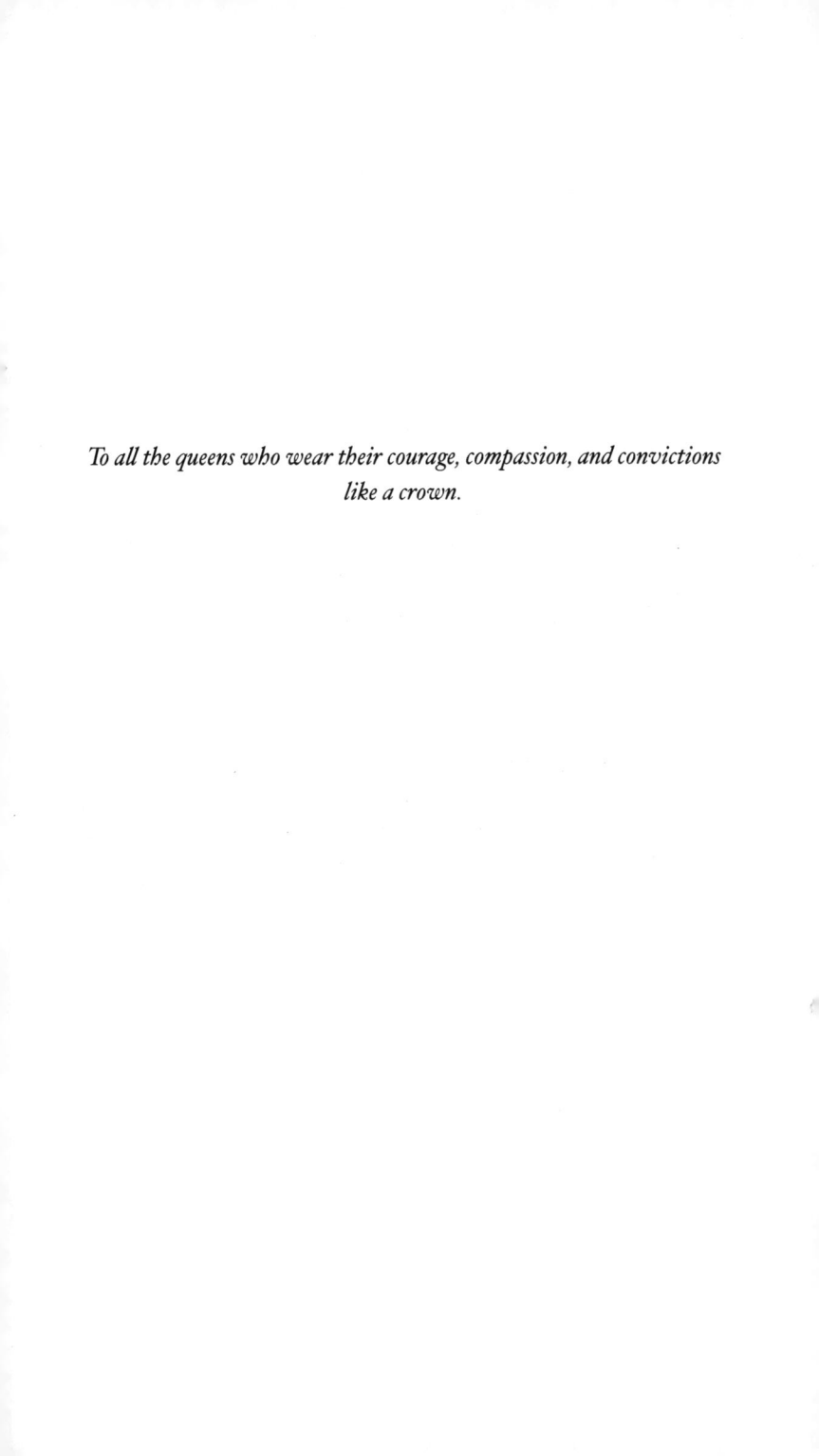

To all the queens who wear their courage, compassion, and convictions like a crown.

"Serendipity, it's one of my favorite words. It's such a nice sound for what it means, a fortunate accident."

— SARA THOMAS, SERENDIPITY

PROLOGUE

Darian – One Year Ago

"No!"

This can't be happening.

This has to be a nightmare. There's no other explanation.

"No." My heart rattles violently before coming to an abrupt stop. I shake her by the shoulders. "No, no. This is not how this was supposed to be. Wake up, right the fuck now, Sonia!" I cup her cheeks, taking in her expressionless face. "Please. I can't do this without you. I can't raise him without you, sweetheart."

I feel the gentle caress of someone's fingertips—the doctor, maybe—on the back of my arm before she squeezes my elbow softly. "I'm sorry, Mr. Meyer. We did everything we could."

A tear lands on Sonia's face and I track it down her neck. It creates a damp spot on the hem of her hospital gown before I realize it's mine. My vision blurs as the knot in my throat threatens to cut through my skin. "Please. Please wake up."

"We'll step out and give you a private moment with her before . . .." I hear the doctor's voice trail off behind me before the entire team shuffles through the door.

Private moment? This wasn't the private moment I'd ever anticipated. One with my wife's lifeless body after celebrating the happiest moment of our lives together–her giving birth to our son.

Our son.

The wish we made together. Our hope. Our fucking prayer.

And now he's sleeping alone in the nursery, without the comfort of his mother's arms around him. *He'll never have the comfort of his mother's arms around him.*

How could this be happening? How could a day that was meant to be the happiest in our lives turn into a nightmare? A catastrophe?

I'm not a stranger to nightmares, the vivid dreams that have me waking up in a cold sweat right before daybreak. The kind that feel so real, so intense, that long minutes pass before I figure out where I am and how I got there. I've learned to jolt myself out of them before they have me facing the worst part. Before I hit rock bottom.

Before I find his lifeless body floating in the river again.

So why can't I do that *this* time around?

I run a hand over Sonia's forehead, caressing her hairline and feeling her clammy skin under my fingertips. "I'm sorry," I whisper, hoping that somewhere, somehow, she might still hear me. A sob pulls from my throat. "I'm so fucking sorry, sweetheart. This wasn't how it was supposed to be. We were supposed to leave here as a family, remember?"

Today was supposed to be our *new* beginning. A fresh start after the months of confusion and strain between us.

Sure, we'd been more distant than we've ever been over the past ten years, but this baby was supposed to change our trajectory. He was going to renew us . . . *fix us*. It's why we decided to name our little boy Arman. A name with the same Persian origin as my own, meaning 'hope.'

But I feel nothing but hopelessness seep in.

The doctor said it was a pulmonary embolism—a blood clot that likely started in her leg and traveled up to block an artery in her lung. They weren't able to get to it in time to save her.

Or the new beginning we were supposed to have together.

I lift her cold hand and press a wobbling kiss over the backs of her long, listless fingers, staring at her face, completely devoid of its usual animation. I used to tease her that even when she wasn't speaking, her face would do all the talking for her. I'd know exactly what mood she was in by the shift of her eyes and the twist of her lips. She never needed to utter a single word, and everyone would know exactly what she was feeling. She was loud without being so.

God, what I'd give to hear her complain about my shitty dishwasher loading technique or my inability to disconnect from work.

I puff out a trembling breath. Where do I go from here? How do I cope with something like this? Nothing and no one prepares you for this day—a day where you have to walk over the jagged rubble of your shattered life and accept this new war zone as your home from here on out.

Bile rises to the back of my throat and I lift myself off the side of her bed, falling into the vinyl-covered excuse for a chair beside her inside the delivery room. Another sob emits from the depths of my stomach as I take in her lying form on the bed once again.

Rubbing a hand over my mouth, I press my fingertips into the edges of my jaw before rolling Sonia's phone in my hand a couple of times. Taking in a shaky breath, I stare at the picture of us on her lock screen—the one we took six years ago at the foot of Heavenly before we went up to spend the entire day skiing and celebrating. We'd just secured a loan for our own ski and kayaking school that day, and we wanted to commemorate the occasion in the only way we knew how—on the mountains.

In fact, this was the same mountain we'd met on almost ten years ago, when I was just a twenty-two-year-old ski instructor with nothing to my name besides my beat-up old truck and my skis. I lived for those damn mountains, like a snow leopard who refused to venture anywhere close to the warm land.

Sonia and a couple of her college friends had booked a private skiing lesson with me as a graduation present for themselves, and by the time our three hours were up, I'd found myself asking her to dinner.

A dinner that led to a year of dinners and wedding vows taken selfishly in private. A dinner that set fire to every bridge in her life. A dinner that had cost her her family.

And I was culpable for it.

I unlock her phone using the same passcode she's had over the past ten years—her sister's birthday—and scroll down her contacts list until I find the name I'm looking for. A name—a title—she no longer used after marrying me.

Mom.

My finger hovers over the call button before a cough rumbles through me, inciting another wave of tears. How am I going to tell them? No matter how estranged Sonia and her mom are, no parent can endure such a phone call.

Before I can press the button to make the inevitable phone call, my own phone buzzes inside my pocket. It's been vibrating nonstop with congratulatory texts from my brothers and our team at the ski school. I'd sent them a picture of the three of us—me, Sonia, and Arman—smiling into the camera right after Arman was born last night.

Who would have thought *that* would be the last picture I'd ever take of us together?

I run a hand through my hair before pulling out my phone.

Garrett: Yo, bro! What's the latest? How's my nephew! When can I come see him? How's Sonia?

Feeling the contents of my stomach rush up my throat, I toss my phone onto the chair and race to the toilet in the ensuite bathroom. Tears spring back to my eyes as I cough into the bowl, but I'm not sure if they're ones inspired by the vomit or the ones I'd been stowing away to use later.

I rinse my face and mouth in the sink before finding my way back to the chair next to Sonia. I unlock her phone again before clenching my eyes shut for a few seconds and taking in a deep breath.

My heart hammers inside my chest, almost drowning out the ringing of the phone against my ear. And when the click registers, we both wait for a moment—breathing loudly—for the other to speak.

There's no denying the surprise in her mother's voice when she finally breaks the silence. "Sonia?"

I swallow the sob threatening to erupt from me again. "Mrs. Shah, this is . . . this is Sonia's husband, Darian. We haven't spoken in a while, but I . . . I have bad news."

Chapter One
RANI
Present

"Girl, look at you! You look scrumptious." Melody pulls the side of my bikini bottom before releasing it with a snap on my skin, making me yelp.

She comes to stand next to me in front of the full-length mirror while I rub the spot on my hip that's now stinging. We're both wearing light gray, long-sleeved rash guards, given to us by our instructor, that display the words *Truckee Sports* with different colored bikini bottoms we'd brought from home.

As of a couple of years ago, I wouldn't have worn something so body-hugging—even if it was to get into the water—or shown the sliver of my midriff currently on display. But, I've come to appreciate my curves and my not-so-flat stomach. They make me who I am.

Who gives a shit that I'm not a size six or eight? At least I'm healthy and can enjoy food without feeling guilty—or starving myself for days afterward as punishment for my overindulgence. At least I can live life without burdening myself with calorie counting or constantly checking my weight.

I mean, to hell with that noise. Who needs it?

If this past year has taught me anything, it's to let go of the superficial bullshit I've ladened myself with for so long and to start living. *Really living*. Because who knows what life has in store and which breath will be your last? And if you've spent the last nineteen years of your life worried about what others think, then you've effectively given those nineteen years to them, haven't you?

Well, fuck that and fuck them. I won't be giving away another precious minute to assholes who make me feel shitty about myself. I'm content with everything I am and everything I'm capable of; I'm content to just be living.

I suppose loss can put a lot into perspective

"I don't know about scrumptious," I say, turning to glimpse how my ass looks in my new red bikini bottoms. "But I'm happy with the way these fit."

"Good! Now, let's go before we miss our damn class because we were too busy checking ourselves out in the locker room mirror." Melody giggles, her bright smile lighting up against her ebony skin.

I pull on the life vest the instructor gave us before following my best friend out the door, admiring her waist-length box braids. With her long and lean legs, tiny waist, and sharp features, she could be Zoe Kravitz and Tyra Banks' love child, if it were anatomically possible.

She's been my ride-or-die since Ruby Mallory shoved me on the playground in third grade before calling me "Queen Piggy." *Yeah, ten points for originality there, Ruby*. Melody had stepped in and pulled me to my feet before she shoved her tight fist under Ruby's chin and told her that if she ever bothered me again, she'd let the entire school know that she saw Ruby pick her nose and eat the 'biggest booger in the history of mankind.'

And while I didn't know my best friend well at the time, I

did know that no one questioned Melody Matthews. If she said the sky was green with lavender polka dots, then it might as well have been written in stone.

We've been inseparable ever since.

As we come out of the locker room, my cousin, Bella, waves us over to the group of more kayakers. She had dressed with us in the locker room earlier, but then left to fill out her paperwork. "Hey! Right on time. He's just about to start giving us a rundown of the safety measures."

Both Melody and I find a spot next to Bella and look toward the instructor, a young Asian man named Felix. "Hey everyone! Thanks for being here on this lovely Saturday morning. It's a bit breezy today, but nothing we can't handle, right?"

A few of us respond with weak "Yeahs" before Felix continues, "Alright, so who here is brand-new to white water kayaking? Raise your hands."

Melody, Bella, and I all raise our hands, looking around the group. A middle-aged man standing to our left raises his hand, smiling at us in companionship.

The three of us drove to Tahoe early this morning from the East Bay. My cousin had suggested taking white water kayaking lessons as a fun way to start the summer, and since I've been on this *live-for-today* kick and all that, I figured, why not?

I was hoping to see my one-year-old nephew—my late sister's son—who lives here in town with his dad and grandparents while I was here, but Melody has to get back for a big family dinner this evening.

I make a mental note to text Karine, my sister's mother-in-law, when I'm done kayaking to let her know that my plans have changed and I won't be able to visit like I originally intended. She's the only reason my family and I even have a relationship with my nephew, and I owe her at least that simple courtesy.

"Okay, great! Well, there's nothing to worry about. I just like to have a sense of the skill levels I'm working with. I'll be your instructor and guide on today's four-hour tour of the Truckee River, so feel free to ask me any questions as I explain the basics of kayaking, but we'll also have a safety patrol hanging out with us, in case we need him." Felix looks past our shoulders to a man standing at the reception desk with his back to us. "There he is! Hey, King, do you mind raising your hand so these lovely folks know who you are?"

Said man—King?—peeks over his shoulder and eyes us briefly from under his ball cap. He raises a rather large and veiny arm in the air, giving us a quick wave before turning back to the paperwork in front of him. The receptionist standing in front of him, facing us, gives us a bright and hopeful smile.

I couldn't get a good glimpse of the man's face, but if his front is anywhere near as beautiful as his backside . . . well, I might just have to make my way over to Truckee for more kayaking lessons.

Lord, what department in heaven do they make men like him? I wonder if there's a special application process to work there, maybe as a seamstress or a photographer. God knows I'm a decent journalist, too. I mean, I'm getting a degree in journalism and marketing, for crying out loud. Surely, The Almighty could use my talents to advertise His masterpieces.

My eyes stroll down King's back languidly, starting from the dark hair curled under his cap. His broad shoulders and upper back are taut under his blue short-sleeve shirt, while his biceps are beckoning for a zip code of their own. They're practically tearing the sleeves with their girthiness. *Indecently*, I might add.

Quite indecently.

I vaguely hear Felix give instructions on how to hold the paddle—something about a shaft and a grip and keeping it 'right side up'—while my eyes devour King's cinched waist and possibly the most incredible ass I've seen in my life. I honestly can't imagine the number of buttock exercises he has to do every day to keep his ass so high and firm. I mean, it *looks* firm. Not like I've touched it to know for sure; not like I'd *ever* even dream of touching it.

Or holding it.

Or squeezing it.

Or . . ..

I'll stop now.

Plus, one of my asscheeks is getting a cramp just from looking at him. I'm perusing the backs of his long lean legs—like the kind you see on soccer players—when Melody elbows me in the ribs, making me groan.

"Pay attention, drooler. You can admire the fine piece of man-meat later. This is important."

"*Pssh*. He just seemed familiar, that's all." I hold the back of my neck and stretch it out from side to side, trying to get the crick out. All that twisting and turning to get a better look at this Hottie McHotterson has me needing an ice pack.

This is why I never date overly good-looking men. Not like I'm getting a million offers, but still, it's a matter of principle. A girl is nothing without her principles, and one of my principles is to never let a good-looking man sway my sound decision-making skills.

Ten minutes later, we get our helmets on and head toward our kayaks on the riverbank. Felix wasn't kidding. The breeze has definitely picked up, but the warm June day counters the morning chill. Bella, Melody, and I find three empty kayaks, lined up in front of each other, parallel to the shore. We follow along as Felix tells us how to get in and out of the kayaks, but my gaze wanders again, trying to find King.

When I can't find him anywhere, I drag my kayak out to the water, feeling the freezing sprinkles on my bare calves. The current isn't fast near the shore, but with the wind picking up today, I can see the white water rushing over the jagged rocks in the stream.

I take in a long, rejuvenating breath, trying to steady my heart rate and reminding myself of my new motto. *Live for today*. It's going to be fine. Everything is going to be fine. I have my friends, an expert guide who likes to give a lot of instructions, and a well-trained safety patrol, who I'm sure is somewhere around here.

Nothing is going to go wrong.

Felix yells at us to follow him with a wave of his arms as he paddles his kayak farther into the water. Even though there's a steady breeze, the temperature is pleasant and my body is already starting to warm up, so I force myself to relax in my seat.

Melody moves ahead of me, seeming way more comfortable on the kayak, while Bella and I are more or less next to each other.

"I think I'm getting the hang of this!" Bella calls, smiling. Her long, straight black hair with purple tips is pulled into a high ponytail, and she leans back in her seat, paddling comfortably.

"Me, too," I lie with an all too confident smile. "Easy-peasy!"

Of my four cousins, Bella and I are the closest. It might have had something to do with us being only a year apart, but it's also because Bella has a huge solid gold nugget in place of where her heart should be. In fact, I bet if she were to get an X-ray, she'd break the damn machine. The girl is so generous and kind, you'd think she was training to become a nun.

When my sister eloped with Darian ten years ago, my parents were a mess. My mom and sister had an awful and irrevocable exchange of words where my mom called Darian a "useless junkie and piece of trash," and my sister vowed to never speak to my parents again. Yeah, she was an extremist like that.

And she stood by her word until her dying day.

My nine-year-old world crumbled the day my sister left because, regardless of our almost eleven-year age difference, she was the one I relied on to hold me during scary movies. She was the one who wiped my tears when Ruby Mallory called me 'blubber legs.' She was the *only* one who understood what it was like being raised by a controlling, sometimes insensitive, mother and a spineless father.

For almost six months after Sonia left, I'd wake up in the middle of the night to find my way down the dark hallway to her room. I'd roll down her comforter and sleep in her bed, breathing in the faint scent of her shampoo on her pillow.

I remember wondering how she could have just left us.

Did my parents mean so little?

Did *I* mean so little?

How could a man she met only a year before mean more to her than us?

Between my mom popping sleeping pills like they were breath mints, and my dad's complete withdrawal from life, I practically raised myself for the next couple of years until my parents finally got their act together. It was then that Bella and I became closer. With our extended Indian family hovering over my parents, Bella was the only one who made *me* a priority. She was the only one to ask how *I* was doing. Aside from Melody, she was the only one who made me feel like a nine-year-old.

My sister held steadfast to her word, not speaking to my parents over the next ten years. She and I connected a few years ago, when I was in high school, but she was so flaky that the two times we scheduled to meet, she didn't even show up. Even her texts and messages were sporadic.

Especially the strange text she sent me a couple of months before she died.

What the hell was that?

I shove the thought of the text I'd spent way too much time pondering aside to focus on keeping my damn kayak steady, pretending to know what I'm doing. Felix yells back to the group, letting us know the areas to avoid and reminding us to keep our paddles face up. "Let's head over to where the water is a little deeper and calmer. We can practice our wet exit. It's the safest way to get out of your kayak in case you roll over, so I want to make sure we practice it a few times."

My heart speeds up when I see the first current of water in front of us. Felix guides us over it, and the rush of getting through it has me feeling more confident. For the next half hour, we practice the wet exit by pulling the kayak skirt in the water and swimming back to the surface. I'm not going to lie, I'm not a fan. It makes me feel dizzy and disoriented both times I try it, but at least I know how to get myself out of the kayak if it rolls.

While Bella and Melody are doing the same thing, I look around to see if I can find King again. I see him far in the distance, tailing the group, but he's still too far away for me to see his face. His arms flex rhythmically as he paddles around, and something about him seems keenly familiar, even from here. It's like examining a pencil sketch before it's been colored in–the details aren't there but the image is taking shape.

The water starts to get choppier as the current speeds up, and we make our way down the river.

"You doing okay, Rani?" Melody's voice resounds in front of me over the rushing water.

"Just peachy!" I yell back, trying to keep my grip around my paddle, telling myself to be one with the river every time my kayak bumps and slides over a white water rapid. The rush is a mixture of exhilaration and intimidation, but I can see why kayakers come back to do this time after time.

"Alright everyone, there are some strong currents headed our way." Felix's voice sounds far away, overpowered by the wind and rushing water, but I get the jist of what he's trying to convey. "The best thing to do is face the wave . . .."

I don't hear the rest of his sentence but try to follow along behind the group. My arms feel tight and sore as my pulse spikes. The group pulls to the left, going down speeding currents, and I try to keep the same pace. But as I paddle forward, a rush of the water shoves my kayak hard toward them. My kayak flies a few feet into the air and lands awkwardly back into the rushing stream, making me roll over into the water and lose my grip on my paddle.

Before I know what's happening, I feel icy-cold pressure around my head and the bubble of water inside my nostrils. The feeling is akin to being punched in the nose by a sledgehammer. I squint my eyes open to a wall of blue with trains of white bubbles, and I know I've rolled over. My lungs burn as I struggle to hold my breath, and my hands wave around wildly, trying to find my paddle.

I try to remember what we had practiced earlier. I have to pull the skirt and exit the kayak, but my heart is racing so fast inside my chest, it's ready to keel over and accept defeat, and all my senses are drowning.

Fuck, I'm going to die.

Chapter Two
DARIAN

"Darian *jan*, I need you to stop calling me every hour like an obsessed teenage girl. I'm fine, sweetheart, and so is my Arman." My mom sounds exhausted, even though she used the Armenian endearment with my name. I can't tell if the exhaustion is from me calling her again or from taking care of my son day in and day out for the past year.

I lift the cap off my head and run a hand through my hair, looking around my office. This isn't sustainable. I really need to find a nanny for my son, but trust isn't something I store extra of, and the only person I trust to take care of him is my mom. "I get it, Mom. I'm just . . . worried."

"Don't be! It was just a dizzy spell. The doctor said he needs to increase my blood pressure meds and I should be as good as new." Her voice hitches up toward the end–something she does when she's trying extra hard to convince the person she's arguing with.

"He also increased your osteoporosis meds, which means *that* is getting worse, too." I pinch the bridge of my nose, feeling guilty for the thousandth time for asking my aging mother to take care of my one-year-old when she should be out touring the world with my dad like they always planned for their retirement.

Mom makes a shushing sound. "Don't be so dramatic. So what if he increased the meds? I'll take what he tells me to, and we can all move forward."

"What about the strength training and physical therapy he told you to do? How can you focus on yourself when you're with Arman all day? Plus, he's trying to walk. He's just going to get more active day by day. You can't be chasing after him."

"*Tsavet tanem*, Darian *jan*," Mom pleads in Armenian. "Let me carry some of your burden. You already have a lot on your plate. If and when I can't handle it, I will tell you."

While my mother is of Armenian descent, she grew up in various parts of the world, including Iran, where she picked up the Persian language as well. Which is the reason she gave me a Persian name.

"You've already helped me so much over this year." I look at my watch, noticing it's time to join the new kayakers outside. Our regular safety patrol called in sick this morning, so I'm subbing for him today. Just the thought of pushing off the mountain of paperwork and payroll changes for even another few hours is giving me heartburn, but I'm short on staff this week. "Listen, Mom. Let's talk about this tonight when I get home. I think we need to figure out long-term—"

"Darian—"

"Mom," I cut her off, knowing she's gearing up to argue with me again, but this isn't a conversation we can have when I'm already running late. She's just as protective of Arman as I am, so I know telling her I'm thinking about getting a full-time nanny for him won't go over well. "I need to get out to the river for a class. Let's talk tonight."

I hang up the phone before glancing at our company website once more. *Jesus. What a fucking mess.* The pictures and blog are all so outdated, you'd think we haven't had a thriving business in years. And hell if I have any time to do marketing or run ads on top of running the company. These were all things Sonia used to manage.

Leaving my office, I head toward the small group standing with Felix when Olivia calls me over. "Hey, King, got a sec? Just need you to sign off on the new ski gear before I place the order. Some of this stuff is priced well right now, so I figured I'd get us stocked up before winter."

Turning toward the reception desk, I hold in my internal groan as I move to meet her. Olivia and her husband Greg have been instructors at my school since Sonia and I opened it six years ago. Whenever they're not booked doing private lessons, they both help manage the reception desk and gear rentals.

And while I absolutely love Olivia—the woman would give her right lung to help me out in a pinch—she tends to be a bit of an overtalker. All joking aside, she can easily fill up hours upon hours with a damn-near-monologue. So, I always cringe whenever I get curtailed by her, especially when I'm already on a tight schedule.

"Hey, sure. What do you have?" I ask, giving her a curt smile before reviewing the order list she has printed out for me.

"Well, some of our snow goggles are scratched up, and some of the bibs really should be replaced since they have holes in them." She takes a breath before shoving her index finger on a line item. "And if you look here, I added some new helmets, too. I mean, we can always use new helmets, so I figure—"

"Yeah, I'm fine with it," I cut her off, turning the paper over to note the final price.

"There he is!" I hear Felix behind me. "Hey, King, do you

mind raising your hand so these lovely folks know who you are?"

I give a quick wave to the group of six or seven students behind me before turning back to the list, examining it once more. "Hey, listen, I told my mom to call the front desk in case she can't reach me while I'm out—"

"Oh, it's no problem! I completely understand. I'll be here if she calls. By the way, how is she doing? Greg told me she fell the other day. Is she alright? Will she be able to take care of Arman?"

Christ. I wonder if she even breathes when she's talking. "Yeah, I'm trying to figure all of that out."

"Well, you know . . . .." Olivia gets a glimmer in her eyes before her eyebrows rise. You'd almost think she was happy with my fucking plight of potentially not having childcare for my kid. "My sister, Violet, would be more than happy to help you out. She even has a degree in child development—"

"Uh—" I look behind me to see that the class has already left to go to the kayaks. I scratch the back of my neck, even though it isn't itching, hoping for an escape hatch to open up below my feet.

"King . . . . Darian, hear me out real quick. I know things didn't go as planned on the date I set you two up on last month. Maybe the timing was off, maybe it was too early for you." She looks down at the desk, disconnecting eye contact with me. "But Violet is a real sweetheart. I think she might have just been nervous that day. She really likes you."

Nervous? I would hardly call groping my dick uninvited as a sign of nerves. Most people would consider that shit sexual harassment or a sign of overconfidence or I don't know . . . not reading the fucking room right!

After weeks of Olivia begging me to go on a date with her sister, I caved. Olivia and Greg had stepped up and had taken on way more than their share for me here at the school after

Sonia died. I even took an extended paternity leave just to get Mom situated with the baby before we got into a regular schedule with Arman.

I'd been buried in work and diapers over the past year without a fucking day off, and the last thing on my mind was starting a relationship or even getting in a casual fuck. I had no room for it, no energy left. With lack of sleep mixed with the constant ache in the cavernous hole where my fucking heart used to be, I basically did things on autopilot. Wake up, work, relieve Mom of her duties with Arman in the evenings, take care of him through the night, then wake up in the morning to do it all over again.

Rinse and fucking repeat.

Olivia caught me on a particularly shitty day where I wasn't sure which side was up or down. Somehow—probably with her talking a mile a minute and not giving me a chance to think—she convinced me to take an evening off to get out of my 'rut.' She took care of Arman that evening and set me up on a date with her sister.

The woman didn't fucking speak. It was as if the disease of verbal diarrhea had only affected one sister—and it wasn't Violet. Where Olivia couldn't shut the fuck up if her life depended on it, Violet was practically mute. Maybe she was forced into silence early on in life because her sister never gave her a chance to speak? I don't know. It doesn't matter anyway, because the date ended as soon as dinner finished.

Or so I thought . . ..

I'd just pulled into Violet's driveway to drop her off when she unbuckled her seatbelt and practically leapt for my dick. I swear, I've never been so fucking scared in my whole life.

Needless to say, we ended on awkward terms.

"I don't think that's a good idea, Olivia."

"Darian—"

I do the only thing I know works with Olivia—something I

don't love doing because despite her overbearing persistence, she's still my friend and I'm not an all-out asshole. But she's left me no choice. I clench my jaw and give her a no-nonsense look, one that has her swallowing the words she was about to say. "I need to go. Thanks for the offer. If I need your sister's help, I'll ask for it."

Feeling like shit at the way her face drops, I hurry toward the exit, swinging my life vest over my shoulder. I know I need more help—at work and in my fucking life—but I've managed figuring shit out on my own most of my life, and especially over the past year.

And I'll do it again.

∽

I SEE the group spread out over the water, practicing exiting their kayaks when it's rolled over in the water. It's the first technique we teach beginners.

I paddle toward one of the stragglers—a middle-aged man with blotchy skin. He seems to have gotten stuck around a small eddy and can't get his kayak faced the right way to get to the rest of the group. I wave to Felix, letting him know I've got it.

"Remember, speed and angle," I yell, getting his attention. "You'll want to use a little more speed and not quite as much of an angle to get over this eddy. Stay calm and use the momentum of the current and a good few pushes with your paddle to get yourself over."

I paddle toward him to show him by doing it myself. After a long minute, he gets himself righted and paddles toward the rest of the group.

They're making their way over a downstream current, and then on to their first drop with the white water. This is usually when most beginners get anxious. After doing a few of these, everyone tends to feel more comfortable, but it's always a little intimidating when the kayak picks up speed before the first drop.

A few of them make it and I'm glad to hear a couple of happy yelps in the process, but then I notice a woman angled too far to the left with her paddle too far above the water. I immediately know she's going to land on her side, and if she's a newbie, she's going to roll into the water instead of being able to quickly right herself and balance over the current.

I rush toward her as she rolls into the water, the current still pushing her downstream. I don't have time to figure out where anyone else is or if Felix has noticed her rolling—my focus is completely on getting to her as fast as I can. Rolling your kayak over is always easier in calmer waters but with her going downstream, I know panic can set in pretty fucking quickly.

I've seen the worst of what can happen. This river may be something I've mastered, having grown up around it, but I'll never make the mistake of trusting it again.

Never again.

She's still rolled over in the water, caught up in a current, when I reach her. I don't see any signs of her above the water so I know she hasn't successfully done the wet exit they had worked on earlier.

Time seems to move both fast and slow, but in situations like this, even a second lost can mean the difference between life and death or even serious injury. Pulling my kayak to the side, away from the current, I get out and rush toward her. The current pushes its weight against me, but I've done rescues like this before and know enough to manage getting to her kayak.

Right as I get my hands under the water to help her out, her head pops out and then her body. She must have pulled the kayak's skirt as she was taught, right in time. Bent over, she coughs as her whole body shakes from both the adrenaline surge and the freezing water in her system. I know the feeling well—I remember it from my first few times when I was learning to kayak—and it feels like your heart is going to explode.

She gasps for air, clutching her chest and coughing, and the slight tinge of blue in her lips seems to be dissipating. "Oh my God! I'm dying. Am I dead? Did I drown?" She turns toward me, and I swear, I see a flash of someone I haven't seen in a year. The woman I spent close to a decade with; the woman I have a son with. The same damn pert nose and flawless tan skin, the same scowl and set of her jaw. Her mouth hangs agape as recognition settles over her features. "Darian?"

"Rani? What . . .?" I look around, noticing this isn't the best location to exchange pleasantries.

Holding on to her with one arm so she doesn't slip on the rocky surface, I get her kayak upright and empty out the water in it before pulling them both out of the current and to the side. She hobbles a little and I turn to examine her bare legs. One of them appears slightly scraped up—possibly from hitting a rock—but it doesn't look like she'll need stitches.

She's still coughing and shivering, heaving in big breaths. Her face is flushed when she looks at me. "I swear, I thought the wish I made came true. I thought the Big Guy had accepted my application to work in his masterpiece department."

She places her wet fingers over her lips, closing her eyes momentarily as if she can't believe she said whatever she just said out loud. And even though I have not a fucking clue what she was talking about, I'm starting to wonder if maybe she took a hit to the old noggin, too.

I look at the helmet on her head to see if it's cracked. "Are you alright? Can you stand on your own?" I ask, pulling her kayak over to mine, while still tentatively holding her arm.

Her face picks up more color as she nods. "Yeah, but I think I twisted my wrist. It might even be broken. I might not be able to use it after this. What if I need surgery? I think I'm done for the day."

I can't help notice the way her eyes flit to the side, and I know she's hoping I won't guilt her into trying to get back in the river again. "Okay, let's get you over to the ground where you can sit and catch your breath for a minute."

A look of relief washes over her before she follows me over the rocks and to the side of the river, taking tentative steps before capturing my forearm in a vise grip with her good hand. I help pull her to the wet ground before she sits. "I don't know where my paddle went."

I look down the river, but I don't see her paddle anywhere. "Don't worry about it. It's not the first time we've lost a paddle."

Felix makes his way over a minute later, and I yell down at him to let him know I'll be back after getting Rani situated in the building.

Rani takes off her helmet—using both hands but wincing a little—letting her long, dark curly hair loose before turning her flushed face toward me again. "Is this your school? Is this the school you and Sonia started? I can't believe I didn't know that." She regards the currents before looking back at me incredulously, as if it's somehow *my* fault she wasn't informed until now. "But then again, I shouldn't be surprised . . .. It's not like I knew much about my sister."

Not knowing how to respond, I point at her wrist. "That seems to be swelling. Let's get you inside. I'll need to come back to finish up with the class."

I help her up, holding her other hand but she seems to be intent on finishing her thought. "I thought you owned a ski school? That's what your mom told us." I leave our kayaks where they are and turn to answer her when she continues.

Jesus. Is there something in the fucking Tahoe air that makes women talk non-stop? "And why did Felix call you 'King'? Do you rule over them or something? It seems a little on-the-nose and arrogant, don't you think? Just saying."

I look over my shoulder at Rani, walking slowly so she can keep up. Her hand is still latched onto my arm like a metal forcep and my blood circulation to the area has dwindled considerably. The corner of my mouth tips up, but I wouldn't be surprised if she can't tell. The muscles used to pull my mouth into a smile have atrophied over the past year from lack of use. Still, something about this woman's dramatics, her youth, and innocence has me teasing her back. "Are you done?"

"No, I was just getting started," she mumbles. "I talk a lot when I'm nervous."

The last and only time I met Sonia's sister was a little over a year ago, at Sonia's funeral. And while we both exchanged condolences somberly, there wasn't much of a conversation to be had. Her parents made sure of that by pulling their younger daughter out of the funeral home as soon as it was finished. They didn't even stop to say three words to me.

It served me just fine, too. I had no desire to start a relationship with them where there hadn't been one in ten years. But my mother saw it differently. Her Armenian heritage refused to let a chance to build a familial connection go.

She exchanged numbers with Rani and has been in touch with her ever since. I know that because my mom drives to the East Bay with my son so Sonia's family can see him at least once a month.

And as much as I want to object as a way of extolling vengeance on them for their disapproval of me and Sonia by keeping my son from them, I can't.

I won't.

Fuck them for their hatred toward me—blaming me for

taking their daughter away all these years ago. Fuck them for not giving her the love she deserved. Was it selfish of us to have done what we did—marry without their approval and blessing? Yes. But you'd think they'd absolve us of the crime after ten years.

Even on that day—and for months after—when I was mourning my dead wife, I knew I wasn't going to do what they did to us. I wasn't going to stoop to their level. They'd foregone a relationship with their daughter over the years because of their pride, but I wasn't going to do the same to them with my son. If they wanted to be in his life, then they could be—I just wasn't going to go out of my way to make it happen.

Apparently, my mom was okay with taking on the task.

We make it to the building, and I decide to answer Rani's question. "Sonia and I started an all-weather school and decided to run skiing instruction over the winter and kayaking during the summer. And as much as it'll surprise you, the reason they call me 'King' isn't because of my ego—"

"Oh, that *does* surprise me," she interjects, smiling, and I find my mouth quirking back up again at her snark.

"It's because my name means king or kingly."

She pulls my arm abruptly right as we enter the building, her mouth hanging open again. "Your name means king?" Her huge brown eyes roam over my face in disbelief as if I've just told her I'm the reincarnation of Albert Einstein. "That's crazy! My name in Hindi means queen!"

And for the second time since meeting her today, I'm left speechless.

Chapter Three
RANI

I look around Darian's small office. There's a light blue wall covered with pictures of different sizes in the same black frame, arranged in a perfectly haphazard, yet aesthetically pleasing, way. On the opposite wall is a large corkboard with calendars, flyers, and various other items pinned to it. A large poster of a skier wearing a red jacket and full ski helmet and goggles is mounted on the same wall. The dark curls under his helmet indicate it may even be a picture of Darian himself. He's mid-air, with his ski-poles tucked behind him, focused on landing in the blanket of snow below.

My gaze travels to the nice mahogany desk in the center of the room with a laptop and some papers strewn upon it. It's in front of a massive window overlooking the river. The sounds of nature outside—the rapidly flowing river, along with the discordant calls of various birds—flood the room with white noise. And even though it isn't incredibly spacious, it's cozy and serene.

A couple of frames on one corner of the desk catch my attention. Pictures of Darian and my sister, and one of him with his lips pressed against my nephew's temple. My heart picks up as I put my ice pack on the chair beside me and stroll over to take a better look.

I lift the one of Darian and my sister. Aside from a random picture she sent me a few years ago of her skiing on some mountain and a snapshot of her pregnant belly last year, it's the first glimpse I've had of my sister's life in over ten years. She appears happy in Darian's arms, crinkles creasing the corners of her eyes as she looks at his face, smiling from ear to ear. He's facing the camera, smiling as well, but he seems so much younger than the man I met just a few hours ago.

Maybe it's the camera work but in this picture, I don't see the dark circles under his eyes or the sag in his shoulders. I don't see the weight of anything but his wife's arms around his waist. He looks content.

Free.

God, I can't believe I was checking out my brother-in-law in the damn lobby earlier. I definitely stared at his ass longer than anyone would consider appropriate. And then I babbled and blushed like a tween at a Harry Styles concert when I saw him face-to-face. What the hell was I even going on about?

My face heats as I put the frame back on his desk and walk back to my chair to wait for my cousin and best friend to get back. What must Darian think of me? It was like I had no filter–telling him about my wish to work in God's masterpiece department. The fuck? And then I called him arrogant! I palm my forehead, squeezing my eyes shut at the thought. He must think I belong in a loony bin.

I probably do.

I think it was all too much at that moment. I'd just rolled over on my kayak in fast-moving, icy-cold currents. I was truly thinking I was going to drown, and my heart was racing like a prized horse in the Kentucky Derby. Thank God I had enough wherewithal to finally get my shit together and pull the damn skirt on the kayak and get myself loose. But as soon as I came up for air, I was met by my hot-as-motherfucking-sin brother-in-law standing in front of me like a Roman guard, all wide-eyed and muscular.

Honestly, I thought I was hallucinating.

I look back at the wall of pictures and note several with the same three men in them, Darian and two others. I vaguely recall their bright blue eyes and honey-blond hair—much the same as Darian's dad's—from Sonia's funeral. From my brief conversations with Karine, I know they're Darian's twin half-brothers from his dad's previous marriage. And where Darian takes after his mom—with his dark hair and Armenian features—his brothers are a spitting image of their dad.

I don't remember much of anything else from that day—not unless I include the feeling of being disconnected, like one feels watching a television show, invested but not experiencing. It all felt like it was happening to someone else. And even as I watched my mother break down inconsolably while my father held her to his chest, I felt like I was watching someone else's life.

And it wasn't because I didn't feel close to Sonia—I think you feel the loss of a sibling regardless of how estranged they are—it was because I didn't know *how* to process it all. I recall just staring at my newborn nephew in Karine's arms, thinking the whole thing was a dream.

Or a nightmare.

I scroll through my phone to distract myself from my thoughts—thank goodness the slight sprain is in my left wrist and not my dominant one—before remembering I needed to message Karine. I lift the phone between both my hands, testing to see if typing out a message using both my thumbs feels comfortable. The pain is bearable.

Me: Hey, Karine. I'm sorry to cancel, but I won't be able to swing by to see you and Arman today. The friend I drove here with has to get back tonight.

I switch apps and start scrolling through my social media when her response comes in a few minutes later.

Karine: NWD. I understand. Next time. <hug emoji>

NWD? I bite my lip, smiling at her response. Ever since I've been messaging with her, Karine makes me laugh with her unique definitions of acronyms and her overuse of emojis. It's as if she's created her own texting language and thinks everyone should be fluent.

Me: NWD?

Three dots appear on the screen before her response comes through. I can practically hear her sighing with exhaustion.

Karine: No worries, dear. <hug emoji, flower bouquet emoji>

I laugh, shaking my head and slowly typing out another response.

Me: Ah, got it. Btw, we took a kayaking lesson at Darian's school today. I didn't know this was the one he and Sonia owned. Unfortunately, my kayak rolled over and Darian had to help me out. Now I'm

sitting in his office with a bruised
wrist.

Karine: Oh no. LOL. <frown emoji>. I hope it
heals quickly. I'm glad Darian was there to
help. <bicep curl emoji>

I stare at her message, knowing she definitely has a different definition of LOL than I do. Even as I'm typing out my next message, a laugh bubbles out of me, knowing she'll be rolling her eyes this time.

Me: LOL?

The bubbles appear for a little longer, giving me an indication she's typing a lengthier response.

Karine: Lots of love. <heart emoji> Really,
jan, you should know these shorthands. All
the kids your age are fluent in them.

As much as a part of me wants to correct her and tell her that she's been using the wrong definition of LOL, I can't seem to find the heart to do so. It's so endearing, and she is such a sweet soul that I just leave it be.

Me: You're right. I should work on that. How
are you and how is my little man? Is he
feeling better from that cold last week?

For the past year, Karine has been bringing Arman—the cutest baby on the planet and the love of my life—to see me and my parents in the East Bay. She actually has a good friend who lives near us, so we always coordinate a day that works for us and meet at her friend's house. I get the feeling that Karine doesn't feel completely comfortable with my mom.

Though, I can't say I blame her.

Over the years, Mom has done nothing but denounce Darian. And though she doesn't say it outright to Karine, it's obvious with the way she belittles his job, or the fact that he's not of Indian descent, or the snide remarks she makes about my sister's marriage with him.

Karine is a true saint for not snapping back at her, however veiled my mom thinks her comments are under her saccharine smiles.

The notification of Karine's response comes through, along with a new picture of my nephew. He's holding a teether in his mouth with his hand and smiling at the camera, showing off his one tiny top tooth. His nose is crinkled adorably, reminding me of the way my sister's used to whenever she smiled.

Karine: Arman is as good as new from last week. No more coughing. He's such a good baby, so easy. And I'm doing okay, too. Darian is being overly concerned about my health, but he tends to do that.

I'm about to respond, wondering what she means about her health, when the door to Darian's office opens. I put my phone on my lap, watching him traipse in with Bella and Melody in tow. My cheeks immediately heat at the recollection of me telling him my name meant 'queen' in Hindi.

Seriously, why?

Why did I feel the need to tell him that? Was there any point to it? And what did that do besides force him to give me an awkward smile? If *that* wasn't a clear indication of my youth and immaturity, then I don't know what is.

I wasn't lying when I told him I tend to be an over-talker when I'm nervous—it's just something I've never overcome. It's also another reason I won't date good-looking men. Not that I'm even remotely thinking about Darian in that way—*eew, he's my brother-in-law!*—I'm just stating the reason why.

I can't be with someone and lose control of the shit that comes out of my mouth because I'm too flustered around them. I like to sound mature, like I have a well-developed frontal lobe, and be in control of my speech. It's part of my guiding principles. I can't do that when someone is so distractingly beautiful.

Again, not that I think Darian is distractingly beautiful or anything. He's just an average man with above average height and features.

And biceps.

And ass.

That's it. No big deal. Lots of men have that.

I just don't date them.

"Hey! Are you okay?" Melody takes a seat beside me while Bella stays at the door with a concerned look on her face. They both seem to have dried off, though Bella's long locks are still dripping down her back. Her purple tips look almost as black as the rest of her hair.

I put the ice pack back on my wrist. "Yeah, just a minor sprain, I think. Nothing these big bones can't handle."

Darian comes to stand in front of me with his eyebrows pinched and his arms crossed in front of his chest. His *average* biceps flex, distractingly. "Pretty sure that's not how bones work." He gestures to my wrist under the ice pack, before pulling out a brace from his pocket. "This should help."

He drops to one knee before locking his coffee-colored eyes with mine, and I blame the drafty building for the traitorous shiver that rolls down my spine.

I shift uncomfortably on my seat, pretending not to

notice Melody softly clear her throat beside me. "I can get it on myself."

Darian ignores my feeble objection and gently takes my bruised hand in his, examining both sides. Goosebumps litter my arms as his warm touch electrifies my skin. Jesus, is it hot in here? Why is this man radiating heat like a damn furnace?

I wonder if people who are always this warm need to reapply deodorant often . . ..

I inadvertently lean forward, trying to get a hint of his deodorant. He doesn't smell bad at all for someone who just came back from doing a strenuous activity. In fact, he kind of smells good. Really good, like pine and oranges.

I go stock-still.

My eyes collide with Darian's, and I notice that somehow, in the span of five seconds, my nose has physically drifted well into his personal space. Anyone else watching us, including Melody and Bella, would think I was about to whisper in his ear. I'm sure *he* is wondering the same thing.

God, what is wrong with me?

Why am I acting like such a nutcase?

I lean back abruptly, flicking my eyes to Darian's face before peering down to my bruised hand inside his large one. His lips twitch as he focuses on getting the wrap over my hand, velcroing it on the side, and if I didn't know better, I'd say he was trying to hide a smile.

Honestly, that makes me feel worse.

How pathetic must I seem right now, sitting here with a bruised hand—though not nearly as bruised as my ego—after only an hour on the river, leaning over to get a whiff of this man like a malnourished dog in front of a steak dinner?

I'll answer. Very, very pathetic!

"Thanks," I whisper, feeling my cheeks burn.

"You're welcome." Darian gets up to walk back to his desk.

Melody clears her throat again, and I'm inclined to ask her if she has something lodged in there. "Since you're already ready to go," she scans my jean shorts and sleeveless shirt, "Bella and I are going to change into some dryer clothes. See you out in the lobby in like, fifteen minutes?"

"Sounds good." I smile at both my friend and my cousin. Bella winks at me before her and Melody leave, and I mentally prepare myself for an interesting conversation during the drive back home. I turn back to Darian, remembering my chat with his mother. "Is there an issue with Karine's health?"

He moves some papers around his desk before giving me a confused look. "How did you hear?"

I squint at him. Does he not know that I chat with his mother frequently? "I was texting with your mom, and she said you've been concerned about her health. Is she okay?"

Darian sighs before sitting on his chair and lifting his cap off his head. He runs a hand through his thick dark hair before putting his cap back on and turning to me. His eyes look weary, as if he hasn't had a full night of sleep in years. "She fell a couple of days ago and passed out for a few minutes."

"What!" My eyes are saucers as they bore into him.

"Yeah. Thank goodness she wasn't with Arman at the time. My dad was there to drive her to the emergency room, but it was quite a scare."

My heart speeds up at the thought of Karine being sick. I suppose since my sister's death, I tend to jump to the worst conclusions and have the worst thoughts when something like this affects someone I care about. "Oh gosh. She never said anything to me about it in her messages. Is she okay now? What did the doctors say?"

"They said her blood pressure dropped somehow, so they increased her medication. But then, just two days ago, she had a full work-up done, and they've increased her osteoporosis medication, too." He runs his hand over the stubble on his jaw and the movement alone almost makes me forget what we were even talking about. "It's just . . . I know taking care of a one-year-old isn't easy for her. She may act like she's still in her thirties with great health, but she's not. I need to look for a nanny to take care of him so my mom can go back to being his grandma instead of his full-time caretaker and focus on herself."

I search his face for a moment. "How do you feel about that? Leaving Arman with a nanny?"

Darian puffs out an incredulous laugh, and I immediately regret asking the question, knowing I've hit a nerve. "It's not like I have much of a choice in the matter, Rani. Both my brothers are busy with their jobs, and I don't have any other family around to help." His eyes land on the picture of my nephew on his desk, and my heart immediately launches toward him. I can see how much this is wearing on him. "I still have to run this place; I still have to provide for him."

"I know," I whisper, looking down at my hands on my lap, wishing I lived closer. "I wasn't trying to offend you with that question."

His shoulders sag. "I'm sorry, I didn't mean to sound like a defensive prick. This wasn't how it was all supposed to be, you know? Sonia and I decided that she'd stop coming into work after Arman was born. She was supposed to just maintain the website and run ads and campaigns from home while she took care of the baby. She was supposed to raise him with me. We were supposed to be in this together. And not having her . . .." I watch his Adam's apple bob and a pang of sadness spears my chest. "Not having her is just something I never considered."

"I know," I repeat in a shaky whisper. I pull my bottom lip

into my mouth to keep it from trembling and get off my seat to move toward him.

I can't not.

He's broken.

Broken and hurt. Even after a year, he's still reeling from the loss of my sister. I can't imagine how hard this has been on him—having been left with a newborn without the companionship of his partner.

Darian tracks my movement toward him and his body tenses slightly. I get on my knees in front of him—similar to the way he did moments ago for me—before picking up his hand with my good one and gently placing my wrapped one on top of it. "I can't fathom how you've managed it all practically on your own, Darian. With a newborn at home as soon as you got back from the funeral . . . well, I can't imagine you even had a chance to grieve properly."

He contemplates our connected hands, lost in his thoughts. "What alternative did I have? What other choice do I have now?"

God, I want to hug this man. This man, who has the weight of the world on his shoulders. They may be broad, but I imagine that even they get tired, even they can collapse.

The words escape me before I even have a chance to think about them. My heart and mind battle to decide if I've said the right thing—if I even know what I'm doing—but they're too late. They're too late because my mouth has already made the decision for me. "You *do have* another choice."

His eyes—dark centers with a rich cappuccino-brown around them—search mine like he's trying to solve a puzzle without any clues. "Oh really? And what is it?"

"Me."

Chapter Four
RANI

"Wait, don't say a single word until I've filled up the gas in my car and can get back in to listen to this whole story." Standing with her driver's side door open, Melody leans in to make eye contact with me in the passenger seat. Her box braids swing over her shoulder before she flips them to her back. She looks in the backseat at Bella, who's chewing her thumbnail as if it were a fruit rollup. "Don't let her speak. I need to hear every word of this."

Bella nods at her so strenuously, her head is at risk of toppling off. I don't blame her. Almost everyone I know, including me, is a little scared of my best friend. She has never hurt a fly. *Never.* But could she? You better fucking believe she could. If she wanted to, she'd probably make that fly suffer, only to die a prolonged and painful death.

So, it's best just to nod and safeguard your life.

Five minutes later, we're back on I-80, driving toward the East Bay. All of us quietly take in the scenery—the serene, majestic green mountains touching the bright blue, late afternoon sky. It's picturesque and transcendental. So much so, that for almost those five whole minutes, I forget that my best friend is waiting for me to speak and glancing at my profile every few seconds from the driver's seat.

I sigh, doubt creeping up inside me. "I don't know. Maybe I got a little caught up in the moment and made an impulsive decision. Maybe this is all a bad idea. I mean, I don't even know this man." I look down at my wrapped hand as thorns of doubt prick my body.

He seems nice. He helped me in the river without batting an eye and then cared for me when my wrist was hurt. Sure, it was part of his job, but there was a bit more sincerity to it, too. I could feel it.

And now *he* needs help.

At the end of the day, I'm family. Arman is my family, and I can't just sit on the sidelines and not help when he needs me the most. That little boy is so precious, he deserves to have someone who loves him take care of him instead of someone who's just doing it as a job.

But now that I have a bit more separation from the situation, little seeds of doubt seem to keep sprouting.

What if I don't know what I'm doing? What if he gets sick under my care? What if I don't feel comfortable living in Darian's house?

How am I going to tell my mom?

God, how am I going to tell my mom?

After I proposed my idea to Darian, he thought about it for a few minutes. I watched as he weighed out the possibilities. His mom needed the rest and relaxation, and taking Arman off her hands would give her a chance to focus on herself more. And since I was only going to be able to help for the next eleven weeks until I had to go back to college, it would give Darian some more time to find a suitable nanny, instead of rushing into finding someone who might not be the right fit.

I knew the moment he made the decision. There was a

brightness in his eyes that I hadn't seen before, and he finally smiled–okay, a tentative smile but it was real, nonetheless.

"You're sure about this?" He leaned his face closer to me, gauging my expression while I sat kneeling in front of his chair.

"Yes, I'm sure. I love that little boy with my life, Darian. I want to be the one to help you out for as long as I can before I have to go back."

Darian sighed, a weight lifting off his shoulders. "What about your mom? She's not exactly lining up to get my autograph."

I huffed out a laugh. "Please. *No one* is lining up to get your autograph, old man. I'll figure out how to deal with my mom." I sounded more confident than I felt, but I didn't want Darian to have a change of heart from seeing any of my hesitation. Plus, I was a big girl. I'd need to step up to my mother and do the things I wanted to do, with or without her approval.

He surveyed my face for another moment. "Okay, but I think you should take this weekend to think about it once mo–"

"I've already thought about it," I urged, squeezing his hand in mine for emphasis.

"Rani, this is a big commitment. While Arman is a relatively easy baby, he's still a lot to handle for someone so young. You haven't spent an extensive amount of time with him. Plus, I'm sure you had other summer plans." He waited for me to object, but then continued with a glimmer in his eyes when I stayed quiet, "What'll happen to all those plans to party it up and the dates you wanted to go on this summer?"

"First, I'll have you know that my summer *is,* in fact, booked to the max with parties, plans of debauchery, et cetera." It wasn't, and based on the twitch of Darian's lips, I knew he caught my sarcasm. "And though I'm on several VIP lists at the very exclusive establishments around the East Bay, I've decided I'd rather party it up with my one-year-old nephew instead." I smiled at Darian, watching his smile finally come to life. "And second, I'm not *that* young. I'm a well-established adult of nineteen years. I'll be twenty in early September."

Darian's eyes lingered on mine for a moment before they flicked to my lips and then back again. I wished I could read what he was thinking. "Sleep on it, Rani. Text me on Sunday night with whatever you decide. If you haven't changed your mind, I'll have a room ready for you at my house."

A tap on my shoulder pulls me out of my thoughts before I see Melody's hand waving in my face. "Earth to Rani. You still with us, woman?"

I tilt my head at her, giving her my best 'go on' look. "Yes. What?"

"Girl, listen." Melody uses the tone I recognize as the one she uses when she's going to give me her honest opinion—not like she ever *refrains* from giving someone her honest opinion, but still. "You volunteered for this for the right reasons and you are *not* backing out now. That hot-ass man needs your help, and so does his adorable-ass kid. So, do what you promised and help them."

A few of the thorns piercing my insides let up as I turn to her. "You're right. I *can* do it. And it's not forever; it's only eleven weeks. I can do eleven weeks."

"Yes, you can."

"What about that photojournalism project you'd signed up to do over the summer?" Bella asks, sitting with one of her knees up, still chewing her thumbnail. I can't get an exact read on her, but if I know my cousin, she's already making a pro and con list in her head about this whole thing.

I shrug. "I just have to find a live event and document it. Then, I have to submit it online. I can do that from Tahoe."

"Yeah, that shouldn't be too challenging. Will you get weekends off? I mean, I know this isn't a job in the same sense, but will you have any time for yourself?" Melody eyes me before looking back at the road.

"We didn't talk about it, but I'm sure I could take days off as needed. It's not like Darian's mom isn't willing to help here and there; she just shouldn't be doing this full-time."

"And how are you going to tell Mona *masee?*" Bella asks, referring to my mom. "She is going to freak out."

I stretch my neck, pinching the skin at my nape between my fingers and exhaling a long breath. It's a question I keep avoiding, and I don't even know if I have an answer. No matter how I break this to my mother, she's going to lose her fucking mind. "I don't know. I'll figure it out."

Melody laughs, shaking her head. "Girl, those are some famous last words. You better start strategizing like you're planning a bank heist. This shit needs to be bulletproof before you get in front of your crazy mom." She turns to me. "No offense."

"None taken." It's not news to anyone that my mom is a bit on the extreme side. I look back at Bella, who is still watching me with concern. She knows exactly how much my mother dislikes Darian–how she still blames him for brainwashing Sonia and taking her away all those years ago. To some degree, I think she blames him for her death, too.

It's completely unfair and utter bullshit, but convincing her otherwise is like ramming your skull into a wall of spikes. There would only be one loser and it wouldn't be the wall.

We drive another few minutes, listening to some song by Taylor Swift and Ed Sheeran that Melody plays off her phone when she turns down the volume and regards me seriously. "I'm not trying to deter you or anything because you're doing the right thing, but you do need to consider the amount of shit you're about to be in."

"You mean with my mom? Yeah, I know."

"No. Not with your mom. With your nephew." She smiles, her beautiful white teeth gleaming against her dark skin and beautifully glossed lips. "You know one-year-olds don't have normal 'milk diapers'?" My nose wrinkles at the thought. I hadn't thought about that. I've only changed Arman's diaper once when Karine brought him over, but it was just a pee one. "My sister told me her one-year-old poops like an eighty-year-old man with indigestion from eating lasagna with spicy arrabbiata sauce."

"That's disgusting." My nose wrinkles further, and I hear Bella gag in the backseat. "I thought you weren't trying to change my mind."

"I'm just keeping it real with you, that's all."

"Yeah, well, that's not going to be my Arman. His poopy diapers are going to smell like the sea breeze and lavender."

Both Bella and Melody burst out laughing. "Oh, you poor thing. You are going to have such a rude awakening."

"Whatever, it's fine. I'll do it because it's him."

Melody and Bella exchange a mischievous look in the rearview mirror, and I raise my eyebrows, silently asking them what it's about when Melody answers, "You'll do it because it's Arman, but you'll also do it because his dad looks like he should be modeling men's underwear."

I glare at my best friend and her implication that I volunteered to help Darian for any nefarious or insincere reason. But as Bella giggles, Melody continues, unperturbed, "I mean, the man could be a Grecian god. Like freaking Poseidon, the god of the sea, if he were a bit hairier in all the right places. You know what I'm sayin'?" Melody whistles, making Bella collapse in a fit of laughter.

I laugh, but I also roll my eyes in annoyance. "Shut up. You're so stupid."

"Girl, I'd let that man glide through my rapids any time of day, if you get my gist." She smiles at me with maniacal trouble written all over her face. "Especially if my V-card was on the line like yours is."

"Oh my God!" I backhand Melody's bicep with my wrapped hand and immediately wince while Bella wipes happy tears off her face in the backseat. "You are so over the top. My V-card is definitely *not* on the line."

"Well, it needs to be." She tries to give me a serious look but fails miserably when a giggle slips through. "With that man, it needs to be."

I roll my eyes, huffing out a laugh. "You are so inappropriate. I don't know where to even begin, but let me start by reminding you that he's my *brother-in-law*!"

"Brother-in-law, schmother-in-law," Melody mocks. "It would be one fucking gray line I'd cross over, again and again."

Bella chimes in, egging Melody on further, "I mean, we totally picked up that vibe you were putting down in the lobby. I *saw* you checking him out."

My mouth hangs open. "*Me? I* was putting down a vibe?"

"Yeah!" She smiles and it's all mischief. "I've known you practically my whole life, and I know when you're crushing on someone—"

"I am not *crushing* on Darian, Bella." I emphasize as many words in that sentence as possible, feeling all my defenses rise a thousand feet in the air. "What planet are you on? I didn't even know it was him in the lobby."

I can't believe I'm listening to this right now. Is she for real? That is the most preposterous thing that has ever come out of her mouth. I am positive that after I left the river, Bella rolled over and hit her head on a big rock.

And honestly, now that I think about it, so what if I think Darian is good looking? Are brother-in-laws off-limits to even be appreciated from a distance? Why is it considered so untoward of me to think my brother-in-law is a handsome man?

I bet if my sister were still alive and we had a better relationship—*any relationship at all*—I could give her a high-five and tell her she did well for herself. I wouldn't think she'd find that perverse or forbidden.

"Who knows . . ." Bella continues, shrugging while Melody whistles a nautical tune in the background, "maybe *everyone* will benefit from this arrangement—Arman, Darian, *and* you."

∼

"So, how was kayaking?" My mom scrutinizes me sternly across the table before gesturing toward the bowl of potato curry. The watch on her wrist *clinks* with her bangle, making a tiny metallic sound, and I can't help but note how the room is always charged with tension whenever she's in it. "Ramesh, can you pass me the *sabzi*?"

My dad wordlessly hands her the bowl of vegetables cooked with Indian spices before going back to his meal. His eyes are withdrawn behind his black-rimmed glasses, his silence even more pronounced over the past year.

I know my dad never agreed with the way things went down between my sister and my mom all those years ago. Maybe for a time afterward, he thought they would patch things up and pull through. But as the years went on, and neither one of them backed down, he lost a part of his heart. He even tried convincing my mom to let things go, to be bigger than her ego, but with one sharp, unwavering glare from my mother, he fell silent.

And he's been relatively silent ever since, speaking only when absolutely necessary.

Bella, sitting next to my mom, gives me a meaningful look across the table before pursing her lips to hide her smile. I almost kick her in the shin but decide it's not worth the effort. Since my aunt–my mother's sister and Bella's mom–Jaya *masee* is an ER doctor and often ends up working late into the evenings, Bella often eats dinner at our house. Bella's dad passed away a few years ago, and with their house being only a couple of streets over from ours, I try to call my cousin over as much as possible.

She also helps to reduce the tension since my mom seems to be a little less critical whenever she's around–not that Mom holds back the underhanded, snide remarks she thinks I can't understand.

After Sonia left, Bella's been more like a sister to me than a cousin, and since she has no siblings of her own, I know she feels the same way about me.

"It was good. A fun start to the summer." I tilt my head to my left hand lying on the table next to my plate. "Aside from the little sprain, I suppose."

My mom scans my wrist, disapprovingly. "And how do you plan to lift your camera and take good photographs for your journalism project this summer if you've hurt your hand?" She doesn't let me answer, bulldozing right over. "Have you given any thought to the event you'll cover?"

I grind the *naan* and curry in my mouth extra hard, reminding myself to stay calm. This is just my mother being my mother–pushy, naggy. She cares less about my wrist or my answer to her questions than her need to exert her authority. "It's the first weekend of the summer, Mom. I have weeks left before it's due."

"I'm just reminding you, that's all."

I decide not to argue, leaving the subject where it is.

Sometimes it's better not to rile her up, especially given that I'm about to tell her about my decision to move in with Darian.

I go to grab another piece of *naan* when my mother clears her throat. "You've had three pieces already." She examines me, her sharp gaze lingering on my chest and torso. "That's plenty for today. You need to focus on your figure, Rani. You can no longer afford to eat unnecessary calories."

Well, there goes the restraint to not rile her up.

I feel the heat rise over my chest and neck, seeping into my cheeks. It's not the first time I've heard her tell me to eat less or make me feel shitty about my body with her belittling remarks, but she usually suppresses them when others are around. I push my plate away, leaving the unfinished curry and refusing to meet Bella's eyes, even though I know they'll reflect nothing but compassion and tenderness.

But right now, I don't want anything to sway the tiny bit of courage and resolve I'm hanging on to by a thread. I know if I look into Bella's eyes, I'll end up feeling sorry for myself with how I let my mother speak to me—at how I've *ever* let anyone body-shame me.

I love the way I look. I may not be a contender on America's Top Model, but I've worked hard to get to where I am, both physically and mentally. I've worked hard to not let others' cruel judgments and criticism take away from me appreciating my curves.

"Oh, stop it." My mom snaps from across the table. "It's hardly as if I've committed a crime by telling my obese daughter to be more cognizant of what and how much she's eating. Don't make that pouty face." She moves on, as if the entire conversation has been swept under the rug, and turns to Bella. "Now, tell me what other plans you both have for the summer."

Obese? By whose standards? The fucking magazines that

line my mother's nightstand, portraying unhealthy women the size of anorexic toothpicks, who probably feel nothing but self-loathing and misery everyday?

Bella clears her throat, putting her spoon on her plate, and I know she wishes she refused my invite to come to dinner today. "I'm starting that internship with Beam Systems in a week, and aside from that, just catching up on reading."

"Oh, that's right! Did they tell you which group you'll be joining?" My mom plasters on a smile, but I know she's still trying to diffuse the tension that's lingering in the air between us. I know she can see me still glaring at her from my seat.

It's all I can do to hold my tongue, because she doesn't realize I'm about to light a motherfucking match to the napalm and set this table ablaze.

"From what I was told, it'll be somewhere on one of their hardware engineering teams," Bella answers.

Mom runs her hand over Bella's bicep, oozing pride and affection—something she only doles out to me when I've met one of her bullshit standards or when she's under the spell of the sleeping pills she often takes. "I am so proud of you, sweetheart. You truly do have it all, beauty and brains."

I crack, severed right down the middle.

Not because I'm jealous of my cousin, but because I just can't take another minute more. My mother knows *exactly* what she's doing, and her relentless effort to light a fire inside me has finally come to fruition.

I was always intent on telling her, but maybe I wouldn't have ice running through my veins when I did it.

So, happy birthday and merry fucking Christmas, Mom. Hope you like your gift!

"I'm going to live with Darian in Tahoe to take care of Arman."

The sound of my voice—thundering through my ears like a freight-train—seems to have stopped all movement around the table. It almost seems like no one even blinks for a few moments before my dad raises his eyes, setting his spoon down while my mom looks like she's stopped breathing. "Excuse me?"

I raise my head, keeping my tone even and my eyes steady on hers. Both Sonia and I have—or *had*—eyes like our mother's—large, almond-shaped pools of chocolate with a thicket of lush eyelashes around them. "Karine's health is deteriorating, and Darian needs someone to take care of Arman. I offered to help him through the summer."

My mom just stares at me, seemingly still in shock and processing my words when my dad chimes in, surprising us all, "That's kind of you, Rani. I'm glad you'll be there to help him when he needs it. His family shouldn't be the only support he has."

At this, my mom seems to have found her voice again. "What the hell are you even talking about, Ramesh?" She snaps her gaze back in my direction. "Are you out of your goddamn mind? You're *nineteen*! You have no idea how to take care of a baby. If he needs help, then I am happy to take care of *my* grandson. I am happy to take Arman off his hands, but *you* will *not* be going there to help."

I scoot my chair back from the table, having lost my appetite. *Mom should be happy about that, if nothing else.* I get up and stare down at her. "You know better than I do that Darian would die before he gave you his son. Not after the way you've stonewalled him, not after the way you couldn't offer him even a single hug when his wife died."

"His *wife*?" My mom's jaw sets as if it's made with stone. "I lost *my* daughter that day."

"No, Mom." I smile, mirthlessly. "You lost your daughter *years* before, and you continued to lose her every day since.

You continued to lose her by doing nothing to patch things up between the two of you."

"Rani, don't you dare speak to me as if everything was black and white. Don't you dare imply that I chose the wrong side . . . it was *never* that simple. She hurt me to my core when she chose to marry someone who wasn't worth the dust on her feet. He didn't even have a real job; he was just a loser who taught people to ski. He lured her into his trap, and now he's doing the same to you by giving you a goddamn story about his mother being unwell." My mother slaps a hand to her forehead dramatically. "God, why is this man after both my daughters? Why can't he let us live in peace? Wasn't taking one–*killing one*–enough?"

I shake my head incredulously. Disgusted. How can she see this so inaccurately? I know my sister's betrayal hurt my mother, but how can my mother not see *her* fault in any of it? "But it *was* that simple, Mom. Don't you see? It was always that simple."

My mother looks up at me like I'm deranged, her brows pinched in the middle of her forehead. "What are you even talking about?"

"Love. Love is *that* simple."

I start to walk away on shaky legs when her voice halts my stride. "Don't forget, Rani, I'm still your mother and you still live under my roof."

I turn to look at her over my shoulder, lifting my head higher. "Not after tomorrow, I don't. So, you either accept my decision or you'll lose me, too. It shouldn't be a hard decision, Mom. It should be simple. It *is* simple."

Chapter Five
RANI

Rain pelting against a window.

Drumsticks beating against a drum.

A stampede arising over the Serengeti.

And yet, my heart still pounds louder, hammers harder. It reverberates against the walls of my chest like a mechanical device rather than an organ pumping life into my veins.

I'm not sure exactly what the source of my anxiety is. I feel like I'm standing at the cusp of fulfillment and failure. At the median between sovereignty and submission, hoping that after risking my relationship with my parents, I don't fuck this up so badly that I actualize my mother's parting words. *"At the end of this, we'll all be bankrupt."*

With my hands still on the steering wheel, I shake the negative thoughts from my head, taking in the Craftsman-style house to my right. If it's this stunning from the outside, I can't imagine what it looks like inside.

A curved driveway leads to a two-car garage with a beautiful dark wood door at the front of the house. My eyes rise higher to the golden bricks that seem to be housing a room with large windows. To the left of the garage is a large, wrap-around porch—in the same dark brown color—with inviting, golden maple double doors, affixed with opaque glass insets.

And while the modest, two-story house—complete with a dramatic gabled roofline and a perfectly manicured lawn—boasts refined elegance, its setting against the backdrop of tall pines makes it look more quaint and charming.

I make my way out of my old Toyota Corolla with my suitcase rolling behind me as I adjust my purse on my shoulder delicately, so as to not use my still-tender hand more than I need to. It's already feeling a lot better since Saturday, so hopefully, it'll be good as new in a day or two.

I climb the three porch steps before my finger hovers over the doorbell. Darian texted me ten minutes ago to tell me Arman was up from his nap and to ring the bell when I arrived.

My heart still feels like it's going to pelt out of my body and land with a *thud* on this beautiful porch, so I repeat the same thing I've been telling myself since getting in my car this morning. "It's going to be fine. You're living for today and doing the right thing."

My mom sat in the living room, glaring at me from her seat on the couch, as I lugged my suitcase and a few other essentials to my car with the help of my dad this morning. Even when I went to say bye, sitting next to her on the couch in a last-ditch effort to make her understand, all she could muster was, "Why do I feel like history is repeating itself, and the price has doubled? At the end of this, we'll all be left bankrupt."

I sighed. "Mom, I'm not running off to marry a man I just met like Sonia did, far from it. I'm going to help out my nephew, *your* grandson, when he needs me the most. That's not a price to pay; it's a privilege."

She turned her face away from me, accepting defeat, though I know she was still unconvinced. I suppose it was the best send-off I could have hoped for after the way things ended at dinner a couple of nights ago.

I look back at my car parked in front of the house before taking in a deep inhale of the fresh Tahoe air. Releasing my breath, I press the doorbell.

A few seconds later, I hear the telltale sound of a lock unlatching before a figure appears behind the glass and the door swings open. My eyes find Darian's before landing on his light blue T-shirt wrapped around those ridiculous stone biceps, and then move to my nephew in his arms.

He's grown since the last time I saw him, and I can't help the immediate smile that takes over my face. My chubby-cheeked nephew chews on his teether, surveying me curiously, trying to place my face in his short memories. I'm sure I've already been long-forgotten, replaced by the stuffed rabbit plushie he loves so much and that colorful teether he'll never let go of.

Still, my nerves settle at the sight of him. "Hi!"

"Hi." One corner of Darian's mouth lifts before he opens the door wider, inviting me in. His slicked back dark hair appears wet, like he just took a shower, and I try not to embarrass myself by leaning in to smell him again. In fact, I'm happy to report that I don't even need to. The same scent of pine and citrus that I smelled on him a couple of days ago wafts over my nose as soon as I pass. Maybe it's not his deodorant. Maybe it's his body wash? Either way, the man smells divine. "How was your drive here?"

I turn back to him, keeping my eyes on my nephew because I don't trust them not to linger on his father inappropriately. God, I need to get a hold of myself if I'm going to be living here for the next eleven weeks.

Bella's words rang in my head throughout the drive, taunting me about my crush on my brother-in-law. And during the entire drive, I told myself she was being obtuse. Finding someone good looking is *not* the same as crushing on them. I find Zendaya and David Beckham good looking, and I don't have a crush on either of them. I might sound defensive, but I know what a real crush is.

The last real one I had broke my heart into a million pieces at prom, and I've been searching for all the little fragments ever since. Too bad my skin wasn't as thick as the rest of me—something my mom reminded me of often, especially when I winced at her insensitive remarks.

Anyway, I know this has nothing to do with a crush and everything to do with my retinas just finding someone visually appealing.

Period.

End of story.

I reach out and gently pull Arman's tight little fist and place a kiss on his hand, making him giggle. "It was good. Uneventful, I suppose. I was looking forward to seeing this little guy."

"Come on in." Darian locks the door behind me before gesturing to the large living room with a dark wood cathedral ceiling and a massive gray stone fireplace that spans almost an entire wall.

My gaze finds a few pictures of Darian and Sonia on the heavy wooden mantle before taking in the rest of the room. The decor is understated and cozy, with nautical highlights in blues and whites. I can't help but wonder if my sister designed it or if it's changed since her death.

Arman babbles around his teether, taking me out of my thoughts, and I turn to face Darian again. He seems to be watching my movements, tracing my face with his intense hawk-like gaze, like he did when I was in his office a couple of days ago. His face gives nothing away, but I catch the quick stroll his eyes take down to my lips and neck before lifting back up. His eyes seem to widen as if he's surprised himself, as if he's whispered a secret he shouldn't have.

I clear my throat, hoping the heat over my chest and neck doesn't rise to my cheeks. "This is a beautiful home. How long have you lived here?"

"Just about a year."

My brows pinch. "A year?" I look around, noticing the chef's kitchen with black marble countertops and maple kitchen cabinets. This house was meant to be a home for a growing family. "You mean—"

"Sonia never lived here." Darian adjusts Arman in his arms. "We were actually in a slow process of moving into this house from our other one when her water broke. But after the funeral . . . .." He gives Arman a kiss on his temple, seeming to take a breath to cover his emotions. "It's just been me and him. My mom occasionally spends the night in the guest bedroom, especially when I'm having a hectic week at work."

I heave out a breath. "Wow. I had no idea."

I can't decide how I feel about not being able to have more insight into my sister's personality through her decor. All I had to go by for the longest time—until Mom cleared it of everything representing Sonia—was her teenage bedroom. A part of me was hoping to find a little bit more of her here.

Darian gives me a tight smile before nodding to my roller bag. "Leave that here; I'll come get it later. Let me show you around."

As I start to follow him, Arman raises his hands toward me, asking me to hold him. I gasp with a smile. "You finally remember your Rani *masee*, little man? I bet you're wondering if I'll give you another sip of my Sprite—" I blanche at the sight of Darian's eyes bulging out of his head. "Er, *water*," I correct myself all too late as I lift my nephew out of Darian's arms. "Another sip of my *water*."

Shit, this nanny gig might be going belly-up before it even has a chance to start.

"Rani." Darian's voice is a warning, but I definitely notice the same twitch on his lips I've seen before. He can't decide how concerned he should be, and I'll take that as a win.

"Okay, so I gave him a sip of my Sprite when Karine brought him to see me last month. It was just once, and only because he kept trying to pull the can from my hands. I thought I'd just give him a taste. You'll be happy to know, he didn't even like it!"

I can feel myself revving up to babble. I know it because Darian's unrelenting stare has turned the knob on my anxiety to the orange zone, and it's what I do when I'm nervous. "But Darian, that was when I was just his cool auntie. I mean, I'm still his cool auntie, but now, I'm also his nanny, and I have strict principles as his nanny, as I do in life."

"Strict principles . . ." Darian repeats as his dark eyes devour my building nervousness. The bastard seems to like making me squirm under his dark stare.

"Yup. I have strict principles in life. For example, I always wear pink on Mondays. Hence why I'm wearing this pink gingham button-down over my shorts." I look down at said outfit in explanation. "It helps Mondays feel a little cheerier. I also wear glitter eyeshadow on Fridays because it brings a festive vibe to the weekend."

"I see."

"Yup. My face is my mood ring. It's part of my principles to not make anyone guess what I'm thinking. My face will say it all if my mouth hasn't said it already."

Darian lifts his chin but melancholy highlights his

features. "Your sister was the same way . . .. Her face had a language of its own."

"I suppose we got that gift from our mother."

Arman snuggles into my neck and I give him a kiss on his cheek, feeling a bit calmer before I address Darian again, "Anyway, I don't want you to worry about this little guy, okay? He's in good hands."

Darian's eyes linger on me for a long moment like he wants to say something. As if he wants to convey so much more with that one look, but then he thinks better of it and turns his head to the rest of the room. "Let's start with the kitchen."

We walk through the kitchen, with Darian pointing out where the cups and plates are before we walk through to the dining room. A full wall of windows behind the large, raw-wood dining table and elegant white chairs showcases a forest of pines and an expansive deck. The view is absolutely breathtaking.

"Wow, there can't be anything better than having a cup of coffee in the morning with a view like this," I state, my gaze lingering on the koi pond past the covered hot tub.

Darian nods. "Or a protein shake, yeah."

I inhale sharply. Did he just say 'protein shake'? Oh God, maybe I should have done some reverse questioning before I took on this job. It's already unsettling enough to endure watching him be so fit and beautiful, but doing so without coffee? I might as well gouge my eyes out now.

But I swear I saw . . .. I turn to survey the kitchen again and breathe a sigh of relief when I find what I'm searching for–the fancy coffee maker. "Oh, thank God. I thought you were one of those aliens who don't drink coffee."

"I am. I mean, I don't. The coffee machine is for my mom."

I shake my head in mock disappointment. "It's not right,

Darian. It's just plain blasphemy." I look back at Arman in my arms, bouncing him. He grins, showing me his top tooth. "This kind of craziness should be a crime . . . or a misdemeanor, at least."

Shaking his head, Darian turns on his heels, but not before I notice the smile on his face. Arman and I follow him as he shows me the rest of the downstairs—his study and a powder room—before we head upstairs.

"This will be your room," he states, opening the door to a small but cozy bedroom with a four-poster queen bed covered in white sheets and comforter. Thin white curtains line the sides of a large window with a view of the pines outside. Like the rest of the house, each room seems to have minimal touches of color. This one has hints of green—the artwork on the wall and the overstuffed reading chair.

"This is perfect. Thank you," I reply softly, noting the en-suite bathroom and the bouquet of white lilies blooming brightly inside a pretty white vase on top of the chest of drawers. I can't help but wonder if he got them for me? I shun the thought as soon as it enters. *Ridiculous*. His mom stayed with him often enough that he got a coffee maker for her, so the flowers were probably for her, too.

Darian turns to walk us through Arman's nursery, and I admire the giraffe theme—from the wallpaper to the lamp and bedding—noting several vintage accent pieces strewn around the room. There's also a changing table and a rocking chair on the other side of his crib, along with a shelf containing tons of children's books.

Arman babbles, spitting out a couple of incomprehensible syllables, and I nuzzle my nose into his cheek. "Is this your room, little man? It's adorable, just like you."

"Sonia decorated most of it," Darian states, finding my questioning gaze. I thought he told me she never lived here?

"This was one of the first rooms we made sure was ready after we had the keys to the house."

I swivel my gaze around the room once more with the new knowledge of my sister having touched it, having envisioned it, and finding her personality shine throughout it. It's strange that it's in a baby's bedroom that I find my sister again. A tinge of grief pricks my chest as I envision her carefully choosing each item, nesting, and preparing for the little boy in my arms. I imagine her sitting on the rocking chair with her large pregnant belly, whispering her hopes and dreams to the baby inside.

Finding Darian's gaze again, I feel the press of tears behind my eyelids. His frown tells me he's reading my thoughts. "In her last few days, he's all she thought about. He's the only thing we seemed to agree on." His voice sounds rougher before he lets out a soft brusque laugh. "He was the only hope we had . . .."

I stand there speechless, with Arman's small hand fisting a lock of my hair, staring at my brother-in-law with questions written all over my face. What does that mean? Why was this baby their only hope? "Darian, I don't—"

Darian shakes his head, as if he's jolting himself out of memories. His brows rise before they pinch like he's just realized what he said. He gestures to Arman. "Let me take him off your hands. He's heavy and you probably need a break from carrying him." He takes the baby from my arms, combing my nephew's silky dark locks back before turning his attention to me. "Come on, let's get back downstairs. I'm sure you're hungry. We can grab lunch and talk about Arman's day-to-day routine."

Swallowing down a mix of emotions and fiddling with the velcro around my left wrist, I follow Darian back down the stairs.

I don't miss the creases around his eyes before he turns

around or the heaviness in his steps as he makes his way downstairs. I don't miss the way he seems to pitch himself into the past as fast as he hurls himself back to the present, living in two time periods but unable to grasp on to either.

And I definitely don't miss the fact that he never showed me his room.

Chapter Six
DARIAN

I grab the large bowl of the Chinese chicken and mandarin salad I'd prepared while Arman was napping from the fridge, along with the dressing. I'd taken the day off today—getting paperwork and receipts sorted in the morning from home, and letting Olivia and Greg handle things at the school.

The cold air from the fridge wafts over my damn-near simmering skin before I close it and place the bowl on the counter a little harder than I'd intended.

Fuck, why does it feel so hot in here?

"Can I help you with anything?" Rani's voice pulls me from my task. She eyes the bowl. "Ooh! That looks yummy!"

I look back down to finish my task. "I hope you eat chicken . . . .. Fuck, I should have asked before I mixed all this in. I'm sorry. I have other things I can put together if you can't eat this."

She comes to stand near me, replacing the scent of the mandarin oranges with lilies under my nose. "I love chicken, and what you have looks delicious."

She reaches up to open the cabinet above me where I'd told her the plates were earlier. Her arm brushes against mine, sending a familiar but forgotten current zipping through my veins and making me take a step back to give us both some space.

"Sorry," she whispers before grabbing the plates and following me to the dining room.

I already have the *lavash* Mom made, along with some lemonade set on the table. Rani sits down next to Arman, who's happily stuffing fistfuls of macaroni into his mouth, watching her every move like she's some sort of a fairy or nymph.

She'd certainly make a damn good one in real life . . . if there were such a thing.

Since the minute I met her again only a couple of days ago, she's been throwing some kind of damn fairy dust everywhere, even where it shouldn't be.

"Oh, God. I'm so hungry!" She scoots her chair in, sitting in front of me, and I serve her some salad before she lifts the basket of *lavash* my way, silently offering it to me. I take a piece before we both dig in.

"Oh, wow," she moans, her eyes closed as she chews around her first bite. When she finally opens them back up, they lock on to mine—chocolate pools glittering under lashes and brows so thick, you'd wonder if they were painted or glued on. They don't seem to be. "This is so good, Darian! Did you make it?"

I force my eyes back to my plate. "I don't cook much, but I can grill and make pretty decent salads. My mom brought over the *lavash* earlier."

It wasn't an easy conversation to have with my mom this weekend. She made me feel like an asshole for taking her time with her grandson away, but thankfully, between me, my brothers, and my dad, we all managed to get it through her head that this was the best thing for her. So, she reluctantly booked her first physical therapy session today with a place that specializes in working with osteoporosis patients.

"Mmm." Rani hums around another mouthful of food, and I remind myself to focus on my food, though it feels almost unpalatable on my tongue.

Rani coos at my son, pointing to the spoon sitting on his tray, not that he'll use it. The kid likes to dig in with his hands and make a mess of his tray and his bib. She gets up to give him a kiss on his cheek, even though he's covered in cheese, making him giggle while causing the dull, ever-present ache between my ribs to intensify.

A part of me wonders if I'm doing the right thing by employing someone I know he'll get attached to, only for her to leave at the end of summer. Will he look for her everywhere once she's gone? Will he wonder where she went and if she'll ever come back?

But what alternative do I have? Any unrelated nanny could leave just the same. At least with his aunt, Arman gets that unconditional, unadulterated love he deserves. The kind of love that perhaps comes second only to that of his own mom . . ..

Fuck.

An image of Sonia comes to the forefront of my brain, and I feel a boulder settle between my ribs. Even after all this time, I can't wrap my head around the abruptness of it all. How she was there one minute and gone the next.

How everything changed in the matter of an instant.

I stab my fork into the last bit of salad on my plate, thinking about the past couple of years before she died. It felt like nothing I did made Sonia happy. She was either always pissed off or completely withdrawn, and I remember the hopelessness that would settle into my chest as soon as I laid down next to her at night—with her back turned to me—and again when I awoke the next morning.

She was a ghost of herself, physically there, but never present.

Unlike now, where she's physically gone, but her ghost is ever-present.

Sonia blamed all our problems on me working too much—and maybe she was right—but I certainly felt her pull away even when I *was* home. Even when I tried to bring her to bed . . . to make her happy.

It was in the heat of an overblown argument about how I forgot to turn on the fucking dishwasher before bed one night that I suggested we start seeing a therapist. Enough was enough, and I knew we needed help or we weren't going to survive.

I suppose we didn't survive in the end, anyway.

Sonia opened up about issues during those conversations that I didn't even know we had. I swear, there were times I recall gaping at her like she'd grown another head because what she would tell the therapist was so out of left field for me. Like how she felt trapped in our marriage or that she felt unfulfilled.

Trapped?
Unfulfilled?

What the fuck was she talking about? How could I have lived with someone all that time and not have known the basics—the fucking fundamentals—about her wants and needs? Had my head really been stuck that far deep in the sand?

The therapist gave us some methods to help us communicate better—to understand each other's 'emotional calls,' as she had termed it—and for a while, they seemed to work. Things between us, including our sex life, were heading in the right direction.

So when Sonia told me that she was pregnant, I was ecstatic. Hopeful.

She'd often be withdrawn and in her own world during the pregnancy, but I occasionally saw a glimmer of hope in her eyes. I hoped that it—and the baby—was enough to save us.

But I suppose I'll never know.

I clear my throat, putting my fork down and watch Rani finish eating. "I had my mom type up Arman's schedule—nap times, meal times, etc. When he hits growth spurts, all that goes flying out the window, but for the most part, the schedule should help you get into a rhythm with him."

"Oh, that'll be really helpful!" She smiles, tearing off a piece of the bread. "I can always message your mom if I need anything."

"You can message me, too. And please don't feel like you need to take care of him over the weekends. I have it worked out with my staff so I'm usually home during the weekends, unless we're short-staffed, like we were this past Saturday." I eye the brace still on her hand. When she texted me yesterday to confirm she'd be coming, she told me her hand was already feeling a lot better.

She looks over at my son and smiles again. "Well, I'd be happy to help any time you need, but okay, I'll take the weekends off and go check out that nursing home I passed by on my drive here."

My brows furrow. "Nursing home?"

She nods before chewing on her bottom lip, as if she's wondering why she even said anything. "Yeah. I, uh . . .. It all started as a journalism project I did in high school. I interviewed elderly people at various nursing homes and asked them to recount the stories of the greatest love of their lives. Sometimes it was their spouse, and other times it was someone they'd pined for but for whatever reason, couldn't be with. I posted their accounts—with their permission, of course—on a blog I called, *The Soulmate Spiel*." She shrugs. "I've kept it going ever since, and whenever I have a bit of time, I volunteer at a couple of local nursing homes and interview anyone who is interested."

I stare at her. I've realized I have a tendency to do that with her because she baffles me. "I don't mean to sound like an asshole, but—"

Rani gasps, looking over at Arman before giving me a disparaging glare. *"Language!"*

Didn't she just walk into my house like, less than an hour ago? How is it she's already barking out orders?

"Sorry," I reply, not wanting to argue that my son has words like 'daddy,' 'food,' and 'pee pee,' to accomplish before the word 'asshole' makes it into his vocabulary. "But why do you continue to do it? It was for a school project . . .."

She laughs, shyly, her cheeks picking up a rosy tinge. "Yeah, I know what you're asking, but how do I disappoint almost thirty-three thousand subscribers?"

My mouth opens as I process what she's said. "Thirty-three thousand subscribers on a blog that talks about the love lives of the elderly?"

"Well, it's more than that," she defends, her chin tilting up. "It's not just gossip about someone's love life; it's an account of their greatest happiness. For example, I met a man named Murray, who was a prisoner of war during World War II. Before he'd left for the war, he asked Clara, a woman he fell in love with, to marry him once he came back. But when he was captured for well over three years, he was sure he'd lost her." She smiles and her entire face lights up, as if the story is an account of her own. "When he was finally released and returned home, she was waiting for him. They got married some time later and had four children."

I listen, hearing more than the sound of her voice as she

gives me a glimpse of who she is on the inside. A romantic. Someone lost in happily-ever-afters and stolen kisses.

Naive and carefree.

Someone I won't ever be again. Not when I know there's no such thing as happily-ever-afters.

"So, it's not just a frivolous blog about old flames; it's a living journal, a memoir. And my subscribers live for these examples of hope, optimism, and love in a world that sometimes feels like it's lacking it."

As if done upholding her stance, she wipes her mouth on a napkin before turning the linen over and wiping Arman's mouth, too. He tries to push her hand away, but she does it anyway, as if she's done it a million times.

Who is this woman and how is she only nineteen?

From the way she speaks her mind, to the way she doles out hope and sunshine like it comes packaged in a bottle—giving away easy smiles and sprinkling fairy dust on people in the process—to the way she enthusiastically volunteers to help a stranger, who quite possibly was the reason her family broke apart years ago, you'd think she was an ambassador of UNICEF or Mother Teresa.

And she has this instinct and confidence when it comes to my son that I never expected. From the way she holds him, the way she coos and smiles at him, and even the way she took on her duties with him in the matter of minutes, I'm surprised she hasn't done this before—barring that Sprite incident.

In all honesty, I was more amused about the way her voice trembled and her big eyes got rounder when she slipped up about it. I'm a jackass for loving the way I put her on edge, but I can't promise I won't do it again, either.

Arman starts to wiggle in his high chair—his cue that he's either wet or done with his lunch or both. I get up to unbuckle him from his seat when Rani's hand lands on my arm, sending that same zing up my shoulder and down my spine, making me recoil once more.

I'm sure I look like an asshole every time I flinch at her innocent touch, but if she notices, she doesn't show it. "How about you start cleaning up, and I'll see if he needs a diaper change? We'll join you in the kitchen when we're done."

"Sure," I respond all too quickly, picking up our plates and rushing to the kitchen.

I hear them through the baby monitor in the kitchen as I rinse our plates in the sink. My eyes move to the figures on the screen.

Rani says something to Arman, speaking softly before she lays him down on the changing table. She brings her face down to his tummy and tickles him, making him squeal before he grabs hold of her curly hair.

"Ouch!" She giggles before unwrapping his fist and then kissing it. "You little monster!" She nuzzles him again, and the process of giggling and laughing seems to restart.

I don't even realize I've rinsed the same damn plate several times when I hear her sing. Her soft rasp wraps around the words, immediately quieting Arman. It's a song from Mary Poppins called, *Stay Awake*. I recognize it from my own childhood memories when my brothers would come over for the weekend—when my dad had them—and we all sat around playing cards with the movie playing in the background because Mom liked it so much.

Rani quickly changes Arman's diaper before throwing the dirty one into the pail nearby and picks him back up. I watch as she gives him a big kiss on his cheek before they head out of the room. I quickly wipe my hands on a kitchen towel and turn off the monitor.

The scent of lilies comes floating in along with Rani and Arman's giggles, and I focus on wiping down the kitchen counters. Rani sets Arman in his walker, encouraging him to hit the various obnoxious-sounding buttons on it while both of their chirps and cackles permeate the living room.

And they invade the peace I thought I'd finally achieved over the past year.

Chapter Seven
RANI

"Daw!" Arman points to the husky mix with its front paws on a tree while his owner tries to pull him back with the leash, unsuccessfully. The dog seems focused on the squirrel that darted past him.

"Yeah!" I cheer, putting some more Cheerios and blueberries on the tray affixed to his stroller. "*Dog*! Do you like dogs, little man?"

"Daw!" Arman squeals, getting momentarily distracted by his snacks before going back to watch the gray and white husky with the tall, red-headed man.

He's been here the past two days that I've brought Arman for a walk in this park near Darian's house, and I gather the dog might be the alpha in their relationship.

I've officially been living with Darian and Arman for three days, and we seem to have a good routine. I think Arman has even come to expect his afternoon walks. I've noticed they help him relax so he's ready to nap by the time we get back home.

Despite how nervous I was with taking care of a one-year-old, Arman has indeed been the easy baby both Karine and

Darian had described. Even without knowing how to speak, he communicates everything he needs—like when he wants to be picked up or when he's done eating. The times I need to be vigilant are when he starts crawling, trying to get into things—especially that bottom cabinet inside the kitchen island. The kid is convinced there's something important for him in there.

I've been waking up at seven, right around the time Arman does. By the time I get to his room, Darian has already changed his diaper and his bottle is ready. He hands me the baby with a curt smile and heads out to work. And while I'll chat with Karine through our text messages here and there, I don't talk to Darian until the evening when he gets back around six.

And even then, we eat a quick meal together, chatting briefly about the day—mainly anything to do with Arman—before Darian whisks him away to take a bath and put him to bed. He insists on spending that time with him, and I don't mind being able to retreat to my room for the night or chatting with Bella and Melody.

But still, it feels . . . lonely at times.

Last night I came out of my room around nine PM to grab a glass of water from the kitchen and noticed the light on under the study door. I'd gone back to sleep afterward, but I didn't miss the click of Darian's bedroom door, when he seemed to have finally gone in around midnight.

I know he has a lot on his plate with his school and managing the staff, but given the dark circles under his eyes, I get the feeling he doesn't sleep much.

A part of me wants to tell him that I'm here if he needs an ear, that he doesn't have to hold it all in and carry it on his own. But I get the feeling it would have the opposite effect.

Since the first night we chatted freely and he showed me around the house, I've seen a different Darian—a closed-off and tighter-lipped man. If he's not rushing out the front door then he's slipping into his study. It's like he's always finding ways to dodge my presence.

I try not to let his avoidance bother me—he's had a lot thrown at him over the past year—but sometimes I wonder if I'm missing something. Maybe my presence annoys him somehow. Maybe I'm in his way, even when I try not to be. Maybe I remind him of my sister? While we shared similar features, we definitely look pretty different.

The first day, Darian told me I could always call or text him if I needed something, but I haven't wanted to bother him at work. If I do have any questions—like the time I wanted to know if Arman liked his bottles warmed up—I just texted Karine.

I unwrap the granola bar I'd packed in my purse before taking a bite. Arman watches me intently for a moment before making grabby-hands, begging for a bite. I tear off a little piece to give to him, and he immediately puts it in his mouth, tasting around it, trying to figure out if he wants more.

I smile when he spits a piece out before wiping his mouth with a burp cloth I brought along with me. "Yeah, I get it, buddy. Eating healthy sucks."

We're sitting in the middle of a large patch of grass, Arman in his stroller and me on the ground. I pull my knees up, placing an arm behind me and finish my cardboard-flavored snack. I haven't had the chance to go grocery shopping, and all Darian seems to have in his pantry are things only a baby goat would find appetizing.

There are few days as beautiful as the ones I've seen here, where the June sun isn't so hot that it scalds your skin but temperate enough to keep you toasty. My gaze lifts toward an eagle sweeping through the sky before my attention lands back on the red-haired man and his dog, now headed in our direction.

I hadn't noticed him close up the other two days, but he appears to be a little older than I am—in his early twenties, perhaps. His green eyes crinkle at the corners when we both raise our hands simultaneously to wave at each other.

"Cute dog," I call as they come within earshot. Arman watches, transfixed, as the dog sniffs around, pawing at something in the grass. Though he looks so much more like my sister—with his darker skin and pert nose—the intensity in his gaze reminds me of his dad.

"Thanks, but he's not mine. I'm babysitting him for the next few weeks for my parents." He smiles at Arman, dimples forming on both cheeks, making him look younger than he is. "Cute kid."

I huff out a laugh, sitting up a bit and running my hand over one of Arman's tiny socked feet. "Thanks, he's not mine, either. He's my nephew."

"Ah, got it. So, I assume you don't live around here, then."

I shake my head up at him, squinting at the sun, when he notices and moves in a way so his head blocks part of it. "No, I'm just helping them out for the summer. I live in the East Bay."

"Not too far, then. I'm Liam, by the way. I saw you yesterday, too." His cheeks pinken and I can tell he regrets admitting that. I won't deny that it has my intrigue and confidence peaking. It's not everyday that a man blushes around me.

"I'm Rani." I jut out my hand and he wraps his long fingers around it in a shake. "Yeah, we have a pretty busy summer schedule of walks, snacks, and naps ahead of us, so we figured we'd get started."

Liam barks out a laugh. "Doesn't sound like you'll have much time for anything else, huh?"

I lick my lips, caught off-guard with the insinuation, when

my phone buzzes inside my purse. It's an incoming call from Melody.

After two nights of dwelling on Darian's personality disorder, I'd called her last night from my room but she hadn't picked up. Now, I'm desperate to talk to her—to hear her tell me that I'm over analyzing and needlessly worrying myself when he's probably just busy. And she'd be right, of course. I mean, the guy doesn't need to entertain me. I'm here to help my nephew and take a little bit of the burden off him, not to create an additional headache for him.

I look up from my phone to the pair of green eyes still assessing me. "I actually need to take this."

"Oh, yeah, sure." Liam hesitates before pulling his dog's leash. "Maybe, uh . . . maybe I'll see you here around this time tomorrow?" This time his cheeks turn a deep red, competing with his hair, before he takes a feigned casual stance. "Or not. No big deal."

I laugh, awkwardly. Truth be told, I've been the plus-sized sidekick to both my cellulite-free runway model best friend and cousin for so long, I've gotten used to not getting attention from men, so this whole exchange is throwing me off. "Yeah, maybe."

I pick up Melody's call on the fourth ring, just as Liam walks away. Actually, it's more like Liam gets dragged away by his dog. "Hey!"

"Well, you sound awfully cheerful. Let me guess . . . you got laid!"

"No. Is that seriously all you think about?"

"Yes."

"Well, sorry to disappoint, but no. I was just talking to this tall redhead guy I met at the park who seemed a little . . . flustered? I think he was trying to flirt, but then you called."

"Wait, you were about to get laid and I cock-blocked you?" she asks, almost panicking.

I get up and start pushing Arman's stroller toward the sidewalk in the direction of the house. "No, dufus. Why would I be getting laid in a park at one PM in the afternoon?"

She pauses, and I know what she's going to say before she even says it. "Why wouldn't you?"

My mouth twists, holding back a laugh. I already feel ten times better than I have over the past few days. I absolutely love spending time with my nephew, and I know what I signed up for, but Darian's mood swing has definitely given me whiplash.

"What's up, *queenie*?" Melody uses the nickname she gave me in middle school after I told her what my name meant. "How's it going over there? How's that fine brother-in-law of yours?"

I grimace. "Things are fine, I guess. I mean, I'm having a ton of fun with this little cutie." I bend to look at my nephew, knowing Melody knows who I'm talking about. He's happily gazing at the clouds in the sky, chewing on his fingers, but I can already see his eyelids are getting heavier. "I'm just not so sure how Darian feels about it."

"What do you mean, you're not sure how Darian *feels* about it? You generously offered to take care of his son and he hired you, knowing what that would entail. So, what's the problem?"

"I don't know." I tuck a lock of curls behind my ear when it flies in the breeze. "He's just been . . . weird. I mean, I don't know the guy well enough to know what weird really means. This might just be how he operates, but I get the feeling he's avoiding me. Like, aside from the fifteen minutes we spend having dinner together in the evenings—where he's mostly scrolling through his phone—he barely makes eye contact with me. It's like he's scared to be in the same room as me."

I hear a familiar *clang* on the phone, guessing Melody's at the gym. She works as a zumba instructor there three times a week during the school year and full-time during the summer. The misfortune of being her best friend is that I 'get' to attend her classes for free any time I want, so of course, she guilts me into going any chance she gets. And as expected, it takes me a good half hour to lower my heart rate back to non-threatening levels.

I call bullshit on all those people who come out of her class, with most of the fluid from inside their bodies stuck on the outside, pretending it was the best thing they've ever done. It wasn't; it was brutal and inhumane.

"Maybe he is."

"Maybe he is, what?" I take a turn toward the familiar two-story, dark brown house with the massive golden maple doors when Arman squeals, "How!" with his index finger pointed at it. I love how much he's trying to speak, and if I could make a recording of all his adorable first words, I'd play them in a loop.

"Scared," Melody states, like it's the most obvious thing. "Listen, I know you're going to fight admitting your attraction to him, even to me, but you and I both know it's there. But I think—"

"No, it's not! Why are you and Bella so hellbent on—"

She bulldozes right past me, continuing her previous thought, "But I think there's some mutual attraction there from him, too."

"Okay, now you're just being ridiculous. I'm his sister-in-law, almost thirteen years younger than him, and definitely not his type."

Melody makes a 'pssh' sound like she's dismissing the facts I've pointed out. "You might be the first two, but how do you know you're not his type?"

I snort. "Um, because he looks like him, and I look like . . . well, *me*."

"Rani—"

This time I keep going, not letting her speak. "No, listen. I know I'm cute. I'm not saying it to put myself down. I'm just affirming that, given the fact that he was married to my extremely sporty, well-proportioned sister, I can guessteculate his type, and I'm not it."

"First, 'guessteculate' is not a word, and second, hear me out. I saw it when he was wrapping your wrist in his office after the fall you took from the kayak. There was something in his eyes. I know fuck-me eyes when I see them, Rani, and he had them."

"No, he didn't, Mel." I walk up the driveway toward the doors. "You're a lunatic."

"Or I'm right. In either case, you should explore this thing with the ginger you just met."

"Why?" A vision of Liam comes to the forefront of my mind, and I twist my mouth, not knowing what to think.

I mean, he's cute in a boy-next-door sort of way–definitely charming and sweet–but there's something missing. I'm no one to judge someone based on their looks–I've had that done to me my whole life–but while the guy is tall and handsome, I'm not sure how I feel about outweighing him on the scale.

Not that I've encountered a scale in quite some time. I stay away from them like a vampire to sunlight.

All this to say, I'd likely restrict blood flow in the poor guy's legs–and other vital appendages–if I sat on his lap. It would be like sitting on a very tall, thin, young boy. And being able to sit on the lap of the man I'm with is one of my guiding principles. It's something I won't compromise on.

Darian would have absolutely no circulation problems if I were to ever sit on his lap . . .. Which I never would, so I quickly chuck that untoward thought right out of my mind.

"Because A," Melody continues, "you need a distraction during the weekends and in your free time. Be a nineteen-year-old for once! And B, the proof will be in the pudding when you do. You'll see that what I told you about your brother-in-law was right."

Wait, what did she tell me about my brother-in-law? I'm so confused, but I don't have the time to clarify. I need to stay on schedule and give Arman a bottle before putting him down for his nap. Then I plan to fill out the volunteer paperwork online for the nursing home nearby.

I leave my shoes in the foyer after locking the door behind me and look at Arman in the stroller. He's rubbing his eyes, as if right on cue. "Okay, I'll see about Liam. I doubt it's anything, and I was probably just reading into it. But listen, I've gotta go."

I hear a car door slam and know she's heading out from work. "Okay, keep me posted, *queenie*. I just have a feeling this summer is going to be all about you getting your *kayak polished*."

She giggles at her ridiculous joke while I refrain from saying anything more than a "bye" before I disconnect the phone. I'm convinced the girl is on drugs.

But maybe I should find her dealer.

Chapter Eight
RANI

"So, what's his name?" I force myself not to laugh as I watch Liam try—and fail—to control his parents' dog. Said dog is currently trying to jump on anyone who passes by, while said passersby are giving us both derisive looks.

"*Her* name? It's Pepper, actually." He tips his chin toward Arman in the stroller. "What about him?"

"Arman." The sun is beating down on us today, so I lower the shade on Arman's stroller to cover him up. He's been babbling non-stop, waving hi to strangers and pointing out trees—twee!—and the swings in the playground—wins!

I make a note to tell Darian about his new words tonight. He came home last night and briefly said he'd already eaten dinner before he waited for Arman to finish and took him up for a bath.

It's not like we made plans to eat together or anything, nor was there any expectation for him to ask me if I'd eaten—I'm old enough to take care of myself—but I couldn't help feeling like it was a brush off.

I didn't tell him that I made chicken enchiladas for dinner while Arman napped that afternoon. I just warmed one up for myself and ate in my room instead, while I reviewed the directions for my summer photojournalism project online and responded to comments on my blog.

"Nice name. Is he your sister's kid or your brother's?"

I figured this would come up sooner or later. "My sister's," I reply, before adding, "She died last year . . . during childbirth."

Liam stays quiet, seeming to take in my response for a moment, though I see his step falter beside me. He strikes me as the type who stays composed in most situations. "I'm sorry, Rani. That must have been so incredibly hard."

"Thanks," I whisper as a familiar melancholy sweeps in.

For a few moments, only the sounds of Arman's stroller tires crunching along the pebbled path and Pepper's frenzied pants float around us, but for whatever reason, I decide to tell Liam more. I'm not in the habit of divulging my life story to strangers, but there's a sincerity to Liam, a calm presence that I find comforting, like I can unveil myself a little more without being pitied or judged.

"I didn't know her very well, actually." I glance at him. "She eloped with my brother-in-law many years ago, and my parents sort of disowned her. I was really young when it all happened and for many years, we had no contact. Then, one day, my brother-in-law called to tell us she died giving birth."

Liam lets out a big puff of air, and through my periphery, I notice his eyes linger on my profile. "I can't imagine how terrible your parents must feel. They never got a chance to make amends . . .."

I give him a quick shake of my head. "My mom is a very prideful woman, so I doubt she'd ever admit that. But the funny thing is, she thinks she has everyone fooled. She thinks no one knows that she's hurting, that she's scared. And whether or not anyone else knows, *I do*. She's had so many refills of her prescription sleeping pills, you'd think she was trying to start a drug lab in our house." I glance at Liam, who's listening intently, no longer even trying to control his dog. "No one needs that many sleeping pills unless they're running away from their past where it haunts them the most, in their sleep."

"And what about your dad?"

I huff out a laugh, not able to hide my scorn. "My dad has been asleep at the wheel for so long, he can't get himself back to a place he recognizes anymore. Every time he tries to speak up, my mom muzzles him with nothing more than a disdainful glance. I think he's made his peace with his decision to let her control their lives. Her decisions are his decisions; her needs are his to fulfill. The man has no backbone."

"Well, I bet you're glad to have a summer away from them, then."

I ponder his comment for a moment. Am I glad to have a break from my parents? Yes. Was my offer to help Darian a way of getting away from them? Not consciously, but perhaps my subconscious needed the reprieve, too. "I suppose, but my main concern was for my nephew."

"Did his previous caretaker leave?"

We turn to go up a steeper path, and I adjust my grip on the stroller's handlebar. "No. His other grandmother was having some health problems, and Darian needed someone to help out until he could find a more permanent solution. So, I volunteered."

Liam's eyes linger on me once more. "I'm not surprised."

I turn to him with a smile. "Oh yeah? One long walk around the park and you already have me figured out, huh?"

He laughs. "Hardly. I'm just an intuitive person, I suppose." He pauses and I notice the faint freckles on his nose. "But I'd like to get to know you better . . . if you'd let me."

I press my lips together, hoping I don't look like the

blushing idiot I feel like inside. I know what he's hinting at. I get where this is going, but something is holding me back from jumping at the chance to go out with him—an internal voice, perhaps—so I stall. "What do you want to know?"

"Well, for starters, what do you do?"

"I'm studying journalism. I'll graduate in two years and hope to go into content writing or social media planning."

"That sounds pretty interesting. What made you interested in journalism?"

I shrug. "I've always been good at writing and distilling information. I love learning about peoples' lives and experiences, along with keeping up with what's happening in the world. I also find content dissemination through marketing websites pretty interesting, too. So, it just made sense." I squint at him. "You know, I feel like I'm at a disadvantage here. You seem to know a lot more about me than I do about you."

"Well, we're going to need more than a walk around the park for that, I'm afraid. I have a very intriguing and exhilarating life as a business analyst working for a water utility company." He grins playfully. "Perhaps I can entice you to have dinner with me? There's just so much of me to get to know."

When he sees me smile but hesitating to answer, he continues, "Oh, come on, I can't have you thinking of me as the guy who's owned by a four-legged beast pretending to be a dog. It's not a respectable look for me. Give me a chance to redeem myself."

On cue, as if knowing it'll embarrass Liam further, Pepper decides to plop down on the grass and roll over, pulling Liam forward with her. He swears under his breath as her leash gets wrapped around his leg, making me burst out laughing.

I can't help but find Liam endearing. He may not be

exactly my type, but there's no denying he's funny and sweet. "I think you have your work cut out on changing my mind."

∽

Karine: Are you and Arman home? I made dinner and <poop emoji>

I READ the text again to make sure I'm not missing some context before a smile spreads over my face.

Me: We just got home from our walk not too long ago. Come on over. Oh, and what does <poop emoji> mean?

Karine: Chocolate pudding! You'll love it. It's my special recipe.

I'm still giggling about our text exchange when I step out onto Darian's back patio, but I suppress the laugh as soon as I see Karine. "How's your physical therapy going?" I hand the baby to Karine.

Karine pulls Arman into a hug, placing a soft kiss on his head. He seems happy after his nap, bouncing on his feet in her lap.

"Oh, it's good," she says, her unique Armenian accent rounding out the O's in the words. "I don't feel a change besides some soreness in my arms and legs, but the therapist said it takes time." She rolls her eyes. "Who knows? It could all just be a money-making scheme."

I laugh. "I highly doubt that, but I hope you start feeling some changes soon."

"Me, too." Karine's short dark hair—the same color as her son's—whips around in the breeze. She's a petite woman, though rounder around her stomach and thighs. "I've missed my Arman *jan*." Her smile widens as she affectionately squeezes her grandson before she looks at me. "Still not fully walking, huh?"

Arman pulls his grandma's necklace and studies it with intrigue, and I lean over to tickle his cheek with my finger. "Not yet, but he's trying. Yesterday, he stood up on his own a few times and took a couple of steps, but then he got worried and crab-crawled everywhere."

Karine lifts him and blows raspberries on his stomach, making him squeal. "Yup, same as last week. Well, we'll get there soon, won't we, Arman *jan*?" She turns to me. "Darian was the opposite as a baby. He was walking by eleven months and talking in almost full sentences by fourteen months. The boy threw caution to the wind, you know? He was a risk-taker through and through. And once his dad and older brothers introduced him to the snow and the mountains . . .? It was over." She rolls her eyes. "The boy didn't want to come home! He was captivated by the snow, though he loved water sports just as much."

"I'm sure you were worried about him breaking bones," I state, imagining a much younger version of the dark-haired, dark-eyed man I've seen over the last few days.

"Oh, he broke plenty. After the first time he broke his wrist and the time he broke his ankle, I gave up trying to control him. He was going to do it, whether I agreed or not." She gives me a saddened look. "But you know, it's not his bones I'm worried about anymore."

"No?" I ask, knowing what she's referring to.

"No, it's that broken heart he walks around with. The one that carries the weight of two people."

My eyes slide down to my lap. "Yeah, I know."

"He's lonely and stressed, and I don't think he's sleeping much, either. I see it written as clear as day on his face. I'm glad he took your offer to help him but," she shakes her head as if giving up, "I still worry about him."

As if his ears were burning, the backdoor to the patio opens and Darian walks out. His eyes find mine before they drift to his mom. "Worry about who?"

Karine gets up, holding Arman, who is anxious to get out of her hold and into his dad's. "You!" Karine admits, handing Darian the baby before kissing her son on the cheek. "I'm worried about you. You work too much and don't seem to be taking care of yourself. Look at those dark circles under your eyes. Darian *jan*. This is not how a thirty-two year old should look."

Darian sighs, giving Arman a kiss on his temple. "I'm fine, Mom. The past couple of weeks have just been more hectic than usual with us preparing for the kayaking tournament. Plus, I'm still trying to get our website updated and the showers renovated."

"When is the tournament?" I ask, getting off my seat as well.

"Early August. There's just a lot to do by then."

"Is there anything I can help with? I'm pretty familiar with website design, and I can help with marketing for the tournament, if you still need that."

Darian grimaces. "I can't ask you to help with any more than you're already doing for me, Rani. It's not something you need to worry about."

"But you're *not* asking me; I'm offering. If you need an extra pair of hands to update your website and get things ready for the tournament, I can always help while Arman is napping."

"I'll think about it," Darian says, turning toward the house with Arman in his arms.

"Don't be so rigid, Darian *jan*," Karine calls out. "Take the help where you can."

I rush behind Darian and grab his elbow. It seems like the only way I can get his full attention is when I cross our physical barrier. And I definitely have his full attention now.

When he turns toward me, I raise my chin and try not to cower under his penetrating stare, even with my heart rate picking up. "If you don't want my help for free, then give me a part-time job or an internship. I could use it to build my resume, and you'd get what you need. It would be a fair trade."

His gaze steadily holds mine before it lands on my hand on his elbow, and I remove it quickly. God, I wish I could tell what he was thinking. It's so unfair that he gives nothing away through his almost expressionless face.

His voice lowers, almost inaudibly, but I hear it loud and clear, knowing his words will repeat in my head relentlessly through the night. "Let's get one thing straight. Nothing about this—nothing about you—has been a fair trade."

∽

MY EYES FLY OPEN, searching in the dark, when I hear Arman's soft cry. Over the past week, he's slept through the night, but I noticed he was a little fussier during dinner tonight. Maybe he's going through a growth spurt. I'd read about them when I was researching baby milestones earlier.

I fling the blanket off me and adjust my thin tank top strap back on my shoulder before getting out of bed. Rubbing my eyes, I tap on my phone to see the time—it's three twenty-four in the morning. Pulling my door open, I walk through the dark hallway toward his room, which is illuminated by a small giraffe nightlight.

Arman pulls himself up in his crib, showing me his gums and that one top tooth in a massive, heart-melting grin. "*Mas!*"

He and I have been working on him calling me *masee* all week. He hasn't quite perfected the word, but nonetheless, it makes my heart flutter whenever I hear him call out to me.

"I'm here, little man," I whisper, lifting him out of his crib and giving him a kiss on his cheek. His diaper is heavy and it appears to have soaked through his pajamas. "No wonder you couldn't sleep, sweetheart. Let's get you changed."

"*Mas*." He grabs a hold of my curls before palming both my cheeks and bringing my entire face to his, placing a happy open-mouthed kiss near my nose.

My chest heaves at the sweet gesture, making my eyes prick with tears. How the hell am I going to leave this baby after the summer? I'm already falling in love with him so hard and fast, I don't know how to control it. "That's right," I choke out before clearing my throat. "*Masee*."

After changing him and putting him in a new pair of pajamas, I try to put him back in his crib, but his grip is so tight around me that he won't let go. I even try finding him a new plushie from his bin to sleep with, but he throws it across the room, refusing to go into his crib. Even in the dim lighting, I can see his face turning red.

"Okay, okay." I yawn, taking him to the rocking chair. "One song and then you're going to sleep, mister. Okay?" No matter how firm I think my voice sounds, it melts as soon as I hear him giggle. A thousand kisses won't be enough, but I place one more on his chubby cheek. "My little monster."

I sing softly, rocking him as he buries his head under my chin, holding on to a lock of my hair while his white rabbit plushie sits on his lap. I've sung the same song–*Stay Awake* from Mary Poppins–to him since the first day I was here, and I know there's something about the words and the tune that help him relax.

Maybe he can hear his mother's voice through them.

Maybe she sang this same song to him when he was in her womb as she did for me on so many nights.

I remember how I'd insist on watching a scary movie with Sonia and pull her arm over me like a blanket during the scariest parts. When the movie was over, I'd beg her to tuck me into bed. I still remember the feel of her fingertips as she glided them over my forehead softly, foregoing her own sleep to make sure I could find mine. Her raspy voice would float through my room as she sang the words, while I envisioned Julie Andrews—Mary Poppins—putting the boy and girl from the movie to sleep.

Before I knew it, I'd have fallen asleep.

I startle awake some time later, still clutching Arman to my chest. His warm breath wafts over my collarbone before he takes a deep inhale and buries himself even further into me.

I lift my eyes instinctively. It's as if, even in sleep, I could feel someone's eyes lingering on me. Someone who seems to do that a lot but never reveals a single thought. I feel his gaze on me, like I feel the cool breeze coming from the air conditioning.

Darian stands with his arms crossed, leaning against the doorframe, and I wonder how long he's been there. He's already rendered me tongue-tied multiple times over the course of my time here, but with his arms flexing under his gray T-shirt and his hair mussed in the sexiest disarray, I'm as good as mute.

Still, something about him seems on edge and unpredictable as his wild eyes stroll over every inch of me with the precision of a surgeon. He takes in my exposed legs before lingering on my bare shoulders. When he finally reaches my face, his eyes lock on my lips before they move up to my eyes.

I don't know if it's because his perusal has me parched or

crazed—maybe both—but I find myself gliding my tongue over my bottom lip. The movement makes him inhale sharply. It's when I bite the middle of my lip, inadvertently—or maybe purposefully—that I see his entire body go rigid.

Warning bells sound inside my head, alerting me to the fact that whatever is happening at this very moment is toeing a line I should be really sure I want to cross, because once I do . . . there might not be a return trip.

This isn't right. He's your brother-in-law . . . .

My gaze stays trapped on his as I start to rock the chair again, holding the most precious part of his soul in my arms. I don't know if it's the abandon that the shadowed room seems to bring about that vanishes in sunlight or the belief that I'm still dreaming, but I feel like I've sprouted wings, like I'm gliding toward a goal I never set.

It's brazen and breathtaking, but at this very moment, I feel like I could leap off this cliff and soar. Only fate would decide if I'd make it to my final destination or fall into an endless abyss, but I feel daring enough to give it a try.

This want, this insane desire, isn't something I've felt or been compelled toward my entire life. Not at this intensity, with the burner turned all the way up. The only man—a boy, really—who's made me feel anything prior to this, would feel like comparing a feral street cat to a lion.

And if a street cat could have shattered me so inexplicably, then what would a lion do if I let it get close enough?

I watch as Darian's eyes go from dark to boundless, as if they belong on a ravenous tiger. I watch as his nostrils flare and his breathing hastens, for the first time revealing an internal battle he's fighting—a battle I'm not sure he even knows he's having.

I don't know how long we stay there, locked in a dialogue of silent words, before Arman's small, dreamy whimper pulls us out of the haze.

Darian's eyes find his son in my arms before he strolls over to me. Reaching down, he lifts the baby from my grasp before speaking over his shoulder. His brusque tone betrays everything we just wordlessly shared, and I wonder if I imagined it all. "Go to sleep, Rani. Like I've said before, you don't need to worry about him on the weekends."

And just like that, the warm breeze beneath my newly found wings disappears, replaced by an arctic chill.

Chapter Nine
DARIAN

I unzip Arman's raincoat, hanging it on a hook in the mudroom, before getting a towel out of the cabinet to wipe his face and hands. We were expecting rain today but instead of a drizzle, we got caught in a downpour on our way home from the grocery store.

Securing him in his high chair, I tread back to the garage to unload the groceries from my truck. I look down the driveway and up the road to see if I spot Rani's car anywhere but it—nor its owner—has been around much this weekend.

"Fuck," I grumble, running a hand through my hair before grabbing the first of five bags and the handle of lagers for when my brothers come over tonight for our usual Sunday afternoon poker game.

Another pang of guilt stabs me right in between my ribs as I place the bags on the kitchen counter and run out for the others. I shouldn't have been so harsh with her a couple of nights ago.

I'd heard Arman through the monitor as soon as he was up, but I wanted to give him a few minutes to settle down on his own before I went to check on him. Sometimes he wakes up because of a bad dream and is able to soothe himself back to sleep. I've learned the differences in his cries and can usually gauge whether I need to get up immediately or not based on them.

So, it caught me by surprise when I heard Rani's voice in his room through the monitor. All my senses locked on her soft, throaty voice as she sang to my son, and something in my chest constricted while I watched her rock him back to sleep.

A part of me wanted to stomp over and tell her that she's ruining him—making him believe in something she'll ultimately take away at the end of summer. That forming this attachment isn't healthy and will only end in heartbreak when he doesn't see her everyday afterward.

That same part of me whispered that I wasn't just talking about my son.

The other part—the part that didn't care about the repercussions or restrictions—wanted to go to her . . ..

Nothing about this situation—aside from her taking care of my son as if he were her own—is sitting well with me. My mind feels unsettled whenever I'm around her, like it can't decide if I should root myself to my spot and hold my ground or run the other way.

I'm generally good at hiding my emotions—something that's worked to my advantage with my brothers being the card sharks they are. I learned to keep my face impassive and my breathing steady whenever I got dealt a bad hand; otherwise, my brothers would rob me clean and wipe the floor with my ass. My emotions are for me to express in the privacy of my own room, not to be on display under a million lights like something in Times Square.

But with her . . ..

With her, I feel like every fucking emotion parades itself over my damn face like it's some Broadway musical. I lose every hand and fold like the world's most pathetic poker player.

I hadn't seen her properly through the monitor that night. All I'd seen was a shadow of her holding Arman to her chest as she rocked him back to sleep. But when her voice trailed off and the room went silent, I found myself drawn to it . . . drawn to her. Before my mind could tell my feet to stop, I was getting out of bed.

I stood there watching her for a good five minutes. The way her bare legs stretched out in front of her, the way her beautiful curls lay across her exposed shoulders, the way her mouth rested on my son's hair. I wanted to pull out my damn phone and take a picture, like some fucking creep.

But before I could decide what I was going to do, her eyes snapped open and landed on mine. It was as if she could feel me there, as if she'd beckoned me there. Her focus stayed steady on me, daring me to come closer. From the way she bit her lip to the way she lifted her chin, her eyes half shuttered, raking over me—it was a fucking siren's call. And I was entranced.

If it wasn't for my son's sleepy voice pulling me from the fixation, I'm positive I would have either stood there all night or done something worse. *Much worse.* And I would have regretted it.

Not only has Sonia been gone for just a year, but her sister is a mere teenager! What the hell is wrong with me, ogling her like some pervert?

I saw her car parked outside late last night and the lights were on under her bedroom door, but then she was gone earlier than either me or Arman woke up this morning, and I haven't seen her since.

I consider texting her but then wonder what I would even say. I don't want to seem like I'm just checking in—I did tell her she was off the hook from worrying about us during the weekend—but I also want to make sure she doesn't feel so uncomfortable around me now that she no longer wants to come home while I'm here.

I place the bouquet of new lilies in a vase full of water before I start unloading the groceries. Arman whines to be let out of his high chair, so I unbuckle him and leave him to wander around the living room and play with his toys while still keeping an eye on him. Thankfully, none of my furniture has hard edges, and I've childproofed most cabinets—except for the one with all the steel bowls that he loves to get into—so I don't have to worry too much about him getting into anything I don't want.

Scrawling out a quick note and affixing it inside the flowers, I run upstairs and place the vase in front of Rani's door. I'm midway down the stairs when my phone buzzes inside my pocket. A big part of me hopes it's her, but I know the answer to that before I even look to see who it is.

A message from Garrett to both me and our other brother Dean lights up my screen.

Garrett: You good on beer? I can pick some up on my way there.

Dean: You might want to pick some up. The guy's idea of a fun libation is a protein shake or a cup of green tea. I'll pick up wings.

I shake my head, typing out my response to my asshole twin brothers. They may be three years older, but I swear I feel like the only adult in the room when we're all together. It's been that way my entire life.

The three of us share the same father—they even take after our dad with their blue eyes and blond hair—but their mom divorced our dad a year after they were born. My dad married my mother not long after that, and they've been together ever since.

Growing up, my brothers spent as much time with me and my parents as they did with their mother and stepfather. So, while it was known that we were half-siblings, we've never treated each other as anything but full-blooded brothers. My mom has always treated them like her own, just as their mom has always accepted me as an extension of them.

I'm aware of the rareness of our family dynamic, but it's how I grew up—with my family being my backbone. It's also why I always found the animosity Sonia's parents—mainly her mother—had for us and our relationship to be so foreign.

I used to wonder how they could have disowned their daughter for following her heart. How could your family, whom you trusted to love you unconditionally, disavow you at the time you need them to understand and support you the most?

I couldn't understand it for the longest time, but I told myself I'd overcome my guilt of breaking up her family—of taking her away from all the loved ones she knew—by giving her my own. I told myself that, with time, she'd feel at home with mine. And for a long time, she did.

After Sonia died, my brothers were there for me as much as they could have been, given their full-time jobs and their own commitments. And when they weren't here physically, my parents were just a short distance away. So while I spent many long and lonely nights missing the woman who'd been a part of my nights for so long, I knew my days would be anything but lonely.

Me: I'm pretty sure I've had you covered the past few poker nights, and I have you covered today, too.

Me: Also, you studying for the SATs or something? Who the hell uses the word 'libation'?

Dean: I do. :)

Garrett: Alright, alright. Don't get your panties in a twist. Did Ryan confirm?

My recently divorced friend, Ryan, used to come to our poker nights. He'd bring his now ex-wife Emily, and while we played a few rounds at the house, the ladies would take their drinks and banter out on the front patio of our old house.

But ever since Sonia died, and Ryan and Emily separated, we lost touch. But for the sake of trying to get my life back to normal—however normal it can be considering the circumstances—I recently reached out to see if he wanted to join us again. And to my surprise, he accepted.

Maybe I should have thought more about mending that bridge before I sent him the invitation text, but now that he's coming, I can't rescind the offer. I can't say I'm extremely thrilled about it, though.

It's not that he's a bad guy, but it takes a certain level of energy and overlooking of objectionable behavior—followed by at least a day of detox—to be in Ryan's company. The words 'loud and obnoxious' don't quite sum up his personality. Even at thirty-something years old, I'm positive he thinks he's still the president of his old college fraternity. While my own brothers can come across as exuberant and excitable—given how sociable they are—they don't hold a candle to Ryan's thunderous personality. Where my brothers are genuine and adept at reading the room, Ryan lacks that bit of sophistication, wavering on the line of being an outright douchebag at times.

I sigh, typing out my response.

Me: Yeah, he'll be here. Bring ear plugs.

Dean: We might need harder stuff than beer, then. I'm on it.

Yeah, Valium or a concussion, perhaps. I don't type that out, of course.

Dean: Hey so, is your sister-nanny going to be there? Karine has been raving about her non-stop. I'm asking because I wanted to know how best to present myself. Should I come in my Sunday best or my Fuckable Friday Special?

Garrett: Oh yeah. I forgot about your sister-nanny. Is she cute? I faintly recall meeting her last year, but it's all a blur.
Garrett: And hell no! Not your fucking Friday special. No one needs to see that shit again.

I grit my teeth, reading their texts as they come through while I prepare Arman's lunch. Unlike me, my brothers are flirtatious and charismatic. I've gone out with them enough to be privy to the charm they fling on women, making them putty in their fucking hands.

The thought of them getting said hands on Rani or even flirting with her has me on edge. She's too innocent, too fucking sweet for anyone like them.

And as for Dean's Fuckable Friday bullshit—some sorority girl once told my dumbass brother that he'd look great if he wore one of those newsboy hats with his shirt unbuttoned to reveal his chest. Apparently, my brother is not above taking fashion advice from random women at a bar, because the next Friday, Dean went out with the aforementioned outfit and claimed he had a threesome with two women. Since then, he's referred to it as his Fuckable Friday Special.

A tense pressure forms in my jaw as I pound out the message, retyping it a couple of times before sending it.

When it comes to my brothers, I can't come across overly dickish or obvious because if there's one thing they're good at, it's questioning me until I wish for death via decapitation. Like fucking termites to wood, they'll wear me down until I become nothing but dust.

But, I also want to make it clear that my nineteen-year-old sister-in-law is off limits for their thirty-five-year-old asses.

She's off limits for thirty-two-year-old jaded assholes as well, but that's not the point.

Me: This is not a clothes-optional party, asshole. Show up with your shit covered or I'm going to kick you the fuck out. Also wtf is up with you two calling her my sister-nanny? She's not my sister. Anyway, she's not here now, but I'm expecting her at some point during the evening.

Garrett: @Dean, is it me or does our little brother seem a bit . . . defensive? <confused face emoji>

I groan, rolling my eyes before throwing my phone onto the sofa and focusing on my son, who is again trying to walk. I'll have the rest of the day to deal with my annoying-as-fuck older brothers. I'm just sitting down to play with Arman when I see Dean's response come in.

Dean: Definitely not just you. I read the 'she's not my sister' part loud and clear. Looks like we're going to need the hard shit tonight.

Chapter Ten
RANI

"So, you're definitely going to stay there all summer, then?" My mom's face tightens as she leans back against the couch in her living room.

Her FaceTime call had come in as I was parking at the bakery this morning, so I'm currently sitting inside my car, looking from her to the sinister clouds darkening the sky. Given the choice, I'd much rather look at the clouds.

I sigh, exasperatedly, repeating my response for possibly the fifth time in the past ten minutes we've been chatting. "Yes, Mom. How many times will you ask me before you realize I'm not changing my mind? Yes, I'm here through the summer to take care of Arman." *I might get fired after what happened on Friday night, but I'm not going to tell her that.* "He's doing fine, by the way, in case you were wondering about your only grandson. He's trying to walk and talk, and he is making progress every day."

My mother snorts. "Sonia was running by the time she was ten months old. And she was already so articulate, I never had to wonder what she needed."

I stare at my mother for a beat, my anger stirring inside my veins and my temples throbbing with the onset of a headache. "He's *one*, Mom. Many kids don't talk or walk at one. Karine said the pediatrician told them it was completely normal and that he'll do all those things at his own pace."

"Karine will believe only what she wants to hear. She never questions the validity or consequences of anything when it concerns her children—and now her grandchildren. Arman is slow; that's all I'm saying. It's not an insult, Rani, it's a fact. Coddling him will do nothing but make him believe someone will always be there to pick him up. You, Karine, and that useless father of his are only giving him a false sense of security."

My chest tightens, wanting to beat my damn steering wheel with my fist. "Yeah? Well, what does *not* giving your children that sense of security do to them, Mom? You should know; you've perfected the art. There's tough love, and then there's your brand of insensitivity. What has it ever gotten you? What has it ever gotten any of us, besides heartache and loneliness?"

"Rani—" My mother's voice is a warning, her face set like stone.

"You might have had the world's most brilliant child with Sonia, but in the end, what did that get you besides another gold star *you* placed beside your name. Because everyone knows that if you were such an incredible mother, no daughter of yours would have been able to resist not speaking to you, not having you in her life, for ten years."

Tears cloud my eyes and I know I'll regret the words as soon they're spoken, but it's as if I'm possessed. As if something was unleashed inside me the second her vile words against Arman and Darian came out of her mouth. "So, be as haughty as you want, Mom. Give yourself *all* the gold stars for setting the standard on parenting. But we both know it won't bring back the ten years you lost with her, and it certainly won't raise her from the dead."

"Rani!" my mom gasps. Her chest rises and falls as tears drip from her eyes.

I know I went too far. I let my anger get the best of me; I let *her* get the best of me. I allowed her to affect my peace, and that's something I've worked hard to never let anyone take from me again.

Not the bullies and body-shamers.

Not the asshole boyfriend I found on my prom night with his dick inside the girl who practically ruined my elementary and middle school experience.

And definitely not the mother who held her love hostage in exchange for forcing her kids to meet her ever-increasing, impossibly high standards.

Despite having been raised by her, despite the constant scrutiny and mockery, I've worked hard to *not* be a reflection of her. I've worked hard to not be bitter or mean.

This is not who I am—I'm careful with my words and the feelings of others. I might be headstrong, but I'm never heartless. So why am I letting her unravel all the work I've done?

My chin drops to my collarbone as guilt smears across my face. "I'm sorry, Mom. I didn't mean to hurt you."

"Ah, but you did." Her derisive laugh is anything but cheerful. "You did. Just like *she* did."

Tears float behind my lids, too exhausted to fall. "Mom, I don't claim to know it all, but from what I can see, if you're looking to everyone around you to find what it is that you need—whether it be Dad, me, or even Sonia—you won't get it. You won't get it unless you find it in yourself first."

My mother's voice turns more condescending and harsh

as she wipes the tears from her cheeks. "And what does my wise, *teenage* daughter think I need?"

"Happiness, peace, fulfillment, love . . . *forgiveness*."

My mother just stares at me, giving nothing away from her expression. Whether my words have resonated with her or not, I'll never know.

The rain seems to be coming down harder, and I still need to get the doughnuts and muffins to take to the nursing home this morning. "Listen, Mom, I need to go. I'm sorry again for what I said." I wait until she meets my eyes before hanging up. "I love you."

∾

"Well, don't those look scrumptious."

I set the boxes of pastries on the breakfast table and look up at an elderly couple walking toward me. A tall man holding a walker slowly approaches me alongside a tiny woman, who I assume is his wife based on the way she's gently holding his bicep. The couple look to be in their eighties, and even though he's hunched down considerably over his walker, there's quite a height difference between the two.

"Fred." The woman's wavering voice warns her husband. Her hair is almost completely gray, while Fred's is more salt and pepper. "You can just have one, so pick wisely."

Fred scowls, eyeing the boxes of sugar in front of him before raising his eyes to me. "She's a real ball-buster, my wife. I've had to endure this kind of treatment for nearly sixty years."

The woman just shakes her head, but the corners of her mouth tilt up, making her wrinkles shift across her face. "Thank you for bringing these for us, dear." She takes account of the visitor tag above my right breast. "Are you visiting someone specific?"

I shake my head, smiling. My hair is still a frizzy mess from the rain that drenched me on the way inside but thankfully, most of it has dried off inside the cool building. "No, I'm actually going to start volunteering here on the weekends or whenever I can come in." I nod at the boxes on the table. "The staff let me bring these in and stay for breakfast to meet some of you."

Blue eyes under heavy lids sparkle, catching the light. "Oh! Well, that's nice of them and you." She extends a frail arm in my direction, and I notice large brown age spots over her skin. "My name is Lynn and this," she turns to her husband, and my heart melts at the way he winks at her, "is my sweet-toothed husband, Fred. He still believes he can eat sugar like a five-year-old at the carnival, so I have to keep an eye on him."

"I have no problems with you keeping your eyes on me, sweetheart. I don't want them on anyone but me. It's why I still look as dashing as I do, even now at my spritely age. All for you. But a man should be allowed a few indulgences from time to time."

Lynn purses her lips. "Your definition of 'time to time' is *daily*."

"And yours is *yearly*. By your calculations, that doesn't leave very many desserts for me to enjoy."

I giggle as Lynn's exasperated eyes meet mine again. "Do you see what I have to deal with?" She looks back at him, holding back an eye roll. "Well, go ahead, then. Get your sugar fix and leave this poor girl alone."

"Oh, I don't mind at all," I respond hurriedly. "I'm Rani, by the way. It was great meeting you both."

"You too, Rani." Fred smiles, following his wife toward the dining area, before turning back and whispering, "Keep bringing in those treats, okay?"

I laugh, feeling the weight of everything over the past

weekend—from the mortifying way I acted with my brother-in-law to the argument with my mother—melt off me. "I promise."

∽

"So fucking stupid," I groan to myself, taking a bite out of my egg-and-cheese sandwich. "Stupid, stupid girl."

It's been at least two hours since I parked my butt on this sandy beach overlooking the lake, and I've circled through the same loop inside my brain. Embarrassment, confusion, and denial, followed by a healthy dose of pure shame.

Phase one: embarrassment.

What the hell was I thinking? How could I have allowed myself to flirt—almost indecently—with my brother-in-law? God, who was I that night? Certainly not the same girl who chatters uncontrollably when met with a man of Darian's caliber. Though I would argue—with myself—that I've never met a man of Darian's caliber, but still, who the fuck was I? What the hell was all that mumbo-jumbo about me sprouting wings and flying? Was I fucking high?

Here comes the confusion phase . . . .

But then again, did I? Did I *actually* flirt with him? Could a staring contest with someone—a hot someone, who also happens to be your brother-in-law—be considered flirting?

You fucking licked your lips, hussy!

Okay, okay. So, I licked my damn lips. But I mean, in fairness, I lick them all the time.

And, we're onto the denial phase. Why is wetting my dry lips considered flirting, anyway? It seems a little far-fetched to consider such an innocent act flirting.

Now, for shame.

"Gah!" I wrap my hand over my eyes and wish for the

hundredth time that I could dig a hole through this beach and crawl to China. "I'm pathetic. It's the only explanation."

I *eye-fucked* my brother-in-law, purposefully licked my lips in a silent innuendo, and made him feel utterly uncomfortable. I completely misread his reaction—the almost audible groan, the nostril flaring, and sexy jaw clenching. It wasn't because he was affected by me; it was because he was horrified, probably on the verge of firing me on the spot. And the only reason he likely refrained from firing me was *because* it was the middle of the night!

My cheeks flame as I think about how inappropriately I acted. Sure, I didn't *do* anything per se—thank God!—but he *knew*. He isn't stupid. He *knew* I was burning up for him. I acted as if I had zero principles, when, in fact, I live by my principles. I'm a woman who values her principles!

I'm sure he went back to his room, repulsed and in shock. Men like Darian Meyer don't go for women—*girls*—like me. Men like him have a line of beautiful, undernourished, delicate women with perfect BMIs and breast-to-waist ratios waiting on the sidelines.

Maybe I should just quit, hand in my resignation after just one freaking week.

I take another bite of my sandwich, not even registering the taste. *I can't quit*. I can't do that to Arman. Darian would have to ask his mother to fill in again and rush to look for another, more permanent nanny. Karine just started going to physical therapy, and Arman and I are adjusting so well to each other. Plus, quitting would just give my mother more ammunition to berate Darian. She'd revel in my failure, especially after the way our conversation ended this morning.

No, I can't quit. But fuck, I want to hide or disappear somewhere.

"Ugh." I throw the rest of my sandwich back into the paper bag, wiping the back of my mouth with my hand.

Maybe the best thing to do is pretend Friday night didn't happen and move along with just focusing on what I'm here to do. That is, unless Darian fires me before I even get a chance to redeem myself. I've been so worried about him confronting me that I've been sneaking out of the house all weekend before he's awake. I know it's impossible to avoid him forever, but I figure giving him time and space to rethink things can't hurt.

He practically ordered me to leave with his last statement.

Another hour goes by before I finally find the nerve to head back. I'm hoping Darian has put Arman to bed by now and is in his study so I can creep back to my room and avoid him for another night. He's usually rushing out of the house in the morning to get to work, so hopefully, we can just manage another week where we stay out of each other's way.

I pull up in front of Darian's house and note the various unfamiliar cars already parked there. Maybe Darian having company will work to my advantage. Maybe he'll be too distracted to notice I'm even back.

Turning the key inside the lock as softly as I can, I try to tiptoe through the foyer to take the stairs up to my room. Unfamiliar laughter hits my ears as I try to keep my head down and find the steps.

I'm barely a foot from the stairs when I hear an unfamiliar voice greet me, "Hey, Rani!"

Ugh!

I plaster on a casual smile before turning toward the dining table full of men I don't recognize, except for Darian. "Hello."

A man with long blond hair—chopped fine on the sides but held in a bun on the top of his head—gives me a two-finger wave. He's holding a few playing cards in his other hand. I recognize him as one of Darian's brothers from the several framed pictures in his office. "We were wondering if we'd get a chance to meet you. I'm Dean, by the way."

I smile in his direction. "Great to meet you."

"Thanks for helping my brother out with Arman," Dean adds before gesturing to his left. "This is Garrett, the man who shared a womb with me but somehow, didn't turn out nearly as handsome."

Garrett barks out a laugh before turning his blue eyes toward me. He has the same blond hair as his brother, but it's cut close to his head, almost military style. "This coming from a man who can't get laid without flashing his chest."

"Guys," Darian warns.

Not knowing exactly what they're referring to, I widen my smile and work hard to avoid the coffee-colored gaze that's currently set in my direction. "No problem. I was happy to be able to help." My voice squeaks a little as I take a step backward toward the stairs, responding to Dean, "Good to meet you guys. I didn't mean to interrupt your game."

"You're quite the welcome interruption." Another unfamiliar man to Darian's right speaks before I can make my getaway. His toothy grin and dark eyes remind me of the big bad wolf from Red Riding Hood. *And not in a good way.* "I'm Ryan, one of Darian and your sister's friends."

I nod, not knowing what more to say.

"God, I see the similarities between you and her. The same eyes, the same nose. I'm, uh . . ." he clears his throat, "I'm sorry for your loss, Rani. I know you both weren't in each other's lives for quite a while—"

"Ryan." Darian's voice sounds steely, a warning laced in his name.

Ryan chuckles as if caught red-handed. "What I meant to say is, Sonia and I were pretty close." He looks at Darian, whose shoulders seem stiffer compared to the brief glance I snuck toward him earlier. "I mean, my ex-wife Emily and

Sonia were closer, of course, but over the years, we'd all become good friends." He pauses, grinning as if he's waiting for me to catch the punchline of a joke. "Anyway, I don't mean to dampen your mood. I just didn't want to waste a chance to introduce myself to such a beautiful woman. Want to join us in a game of Texas Hold'em?"

I offer him a tight smile. "No, thank you. I don't know how to play, plus I'm pretty tired. It was nice meeting you."

"You, too." His eyes trail down my neck and over my breasts before they flit back to my face, and a shudder runs down my spine like acid on my skin. "Hope to see you around again, Rani."

As much as I've been avoiding Darian, my eyes can't help but seek him out. I don't know if he caught his friend's leering, but his jaw is clenched tight, nonetheless. You'd think he was working on crushing rocks between his teeth. Other than that, his face is a blank mask.

Feeling queasy, I dash up the stairs, hoping to rid my mind and skin of Ryan's unwanted attention. God, some men just know how to give a girl the heebie-jeebies.

Tiptoeing past Arman's room, I walk down the hallway to my own. My attention gets caught on a vase full of light pink lilies at my door. I know exactly who left them, but I still can't help dart my eyes left and right as if maybe I missed the deliverer.

Picking up the vase and opening my door, I pluck the small card attached to them. I head inside before closing the door behind me and place the vase on my chest of drawers. I smile at the fresh blooms as I'd just thrown out the old lilies yesterday on my way out.

My heart pitter-patters inside my chest, and I can't quite reason as to why. Why is a vase of flowers—seemingly here to replace the old ones in my room—constricting my airway? Why are my hands trembling as I pull the small card out of its envelope? Why are my lips turning up at the corners, as if knowing–hoping–that this bouquet is a peace offering? A peace offering for what, exactly?

Turning the card around, I stare at the simple handwritten words, knowing they declare anything but simple thoughts.

I'm sorry.

Chapter Eleven
DARIAN

"King!" Olivia waves at me from one of the supply closets. "The stuff you ordered for the tournament came in today. Come, check it out."

The better part of my morning has been spent negotiating contracts with a well-known sporting goods retailer who would like to showcase *Truckee Sports* as their preferred kayaking and skiing instruction partner. While my school has many business partners, this one is definitely the most lucrative in terms of future growth due to the retailer's brand value. So, as tiring as the call was, I know it's one that will help expand our market footprint.

Sighing, I run my hand through my hair and turn to face Olivia. "Let me get some Vitamin Water from the kitchenette, and I'll meet you there."

A few minutes later, I'm examining the marketing material—banners, poster boards, and pamphlets—I'd ordered for the tournament that will be held at my school in a little over a month.

"The posters look amazing, huh?" Olivia's eyes gleam through her red-rimmed glasses. She doesn't generally wear them but when she does, her eyes always look twice as big. "And look at these stickers and pamphlets! You and Greg did a great job putting these together, King."

I nod, liking the result of what seemed like a million hours of work last month. "Thanks. Yeah, it turned out great. Let's find an hour to discuss other logistics for that day."

"Sounds good. I'll get some time set up for us." Olivia closes the closet door right as I start walking away. Unfortunately for me, she catches up to me quickly. "So, how are things going with the nanny?"

I squint at her. "The nanny? You mean, my sister-in-law, who is helping me for the summer?"

Olivia shrugs with a high-pitched laugh. "Potato, tomato. How is she?"

"All good, can't complain."

Actually I *can* complain, but I won't. Not to anyone. Because my complaints barely make any sense to me, so revealing them to anyone else would just make them think I was a whack job. Which is precisely what I'm turning into.

For example, my complaint with my sister-in-law's silver fucking eyeliner and shiny lip gloss. Why? Why did I loathe the way they highlighted two of her best features? When I caught myself staring at her pouty, glossed lips as she sang to my son in her raspy, whispered voice made me want to jump out of a high-rise.

I hated that I even thought about her full lips. I didn't need to. Just as I didn't need to think about the damn low V-neck, black T-shirt she wore this morning as she pulled Arman from my arms so I could go to work. I got an eyeful of the tops of her heavy breasts, and I swear, I almost dropped my kid in the process of handing him over.

Why the hell did I even notice her breasts?

Better yet, why was I still thinking about her breasts hours later?

Truth be told, it wasn't the first time I'd noticed her curves. You'd have to be blind not to—they were unapologetically obvious and undeniably alluring.

But that didn't mean I was comfortable with anyone else looking at them.

It boiled my blood when I saw Ryan ogling her on Sunday. I about decked him for his comment to her about being a wonderful interruption or whatever the fuck he said. I could tell he made her feel uncomfortable. And what the hell was he on about, referring to her relationship with Sonia? That was none of his fucking business.

The only reason I kept my hands fisted at my sides was because I was battling my own reaction inside my head. A part of me wanted to shove that smirk right off his face as he spoke to her like she was going to be his next meal, while the other part of me wondered if I was just reading it all wrong. I certainly don't remember him being as much of a douchebag before. Maybe he was just being friendly, and I was getting worked up over nothing.

So, since I can't voice my ridiculous non-complaints to anyone, especially not to Olivia, I stick to my original response: *Can't fucking complain!*

"That's good to hear." She snaps her fingers, getting my attention. "Oh, I forgot to ask again! Will you be coming over for Greg's surprise party this Friday night?"

Crap. I'd forgotten about that. "Uh—"

"I know you have Arman, but maybe your nan—uh, your sister-in-law—could pitch in for a night? Or maybe your mom could help out?" Olivia sounds breathless walking beside me.

"I don't know. I haven't asked either of them."

"Darian, you know how much Greg and I care about you. It would mean so much to us if you were there. Plus, you haven't done anything with anyone lately. I know you're a single dad, and I really respect how much you've had to do over the past year on your own, but it's Greg's fortieth birthday. Please come, even if it's just for an hour."

She's right. It's not every day that she begs me to leave my son and mingle at a party. She knows how hard that is for me. But Greg and Olivia—along with the rest of the small team here—have truly been the support I've needed to run this place. They've dropped vacation plans and days off to help fill in for me when Arman was sick or if I just needed a day. I can't not celebrate a big day for them when they need me.

But Mom and Dad leave town this Saturday for a week away. After not seeing her sister for almost a year, Mom made plans to go visit her in Seattle. Asking her to babysit Arman the night before her very early morning flight doesn't seem like the right decision.

I take my cap off my head and run my hand through my hair, thinking about asking Rani to cover for me. She'd offered to take care of Arman as I needed, even on the weekends, but based on the ass I made of myself in front of her last Friday night, I'm not sure that offer is still on the table. Still, it's not something Olivia needs to worry about. "Let me see if I can line up some help. No promises, though."

Olivia's hand lands on my bicep as she eyes me hopefully. "You know, you can even bring Arman with you. Violet will be there if you need help with him."

Um, no thanks.

Gently, I move my arm away. Olivia had a tendency to push and not necessarily know when to stop. "Thanks. I'll let you know what I decide."

Getting back to my office, I pull my phone out of my pocket when I get a doorbell notification from the security system I'd installed a few months ago at the house. I flip on the camera to see who's at the door, thinking it's probably a solicitor or a Girl Scout asking if we want to order cookies. Instead, I notice a tall, lanky guy with bright curly hair.

A few seconds later, Rani opens the door and I hear her chirpy voice. "Hey! I thought I was going to meet you at the park . . .. Did I misunderstand your text?"

Scrawny guy smiles at her before he shrugs sheepishly. "No, you didn't. I hope it's okay, though. I left a little earlier and thought I'd come pick you guys up so we could walk there together."

Rani looks back at something inside before opening the door a tad. My hackles rise when I see the guy step toward her. Is he going to follow her in?

"Give me a second. I need to get Arman's shoes on." I hear Rani say. "I want to take him on the swings today and let him try walking around a bit."

Thankfully, she closes the door while the guy waits outside. I watch as he runs his hand over his face, as if he's frustrated or second-guessing himself. He peers down at something and I notice a leash in his hand, though I can't see what—or who—is attached to it. He weakly commands it something like 'sit' or 'stay' before the door opens again, and Rani walks out with my son in a stroller.

I watch as she locks the door before turning to the guy, giving him a lingering smile. Scrawny guy helps her hoist Arman's stroller over the steps before they leave my porch and the camera goes idle.

Huh. That's interesting. I'm not sure what to make of the entire event, but I sure have a bunch of new questions floating around in my head. Like, when did she meet this guy? Who the hell is he? And why did she give him her number? Is he who she was out with all last weekend? I thought she was going to the nursing home . . .. And why are these questions making me feel murderous? Perhaps that's too extreme of a word. Perhaps a better word is uncomfortable . . . unsettled.

Nope. Still feeling murderous.

Not able to stop myself, I flip to my messages and bring up my conversation with Rani.

Me: `Who was the guy at the door? I got an alert from the security system.`

I wait a few minutes, occupying my hands and mind by opening up the new insurance policy updates I received in my email to read over and sign.

Rani: `Well, hello to you, too! I'm fine. Thanks for asking!`

I bite my cheek, fighting a smile.

Me: `I'm pretty sure I asked you how you were this morning. I'm also pretty sure I said hello.`

Rani: `I believe you said, "Hey. He's been fed and changed," before you handed Arman to me and ran out like you had ants in your pants.`

If she only knew what I had in my pants....

Not able to tell her the reason I ran out of the damn house was to avoid making more of an ass of myself when I saw her tight-as-fuck T-shirt and the ridiculous amount of skin underneath, I decide to concede.

Me: `Fine. You're right. I was rude. How are you? And who the fuck is that scrawny-ass Ronald McDonald-looking dude with you?`

Okay, so that's my version of a concession.

I tap my foot incessantly under the table while I wait for her to respond.

Rani: First, you're STILL being rude. Second, he's not as scrawny as he might look on that tiny camera. His name is Liam. Arman and I made friends with him last week at the park. I hope you don't mind that he came to pick us up. He's a nice guy. We're on a walk with him now, which is why it's taking me time to respond.

How do I respond to that? Do I mind that he came to pick her and my son up?

I don't like that she's on a damn walk with someone I don't know. More importantly, I don't like that she's been texting with him. I'm not ready to answer *why*, so I refrain from letting my brain even go there.

From the quick glimpse I got of him, he certainly seems non-threatening—tall, lanky, and goofy looking. So why is he showing up to my house, taking a walk with my son and my sister-in-law, anything but non-threatening?

Swiveling around in my chair, thinking about how to respond, I settle on not being an asshole. I've done enough of that lately.

It's not fair for me to hold Rani hostage in my house on account of her taking care of my son. She's a smart and capable woman, who has nothing but the best intentions for my son. Asking her to not spend time with a guy she feels comfortable having my son around would make her think I don't trust her, and that's not my intent.

Maybe meeting him in person would ease my concerns?

Me: Yeah, okay. But I'd like to meet him.

Rani: How about Friday evening?

Me: What's happening Friday?

While I see that my text has been read, I don't get a response from her the rest of the day, and I know I'm not going to like the answer, whenever I get it.

∼

I watch as Arman grabs hold of the vertical metal bars on the balcony and pulls himself up. He turns around to give me a toothless grin before trying to stick his face through the metal bars. Thankfully they are narrow enough that he won't get his face through, but I watch him anyway.

"Bo!" Arman points to a red ball on the grass below, bouncing on his feet.

"Ball. That's right." I smile.

The door to the balcony opens and Rani steps out, her long, shiny curls flying delicately behind her. "I made spaghetti and a salad if you're hungry. It's probably not as good as yours, but I figured you wouldn't mind."

"Thanks."

We both stand together in silence for a minute, watching Arman and feeling the light evening breeze against our skin.

"How was your walk with Ronald?" I glance at her before crossing my arms on my chest.

She glares at me. "His name is *Liam*, and it was good. He's a nice guy."

I nod, my jaw clenching. "So you've mentioned."

Rani bristles at my tone and for the life of me, I can't

figure out why I even said it the way I did. "Okay, then. Duly noted. You don't like information or repetitive small talk."

My shoulders slump. "I didn't mean it that way. I'm—fuck."

"Darian, did I do something to upset you? If you don't like me taking Arman on a walk with Liam, I can stop. All you have to do is tell me."

"No. I trust your judgment."

"I hope you know I would never put Arman in harm's way. He's safe with me. You never need to worry about him when he's with me."

I keep my gaze steady on the koi pond just past the deck. Before I can even decide not to vocalize it, I murmur, "It's not him I'm worried about."

I hear her soft inhale before she whispers, "What does that mean?"

I don't respond; I couldn't even if I wanted to. I'm not even sure why I said it. It's like her flowery scent invades my senses and turns my fucking brain into mush.

Rani's quiet next to me while I keep repeating the same words in my head, *She's your sister-in-law. She's nineteen!*

"I feel like things have been weird between us, especially since last Friday night—"

I turn to face her and questions fly through my head. Questions I refuse to ask myself but somehow, hear myself speaking aloud. "What happened between us Friday night?"

A flush takes over Rani's cheeks at my lack of acknowledgment—my denial. "I don't . . .." She shakes her head. "Nothing. I should go back in. I have some stuff to catch up on for my summer project."

God, I feel like such an asshole. No matter what I tell myself, the truth is, I felt it, too. I know exactly what she's referring to when she asks about Friday night. "Rani . . .. Fuck." I try to lighten my tone. "I'm sorry."

She stops on her way back inside, turning to me. "About what?"

My eyes slide past her determined gaze, asking me something for which I have no answer. "Nothing and everything."

Rani nods once, slowly, like she's deciphering the meaning of my response.

We both fall into another moment of silence watching Arman walk toward the stairs, holding the railing. Before I can, Rani rushes toward him and pulls him up in her arms. He wiggles and whines, trying to get back down, so she puts him down at the other corner for him to make his way slowly toward what has become his new goal—the stairs.

She clears her throat. "I looked through the *Truckee Sports* website in depth over the weekend."

I raise my brow, relieved with the change of subject. "You did?"

"Yes. There are several site optimizations I could easily do to make the website more searchable. I could also update the pictures, the blog, and newsletter. I think the last newsletter you sent out was months ago."

"That sounds about right." I watch Arman waddle, holding on to the railing. "It was a lot of what Sonia used to do."

"I know, but I think it might be time to modernize your site and marketing strategy. For example, more and more businesses are getting on TikTok these days. It might be something to consider in terms of garnering more visibility."

"And you have time to do this all during the summer?"

"Well, I can certainly lay the foundation for it."

I study her for a moment, noting the way she licks her lips before sliding her palms over her shorts. She's wearing the same black shirt I've been trying not to think about all day. It snags around her large breasts, revealing the most luscious dip of cleavage I've ever seen.

God, I'm a fucking perv.

I look away, hoping the silence hasn't stretched too long. "I can't let you do any of this for free."

"Darian, I've said it before and I'll say it again. Honestly, I'm happy to help."

"No. It's not up for debate, Rani. My business is doing well, and I've been looking for someone to help with these things, so you'd be doing me a huge favor."

She sighs before her silver-lined eyes turn to me. "Okay. Whatever you feel is right."

"I'll send you all the website credentials and information tonight."

Rani smiles in my direction for the first time since she came out here and something unfurls inside my chest, catching me off-guard. The woman has curves I want my hands on, but there is one curve—her smile—that I know, without a doubt, will lead me into a lot of trouble.

Feeling a little lighter from the rest of the conversation, I let a few moments pass before bringing up the text that went unanswered this afternoon. "So, what did you mean when you said I'd meet Ron—uh, *Liam*—on Friday?"

She chews on her lip for a prolonged second. "Liam's picking me up from the house for dinner Friday night."

I should have known that any of the calm I'd finally garnered around this woman would be wiped clean in an instant.

Chapter Twelve
RANI

I rise up in bed, frantically searching for the sound. My heart beats wildly in my chest as if I've just found myself inside a battlefield like a sitting duck. That noise definitely felt like a gunshot. Or was it a shout?

"What the hell was that?" I whisper into the dark before going silent to listen for it again. When I hear nothing but the air conditioner turning on, I lay back down, trying to recover.

Maybe it was in my dream. It felt real, though.

I search my nightstand for my bottle of water but can't locate it. I must have forgotten to grab one from the fridge last night. "Shit," I mumble, considering just getting a few sips from the tap in the bathroom, but it never gets cold enough.

Quietly making my way out of my room, I'm just about to take my first step down the stairs when I hear a pained wail from Darian's room. "No!"

Okay, I definitely wasn't dreaming.

My breathing speeds up again, and I contemplate whether

I should go and check on him. Being as late as it is, I can only assume he's in the throes of a bad dream. Should I go wake him up or let him come out of it on his own?

I've never been inside his room. It's on the other side of the hall and always closed, but that doesn't mean I haven't thought about peering inside. I have, plenty of times, but I haven't been gutsy enough to encroach. Plus, it's against my principles to snoop around in someone's personal space without their knowledge.

Growing up, I never liked when my mom poked around in my room. It made me feel like she was searching for evidence of a crime I didn't commit. And while she did it out of both curiosity and distrust, it only made me trust her less because of it.

That was just one of many events to stretch the void between us.

So, whether he would find out or not, I can't do that to Darian. It would be beneath me, and I'm not one who can live with guilt. I'd eventually tell him I did it and that would be more embarrassing.

But I'll admit that I *have* had to stop myself from just taking a quick gander—if only to find where that heavenly scent of pine and citrus came from—but again, I haven't done it.

"Jude . . ." Darian whimpers again and it stirs something inside my chest.

I can't just wait and listen.

I *can't*.

Tiptoeing toward his room, I slowly turn the knob and open the door. It's fairly dark inside, save for the red light glowing around the numbers on the digital clock on his nightstand. I hear him shuffle and follow my ears toward the sound as my eyes adjust to the lack of light. "Darian."

"Jude. No . . . wake up."

He's on his back, the covers thrown from his body. I can tell he's still in the clutches of his nightmare, his body rigid and his head jerking from side to side.

"Darian?" I whisper this time, bending over him. I slide my fingertips gently over his arm before following the curve of his shoulder to his neck, noticing it's bare. I raise my fingers to his cheek. I want to wake him up, but I don't want to shake or startle him, either. "Darian."

His skin is damp, like he's been running, but that same pine scent that always surrounds him lingers in the air. It's strange to see this man, who exudes intensity and strength with every fiber of his being, appear fearful and panicky. I hate it. I hate that whatever horror he's stuck inside has the capacity to do this to him.

I gently rub his cheekbone with my thumb, hoping to stir him awake. When he doesn't, I take a deep inhale and am just about to speak his name again when his hand comes up to grasp my wrist in a firm hold.

I flinch, gasping as I find his eyes.

He's breathing hard, his chest—which I notice is also bare—is rising and falling rapidly. His rough voice ghosts a sweet chill down my spine, making my legs clench. "What are you doing here?"

"I'm . . . you were having a nightmare," I stammer. "You cried out, and I wanted to make sure you were okay."

His grip tightens like a steel cuff around my wrist, betraying his gritted words. "I'm fine."

I nod, not knowing if he can actually see me. My face is no more than a few centimeters from his, my breath caressing his skin. "Okay," I whisper. "I'm sorry. I just wanted to check on you."

He relaxes a little, though he doesn't let go of my wrist.

Neither one of us makes an effort to move as we search each other's eyes. "Are you . . .. Do you want to talk about it?"

His jaw hardens below my hand. "No."

"Okay." My nerves tingle throughout my body and I can't stop myself from saying more. I hate this quality about myself, but it's as if the only way to control my anxious heart rate is to keep babbling, my words serving as a pressure valve for my damn brain. "Because when I have a nightmare, it helps if I talk about it. It makes it less real and usually, I never have the same dream again."

"It won't make it less real."

I nod again, twisting my wrist in his grip. "Okay. Well, I'm here if you change your mind. I was just going to grab a bottle of water from the fridge."

He loosens his hold, and I notice a surprised scowl between his brows as he watches his hand release mine, as if he just realized he was holding it.

I take a few steps back, watching him lay back on his pillow, before turning and rushing out of the room. With my heart in my throat, I quietly make my way down the stairs, holding the railing to keep myself upright. I swear, my legs feel like stilts.

In the kitchen, I swing open the fridge door, taking a moment of reprieve to let the cool air wash over my tingly skin. "Holy crapola." I close my eyes for a moment, trying to center myself again. "Breathe. Just breathe."

The first gulp of water down my parched throat feels like an elixir. With my hip against the center island, I take another gulp. Why are my hands trembling? Just nerves. It's fine. Everything is fine.

I saw Darian's chest.

Not a big deal. I couldn't even see that well.

It looked muscular and defined.

That's expected, given his profession. It's a normal chest. Completely average, like his biceps and his ass.

Did I see a smattering of hair?

Geezus. I need to get a grip. These damn teenage hormones should have been out of my system by now. Maybe it's a vitamin D deficiency. Or is it zinc? It's probably a multi-vitamin deficiency, given I haven't taken any since I was a kid.

Multiple thoughts swirl in my head—multivitamins and bare chests—fighting for more headspace. I can't get a hold on any. And honestly, how can I when all I see is the intensity of dark eyes boring into mine? How can I when all I feel are warm fingertips around my wrist and soft breaths skirting over my lips and chin. Strong shoulders—

"Hey."

I jump at the unexpected voice. No, I don't jump. I almost come out of my damn skin as cold water sloshes over my chest and down my tank top. "Shit!"

Darian's hands fly up, open palmed. "Sorry. I didn't mean to sneak up on you."

I quickly glance up and just as soon regret it when I spot his massive bare chest—all man, all firm edges and hard corners, with a delicious happy trail running down from his navel to an unnamed, unimagined region.

A region I *never ever* care to see.

Ever.

I angle my head as far down as I can, practically breaking my damn neck with how my chin shoves into my collarbone. I dab at my chest repeatedly, as if that's going to do anything. "No, it's fine. I was just . . .." To my horror, my mortification, I notice my nipples standing straight out. So sharp and so painful, I'm positive they're going to cut through my shirt. "Uh, I should go change," I say to my chest since I'm still too scared to look up again.

"Rani."

No. Please, just don't say anything. Please don't utter another word and make me feel like a bigger idiot than I already do. I swear, I'm trying to compose myself here. I swear!

"Boy, this water was colder than I expected. Not that I expected it or anything. I didn't come down here to just, you know, throw water on my bre—er, chest. Really wakes you up, though!" I laugh nervously, still dabbing at myself.

What. The. Fuck. Am I doing?

Someone, please punch me in the face and render me unconscious!

"Rani." Darian's voice sounds awfully close, like he's a mere step away.

Oh, boy.

I look up, hoping to appear less mortified than I feel and praying he can't see my damn nipples through my shirt. I already know that's a pipe dream.

His irises darken to an almost espresso color instead of his regular cappuccino ones. The irony isn't lost on me, given he doesn't drink coffee.

I wonder if there's a story behind that. Does he have preconceived judgments for those who partake in caffeinating themselves? Does his bigotry also percolate to chocolate?

Percolate. What an appropriate word, given the whole coffee conversation I'm having inside my head to distract myself from his ridiculously overwhelming stare. I'm pretty proud of my effort, actually, and I barely notice him there.

"Hmm?" I hum.

Darian's lips twitch. They do that a lot whenever I'm around, but he'll never give me the benefit of just letting them curve up all the way. It's as if he thinks once he does, I'll come to expect it. And maybe I would. "Are you nervous-rambling again?"

I shake my head, almost imperceptibly. "No. Was I rambling?" My chin tilts up. "It's rude, you know, to tell someone they're rambling, even if they are. Social norms dictate that you should allow people to ramble and find an excuse to flee instead of telling them they ramble."

He blinks, biting the inside of his cheek. "Noted. It won't happen again."

I straighten, still feeling my nipples rub against the back of the cold, wet fabric of my tank top. It's fine. It's the twenty-first century, and nipples are in sight practically everywhere. So what if he can see them? It's not like mine are anything special. Just another garden-variety set of nipples. Nothing more. "Good."

Placing the cap back on my bottle, I skirt past him, hoping to make a less mortifying exit, when he speaks. "Thank you."

My back faces him so I'm not sure if he's turned to look at me or not. "It was nothing."

"It was something to me," he murmurs. "But even if I talk about it, like you asked, it won't make it any less real."

I turn, no longer worried about my chest . . . or his, for that matter. "What do you mean?"

He looks away, like he's weighing if this is a conversation he wants to have or not, before his eyes swing back to mine. His Adam's apple bobs against the smoothest, creamiest skin I've ever seen.

Creamiest? Wrong adjective; obviously, I meant mediocre . . . unremarkable. His Adam's apple bobs against the most unremarkable skin I've ever seen.

"Fifteen years ago, my best friend and I took our kayaks out to the river."

"The Truckee River?"

He nods once. "It was our summer routine. We were both strong swimmers and had kayaked a hundred times before."

Fuck, I can only guess where this is going. My hand slides up to my ribs as I press against the wet fabric to rub out the constriction that's suddenly appeared.

"We knew we'd chosen a particularly challenging part of the river, but we were ready. It was just going to be a normal day in the water but uh . . .." His jaw clenches and I know it's to thwart the emotion in his voice. "Jude's kayak rolled over when we hit a particularly powerful current. It moved him downstream so fast, I couldn't catch up."

"Oh, Darian . . ." I know I've closed the distance between us again, I just don't know when I did it. Somewhere in the same ten seconds, I've also done away with the bottle I was holding. My hand finds his forearm and I squeeze, unsure whether I'm comforting him or me.

He stares past me as if he hardly registers my presence. "I looked everywhere for him, but the current was so strong and I lost time."

I squeeze his arm again, urging him to continue.

"I found his body, facedown, a half mile downstream, shoved between rocks. It seemed like he made his way out of the kayak at some point, but the autopsy report said his neck was broken."

My eyes prick as a rush of tears well inside my lids. "Darian." I reach up, not giving a shit about my warring senses and thoughts, not giving a shit about right or wrong, surrounding his neck with my arms. There is no right or wrong when all you're offering is friendship and comfort. "I'm so sorry."

Darian stands there motionless, his hands hanging by his sides. His body feels warm and strong—albeit stiff and unyielding—against mine and I almost don't want to let go. But as I gain my composure—and the realization that maybe my comfort was unwanted and unwarranted—I lean away from him.

It's then that his hands find my back.

Sliding up my torso, in a torturous sail over my pebbled skin, his arms cross behind me. I hear—feel—his inhale against my hair before he relaxes in my embrace.

"Darian," I whisper against his neck, "it wasn't your fault."

He's quiet for a moment and I wonder if maybe he didn't hear me. "But I feel culpable for it, just the same. Jude, Sonia . . ." he trails off. "I'm the only one answerable for them, the only one who survived when they didn't."

I lean back, my palms finding his face as I bore into his pain-stricken eyes. "No. You're not answerable for any of it, and you're not culpable, either. You were simply just there, Darian." A tear drops from my eyes and I watch him track it. "And no one should have to carry that weight around like you do." I slide my hand down to his chest, feeling it twitch under my palm, but keeping it steady over his heart. His skin is warm as his heart thuds under my fingertips. "No one is strong enough to carry that around . . . not even you. None of it was your fault."

His eyes skim over my face, landing unwaveringly on my lips as the weight of the moment between us holds us hostage. It beckons me to close the distance and cross the chasm. And when I don't, his gaze slides up to mine, where he sees all the questions, all the reservations that mirror his own.

I close my lids, taking a moment to compose myself before stepping back and releasing him from my hold. He lets me walk away but I turn back to him right as I get to the stairs, remembering a thought that's been swimming in the back of my mind. "Can I ask you something?"

He nods, his face completely devoid of the emotion that was there just seconds ago, and his hands once again rest at his sides.

"The note inside the bouquet . . . .. You'd written you were sorry."

His head tilts up, waiting for me to finish my thought, but I don't miss the slight resolve in his stance.

"Why?" My eyes search his. "What were you apologizing

for? I'm the one who made you feel uncomfortable that night in Arman's room. Why were you the one apologizing?"

"For making you think you could ever make me feel uncomfortable, Rani. Because the only thing I feel around you is unhinged."

Chapter Thirteen
DARIAN

I button up Arman's pants, snapping the suspenders over his short-sleeved, white button-down. It's an outfit that's been hanging in his closet for over a year, received as a gift from someone when Emily threw Sonia's baby shower.

Arman bends over on his changing table to pick up the precious teether he dropped, and I pull him into my arms to head downstairs. We're both as ready as we're going to be for Greg's surprise birthday party.

I'm midway down the stairs when the doorbell rings. I sigh, knowing who it's going to be but holding back my visible disdain. Rani's feet shuffle above us as she bounds down the stairs as well. Both Arman and I look up at her, taking in her strapless, black frilled dress that has some sort of lacy fabric on the top. It accentuates her figure, but I'm not sure how I feel about her baring all that skin on her shoulders and décolletage.

The fuck, though? It's just a first date. Do women get this dolled up on their first date? Especially when the date is with a clown? I clench my jaw to refrain from saying anything because I don't want to tell her she looks beautiful. Or that

I'm intrigued by her damn shimmery gold eyeshadow and the miles upon miles of luminous skin. Or that I wish she wasn't going.

Instead I opt for, "Looks like Ronald is here."

She tilts her head and squints at me. "Darian."

Right. Like using my fucking name as a reprimand will stop me from wanting to shove my fist into Ginger Boy's face.

I unlock the door as she approaches, holding out her hands toward Arman. He willingly jumps to her, hitting her head with his teether a couple of times. She pulls down his arm and pretends to give him a chastising glare, making him giggle.

"Hey!" Ronald says as soon as I fling the door open, giving me a tight nod and smile. His eyes quickly find Rani before they glide back to me. He juts out his hand. "I'm Liam. Rani's told me a lot about you."

I consider not taking his hand. I almost consider breaking his wrist, but then I'd probably get another scornful lecture from my nineteen-year-old sister-in-law and have one more thing to apologize for. So, to avoid all that drama, I grasp his hand firmly in mine before turning around and walking away. He already said she told him a lot about me, so why introduce myself? Seems like a waste of energy to me.

I'm sure they both gaped at me momentarily, but I leave them to chat before heading toward the kitchen in search of a drink. Maybe I'll have a finger of the whiskey my brothers brought over last weekend. Something to take the fucking edge off.

Their hushed conversation in the foyer makes its way to my ears, and I don't miss the hesitation in the lanky kid's voice. Okay, so maybe I was a little rude—I'm sure Rani will express her disapproval of my behavior later—but I have no interest in befriending the guy.

Whatever. I'm an asshole. I'm over it.

"I'm going to leave him in the living room with his toys." Rani indicates to my son before flicking her gaze toward me to see if I'm listening. "Bye, little man." She kisses him on the cheek before wiping her lipstick or lipgloss or whatever off him. "Be good for your dad at the party. Don't drink too much." She giggles at him before straightening up and surveying the glass in my hand with a frown.

She turns to her date just as I turn to the kitchen island. "I'll meet you in the car. Can you give me a second?"

"Yeah, no problem." I hear the door shut before the telltale sound of her footsteps behind me. Of course, I pretend not to notice. I'm too busy clutching the edge of the marble countertop with my free hand.

"Hey, are you sure you'll be okay with Arman on your own at the party?"

I swivel to face her with the glass of whiskey in my hand. Her eyes flick back to the glass. She's as surprised as I am. I don't generally consume alcohol or anything unnecessary for my body. Sure, I'll have the occasional beer with my brothers, but it's rare for me to consume anything stronger.

I arch a brow. "I've taken care of him on my own for the past year. I'm pretty sure I can handle one night without your help."

She frowns again. "That's not what I meant, Darian. I know you can take care of him and you've done a great job of it." She fiddles with her hands, looking down at them. "I just feel bad. If I'd known you had this commitment tonight–"

"What? You would have canceled your exciting date with Lanky Boy?"

A crease forms between her brows and her nostrils flare. "You're not being fair and you know it. *You're* the one who told me you didn't need my help on the weekends. *You're* the one who made it seem like I should be out and about, doing other things, when we first talked. Obviously, I can only do those things over the weekend. I can't sit here night after night watching you avoid me—"

I reel back. "Avoid you?"

She sighs, closing her eyes in frustration before reopening them. "Never mind. I have to go. I can't do this right now. Liam is waiting for me."

Oh, God forbid Liam has to wait.

"What do you mean, I avoid you?" I repeat sternly. I don't mean to sound so irate, but seriously, what the fuck?

The only reason we haven't talked much over the past couple of weeks is because I've been busy with work. Sure, I could do a better job of getting to know her instead of retreating into my study or bedroom every now and then, but fuck, I thought she'd want time to herself after taking care of my kid all day.

Maybe there *is* a small part of me that avoids her? I don't know. Maybe I don't want to get used to having her around. Maybe I'm afraid that if I get attached, it'll be yet another fucking adjustment when she leaves—when I've already had to make quite a few adjustments this past year. I figured I'd take a more professional stance with our relationship.

A voice pipes up somewhere inside my head, wondering if holding her, inhaling her flowery scent, and generally having to hide the constant boner in my pants around her is considered professional, but that voice is an exasperating piece of shit, so I mute it.

Rani opens up her clutch, pretending to look for something in there. Or, at least, I think she's pretending based on how animated she's being.

"Who's avoiding whom now?"

She huffs. "Look, forget I said anything, okay? Have fun at the party." She turns to walk away, exiting through the front door and leaving me staring after her.

I throw my whiskey down the drain—sacrilege, if one of

my brothers were to witness it—no longer finding it helping me relax.

I put both hands on the counter and breathe deeply, knowing I'll be stopping by the florist again on my way back.

∾

"Gosh, you are just so cute and growing up fast!" Olivia coos at Arman, bending down to look at him in her foyer. He insisted on being down on his feet today, so I'm holding his hand above him as he practices walking. "Aren't you, buddy? And you're looking more and more like your mom." Olivia gives me a cursory look to gauge my expression, as if she's said something that might bother me. It doesn't. I'm well-aware my son looks like his mom, and I never want that to be something my friends feel fearful mentioning.

I loved Sonia, and she will always have a place in my heart. You can't take away ten years of memories, even if some weren't perfect. We had to work on our marriage as I'm sure most people do. We had happier years, along with some not so happy ones. Either way, I want my son to be proud of who he came from and who he looks like.

"Well, come on in. I'm so glad you were able to make it." Olivia smiles before gesturing for us to follow her into the living room and kitchen, where the rest of the party is taking place. She lifts the bottle of wine I bought on my way here. "And thank you for this. You didn't have to."

"You're welcome."

We missed being a part of the surprise earlier, but I'm not upset about it. I've never been one to partake in these things. Whether you're the person being surprised or doing the surprising, it all seems a little forced and theatrical. Personally, I'd much rather enjoy an intimate evening with family and friends than something so put-on.

Greg sees us as Arman and I hobble in, Arman still clutching my fingers to waddle ahead of me. He's trying so hard to find his independence, and while I'm happy for him, I can't say I don't miss the times he was more immobile. At least I didn't have to worry about him getting into everything then.

"King!" Greg chimes as he makes his way toward us. "So glad you could join us!"

I let go of one of Arman's hands, ensuring he's steady on his feet, before reaching out to shake Greg's. "Happy birthday!" I look around at the various guests mingling with drinks and hors d'oeuvres in their hands. "Looks like a great party."

"Thanks! It was a total surprise, but you know Liv. She just loves doing this stuff." He reaches down to pat Arman's head. "Glad you were able to bring him. Hi, buddy!"

Arman waves to Greg with a toothless smile, getting a happy reaction. "Hi."

"Liv just told me your nanny wasn't able to keep him tonight," Greg says, apologetically.

I don't know why the word *nanny* in reference to Rani irritates me. For all intents and purposes, she *is* Arman's nanny, but I have the sudden urge to ask Greg why he never referred to my mom as Arman's nanny when she was taking care of him.

Unlike a professional nanny, Rani doesn't take any payment. And I don't know, but the word just makes her seem like someone meaningless to me, like she's only there to do her job.

She's anything but meaningless to me or my son.

"My sister-in-law?" I ask him with my brow arched. Why am I getting a sense of déjà vu?

He hesitates. "Right! My apologies. Come on, let's get you a drink!"

I wave my hand before grabbing Arman's again. "Don't worry about me. I'm good."

A few minutes later, I'm involved in a conversation with Felix and a few other folks from the school. I won't deny that I have thought about Rani over the course of the past forty-five minutes since she left my house.

I keep wondering where Liam took her for dinner. Nowhere she deserves to be taken, I'm sure. What if the guy's an asshole and tries something with her? What if he takes advantage of how sweet she is—all fucking nymph-like—and makes a move on her?

Fuck . . ..

What if she lets him? What if they hit it off really well, and she develops feelings for him?

Shouldn't I be happy for them if that happens? After all, she still believes in eternal love and happily-ever-afters and all that garbage based on the blog she maintains. Shouldn't she get one of those for herself?

Maybe. But I still don't like the idea of Lanky Legs giving it to her.

I don't like the idea of *anyone* giving that to her. Maybe I'm old and jaded, but I'm also wiser and more experienced. So what if she's found a few success stories from her time interviewing old people at nursing homes? That's not the norm. They're just coincidental waves of happy anomalies in an ocean of tragedies.

Long-lasting relationships don't guarantee happiness. Just like chemotherapy doesn't guarantee remission. Just like an inhaler doesn't guarantee impeding an asthma attack.

Just like a team of doctors can't guarantee a mother will walk out holding her newborn.

It's all a gamble; a lottery ticket bought in hopes of winning the jackpot when only a few in a million will guess the correct numbers.

Been there, done that, lost a shitload.

I'm only somewhat focusing on the conversation with my colleagues when Arman starts fussing in my arms. I swivel my nose around behind him to get a sniff and immediately know he's dirtied his diaper.

Excusing myself from the conversation, I go in search of Olivia, waving hello to a few acquaintances along the way. I spot her familiar blonde curls in the kitchen but groan as soon as I see who she's conversing with.

Violet's hazel eyes find mine as she watches me approach. She gives me a shy wave and says something almost imperceptibly to Olivia, making Oliva turn to face me.

"Hey! Are you having fun?" Olivia shoves a tray of eggrolls in my direction on the counter before I can respond. "Here, have one of these. Violet made them from scratch." She gleams at her sister before looking back at me. "You won't regret it."

I fucking regret coming here.

"Actually, I was wondering if you could point me to where I could change his diaper." I tilt my head in Arman's direction in my arms. I left his diaper bag at the front door, so once she directs me to the room, I'll go pick it up.

"Oh, absolutely! You can feel free to use the guest room right around the corner. It has an ensuite bathroom, too."

"Thanks," I say, stepping away when Violet stops me.

"Gosh, is that your son?"

No, I walk around asking strangers if I can change their child's diaper.

I nod, trying not to think about the last time I was in Violet's company. The one and only time prior to this was awkward and unforgettable enough. Maybe I'm being too judgmental; maybe she really was just nervous and read all the signs wrong.

Before I can step away, Violet bridges the gap between us.

She pulls Arman's chubby arm with her hand—her long fake nails giving me heart palpitations. "You are just the cutest little thing." She blinks up at me. "Does he speak?"

Arman pulls his hand away, suspiciously eyeing her before reprimanding her with a firm, "No no!"

I try to swallow the laugh bubbling up at my son's intuitiveness. "He says a few words."

Violet smiles. "Oh, I understand that. I'm not much of a talker myself."

Yes, how could I forget the excruciating one-and-a-half-hour non-conversation at the most awkward dinner in history, followed by the unwelcomed groping attempt.

Without making any more small talk, I excuse myself and rush to the foyer for the diaper bag before finding the guest room Olivia had indicated. After changing Arman and washing my hands, I head back to the kitchen in search of something for him to munch on since he seems hungry.

When I don't find anything he'll like, I reluctantly hand him an eggroll under Violet's satisfied gaze, seating him between my arms on the counter.

"Darian, I, uh . . .." Violet looks around, noting that most of the guests are involved in their own conversations and that her sister is nowhere in sight. "I wanted to apologize for that night again. I honestly don't know what got into me; I've never acted so uncivilized in my life."

"No need. Water under the bridge."

"Do you think," she clears her throat as a flush rises from her neck to her face, "that maybe we could try again sometime?"

I pick up a piece of the eggroll that Arman drops on the counter, chucking it into the nearby sink. "I don't think that would be a good–"

"Darian, listen." She slides closer, placing her hand on my forearm. The gesture reminds me of something Rani did, but

I'm repelling Violet's touch where I was leaning into Rani's. "I know you're lonely—I've heard enough about it from my sister—and I am, too. Look, I'm not looking for anything serious either, but . . . .."

Something about her trailing off has me glancing at her, even though I don't really want her to finish what she was going to say. Clearly, she's still not reading the signs right. Also, what the hell is Olivia's problem? I think her and I are due for a chat soon.

"But I . . . I'm really good in bed, Darian."

I'm glad I didn't have a drink in my hand or in my mouth, because I swear, I would have spilled it.

My face must not be doing a good enough job conveying my shock because to my horror, she continues, sucking her bottom lip and looking up at me with hooded lids. Her long fingernail grazes the back of my hand, and I quickly remove it from the counter. "I may not be adept with words, but I'm highly skilled with my hands and tongue."

On that note, I pick up my son to head back to the foyer. But when Violet follows me, I look pointedly back at her, trying to keep my voice low as to not embarrass her. "I'd say you're quite adept with words, too. Thanks for the offer, but I'm not interested. I wasn't interested last time, and I won't be interested in the future, either."

I hurry forward, not worried if she appears shocked or ashamed. Frankly, she's not my problem.

The only woman who *is* my problem at the moment—who has taken up more space than I care to admit in my already cluttered brain—is currently on a date with a twirp I'd like to break in half like a twig.

Chapter Fourteen
RANI

Bella: Have fun on your date tonight. FaceTime when you get back?

Melody: I doubt she's going to have time for a video call if she's busy finding out whether the carpet matches the drapes.

Bella: LOL! What if it doesn't? That would be awkward.

My phone vibrates incessantly inside my grasp and after Bella's last message, I decide to stow it inside my purse so I don't come off as rude.

I tuck my hair behind my ear and try to relax as I look out the window. I don't know if I'm overanalyzing, but Liam seems to be quieter than I expected ever since I got in the car. I guess I can't blame him, given the awkward greeting—or lack thereof—he received from Darian.

Seriously, what was Darian's problem tonight? Why was he acting like such a manchild? I'm considering telling him he needs to get on mood stabilizers. All the nostril flaring and chest beating is getting exhausting.

How did my sister deal with that on a daily basis?

Whatever. I need to shove him back into a corner in my mind and focus on the first date I've had in more than two years. Putting aside the current awkward silence, I've had really good conversations with Liam. He's funny, sweet, and genuinely shows interest in what I have to say. I never get the sense that I'm being judged or talked down to when I'm around him, and even our text conversations have been pretty light and easy.

I smile, turning toward him. "Quite a nice evening tonight."

He bites his bottom lip, intently focused on the road ahead, but I don't miss the way he white-knuckles the steering wheel. Taking in a breath and releasing it, he offers me a quick smile. "Yeah, nothing beats summers in Tahoe."

We fall silent again. I'm not really sure where he's taking me, but his phone navigation shows another fourteen minutes to our destination. Fourteen long minutes, if it goes at this pace.

"So, I've gotta ask." Liam glances at me. "What was up with your brother-in-law today? Is he always that dickish?"

Yup, it's exactly what I suspected was bothering him.

I puff out half of a laugh, trying to concoct an answer to his question. "Darian's been under a lot of stress lately. He's also not much of a talker." I laugh, letting him know the rest of what I'll say is in jest. "He relies heavily on intense glaring and some jaw clenching. It wouldn't surprise me if his facial muscles have atrophied with the lack of use."

Liam relaxes, finally giving me a genuine smile. "Right? Like, what did I ever do to him? He *really* didn't like me."

"Don't take it personally. I'm sure Darian's reflection asks him the same thing."

Liam laughs and the heavy air seems to have lifted from the car. "Is he nice to you? I mean, he's not like *that* to you too, is he? It would fucking suck to have to live with someone who just glared at you all the time."

I smile, finding the comment amusing and interesting. Does it suck to have Darian glare at me all the time? What a complicated question, but I only have one answer to it. No. In fact, I feel like his intense gaze has become a fascination, an addiction. I don't whither under it, like I saw Liam doing. Instead, I feel empowered and emboldened.

Alive, untethered.

Liam's question brings about the various moments over the past two weeks where I witnessed the soft sides of a man who doesn't leave home without his heavy suit of armor.

The way he sweetly kisses his son's temple. The colorful flowers he leaves on my doorstep. The array of new coffee pods and unhealthy snacks that magically appeared a few days after I arrived. The way he softly shushes Arman in the mornings in case I'm still sleeping.

The way his soft spoken words and raspy voice betrayed the strength he's always projecting when he let me hold him in the kitchen.

He's been broken, not once but twice. He's lost people he's given parts of his soul to, only to have lost those parts with them.

I know all of this—recognizing the quiet beast with a soft underbelly—but I'll be damned if I stand by silently, allowing him to use his pain as an excuse for his poor behavior. We've all been dealt unlucky hands, and we've all been through our fair share of pain in life. But only we are responsible for what we do with that pain—grow from it or succumb to it.

I certainly know which way I lean.

For far too long, I allowed others to be responsible for my happiness. I let them decide who, what, and how I should be, but with the death of my sister came an inner awakening. I can't say I wasn't working toward that even before her death, but her passing was like a catalyst for the new me. The reenvisioned, reimagined, two-point-oh me.

It was then that I decided I'd no longer permit anyone to hurt me just because they had been hurt in the past and I looked like I'd be good target practice. Fuck no. I'd allowed it for too long and I refuse to go backward, be it for my mother or anyone else.

"No, he's not bad. A little complicated, but who isn't?"

Dinner with Liam is fun and easy, as if I've known him forever. He tells me more about his job working for the water utility company and his love for biking. Apparently, he's taken part in several cross-country marathons and even fixes bikes on the side.

I tell him more about my love for journalism and my recent venture into photography. He's fascinated with my blog, *The Soulmate Spiel,* and asks me a million questions before pulling out his phone and subscribing to it.

I honestly can't recall the last time someone has been so attentive and sweet. And I find his boyish charm incredibly endearing. There's a goodness about him—a wholesome guy-next-door quality—that I could see women fawning over, and I know without a shadow of doubt that whoever he ends up with will be a lucky girl.

It just won't be me.

Why? Because clearly, even given the million wonderful qualities about this red-haired, sensitive and gentle man in front of me, my thoughts are irritatingly anchored to a man who is anything but those things. A man so unmercifully broody and immodestly good-looking that I can't decide if I want to clip him or climb him.

So even after Liam and I finish dinner at a beautiful Italian restaurant set at the base of the mountains to take a walk around the stretch of land behind it, my thoughts trail off to the two guys who have burrowed themselves somewhere deep inside my heart.

Liam drives me back to Darian's house, exiting the driver's side as I get out of the passenger's. We spent the drive back sharing our love for music. I played him a couple of my favorite songs, and he introduced me to an indie band I hadn't heard of.

"Can I walk you to the door?" He meets my eyes with a soft smile.

"Sure." I can't tell if Darian is home or not. He often parks his truck in the garage and the lights inside the house are all turned off. I wonder how my little toothless monster did at the party.

"I don't think I had a chance to tell you, and I should have." Liam follows me as I walk up the path to the front porch.

"What's that?" I ask over my shoulder.

"You look lovely in that dress." He purses his lips. "You should consider wearing it on one of our walks to the park."

I'd ordered it a few weeks ago from an online boutique I found that specializes in plus-size dresses and lingerie. And even though I had no one to wear the lingerie for, I'd decided on a whim to splurge on that too, following my *live for today* mantra.

"Oh, should I?" I snort. "I'm sure I'd be well-dressed to play a part in a 1960s film, pushing around a stroller, wearing my short-heeled pumps. Any other requests? Would you like me to put my hair up in a beehive, too?"

Liam gives me a sheepish grin. "If it's not too much to ask."

We climb up the steps and Liam presses his back to the large wooden pillar framing the porch entrance. "I had a really nice time with you, Rani. I don't think I've been on a date before where I paid such little attention to what I said. It was just . . ."

"Effortless?" I supply.

He smirks. "Yeah. Effortless, uncomplicated."

"Ooh, I have another adjective. How about 'comfortable'?"

His smile widens. "I'll see your 'comfortable' and raise you a 'pleasant'."

I giggle. "We could continue this game all night; I'm pretty good with adjectives. I kind of have to be given the profession I'm pursuing."

Liam's eyes search mine for a moment, and if I know anything about searching gazes that heat up like molten rock, something about this adjective game has really turned up the fever inside him. Okay, noted. Liam has an adjective kink. I'm no one to judge, and at least it's not an armpit or an insect kink. Yes, those are real things based on one of my many intriguing conversations with my best friend.

I inch backward as Liam moves toward me.

"I don't want to play games, but I'd like to spend more time with you, whether it be tonight or any other."

I swallow, working hard to steady my nerves. "As fun as this evening was, the truth is, Liam, I'm not very experienced in dating. I've only had one serious relationship in high school, but it gave me little else more than heartache and betrayal."

Liam's hands circle my arms before rubbing them up and down. His face tilts down toward me as he tries again. "I wouldn't hurt you, Rani. We could take it as slow as you'd like."

I look down, disconnecting our gaze and feeling the air in my lungs being compromised. "I don't know . . . .. I'm leaving at the end of summer."

"I only live three hours away."

"Liam, I think—"

"Rani, all I'm asking for is a chance. Whether that means another *effortless* night of conversation, a summer to explore more, or God forbid, something long-term." His brows go up in mocked astonishment. "You don't have to tell me right now. Just tell me you'll think about it."

I nod, hating to see someone care for me in a way I can never reciprocate but not being bold enough to tell him right here, right now, because I don't have it in me to break someone's pride and crush their self-confidence. "I'll think about it . . .."

"Good." He smiles, still grasping my arms gently. "I'm assuming hastening your decision with a kiss is out of the picture? I've been told I'm quite a good kisser."

"Absolutely the fuck not."

Both Liam and I turn—me jumping as if I've been electrocuted—to see a stone-faced, nostril-flaring, jaw-clenching Darian drilling his gaze into Liam. He has his herculean biceps flexing around his chest as he leans back on his heels, pretending to take a casual stance as if this is just another Tuesday.

He can pretend all he wants, but the growl laced around his words says he's two seconds from pouncing on his prey. I just don't know whether that's me or Liam.

"Darian—"

"Get inside the house, Rani."

I flinch. "Excuse me?"

His eyes—not so cappuccino-colored at the moment, but more ebony-colored pools of barely controlled fury—slide to me before his chin tips up. "Whatever your grievances are with me interrupting your *date*," he emphasizes the last word as if he's mocking it, "at my own damn house, please feel free to express them to me inside. I know you will, anyway. But right now, I need you to get inside."

I'm about to lay into him, my skin prickling with a mixture of adrenaline and embarrassment, when something shifts, almost imperceptibly, in his features. It's so subtle that I'd have missed it if I had blinked but it halts the words inside my mouth.

It's a vulnerable plea. A silent request to let him have this.

While I'm mortified by his behavior, I have to respect that this *is* his house, his porch. I had no intention of letting Liam kiss me, and in a strange way, I'm thankful for Darian's interruption, but I also hate the way he's acting like an overprotective parent. How dare he think I will just bend to his demands? How dare he use his house as an excuse to cover whatever the fuck is bothering him about me going out with Liam?

It's not something I can completely put into words at the moment since my brain is on overdrive from the mixed signals, the emotional vacillation, and the fire-breathing dragon still glaring in our direction.

I turn to address an incredulous-faced Liam, who is gearing up to speak. "Liam, can we chat another time?"

Liam's hands fist at his sides as he stands taller, glaring back at Darian, but keeping his voice level. "You're a real asshole."

"Surprising. I've never been called that." Darian's lips lay flat, as if he's already bored with where this is going.

Liam gives me a hard glance before nodding, and I give his arm an apologetic squeeze. "Let's talk soon, Rani."

I watch only for a second as he turns around, taking long strides to his car, before I shoulder-check Darian through the doorway.

Heat, a level one-thousand on a scale of ten, swirls inside my head when I turn around with my finger jabbed into his chest. "What is your problem? Did you learn no common decency and basic manners in life? Even kindergartners behave better than you!"

"Ah, that explains it . . . I skipped kindergarten." He has the audacity to sound amused.

My finger presses deeper into his chest, and I remind myself not to think about what it feels like without the fabric in between. "Don't you dare. Don't you dare try to be evasive and lighten the mood. You can't change the subject."

"I can guarantee I'm not smart enough to do that. I barely know what 'evasive' means."

"Darian."

"Here you go again, using my name as a deterrent." His warm hand finds mine, pulling it off his chest.

"Why?" I grit out.

"Why what?" He's stalling. I can practically see the turbulence in his eyes. While he might look calm and collected, I know he's anything but.

My chest rises and falls, my body trying to prepare for a conversation I know I won't come back from. "Why did you come out there and stop him from kissing me?"

His stance stiffens while his eyes bore into me. "Were you going to kiss him back? Was I the only one standing in the middle of your big night?"

"You don't get to ask me that. You don't get to demand answers when you haven't supplied any yourself," I grind out.

His arms fly up. "What do you want to know, Rani? What do you want from me?"

"Honesty to start with, but I think you need to ask yourself what it is *you* want from me, Darian, because I'm pretty fucking clear about what I want."

He leans forward slightly, invading my senses with his fucking pine and citrus scent. Invading the clarity of my thoughts. Invading my wherewithal and control. His voice is raspy, almost whispered. "Yeah? And what do you want?"

"For you to kiss me." Blood rushes through my ears as I struggle to breathe, hearing my admission after the fact. I don't know if it's the bravest thing I've ever done or the most foolish.

Darian's face pales, his words halting on his tongue. If he had any idea of what was going to come out of my mouth, I doubt he would have asked the question. His shoulders sag as my words ring out between us, hovering in the air like heavy smoke. "Rani–"

"No." I throw my palm up, effectively stopping him. I saw everything in his face before he even knew how he was going to respond. The torture, the questions, the fucking pity. Tears that I didn't even know I had well inside my lids, falling over my burning cheeks. *What has gotten into me? What have I done? My sister. . ..* "Please," I whisper, my voice trembling raw. "Please don't speak."

I rush from the spot in the entryway toward the stairs, taking them two at a time as a dam bursts through my chest, erupting through my eyes.

I force my palm over my mouth to keep in my sob as I pass Arman's room. I barely register the bouquet of orange lilies on my doorstep before quickly entering my room and pressing my back against the door.

Oh God, what have I done?

How could I have been so idiotic? How could I have made such a fool of myself and allowed myself to think that, even for a minute, even for a goddamn second, I could ask something so unseemly, so fucking inappropriate from a man who isn't just broken and on the mend, but a man who also happens to have shared ten years of his life with my sister?

In her bed.

I'm disgusted with myself. Utterly and completely appalled and ashamed as I think about how the shock and reluctance registered slowly on his features. I quite literally stupefied him . . . and myself.

I don't know how long I stand there, pressed against the door, reevaluating all my life choices and licking my wounds before I finally reopen the door and pull in the new vase of flowers–orange lilies with purple sweet pea blooms.

Wiping the dried tears off my face, I pull out the card, wondering if I should even read it, though I do so just the same.

I couldn't avoid you if I tried. And you're right, I've tried . . . but failed.

Chapter Fifteen
RANI

I sit there, re-reading the damn note until I've dissected each word in every which way I can. He's tried to avoid me but failed. What the hell am I supposed to assume from that? That I'm unavoidable? But why? Because I'm in his way? Because he thinks about me the same way I think about him? And if not, then why?

I shake my head, squinting at the paper in my hands, searching yet another bouquet of beautiful flowers for an answer. Maybe it's not as complicated as I'm making it. Maybe his statement is indeed an admission of his feelings for me, but then what about the look on his face when I blurted out the most mortifying request in the history of mankind?

If he did, in fact, admit to not being able to avoid me, not being able to stop thinking about me, then what was with the rebuff and repulsion when I asked him to kiss me? Wasn't it repulsion I saw on his face? Or was he weighing out the predicament I'd put him in?

Shit. I don't know. The man has never made it easy for me to read him.

Either way, I can't fucking live here with this hanging

between us. No matter how much I try, I won't be able to sweep this under the rug and pretend like it didn't happen. I have the rest of the summer to think about; I have my sweet nephew to think about. I can't move forward from this unless I own up to it and clear the air–tell Darian I'd momentarily lost my goddamn mind and possibly had a stroke.

Shouldn't be too hard for him to believe, given the strange things he's heard me say before. I'll just chalk it up to another Rani quirk, but at least I'll address it.

I stand, surveying my dress and running a hand over it, before squaring my shoulders. It's fine. I'm a big girl, and I can fix my mistakes like the budding adult I am.

Swinging my door open slowly, I make my way from my room and down the stairs. He's not in the kitchen or dining room, so I know there are only two other places he'd be–his study or his bedroom. I didn't see his bedroom door closed, like it usually is when he's in there, so I turn down the hallway toward the study.

Releasing a breath and shaking my arms a little to loosen the nerves, I knock on the door. I feel like I'm about to get on stage in front of a million people, without having prepared my speech.

Time to wing it.

"Come in." His voice makes me jump, even though I expected it.

Fucking calm down, Rani. Fix this and move on.

I turn the knob and enter, noting the wall of bookshelves, packed full of books, trophies, and trinkets. My heart hammers as I slowly slide my gaze toward him, watching him get up from his seat and walk around to the front of his desk. He sits against it with his long legs sprawled out. His arms are crossed over his chest, and I note his attempt at a casual stance, even though his shoulders are stiff and his eyes are trained on my every move.

I suppose I'm the one who needs to break this ice.

"Um . . .." I clear my throat, unnecessarily. "I, uh, wanted to come here and say I'm sorry."

"Rani—"

I lift my hand to halt his interjection. "No, please just let me finish. It took me a lot of courage to come here and address the foolish words that flew out of my mouth earlier, and I just want to mend whatever I did." I take a breath and raise my chin. "I don't know what got into me earlier. I'm sick to my stomach that I could be so brazen and impulsive with what I asked of you and I . . .." My eyes fall to the floor as I fiddle with my hands, wishing this dress had pockets.

Why? Why can't all dresses just have pockets? Is it so much to ask that women be given this small concession? If this dress was made for men, wouldn't it come with pockets? I am positive it would. It just boils my blood when I think about the little injustices we have to swallow as women.

I momentarily forget what I was here to say as I get riled up about not having fucking pockets inside my dress so I can rest my hands in there and not fiddle with them like I'm doing right now. "I'd really like for us to forget my lapse in judgment earlier and just move forward."

He's silent for so long that I have to wonder if I've rendered him unconscious. I reluctantly bring my gaze up to his, finding nothing but his impassive expression. He runs his tongue along his bottom lip and oh, *this is not good*. No, no, no. This is very bad, indeed. My eyes adhere to the movement like superglue, and no matter how much I try to unstick them, they won't listen.

It's like he's challenging my restraint, waiting for me to either run out like my pants—er, dress—are on fire or find my way to him. My body sways like a pendulum being pulled in both directions.

Finally, my eyes flick back to meet his when he speaks. "You want me to forget that you asked me to kiss you?"

God, it's fucking hot in here, like a damn inferno.

"Can you maybe *not* remind me of what I asked you to do?" I look away, my cheeks flaming before meeting his eyes again. "Can we just call it the 'thing' I asked you to do?"

His lips twitch. Fucking twitching, glistening, and ridiculously plump lips that no man should have. Women pay good money to have lips like that.

"I'm just trying to make sure I know which 'thing' you're referring to. I assume it's the kiss you requested that you want me to forget about."

I release a hard breath, getting irritated with his use of the word 'kiss.' Why does he even have to say it? We both know what I asked. Is it not humiliating enough for me that I even said what I said? Why does he now have to repeat it over and over again and torture me with it? Whatever. "Yes."

"Why?"

My brows pull up. "What?"

"Why do you want me to forget about it?" He blinks as if he's just asked me how the weather was outside.

I sputter around a laugh and a cry at the same time. "Darian, what the hell? You have me so mixed up and inside my head that I no longer know if I'm even sane anymore." I laugh incredulously as my voice rises. "Why do I want you to forget about me asking you to kiss me? Well, for starters, *you don't want to*! You might say you feel *unhinged* around me or that you can't avoid me even when you try to, but you can't face me, either! You can't face whatever it is that I make you feel, so what's the point? Why disorient me like this? What do you get out of it?"

He pushes off from his perch on the desk as alarm bells blare inside my ears. *Oh boy.* I've either pissed him off or I'm about to get all my answers. He steps forward as my pulse quickens. I'm positive if a nurse were to catalog my heart rate, it'd be well over nine thousand beats a minute, give or take a few. In fact, my pulse is so high that I'm at risk of rocketing into the sky.

With his eyes locked on me, he erases the space between us in just a couple of long strides. I do my best to stay rooted to my spot, but I can't guarantee my feet haven't ripped up the carpeting below me. He lowers his head, his lips only a few inches above mine. "Were you going to let him kiss you, Rani?"

I mumble a response in Gaelic . . . or maybe it's Portuguese? I don't know either of those languages, so who knows what I've just said.

Trying again, I croak, "What?"

"Were you going to let Ginger Boy kiss you?"

I swallow, pretending that my legs aren't mercilessly clenching, trying to squelch the need forming in between them with the awareness of his closeness. "He did say he was a good kisser."

Darian's nostrils flare and his eyes flash with silent warning before he leans in even closer. Goosebumps erupt across my skin as he whispers against my ear, "I'm at the edge of my restraint, Rani. If you don't want to see me lose it, then I suggest you walk away, right the fuck now."

Oh gosh.

Oh man, oh man.

This is not good. This is very, very bad.

I move my face only an inch but it's enough to feel the brush of his delicious scruff across my cheek. It sends a shiver down my spine and I hold back a whimper. The air stands still between us. "And what if I want to see what the *king* looks like when he falls?"

Before I even finish thinking about what I've done, yet again, his lips are on mine with a soft growl. Both of his hands stroll up my bare shoulders, finding their way to the side of my face. He cups my cheeks as his tongue sweeps over my lips, asking—no, *demanding*—entrance into my mouth.

At first, I'm so bewildered by his scent and the feel of his lips on my mouth that I barely respond. But the more he coaxes me out of my stupor—his tongue teasing against my mouth—the more I feel myself give in.

My eyes finally close as my hands slide up his torso, finding purchase on his chest, and I open my mouth, letting him in. His tongue finds mine as it dances and caresses against it while a pool of want collects shamelessly inside my panties. A low, intense need awakens inside my belly as his arm circles my waist and he pulls me closer. The need only escalates when I feel the heaviness of his desire inside his pants rub against my core.

His tongue swirls inside my mouth as he tilts my head with his other hand, pressing down to find more, to suspend me between a state of consciousness and oblivion. A state I never want to come out of. A state I'm perfectly content finding my new existence inside.

The taste of his mouth, the way he sucks on my tongue, and his hand now sliding into my hair, makes me breathless. But if this is what breathlessness feels like, then I'd rather not breathe again.

There's nothing sweet and gentle about this kiss; it's rough and demanding. It orders me to comply as his tongue wars with mine. He pulls my waist in further, plastering my chest against his, and I revel in how he maneuvers my body around, as if I'm pint-sized in his arms. I arch against his chest, rising up on my toes as my arms circle his neck, letting out the smallest of moans.

And just like that, he pulls away from me, making me whimper against the cold air that glides over my swollen lips. I'm panting, as my hands beg to pull him back, as my lips burn for another taste of him. *No!* my body and mind cry out. This can't be all I was going to get.

I sway against him, loosely hanging on to his neck as he stares at my glistening lips. His generally impassive face never gives anything away, but I swear a smug smile pulls at his lips. "Still want me to forget about that kiss?"

"I . . . I think I need a refresher, just to be sure."

His face lights up like I've never seen before, his beautiful teeth gleaming against his tanned skin and pillowy lips. He's breathing almost as hard as I am, though I feel like he has his senses still about him. I, on the other hand, feel senseless.

Helpless.

Endless.

Basically a lot of 'less' while feeling a whole lot *more*.

If that kiss was his way of clarifying himself and setting the record straight, then I'm going to award him with an A-plus. A job very well done, indeed! As of this moment, there's no confusion in my mind as to what just happened, though it still feels surreal. But, I suppose this moment paves the way for the million other questions that will race through my brain once I step out the door, starting with, what happens now?

Darian's forehead meets mine while he studies my face. His hands rest around the base of my neck and shoulders as his thumb slowly circles my skin. His lips glide against my forehead softly as we gather ourselves, catching our breaths. My nipples feel tight inside my dress and the dampness between my legs reminds me that I'll need to change my underwear tonight.

"Rani–" he starts, right as the baby monitor atop his desk signals a waking baby's cry.

Darian's smile vanishes and it's as if he's been awakened from a spell. As if the snap of a hypnotist has brought him back to reality. His eyes lock with mine, slightly widened, as the entire moment transforms into one washed with guilt and doubt. As if what we just shared was nothing more than a blip in the normalcy of our relationship.

He pulls away from me as my hands slide back to my sides, and I'm once again cursing dress designers everywhere for not giving me the one thing I truly want at this very moment. "I'll go check on him," he supplies through an unmistaken rasp in his voice. "It's Friday and you're still off the clock."

With my stomach at my feet, I watch him leave the room, once again convinced I should check myself into a mental asylum.

Chapter Sixteen
DARIAN

"Yo!" My brother, Dean, peeks his head into my office, making me break my attention from the contract I was reviewing. His blond hair is a messy bun on his head, his teeth gleaming the way they do whenever he's here to ask for something.

Dean is a firefighter in our local fire department. Sometimes when he's not on shift, he'll drop by to bum kayaks off me.

I turn back to my computer screen. "Let me guess . . ." I don't have to finish the sentence.

"Any chance Mala and I can grab some kayaks for a couple of hours?"

We've talked about this before, but my brother is nothing if not persistent. That's another way of saying he's good at pestering until you want to ram your head into a wall.

I sigh. "My school can't afford the liability if something were to happen to either of you in the water without an instructor or a safety patrol present." I wheel my chair over to the middle of the desk and stretch my neck. Fuck, I'm exhausted. "Buy a couple of kayaks and store them here. You know I don't mind that. But I can't have you out there in the water with the ones with our emblem on them."

"Dude, both Mala and I are skilled kayakers. You know this." When he sees me give him an exhausted stare, he adds, "Alright, just this one time, and I'll buy a couple. I'll even purchase my own life vest and helmet. Come on, I'll buy you a smoothie or some shit."

"Tempting," I deadpan.

He shifts into the middle of the doorway, with his hands inside his pockets, taking up most of the space. The three of us got our six-foot-plus frames from our dad since both our moms are on the shorter side.

"Please." He drags the word.

I shake my head. "Fine. Whatever. If you guys die, that's on you."

"Got it." He smirks.

I peer behind him. "Where is Mala, anyway? And what about Jessie?"

My brother's best friend for the past five years, Mala, has become more like family. He brings her to our family gatherings and Christmas dinners, and she's been his plus-one for weddings and other formal events.

I can't count the number of times we've asked him about taking things further with her—she's gorgeous, smart, and has an incredible personality—but he dodges the question every time. He's even claimed she's like the sister he never had.

The guy is smoking crack. If the way he looks at her and acts around her is any indication, there's nothing brotherly about it.

Recently, his excuse was that he got back together with his on-again, off-again girlfriend Jessie. I hold in a groan even thinking about her. The woman is a needy narcissist. She constantly uses him as a cash cow, fluttering her eyes at him whenever she's in trouble because for whatever reason, my brother cannot say no to her.

If I were to get started on all the reasons Jessie is wrong for him, it would take me all night to get through the list, but I guess some people have a thing for learning shit the hard way.

"Mala's changing in the locker room." He winks at me. "And Jessie's at work."

"Jackass," I grumble. He planned on me saying yes even before he asked me and directed Mala to get changed.

"Too bad we share DNA." He chuckles before his smile fades a little. He assesses me with an arched brow. "You okay, bro? I mean, you *were* born with that scowly-ass face of yours, but it seems worse today. Everything alright? How's my nephew?"

I lift my cap off my head and throw it onto the desk, leaning back in my chair. "Yeah. Fine."

"Nuh-uh." He shakes his head, strolling into the room and taking a seat on the chair in front of me. "Don't do that. Tell big brother what's up."

Fuck, I wish I knew myself.

It's been almost a week since I kissed Rani, and she's been giving me the cold-shoulder ever since—leaving the house as soon as I get home, eating dinner in her room, and leaving my texts on 'read' if I haven't specifically asked about Arman. Every passing day has been more excruciating than the one before it.

I don't blame her. I probably didn't give her any reassurance that our kiss wasn't something I regretted—not with my rigid body language and clipped tone the next day. Because, honestly, I didn't know what to think of it. One minute I was still fuming inside my study at finding that red-headed tool's hands on her—I might have peeked proactively through the camera at my door—and the next minute, she was shuffling into my space, enveloping me with her lily scent. She was so nervous and wound up, it was adorable as hell. And the next minute after that, my lips were locked with hers.

I didn't think—even when I told her to do so herself—I just acted. It was almost instinctual and impending, like it was bound to happen. I took what I wanted, without any fucking thought of the consequences. Without a thought about the fact that she was my sister-in-law, the fact that she was nineteen, or the fact that I had promised myself I wasn't going to go down a path like this with her.

I devoured her exquisite mouth and those sinful lips as if they belonged to me, as if they were only mine for the taking. I took, and I took without giving two shits about remorse or regret.

And I fucking liked it.
Nix that. I loved it.

The way she molded to my body, arching to let me taste more. The way her hands pressed against my chest, telling me exactly how much she was enjoying the taste of me, too. The way she panted softly when I pulled away, like she'd forgotten how to breathe.

And then, with the sound of Arman's voice on the monitor, it was as if the lights had been turned on in a movie theater and the best movie I'd ever seen in my life was nothing more than a blank screen in front of me. In that kiss, I'd seen a different life. In that one kiss, I'd almost allowed myself to imagine that I could have more.

But it was as if my son's voice was a wake-up call, a jolt out of the fiction I'd allowed myself a moment's reprieve inside. A moment where I wasn't struggling to manage my one-year-old son and my business without his mother. A moment where I didn't have to worry about the morality of being with my dead wife's teenage sister. And a few seconds where I could pursue something without the handcuffs of my life and my own disillusionments keeping me tied.

But like every good movie, that ended too, making the void in my life even more evident.

I squeeze the bridge of my nose between my thumb and index finger before running a hand over my face. "I kissed Rani a few nights ago."

Dean slumps back in the chair before he exhales loudly. "Wow. I knew I was onto something with the sister-nanny."

I flip him off.

He chuckles again. "I'm guessing she was game for it? I know you wouldn't do anything unless you got a clear signal from her."

Rani's breathless request spins in circles around my head. *"For you to kiss me."*

I nod at Dean, not feeling any better about his confidence in me. "Yeah . . .."

He searches my face. "I hear an unspoken 'but' in your response."

I clench my jaw, unsure of how to respond, but luckily, Mala pops her head in. "Hey, Darian!"

"Hey, Mala. Good to see you."

"You, too!" Her eyes flick to Dean before a coy smile plays on her lips. "Well? Did he say yes?"

"Of course he said yes. Did you honestly doubt me, woman?" Dean chimes in smugly, and both Mala and I exchange exasperated glances. "Hey, will you give me a few minutes, though? I just need to bestow some of my profound wisdom onto my little brother."

I scoff. "Get the fuck out of here. The minute I start taking advice from you is the minute I've officially handed in my adult card."

Dean places a hand on his heart. "You wound me, Brutus."

Both Mala and I look at each other, holding back our laughs.

"Pretty sure you've mixed up a couple of Shakespearean plays there, Dean, but you definitely deserve an A for effort. I'll see you out there in a few." She throws a thumb over her shoulder before her gaze meets mine. "Thanks for letting us use your equipment."

Dean sighs, turning back to me when Mala disappears. "Dar, listen, I'm not an expert in relationships–"

"Rani and I aren't in a relationship," I clarify, quickly.

"Right. I suppose what I'm saying is, I can understand your dilemma without you having to spell it out. She's your sister-in-law, helping with Arman, and living at your house. If something goes sideways between you two, it could really make for an awkward summer."

"She's also fucking nineteen years old. She's practically a child."

Dean shifts in his chair. "I'm assuming that nothing's happened since you guys kissed, so let's talk about the *why* before we talk about the *why not*."

I frown. "What?"

"Tell me *why* you kissed her. What brought on that spontaneity and that desire in you? Don't get me wrong, she's a pretty girl–I may have even checked out her ass as she went up the stairs that day we were all playing poker."

I glare at him, knowing he's goading me, yet I still just barely resist throwing a punch to his pretty-boy face.

He laughs, knowing he's done exactly what he set out to do. "In all seriousness, brother, I was hoping you'd find this side of you again. I don't think it was even there when Sonia was around. At least not . . . in the end."

I bristle. "What does that mean?"

Dean tilts his head, his blue eyes examining me, weighing out how to say what he wants to. "Look man, I don't think it was much of a secret that you both weren't seeing eye to eye on things. She was constantly on your case about shit—from working too much to not working enough—and she didn't mince her words, even in front of your family."

My thoughts wander off to the last Christmas before she died. I'd thought our therapy sessions were working and things were getting better. We'd found out we were pregnant only a few weeks before that, and we were hopeful the baby would bring us together like we had been in the past.

"So, Sonia, have you and Darian decided on baby names yet?" My dad was always good at getting Sonia out of her shell at family gatherings.

While she wasn't anti-social, I think being apart from her own family for so long had made her aloof. And whatever I did to help her—whether it was trying to bring her into a conversation or even holding her hand in companionship—made her feel like I was trying to 'change her.' So, after a while, and a thousand arguments later, I stopped trying.

She smirked, without a sign of happiness, and glanced at me. She'd always been good at conveying a thousand emotions just with the tilt of her head or the set of her jaw. "If Darian was ever home to discuss mundane things like our child's name, then perhaps we'd have one picked out. But between our school either doing so well that he needs to backfill the open positions or not doing well enough to where he's having to do the work of employees we've had to let go," she looked at me pointedly, "the baby and I take a back seat."

"Well, I'm sure that's not true," my dad had argued, congenially. "Darian loves you to the moon, and he'll love this baby just the same. I know you understand this, since you're a big part of the success of the school, but running a small business is no joke. Staffing is hard and the hours are always long."

"With all due respect, Marvin," Sonia's voice was stern and made everyone at the dinner table turn to listen to our conversation, "I'm not a woman who values useless words. I value actions and effort—"

"Effort?" I finally questioned, my patience failing me. "You value effort? What have I been showing you, if not effort? *From the therapy we've had, to the times I've left the school early–knowing I'd have a pile of work waiting on my desk the next day–to committing to go to every appointment with you. If that's not effort, Sonia, then what is?"*

Of course, I wasn't going to mention the times I'd try to coax her into our bed. Not because I wasn't tired, but because I wanted to show her how much I loved her.

"Vacations!" She'd raise both palms, shrugging in exasperation. "A getaway, away from this small, goddamn mountain town I've been trapped in for so long!"

I'd reeled back, pointedly ignoring my mother's gasp. "You wanted to stay here. You loved the mountains and the lake . . .. Why does it feel like you're turning the story around to make it seem like I'm forcing you to stay here?"

She gawked at me in shock, and I realized my words hadn't come out the way I'd intended. "Oh, so you'd let me leave? You'd let me walk right out this door and cut off all ties?"

"Sonia, you know that's not what I meant."

As much as Sonia hated her mother, as much as she complained about the way her mother had perfected the art of gaslighting, she'd slowly turned into a version of her over the years.

Maybe I just hadn't seen the slow transformation or maybe I'd been in denial from the very beginning. There was no use in overanalyzing it.

The rest of dinner progressed like nails on a chalkboard–painstakingly. Dean and Garrett both tried to change the subject and made jokes to lighten the mood, but I decided to cut the night short and left early with Sonia, in a familiar but torturously silent car ride.

My brother gets up from his chair, jostling me back to the present. "You haven't answered my question about why you kissed her, and I suspect you won't. What triggered your decision and that spontaneity inside you? I think it's time you were honest with yourself."

When I just stare at him blankly, he continues, "Dar, it doesn't matter how she's connected to Sonia. It doesn't even matter that she works for you or that she's nineteen—a consenting adult, by the way. You need to stop questioning any of that." He focuses his gaze on me. "The only question you should be considering is whether you'll regret letting the first person to light a spark inside you in a very long time go without giving it an honest shot."

My brother walks out of the room and I don't know how long I sit there, in the same spot, staring at an empty doorway.

Chapter Seventeen
RANI

"Thanks for letting me visit again, Lynn. I hope you don't mind me taking up your time, especially this late." I hand Lynn the small cheesecake I picked up on my way here.

She hesitates before taking the box from me, giving me a reproachful look. "Well, it's no bother at all, dear, but I will have to rethink any future invitations if you keep bringing sweets."

I wince. "I'm sorry. I just can't help bringing in something for Fred."

"She has a crush on me," Fred yells from his seat in the living room. "I'm used to this with the ladies."

Lynn rolls her eyes, her heavy lids setting back in place, but the ghost of a smile buds on her face. She sets the box on the counter and gently rips it around the sides. "You're spoiling him, along with playing to his ego. The man doesn't need any more of either."

I smile, watching her take down three plates from the cupboard. Her hands tremble slightly, and I almost move to help her but decide against it. I don't want to make her feel incapable in any way.

She gets a cake knife and cuts three slices of the cake, one larger than the other two, placing them on the plates before closing the box and putting it into the fridge. She comes back with a bowl of blueberries and raspberries, placing a few on each plate.

She gives me the plate with the thickest slice, gesturing to the drawer behind her. "The forks are in there, if you don't mind getting them for us."

I pull three forks out, then follow her into the living room with my plate in hand.

Fred straightens, eyeing the two plates in Lynn's hand. "I want that one," he declares, pointing at the plate with a slice hardly a centimeter thicker than the other. I can't help the giggle that escapes me, which earns me another chiding look from Lynn.

She hands him the plate before pushing back the uniformly white hair brushing her shoulders. "You are such a child."

Fred ignores her, happily taking his plate and the fork from me before digging in. "Mmm. This is something." He hums around another mouthful as I take my seat on the couch.

I'd called the nursing home a couple of days ago to see if they'd let me help out in the evenings, even though that wasn't my scheduled time. They were happy to have me come in, telling me they were actually low on staff that day. So, I helped run meals to the various independent units throughout the property, introducing myself to residents and chatting with some as I dropped off their dinner.

When I brought a bag of groceries and another bag of dinner to Fred and Lynn's unit, they recognized me immediately. We started chatting and before I knew it, I was telling them about my blog. I took a chance at asking if they'd let me document their story and surprisingly, they both said yes.

So, here I am, on my second visit with them—and my third evening at the nursing facility.

I've been making a conscious effort to be out of the house as much as possible as soon as Darian comes home. I generally mumble a quick recap of the day with Arman—what he ate, how he did, words he said—and then slip out of the house. Several times, I've seen an apology in Darian's eyes. Several times, he's tried to interrupt while I'm speaking, but I bulldoze past him.

I don't want to talk about what happened. I don't want to hear him express his remorse or tell me it was a big mistake. I don't need him to say any of those things because his demeanor the day after we kissed said it all.

He'd practically run out of the room whenever I was in it or he'd mumble about checking on something before hiding out in his study for hours on end. He was back to doing that whole avoidance dance, so I figured I'd join him.

Two can tango, and I'm not a bad dancer.

If he wants to avoid me for the rest of the summer because I make him feel something—because I make him face his own desire—then that's on him. I don't regret our kiss. It was single-handedly the hottest moment of my life, and now, I feel like I'm starving around him.

I want more. God, I want so much more, but not at the cost of my dignity. Not at the cost of being treated as anything less than I know I'm worth.

I set my phone on the table and click the record button on my app before leaning back to look at Fred and Lynn. Fred is already done with his cake, giving me a satisfied and grateful smile. "I know I spent a lot of time talking about some of the other stories in the blog last night, so we didn't quite get into everything—"

"Well, that and Fred fell asleep, having no regard for his manners," Lynn supplies, side-eying her husband.

I laugh. "Right, that too. Fred, I hope I can keep you awake today."

Fred smiles, winking at me. "Well, another piece of cake might help."

"Absolutely not." Lynn keeps her eyes on me, addressing the man beside her. "Now, let's begin, dear. What questions do you have for us?"

The warmth that radiates between these two is unlike anything I've ever seen. Their banter and love for each other—despite their bickering—is so heartfelt and sincere, I wish I could be a fly on their wall all day long. This is what true love looks like. It's what it feels like and it's what we were born to find, I just know it.

I clear the emotion building in my throat. "Well, I don't have a predetermined set of questions. I want this to be as organic as possible. Perhaps you could start with telling me how you two met."

Fred slides his hand into Lynn's and I watch her squeeze it back, turning her head to admire him over her shoulder.

"Do you want me to start, and then you'll correct me like you always do?" he quips.

"I correct you because you exaggerate the truth."

Fred mocks offense with his mouth hanging open for a second. "I merely give color to the gray parts of our story."

"With you, there's never been any gray."

He slips an arm around her, squeezing her to his side. "Mrs. Cox, I do believe that is the sweetest thing you have ever said to me. This whole time I was convinced you'd married me for my looks."

Lynn smacks his arm playfully, settling her gaze on me while I observe their exchange in awe.

Fred regards Lynn affectionately. "I met this wonderful woman almost at the end of my senior year of high school.

You see . . ." he hesitates with a smile tipping up the corners of his mouth, "she was my English teacher."

My eyes widen to saucers as his words hit me. "What?"

Fred chuckles as Lynn focuses on their tangled hands in her lap, smiling to herself. "I was eighteen, and Lynn was twenty-five . . . practically an old maid." This earns him another playful slap. "My regular English teacher was in an awful accident and could no longer teach for the rest of the year. The school had to find someone to cover for her for the last six weeks before the school year ended."

He caresses Lynn, sliding his hand up and down her arm. "I knew the moment she stepped into the classroom that I'd marry her. Come hell or high water, I was going to make this woman mine, whether she knew it or not. She was—and still is—the most beautiful woman I ever saw. She was gentle and kind, and boy, was she whip-smart. But if you got on the wrong side of her, she wouldn't be afraid to show you the door."

I could see that. Lynn had a no-nonsense air about her, and I'd be lying if I said I didn't want to stay on her good side.

"So how did you approach her? How did it all begin?" I'm giddy with excitement. Even knowing they ended up together, I want to hear every detail, every part of their story.

"He kept failing the assignments I was sending home. I didn't know it at the time, but he was purposely writing in the wrong answers and even failed two quizzes I'd handed the class," Lynn adds. "So, I offered to tutor him."

"Which was my plan all along." Fred winks at me. "I gradually worked my way up to seeing her for tutoring three times a week, rather than the once a week she had originally suggested. And during those sessions, I'd find ways to slip in personal questions, trying to get to know her. I'd share unnecessary details about my life too, just so she could know them, hoping she'd think about me even after the tutoring session."

I regard Lynn. "And did you?"

She inhales. "Well, I didn't want to, you know. He was seven years my junior and still had to figure out what he was going to do in life. My parents were bugging me to find someone and settle down, and while they were liberal, I knew they wouldn't approve of a relationship between us."

"What happened after that?" I ask Fred.

"Well, one day, I told her how I felt." Fred smiles. "It was the last day of school, and magically, I'd passed English–"

"*Barely*."

Fred continues, unperturbed by Lynn's interruption, "I told her that I'd fallen in love with her and I wanted to marry her. Just like that."

"It wasn't 'just like that.'" Lynn scowls at him. "You were sweating bullets."

Fred shakes his head. "See what I mean? She can't just let me have my moment of bravado." At the roll of Lynn's eyes, Fred continues, "As I was saying, I professed my love to this woman, who, for all intents and purposes, had already become my girl . . . in my mind at least."

He pauses, so I look between the both of them, waiting for one of them to continue. When I don't see either of them give me a reaction, I ask, "And? What did she say?"

"I said no," Lynn answers.

"No?" I ask, my brows raised.

"Yes, I said no. I told him that he was out of his mind if he thought I'd marry him when he had no idea who he was or what he wanted to do with his life." Her eyes stay on him endearingly. "So, he asked me what it would take."

"And she said it would take me figuring out my life, getting a job, and being able to afford to buy her a ring before she'd say yes." He sighs. "So, I did just that. I got a job as a car mechanic and slowly moved up to supervisor. Four years later, I became part-owner of the same repair shop. And when I could finally afford that ring she'd asked me for, I asked her again."

"And I said yes."

"And she said yes," Fred repeats in a whisper. "She'd waited for me. We got married in her parents' backyard six months later, and Lynn gave birth to the first of our three children a year after that."

Heartwarming tears of joy gather inside my eyes as their story sinks into my bones. When a tear slips down my cheek, Lynn comes to sit next to me. "Oh now, you've interviewed so many couples before, and I'm sure they've all had wonderful stories. I can't imagine you crying with each one."

I blubber out a laugh, wiping my tears with my fingertips. I remember to stop the recording before taking a breath. "I guess this one just spoke to me. I'm so happy to see that you both got to spend your lives together."

Lynn leans in, searching my eyes. "Is there anyone you've found to spend your life with?"

I meet her gaze. "I . . . I don't know. The way it appears right now, I don't think so."

Over the next few minutes, I tell them about Darian–who he is to me, why I'm in Tahoe, how we kissed exactly one week ago.

When I've finished, Fred regards me seriously. "It seems you've put this Darian man in quite a state, Rani. As much as I want to call him a jackass for not giving in to what his heart clearly wants, I think I'd respect him less if he didn't get wound up in his head about it. Wouldn't you?"

Lynn hands me a tissue, and I swipe it over my nose. "What do you mean?"

"Well, I'm not saying I loved the time I spent apart from my Lynn. It was a hard four years trying to prove myself to her, but had I told you that she was willing to jump into a relationship with an eighteen-year-old—no questions asked—I don't know that you would have seen her the same way. Maybe it wouldn't change where we are today, but we may have taken a different journey. Instead, she weighed out what she wanted with what she needed. She made sure we were both ready for each other before she allowed me into her life. She had principles that she couldn't disregard."

His words, spoken with gentle concern, center my thoughts. *Principles*. Just like me, Darian had his own principles and I was tempting him to break them. I was asking him to put them aside for me. Was that fair?

Was it fair for me to expect him to go at my pace? To see things the way I see them, when he still has wrinkles he's ironing out in his head. Didn't the timing have to be right for both people in order to take a step together long-term?

And what if Darian hadn't shown restraint from the beginning? Would I have respected him the same way? Would I have come to care for him the same way?

I hug Fred and Lynn, take my leave from their home, and walk back to my car. I'm just turning the engine when my phone vibrates in my purse and I take it out.

A text from the man who has tainted all my recent thoughts stares back at me.

Darian: Did you know there are over one-hundred types of lilies?

A frown forms between my brows, and I know my mouth probably has one, too. The hell? Did he accidentally send me a text that was meant for someone else?

I'm staring at the text in confusion when another one comes in.

Darian: Did you know that the Romans found the scent of lilies so intoxicating that they used to fill their pillows with lily petals?

My mouth twists. This is just a strange way of breaking the ice, if that's what he's doing. I realize he probably knows I'm reading his messages given the read-receipts I have turned on.

Darian: Did you know that lilies primarily come in six colors, and that each color has a certain meaning?

Lord, how long is this going to go on? I turn down the air conditioning in my car, chewing my bottom lip, before typing out a message.

Me: Thank you for the incredibly useful information. I'll be sure to file this away for the next Trivial Pursuit night.

Dots jump on my screen as he types.

Darian: That would be considered cheating.
Darian: What you should be asking me is which color lilies are sitting at your door right now.

Wait.
Wait just a damn minute.
I raise my head and look out my windshield toward the illuminated nursing home. Darian has left me a bouquet each week–the white ones already in my room when I arrived at his

house, the pink ones the week after, and the orange ones last Friday.

Is he implying that he *chose* the color of the lilies because of their meaning?

No. No way.

Me: What color lilies are at my door

Darian: Come home . . . you'll see.

Chapter Eighteen
RANI

I slam my car door, swinging my purse onto my shoulder, before practically running to the front door. I can't quite pinpoint the urgency, but my racing heart tells me there is one.

One by the name of Darian Meyer.

My hands shake as I unlock the door, seeing only a lamp illuminating an empty living room. Darian's study door is open and the lights are turned off, so I know he's not in there. But even as I search for him, I ask myself why.

Why is my heartbeat surging through my body, eviscerating any other sound inside my head? Why am I searching for a man who has baffled me since the second I stepped foot into his house? Why am I desperate to find him . . . to see him?

And once I find him, what do I even plan to say?

I make my way up the stairs and find him leaning against my doorway with his arms crossed. The dim lighting in the hall does nothing to dull his imposing and aristocratic form. I do a shameless perusal of his bare feet, his long black pajama bottoms that cinch around his lean waist perfectly, and a white T-shirt that stretches across his wide chest. My eyes snag on his biceps—of course, they do—before slipping up to his face.

He looks calm and focused—and that focus is set firmly on me. I stand rooted to my spot, listening to the rhythmic hum of Arman's sound machine vibrating in the air between us.

Darian raises his chin and the low timber of his voice hits me below my belly button, swirling heat inside my stomach before pooling between my legs. "Did you know that lilies—the scent of them, the feel of them, the fucking taste of them—have the ability to make a person go insane?"

With his hands now in his pockets, he takes a step toward me as the air charges between us like uncontrolled electricity. "It's not a written fact, but it's one I've personally experienced. One I've become dependent on, like a potent drug." He takes another step toward me, and I positively tremble with his closeness. "One I haven't stopped thinking about since my first whiff . . . the day on the kayaks. One I can't get out of my fucking head or my senses now that I've had a taste of it."

His eyes caress my lips, boldly staking their claim, unwavering. "Did you know that the lily is considered one of the most powerful aphrodisiacs, awakening a desire so deep, it's almost impossible to ignore?"

He covers any distance left between us as his large hand wraps around my neck. His thumb runs along my jaw, making my eyelids feel heavy, as my breaths come out in soft pants. "I've tried. Believe me, I've tried to remove the scent of lilies from every inch of my skin that's been exposed. But there's no way to scrub my fucking veins. There's no way to cleanse my mind. It's infused in *everything*."

His other hand wraps around the other side of my neck and I whimper, leaning into his touch. "So," he whispers, his lips a mere inch from mine, "I give up. I can't fucking breathe without the perfume in the air. I can't fucking breathe, Rani."

My hands wrap around his shoulders. "Then just breathe."

Darian's fingers tighten slightly around my neck as his lips descend upon mine. He takes my bottom lip between his before pulling it gently between his teeth. I moan as his tongue sweeps inside my mouth and his arm drops to my waist, pulling me into him. I'm pressed to his chest, sliding my fingers around the back of his neck to play with the curls at his nape.

He tilts his head, and I turn mine in the opposite direction, as his restless tongue dives further into my mouth. He sucks my tongue, groaning into my throat. I feel the vibration of his voice well inside my belly as butterflies erupt, sending heat coursing through my veins.

His mouth fits mine perfectly and his hands keep me exactly at the angle he wants. There's no exchange, no give or take with him. He gives and he takes, and I want more of it–I want all of it. I can feel his heart hammering against his chest, reverberating against my own.

His hard-on, deliciously protruding through his thin pajamas, presses exquisitely against my belly, and I almost ask to climb him so I can rub myself shamelessly against him and satiate the need building inside me. My nipples ache painfully inside my bra, begging to be let loose. Begging to be touched and licked, to be pinched and bitten.

The more he delves in with his tongue–refamiliarizing himself with my mouth–the more I reciprocate, massaging the side of his tongue and pulling in the sweetness from his lips. His hands tangle inside my long curls, and he wraps them around his fist. I'm going to collapse. Right here, right now. I'm going to die, but at least it'll be happily in his arms.

Neither of us has taken a breath in God knows how long, and we're in serious risk of asphyxiating, so I pull away from him slowly, leaving lingering kisses on his lips. Both his hands slip to my waist while I continue to softly tug on his hair. We're both breathing hard, holding each other up and taking each other in.

Darian's forehead meets mine. "Rani."

I nibble on my bottom lip–tasting him on me–as the weight of the moment hits me. I recall Fred's words and the subsequent thoughts I had about not pushing Darian into something he's not ready for. Something I might not even be ready for. "Darian . . . I don't know what this is. I don't know where we are or how we got here, twice. And I'm . . . ."

He kisses up the side of my neck, inciting goosebumps all across my body and making me forget my train of thought. My legs clench, begging for relief. I'm shamelessly aware that he can probably smell the desire pooled inside my panties, but I'm beyond the point of caring.

"And you're scared," he finishes my thought.

I nod, squeezing my eyes shut.

I used to do it a lot when I was younger–squeezing my eyes shut to capture the moment in a mental picture. I can only recall a handful of happy moments from my childhood, but one was when Dad took Bella and me to a water park with roller coasters that dumped riders into enormous pools. It was a simple outing–one many kids spent their summers doing–but for me, it was a day of freedom. A day without my mom nagging me about something or another. I can't recall the reason she couldn't come with us, but I remember squeezing my eyes shut tight before opening them up, taking in the monster roller coaster in front of me and squealing in disbelief.

I want to squeal in the same way now, but I'm afraid I'll completely ruin this dream if I do. Because how could I not be dreaming?

I open my eyes to see that he's watching me, his usual

blank mask back on his face. I should get my head checked for finding his unruffled expression so incredibly sexy. I know he feels a lot—it's obvious with the way he guards himself—but he uses his inscrutable face as a shield that I find both irresistible and heartbreaking. Call me crazy.

"You don't think I'm scared?"

Before I can answer him, he pulls me by the hand to his bedroom, turning on the light. I scan his neatly-made bed with navy linens and a fluffy white comforter. It's large enough to fit an entire family on. Aside from that, there are two nightstands with oversized lamps and a couple of chairs placed for both form and function inside a bay window nook. Set against the light blue accent wall, the entire room feels subdued but deliberate—a lot like Darian himself.

The door clicks closed behind me, and Darian's hands find my face again, imploring my eyes. "You don't think I'm scared?" he repeats.

I nod, looking down at his chest. "I know you are, just like I am. I'm terrified that if things go south between us, I won't just lose you, but I'll lose Arman, too."

He places a kiss on my forehead. "Sweetheart, I would never take Arman from you. I know how much you love him."

"Maybe we should just take things slow." I search his eyes again.

"Rani, I'm not scared of the physical stuff between us, so I hope that's not what you thought I meant. You are so fucking beautiful, I haven't quite found the right words—"

"I'd say you did pretty well with the whole lily analogy," I quip, smiling shyly.

His intense gaze pins me to my spot again. "I'm scared of everything in-between."

"The emotions," I state, understanding him.

His thumbs gently soothe my cheekbones. "I didn't want

to go down this road again. I was starting to become settled in my single-dad life. Frankly, I'm terrified to take the path again." When he sees my questioning gaze, he continues with the typical twitch of his lips, withholding his smiles from me, "But I couldn't ignore the scent of lilies any longer."

I wrap my hand around his wrists and fall into his beautiful cappuccino eyes. "So, are you saying you want to try?"

"I think I'd be a fool not to."

My heart soars and I can't hold back my grin. "I think you would be, too."

He gently pushes me against the wall next to the door as he takes my lips again. His hands stroll up the sides of my torso as his tongue once again finds mine. My fingers skate along the hem of his shirt before I slowly dig them underneath, feeling his warm and taut skin. He groans at my touch, as the bulge inside his pants thickens. He grinds into the sweet spot between my legs before placing his hands under my ass, lifting me against the wall.

I yelp into his mouth as my face heats up in embarrassment. No one has ever tried to lift me before, and I feel incredibly conscious of the way his biceps flex around me. What if he tears a muscle? "I'm heavy, Darian," I breathe, breaking out of our kiss.

"Do you doubt me?" His voice is low and gritty, making the throbbing in between my legs unmerciful. When I shake my head, he demands, "Then give me that mouth."

I kiss him as his mouth covers mine in the most exquisite balance of too much and not nearly enough. His erection digs into me, rubbing against my swollen clit, and I moan into his mouth again. My nipples pebble so hard, they feel like they're made of stone. I squeeze his waist with my thighs as he continues to grind against me.

His lips drop to my neck, sucking and coaxing the softest of moans from me. I feel his tongue over my skin before he slides up to grasp my earlobe between his teeth. Oh, God. I feel like I'm going to combust. He expertly sucks and pulls on my earlobe before moving to my jaw—biting, licking, and sucking.

"Darian." I stall against him, my fingers inside his hair. I can't decide if I want to press him back to my neck or pull him off.

"Fuck, Rani." His eyes are half-lidded. "How the fuck am I supposed to slow this down? I want to fuck you right here, right the fuck now. I want to bury myself inside you until we can't see straight."

The images his filthy words paint in my mind have me arching further into him, taking just a little more. Moaning just a little louder. God, I want him inside me more than I want to breathe. "Darian," I warn again, squeezing my eyes shut before reluctantly restraining my body from moving. It's the hardest thing I've ever had to do, and every nerve inside me—and my slick, swollen, needy center—riots against me. "We need . . .." I try to catch my breath. "We need to slow down."

Darian halts, but I don't miss the look of pure agony on his face. He nods before pressing his forehead against mine. We both clutch each other—my fingers digging into his shoulders and his still under my ass—as we quell our racing hearts, our chests rising and falling hard. He puts me back on my feet, scanning my face for a moment. "You're so beautiful."

I still have my arms loosely around his neck. "I'm not for everyone."

His jaw clenches. "I'm *not* everyone."

I gently scrape my fingernails against the nape of his neck. "No, you're not." I cut our locked gazes to look past him before coming back to scan his face. "But I'm not exactly experienced in the physical department, Darian."

His face is blank, but I know he's piecing together what I'm saying.

I clarify for his benefit, "I'm still . . .. I've, uh, never had sex."

He inhales as if he'd been out of breath this whole time. "Okay."

I bite my bottom lip as anxiety courses through me. "Does that bother you?"

He's quiet, though his gaze never leaves mine. "It just makes taking things slow even more important. You haven't given it away for a reason, and I don't want you to have regrets."

"I wouldn't," I insist. "Not with you."

He leans down to kiss me. His lips linger softly over mine, and even as he pulls them away from me, I want to reach out and bring them back. He stretches his arm toward the door behind me, opening it. "You need to sleep."

My heart thuds in my chest at what seems like a brush off. Did I say the wrong thing? Should I not have mentioned my lack of experience? I look at his face—impassive as it always is—before squaring my shoulders and heading to my room.

My experience is what it is; I can't do anything about it. I come with it, whether he likes it or not. Feeling a mix of emotions from elation to confusion, I walk down the short hallway to my room.

My eyes stall on the image in front of me as I flick on the lights.

There, spread around my entire room, are at least ten vases full of deep burgundy lilies. From my nightstand, to the dresser, to the windowsill, the room blooms with the gorgeous flowers and the scent fills the entire space.

The one on my nightstand has a note affixed to it.

This is the only color for you.

I'm just about to pull up my phone to text him a *thank you* when there's a soft knock on my door. I haven't moved from the spot, so I turn around, knowing who to expect.

His hands are in his pockets as our eyes meet, his lips a shade pinker from our kiss. A vulnerable look passes over his face as he takes me in, as if he hadn't just seen me a minute ago. "Goodnight, Rani."

I can't even help it. I throw myself at him, giving in to everything my heart wants to tell him but can't. He catches me by my waist as I lock my arms behind his neck and press my lips to his. This delicious and confusing man has my mind buzzing with thoughts of him and my tongue tied.

He opens his mouth to let me deepen our kiss, and I suck on his tongue, relishing its sweetness before moving back to his bottom lip, pulling it with my teeth. He smiles against my lips, and another swarm of butterflies flutters through my stomach.

Kissing him might have become my most favorite thing, but kissing him while he smiles against my mouth just took first place.

Chapter Nineteen
DARIAN

I PLATE SOME SCRAMBLED EGGS, HASH BROWNS, AND BANANA pieces for Arman and place it on his high chair tray. He lifts his arms, squealing with delight. There's no doubt about it, my boy likes his food. I ruffle his hair and let him go at it, which he does with fervor.

I hear Rani's footsteps upstairs and before long, she's coming down the steps. Her eyes lock with mine instantly. Her hair is half-up in a clip while the rest of it lies down her back. It's one of my favorite features about her—thick, curly, and so long that it hits the middle of her back. Her hair is jet-black and the curls are so fucking wild and luminous, I get a hard-on just thinking about them around my fist.

Which is exactly what's happening, because just the sight of her, the memory of her lips on mine, her body writhing against me last night, has my dick stirring in my pants.

Last night.

Another taste, another test. One of which I failed miserably.

I just couldn't fucking do it anymore. I couldn't stand the cold war she was waging inside my house. I couldn't stand her flowery scent lingering in the spaces she'd just left, only for me to find them empty. I couldn't allow myself one more day without her.

Fuck, I grappled.

I grappled with it all—my guilt, my reservations, the weight of the consequences I knew we'd face if I were to keep going. But her pull was stronger than any reasoning against it. She'd thrown her damn fairy dust on me, and I was fucking enchanted.

I turn to grab a coffee mug from the cupboard behind me. Using the mug she brought with her from home, which says, *I have principles, but only after my cup of coffee*, I pour her a cup I just brewed. I add a small amount of creamer and a teaspoon of sugar, like I've seen her do many times.

She's talking to Arman behind me, asking him what he's going to do today. When I turn around, she's kissing his face and pretending to eat his eggs. He giggles before reprimanding her with his standard, "No, no!"

I see it.

In just a little over three weeks, she's taken over his smiles. Even when I got home last week to take him from her so she could leave to do whatever it was she was doing, Arman searched for her—crawl-walking to the window to watch her drive away, saying bye-bye long after she'd left. Fuck, it's everything I worried about. He can feel her sincerity and love, and it makes whatever her and I are doing so much more complicated.

She has to go back, that's a fact. Whatever this is between us can't last—and that's the hardest fact to swallow. Between her mother ready to snap my neck if I touch her—I don't need her to tell me to know it—to her needing to finish school, to me being a single parent with long hours at work, how the fuck *could* this last?

I take a sip of my smoothie, watching her straighten up

and find my gaze on her again. She gives me a hesitant smile. "It smells good in here. I thought you said you only knew how to grill and make salads."

I put my smoothie on the counter and serve us both some eggs, toast, and hash browns on the two plates I'd gotten out earlier. "I'd hardly call scrambling eggs and making boxed hash browns *cooking*."

She inches closer to me and eyes the coffee sitting out on the counter in her special cup. A smile graces her lips, and I practically white-knuckle the spoon I'm using to scoop the eggs. Her voice is soft, like the lips I tasted last night, like the way she felt against me. "I'm assuming this is for me?"

I nod.

Her nearness, almost close enough that she's touching me but not actually doing so, is making every brain cell and body cell and whatever other fucking cell I have go haywire. They're crisscrossing and getting all sorts of scrambled like these damn eggs in front of me.

I want to touch her. Grab her and press my lips to hers again, but I don't fucking know what going slow means.

Am I going slow enough? Am I going too slow? I feel like I'm moving at a snail's pace. Does this going slow thing apply to everything or just sex? I honestly don't know when to hit the brakes, when to just coast, or when to slam the pedal to the floor.

I barely slept last night as I weaved in and out of lucid dreams about her. At times I felt like I was clear; I knew exactly what I wanted–*her*. But then the dark room would dim my thoughts, and I'd feel confused all over again. But one thing remained . . ..

My craving for her.

I can't say it didn't bother me when she told me about her being a virgin, because it did. It was another reminder of the differences between us–age and stage in life. I didn't know how to take her words when she said she wouldn't have regrets if I was the one to take her virginity. On one hand, I couldn't stand the thought of someone else touching her—*taking what was mine*—but on the other, I felt like a bastard for wanting to desecrate someone so fucking innocent and beautiful.

I know which side will eventually win.
There's no fucking question about it.

She takes a sip of her coffee, closing her eyes for a moment. "Mmm. This is perfect." She examines my profile like she's trying to find something under my skin. "You've been watching me. Restocking the Funyuns and the ice cream, keeping the house a little warmer because you saw me wearing my fuzzy socks and long-sleeved shirt, and now you're making me the perfect cup of coffee, exactly the way I take it."

I meet her eyes, standing face to face with her, when she scoots in just a little closer. Her coffee cup held between us—like some sacred potion—is the only thing that keeps her chest from meeting mine. The backs of her arms brush against me, tilting her chin up at me, awaiting a response to all her accusations.

"I couldn't miss you with my eyes closed, Rani," I murmur.

She presses her lips together, holding in a smile, but I see the blush creep up her face. "You're pretty hard to miss, too, Mr. Meyer."

She turns, putting her precious cup on the counter and takes the plate of eggs I made, shoveling a couple of forkfuls into her mouth.

I eye her flowery dress, noting the purse and camera she brought down and left on the table. "Where are you going?"

"To the nursing home. Today is Anabelle's eighty-fifth birthday, and we're all decorating cupcakes in her honor." She takes another sip of her coffee, watching me. "How did you sleep?"

I scoop up some eggs on my fork, turning to watch my son sing while he continues to eat, before talking into my plate. "Shitty.'

Rani's gaze turns concerned. "Bad dreams again?"

I shake my head. "Good ones."

She gives me a smug smile that I want to kiss right off her face. "Were they about me? Want to tell me about them?"

I just stare at her; it's like my brain freezes whenever I'm around her.

When I don't offer an answer, she faces me again and squints. "You know, as much as I have an unhealthy fascination with your blank expressions and those lips that seem to do nothing but lay in a permanent frown on your face, I wouldn't mind seeing a smile here and there."

My lips twitch, if only to irritate her more. Leaning down, I brush her face with the side of mine before finding her ear and revel in the shiver that travels through her. "I'm pretty sure you have a decent idea of the other things my lips can do, don't you think?"

She lets out a staggered breath. "Yes . . .." Her eyes get a faraway look in them before she grazes her face against mine again and whispers, "No."

"No?"

She shakes her head. "I mean, I have an idea, but by all means," she swallows, "if you have more you want to do . . .." She trails off like she's imagining all the things I've been telepathically planting in her head.

My lips are right above hers. "What I *want* to do and what I *should* do, based on our little agreement, are two very different things. For example, what I want to do is take you upstairs and fill you up with my tongue and my cock so you'll be dripping *my* spit and cum for days."

She gasps, her eyes giving away the shock and lust building behind them.

"But I wouldn't call that going *slow*," I add with a raised brow. I inch closer, my lips almost laying on hers. "So, unless you've changed your mind . . .."

"You," she says breathlessly, pressing her finger into my chest, "are not playing fair, Mr. Meyer."

I chuckle, closing the millimeter of space between us with my lips. I taste her after an entire night of dreaming about doing it again. I suck on her bottom lip, teasing her, before bringing my hands to cup her face. Her eyes close as she opens her mouth to let me pull her into a deeper kiss, and I do so wholeheartedly, tightening dangerously inside my pants.

God, she tastes delicious. So much so that I reconsider my stance on coffee.

I've wanted her–thought about this–since the minute I got into my bed last night. I'd wondered what this morning was going to be like. Were things going to be awkward in the daylight, cured of the carnal hunger the night seems to breed? Were we going to have another conversation about what had happened? Was she going to withdraw? Was I going to be able to handle not touching her again?

My mind had buzzed with anticipation and anxiety before I succumbed to a frustrated sleep. But my worries dissipated the minute I saw her smile this morning. I still don't know how I'm going to take this slow–physically or emotionally–and I have to question my sanity when agreeing to do so, but I'm glad to see I'm not the only one who's having a hard time with it.

Pulling her into me by her waist, I linger another kiss on her lips and meet her deep chocolaty-browns. "Who said this was ever going to be fair?"

Chapter Twenty
RANI

I get home later than I had intended. Turns out, seniors at a nursing home can party like it's nineteen-ninety-nine even better than an almost twenty-year-old. A few of them were still up and chatting in the common area when I slipped out at nine PM.

Unsurprisingly, I notice the lights on in Darian's study, so after taking off my shoes, I pad over to see him.

I thought an entire day away, doing things with other people, would quell the frenzy inside my head to see him, to be with him. But I was so wrong. I found myself staring at Fred and Lynn even more, wishing things for myself that I know Darian can't guarantee. *I wished for them anyway.* Even when we were all decorating cupcakes, I found myself smiling, wondering if Darian liked cake with how nutty he is about nutrition.

I push the study door open since it isn't closed all the way and find him asleep on his chair. His head is tipped back, his arms resting loosely on the armrests. His broad chest takes up the entire width of the chair, while his neck stretches so temptingly, I want to run my tongue along it.

The hum from the baby monitor echoes through the room as I tiptoe closer, until I'm mere inches from him. I need to get him to his bed so I know I have to wake him, but I take a second to marvel him. He's so gorgeous, it's no wonder my sister fell for him in mere hours. I've seen the pictures of him from a decade ago, and I can firmly say he looks as good, if not better, than he did then. He's filled out and takes over the space in almost any room. The lines around his eyes that likely weren't there ten years ago don't make him look aged but rather refined.

I gently skate my fingers into his thick wavy hair, watching his eyes twitch and his lashes brush against the tops of his cheeks. His hair is so thick and luxurious under my fingertips, I feel like I'm touching strands of silk. I do it again and he opens his eyes, taking me in.

"Hi," I whisper, keeping my hand in his hair.

His hand wraps around my wrist before he pulls my hand down to his mouth, pressing a kiss to the center of my palm. "Hi."

"I thought I'd get you to bed. I didn't want you getting a crick in your neck."

He rubs the inside of my wrist with his thumb. "What time is it?" His voice is gruff, sparking goosebumps across my arms.

"Just about nine-thirty."

His eyes are still on me and his head stays tilted back in the same position as he pulls on my hand, drawing me closer to him.

I rest a hand on his shoulder while my other one wraps around the base of his jaw and neck. I lean in and press my lips to his. It feels natural to do so, as if the barriers to be closer to him have lifted. As if his lips were made just for me to kiss.

It's hard to believe it was only yesterday that I was so

unsure about it all, worried I wouldn't be able to last inside the ever-changing hot and cold temperatures between us. But now . . ..

Darian's confession, his honesty, changed everything. His disclosure that I was on his mind, even when I didn't think he thought about me, made it clear that I wasn't the only one suffering, fucking tortured, at the sight of him.

His hand travels the length of the back of my thigh under the dress I'd worn to the nursing home today, and it drives me wild. Our lips mesh together and our tongues dance against our moans as his hand continues its slow upward perusal. His eyes fly open in alarm just as he finds my bare ass.

He pulls away from my lips. "You're not wearing any underwear? What sort of nursing home party did you attend?"

I giggle, leaning further in to press another kiss to his lips before covering his hand—the one still on my bare bottom—with mine and scooting it further up so he finds the top band of my thong.

He groans, running his hand over my ass cheek before pulling me onto him. "Fuck."

With minor adjustments to our positions—and a mini panic attack that the chair is going to break with our combined weight on it—I straddle his lap. My hands can't decide where to be—starting on his chest and sliding to his neck, feeling his delicious scruff under my fingertips, before settling inside his hair. I pull it gently as he groans into my mouth.

We're ravenous, our tongues colliding, exchanging each other's air. With my dress covering his lap, I grind into his hard erection, shamelessly rubbing my swollen clit against the thin material of my thong and the rougher material of his shorts. His hands guide me over him, creating a rhythmic symphony that starts pulsating in my core. While squeezing my ass in one hand, he skates the other out and slides it over my breast, palming me.

"Jesus, Rani." He speaks low against my mouth, and I force myself not to scream from the pressure he's inciting inside of me. "Tell me you want this because I might be getting past the point of stopping. But, baby, I need you to think."

"Yes," I hiss into his mouth, undulating over him. I'm seconds from shattering, the friction too much, lighting up my body like it's in a firework display on the Fourth of July. "I want this." I cup his face with my hands, my eyes hooded. "You're the only one I want this with."

Needing more traction, I rock over him more fervently, groaning as the rough fabric under me scrapes against my most delicate skin. The torture is both excessive and insufficient, eliciting a guttural groan from my throat.

Darian continues to guide me against his erection before his thumb comes around to my front. He slides it into my panties, finding my clit, before pressing it with the perfect amount of pressure. He circles my slick center while letting me rub myself on top of him. I scream, feeling the overwhelming lust build up inside me, ready to pull me completely under.

My forehead rests on his shoulder as he alternates between flicking and rubbing my swollen nub, still pressing into me from underneath, and I keep grinding down on him. "You want to come?"

I mumble incoherently, biting into his shoulder. I've never wanted anything more.

I'm a shameless mess of desire and need. My body feels like it's on fire, and he's the only one who could douse it out.

His other hand on my ass, pushes me against his thumb on my clit, while his lips land on the side of my neck. He sucks gently, creating a full-body experience so potent that the memory of this will live inside me forever. His tongue glides to my earlobe before he bites it, making me groan in ecstasy.

"God, you smell good. The scent of your juices mixed with the scent of flowers . . . . I'm going to put my nose directly inside your delicious pussy and inhale you."

"Oh, God!" I moan, giving into his filthy words and my orgasm. My nipples tighten against the fabric of my bra so painfully that I think they'll cut right through. I squeeze my eyes shut as wave after wave of pure euphoria vibrates through my core, and I come for what seems to be forever.

I'm still gliding on the inside of my wet and tattered panties, sure that I'll see my arousal stained over his erection, when I finally come to. I've orgasmed before—plenty of times on my own and a few times when Patrick fingered me—but never like this. Never this unrestrained. Never this wild.

I lift my head, my cheeks burning with shame, to look at him. I close my eyes as soon as I see him assessing me and I try to get off him. But he holds me firm, his hands around my hips, pressing into my skin.

"Rani."

I squeeze my eyes shut, like I've always done when I'm taking in a moment, but this time I hope it's not real. Because if it's real, then I've truly broken my own rules, forsaken my principles.

"Rani, look at me." His voice is firm and there's no question he's going to wait until I either open my eyes or pretend to have a stroke. When I finally open them, he pulls his hands out of my dress and rounds my neck, lifting my chin with his thumbs. I vaguely register that one of those thumbs has my juices all over it. "Don't." He shakes his head. "Don't do that. Don't be embarrassed or ashamed or whatever it is that you're feeling right now."

My cheeks burn like they're on fire. "I did exactly what I

told you we shouldn't do. I went too fast, and now I'm afraid you're going to pull back—"

He stops me by putting his mouth on mine, kissing me softly, before breaking away. "We went at the pace that felt natural for us. I was right there with you, baby. You didn't force me into it. I'm not going to pull back because I felt everything you did."

I search his eyes through a frown. "But you told me you were scared."

"Of what I *feel*, yes, but I can't deny what I feel, either."

I'm tempted to ask him what he feels, but I'm so drained at the moment that if I found out he didn't feel the way I did, I'd probably burst out crying. I look down at the stain on his shorts and wince. "I'm sorry."

"I'm not," he replies without hesitation.

I get off his lap and straighten myself up, brushing my hands down my dress. "I'm exhausted."

He bites his bottom lip, but I see the smile he's hiding. "I'd imagine you are."

My cheeks flame again. "I'm going to bed. Um . . . thank you for," I wave in his general direction, "that."

"The pleasure was all mine."

I nod, feeling a little at a loss of words and unsteady on my feet. "Are you going to bed soon?"

He pauses, staring at me intently. "After I take a shower and try to rid my brain of you for a night."

Chapter Twenty-One
DARIAN

"How is my Arman *jan*! Did you miss your *tatik* this week?" My mom bounces Arman in her arms. "*Tatik* missed you! So much, my sweet boy. I couldn't wait to run back home from Seattle to see you again."

I stir the creamer inside the cup before going to the fridge to grab some raspberries to put onto the bowls of greek yogurt, oats, and honey. "How's Aunt Anush?"

My mother watches me curiously, ignoring my question. "I've already had my coffee today, Darian. Are you making a cup for yourself? When did you start drinking coffee?"

"It's for Rani." I don't make eye contact with Mom, moving to put the raspberries back inside the fridge and putting a couple of spoons into the parfait bowls.

"I see." Mom stands there a moment longer before retreating into the living room with Arman.

It's too early in the morning for me to think about the consequences of my mother watching me perform what I'm sure she thinks is an intimate act, so I go about preparing my smoothie instead.

A few minutes later, Rani comes down the stairs to the

kitchen and we both bestow each other quiet smiles. We haven't discussed keeping things private specifically, but I would assume taking things slow entailed that. I make a mental note to talk about it with her later, just to make sure.

She's wearing a white crop-top that hangs over one shoulder, revealing the bright blue strap from her sports bra, over black tights. Her ass looks so fucking scrumptious in them, I have to turn around and busy myself with the bowls to stop from springing another hard-on at the sight of her.

Rani's eyes find my mom. "Oh hi, Karine!" She walks over to give my mom a hug. "How was your trip?"

"It was so good, dear. It was nice to see my sister again after so long." Mom settles Arman down near the window. He has a toy car in his hands that he wheels over the sill and it drops to the ground. He wobbles to it on his own and picks it up, then holding the sill to steady himself, he does the entire thing all over again. I see the little amounts of progress he makes everyday, and I can tell he's determined to become more and more independent.

"How is she doing?" Rani asks.

"She's doing okay, but you know, each healthy year after eighty is a blessing." My mother's expression becomes grave. "She has severe osteoporosis—it clearly runs in the family for us—and arthritis, so it's hard for her to be too mobile."

Rani nods, turning back to me when she hears me place the bowls on the table. She has a questioning look in her eyes as she walks over to see what they are. "Is that for me?"

I nod, handing her her coffee.

"Thank you," she whispers, taking a sip. Her eyes stay glued to mine, and I wonder if she's thinking about what happened between us last night.

Because I sure as hell am.

That's all that's been on my mind from the moment I fell asleep—after jacking off so hard that my dick almost fell to the shower floor—and again the moment Arman woke me up early this morning.

If I'd had fantasies of seeing Rani come on my fingers, what happened last night blew those out of the water. The way her skin flushed—tiny droplets of sweat forming over the base of her neck—the sounds she made as I helped her find the perfect rhythm, and the sheer amount of wetness I felt dripping from her. Sweet Jesus. I think I'm going to need to excuse myself and go take another fucking shower.

She was mind-blowingly sexy as she came over my pants from the mere touch of my thumb on her. If that's what she looked like—if that's how responsive she was to my damn thumb—then I can only imagine what she would look like coming on my tongue.

I clear my throat, sitting with my smoothie and my parfait before taking out my phone to distract myself. Rani takes her breakfast to the living room and chats with my mom for a little longer before Mom gets up, heading to the door.

"So, I'll be here around seven-thirty tomorrow morning, then." Mom kisses Arman on the cheek before placing a kiss on Rani's cheek as well.

Huh? That's interesting. Not that my mother showed affection to Rani, but the fact that over the course of our ten years together, that was one of Sonia's primary complaints against my mother—that she didn't show a whole lot of affection toward her, even though she showed it to other people in the family. The fact that Rani has garnered my mother's adoration so quickly is something I can't help but notice.

"What do you mean you'll be here tomorrow morning?" I hear myself ask, pushing away my observations to be pondered upon at another time.

"Karine's coming over tomorrow because I'm going to work with you," Rani states.

"You are?" I might have said it like a question, but I know

there's only one answer for it because once this woman has made up her mind on something, she seems to be hellbent on doing it.

Not that I object to her coming to work with me, and even if I did, I'm positive my objections would be dismissed as nonsensical complaints. Since the minute she showed up at my house, she's taken charge of things without my input— whether it was encouraging me to take her help with Arman or practically forcing me to take her help with the school.

She nods enthusiastically. "Yup! I want to come take some pictures for the newsletter. I already have a really great idea for a new series we can send out. And I got a chance to create a mockup of the new *Truckee Sports* website, so I want to show that to you."

I squint at her. "You already have a mockup done?"

"Yeah. And I looked at the ad space you have and the subscriber flow to sign up for the newsletters. I think we can optimize that, too. I figured I'd give your mom a chance to hang out with Arman for a day since she hasn't started her therapy sessions again yet and I'd come help you." Rani's brows fold. "Unless you have meetings and you can't tomorrow. . . .. I didn't even think to ask you."

"Tomorrow's fine," I say, waving to my mom.

Rani shuts the door behind my mom and checks on Arman to see him happily playing with his toys. She walks into the kitchen to place her dishes into the dishwasher, and I lift off my chair. I amble up behind her, caging her in with my arms. I place a featherlight kiss on her bare shoulder, listening to the soft pant that escapes her mouth.

She turns around and I press my lips against hers, relishing the fact that I can finally do that without feeling pulled in different directions about it. Her mouth opens, welcoming me like it's come to expect me, and I happily dive in. A groan leaves my throat as I delve deeper into her mouth, tasting the honey from the parfait on her tongue. My hands white-knuckle the edge of the counter. I'm trying hard to not touch her yet, because once I do, I'm not sure I'll be able to stop.

Her arms curl over my neck and I can't resist. My hands find their way under her crop-top, gliding over the smooth skin of her torso. God, there is nothing I like better than her curves and her skin. I like them even more than her luminous hair, which is saying a lot because I love her fucking hair.

Feeling her warm skin underneath my palms, I slide a little further up, skating the tip of my thumb under her breast. A shiver travels through her as she opens her mouth further for me, letting my tongue snake inside again.

Her arms tighten around my neck and she arches into me as we kiss, deep and long. Her lips move against mine and she moans into my mouth. I pull her closer, digging my erection into her again, leaving no doubt as to how much I want her.

I break away to kiss her jaw, moving down her neck. Jesus, I want to turn her around, pull down her tight leggings, and smack this voluptuous ass before fucking her into oblivion.

I know how wet she'd be for me. I had a front and center seat to that show last night, and she's wet again for me now. I can tell just by the way her body shimmies against mine, like she's trying to sink into my skin.

She has no idea that she already has.

And fuck, I'd be ready to give in to her need—the same as mine—but I promised to take things slow. I just don't know how long I can be a fucking gentleman about it because my restraint is at the sheer end of its rope.

"Darian, I–" Her breathy words are interrupted when her phone rings on the table. She groans, stepping away from me to pick it up. Her frown deepens when she reads the name on the screen. "It's my mom."

I nod. "Take it."

She sighs, carrying the phone to the living room. "Hey, Mom."

It looks like they're on FaceTime because her mom's voice comes through the call. "What is *that* you're wearing?"

I rinse some dishes off before putting them into the dishwasher, glancing at Rani through the kitchen.

She regards her clothes. "Just a workout outfit."

Her mother chortles, as if she's watching a comedy routine. "Oh my goodness!" She laughs again. "My dear daughter, if only you'd make use of such outfits to do what they're *designed* for, then perhaps you wouldn't be in the state you're in."

Rani's eyes find mine and instead of looking away, I hold hers steady. I don't need to touch her to know that her face is heated and a pang of hurt and embarrassment just ripped through her chest.

My jaw tightens as Rani turns back to the camera, plastering a smile on her face. "How are you doing, Mom? How's Dad?"

"You dad is what he always is . . . in his own world. He doesn't realize there is someone living with him. Anyway, how is my grandson? Has he started talking or walking yet? Please tell me he's not–"

Rani immediately interrupts her mother, and I get the distinct feeling it's for my benefit. I also get the feeling that had her mother finished her thought, I would have felt murderous.

"Yeah! He's saying a lot more this week! He likes to tell people no, and he's really not good at using that word in moderation." Rani giggles airily, though I can't tell if it's genuine. How could it be, especially after being degraded like that by her mother? "He's also been asking for ice cream and chips. And he knows how to tell me to pick him up pretty clearly when he wants to be picked up."

"Of course he does, because he knows you will, and that's why he still can't walk." Her mother's spiteful tone has me on edge, and Rani gives me an empathetic look.

I slam the dishwasher shut a little harder than necessary, contemplating walking over there and snatching the phone from her hands, giving her mother a piece of my mind.

One more fucking thing out of her mouth . . ..

"Actually, Mom, I was just about to head out to the nursing home. Can we chat another time?"

"Well, I would love to see Arman. That's why I called. I know since you're there, Karine won't bring him to see me. I don't want him to forget me."

If only we'd all be so lucky.

Rani hesitates, catching my eyes again, and I nod in consent. I finish up in the kitchen and head over to the floor to sit near Arman. I'm sure she's a little surprised that I'd want to be on camera when she brings it over, but I need her mother to know that I won't let her say a single fucking thing about my son. And if that means that I have to be sitting right next to him like his security detail to get my point across, then I will.

Rani brings the phone toward us while Arman works on putting large wooden puzzle pieces inside the board. "Here he is!" Rani chirps. "Arman, can you say hi to *Nani*? Say hi!"

Arman continues to focus on his task but says, "Hi!"

"Good job, little man," Rani cheers. "Can you say, '*Nani*'?" She articulates the word.

She repeats it a couple of times and I'm positive he isn't even listening to her, too focused on his puzzle, but to my amazement, he looks up and says, "*Nunnee*".

Rani squeals, placing a kiss on his cheek. I can't help the smile on my face as I observe them. It's been amazing to see how much progress he makes every day, and it has a lot to do with all the attention and love he gets from his devoted aunt.

She's constantly singing to him or playing games with him—completely in-tune with his needs.

Rani and I exchange a look, and I know she can see how fucking crazy she drives me. I know she claims she can't read my face, but I swear, she's the only one who can. And if she's reading it right now, she'd know this whole going slow thing isn't going to last long between us because I can't rein this feeling in much longer. It's like an untamed horse, unpredictable and ready to buck me off.

She makes me feel wild.

Wild, like her fucking hair. Wild, like my racing heart and sordid thoughts. Wild, like the way she rocked over my dick last night, coming all over my pants.

"Yay! Good job, little man! See, Mom! He is learning so fast!" She turns the camera back to her.

Her mom makes a *pfft* sound and before she says another word, Rani interrupts again, "Anyway, I have to go now. Let's talk soon."

"Rani." Her mom's voice suddenly has a different sort of ice around it. "Can you please call me when you're . . . alone? I'd like to discuss something with you."

Rani regards her mom dubiously. "Um, sure. Maybe I'll call you Monday evening? It's just, I have a few things planned for today."

Her mother is silent on the phone, and since I can't see her face, I continue to watch Arman practice his fine motor skills. "Remember my words the day you left. I don't want history repeating itself, because this time, we'll all be left bankrupt."

Rani straightens, catching her meaning. "Talk to you later, Mom."

As soon as her phone is off, she scans my face. She lets out a puff of air. "I'm sorry." She presses her fingers to the middle of her brows, closing her eyes. "My mother is just a lot."

I make my way to the couch and wait until she looks at me again. "Come here."

She hesitates for a second before taking a seat next to me. I find her hand and gently weave my fingers through hers. "Why do you let her talk to you like that?"

Rani huffs out a laugh. "You mean, why do I let her talk to me like she has been for the past nineteen years of my life?" When I stay silent, she continues, "Did Sonia ever tell you about my mother and her strained relationship?"

I nod. "A little. It used to piss me off, the same way it is right now after witnessing what I just did."

Rani regards our entangled fingers distractedly before leaning her head on my shoulder. "I don't remember all the issues they had, but as you know, my sister was more of a wild child. She wanted to do things on her own terms, and my mom was just as much the dictator. They'd bicker all the time." Her voice seems a little faraway, like she's somewhere else. "One time Sonia took Mom's car to someone's house party at the age of fourteen. She didn't know how to drive, but since Mom forbade her to go, she was hellbent on doing it even more."

"Sounds like Sonia," I admit, thinking about my late wife's determination. She couldn't accept no for an answer, even to her detriment.

"My sister's worst fear was being caged. She'd say to me, 'I feel like my wings are clipped, Rani.' And with our mother, that's how she always felt."

My thoughts trail to our sessions with the therapist, where Sonia admitted to a similar feeling—that she felt trapped.

"Anyway, when Sonia left with you, my mom had no one else to bicker with. My dad is a punching bag that has no give, no resistance, so to punch him down wasn't satisfying enough for my mother. So, she turned to me. She's always been after me for being overweight, but after Sonia left, Mom channeled all her frustration into me."

I bury my nose inside her hair, breathing in her flowery scent. "I can't stand the way she talks to you, and I hate that you let her." Rani's shoulders sag, and I immediately regret making her feel worse. I haven't been in her shoes, and I haven't lived with her mother to know what sort of mental abuse she's had to endure. It's unfair of me to expect her to just be able to stand up to her mom, even though I notice so many glimpses of her courage. "Rani, look at me."

She lifts her head and her glassy eyes find mine. I almost lose my shit all over again, tempted to call her mother and scream at her myself.

How? How can someone hurt this gorgeous, unselfish woman who would drop everything at a moment's notice to help someone else? Who smiles in spite of the heartless things said to her.

I reach for her, grasping her face in my palm lightly and stroking her cheek with my thumb. "You are so fucking beautiful, you have no idea. I love what you're wearing and the way you're wearing it. I love your curves as much as I love your smile and your fucking tantalizing hair." I wrap a curl around my index finger. "I'm sorry your mom doesn't see you for the perfection that you are, but . . . I do. I see *you* and I hope that's enough."

Rani's bottom lip trembles before she sucks it in, her chocolate eyes searching mine as they swim inside a well of tears. "Thank you," she whispers before leaning toward me.

I kiss her gently, wanting to make it a little more when she breaks out of it abruptly.

"Shoot! I need to get going. I promised the nursing home I'd be there to help from ten to three today." She lifts my wrist to scan my watch. "I'm going to be late."

She gets up to gather her purse and her phone when I

remember. "Oh, my brothers are coming over tonight for poker."

"That's cool. I really like them. Is . . ." she stalls for a second, "is that other guy going to be here, too? Ryan?" Her nose wrinkles.

"Yes, but I can tell him not to come. He's kind of a douche so I don't mind, but he evens out our group, so my brothers wanted to invite him."

She shrugs airily. "No, don't uninvite him! He's fine. He just weirded me out the first time I met him, that's all."

"Yeah," I agree, pinning my gaze to a spot behind her as memories come flitting in. I remember it took Sonia a little while to warm up to Ryan, but she eventually did. By the time we were all good friends, she claimed he was just misunderstood. "He's always been an interesting guy . . . and not always in a good way."

"I might head to a coffee shop after and try to start my photojournalism project. I'm still searching for events in the area to document."

I get up from my seat, finding a way to be closer to her. I lift my hand to her jaw. "I don't want you to not be able to come home because you feel uncomfortable."

She wraps her hand over my wrist. "It's not that at all. I sort of love working in coffee shops. The smell of coffee just helps me think better."

"Okay," I acquiesce softly before recalling what she said she'll be researching. "You know, we have that kayak tournament in early August. If it won't be too late for you to get it all done, perhaps you could document that?"

She wrinkles her nose. "No offense, but I might have had my fill of kayaks, so if I have to document it while atop a kayak, that's going to be a big no from me."

I chuckle. "You don't have to be on the kayak to document it. There are great trails right next to the river where you can take good pictures."

She twists her mouth, thinking. "Okay, that might work. Then I'll start my introduction and a potential outline on that tonight."

I trail my hand down to her waist and pull her in. "You know, you're supposed to give any activity at least three tries before quitting."

"Not if that activity is hazardous to your bones."

I laugh, throwing my head back. "You're cute when you're ridiculous, but I'm going to get you back on a kayak once more this summer."

"Challenge accepted."

Chapter Twenty-Two
RANI

Darian helps me into his truck before closing the passenger door. Lord, it's like a hop, skip, and a jump to get into that thing. I feel like I've had my workout for the day.

He walks around the front of the truck to the driver's side, and I ogle him like a lovesick puppy. It doesn't help that he looks excruciatingly delicious in his cap. It somehow makes his scruffy jawline look even more tapered, and that just does things to me. *Filthy, panty-melting things.*

He smiles over at me as we both buckle ourselves up before he waves out the window to his mom holding Arman. When he turns the truck around, I open my window and blow my little man a few kisses.

A few moments later, I side-eye Darian, who is focused on the road, before I walk my fingers ever so slowly over the center console and to the hand resting on his thigh. I tickle the side of his pinky finger and notice the familiar tug on his lips. He weaves our fingers together without even shifting his gaze.

He clears his throat after a moment, while I relish in the feel of his fingers around mine. "I know we haven't spoken about it, but how do you feel about keeping things quiet about us?"

I grin, looking over at him. "I like the sound of the word, *us*."

He glances at me and this time, I see a rare smile on his face. "Yeah? Me, too."

"I think it makes sense to get to know each other without the scrutiny of anyone else. I like the idea of keeping things just between us."

He seems to relax physically, but a frown has replaced the smile that was there. Is that not the answer he wanted? I'm about to ask when my phone buzzes in my other hand.

Liam: Hey, Rani. I gather from the fact that you never responded to my last text that we ought to talk. Any chance you'll be taking a walk with your nephew today? Or maybe we can grab coffee some evening?

I sigh, reading Liam's text. He'd texted me last week to ask if I wanted to go on a walk, but I just needed a break from everything. Between worrying about his feelings for me, his feelings with the way Darian had treated him, and avoiding Darian myself, I needed a break from the boy drama. In hindsight, it wasn't cool of me to ghost Liam because at the end of the day, he's a good guy and not someone I want to hurt.

Darian glances inquisitively at my lap as I untangle my fingers from his. "What's wrong?"

"It's a text from Liam. He wants to talk."

Darian snorts. "Tell him to fuck off."

I give him a stern look—one I know he's familiar with. "Darian, I am not going to tell him to simply fuck off. He's my friend, and he's a good person."

"He tried to fucking kiss you after you made it clear you didn't think being with him was a good idea!"

I scoff, incredulously. "Just how much of my conversation did you listen to?"

Darian presses his lips shut, his jaw flexing.

"Darian?"

"Enough of it." He regards my mouth hanging open with a shake of his head. "Look, it's not like I tapped your phone! The asshole was on my property, daring to touch what's mine—"

He stops himself abruptly, and as much as I want to punch his arm right now—though, I'd probably just end up breaking my hand—I can't help but grin. Like from ear to fucking ear. Like Jack Nicholson from *The Shining*.

Yeah, I look insane.

"He dared to touch what's *yours*?" I emphasize his words.

Darian sucks on his cheeks, glaring at the road. I can tell he's holding in both an eye roll and a smile. "Just shut up and text the asshole back." When I smile down at my phone, he adds, "Are you going to meet him?"

"Yes. I have to. I care about him."

He huffs. "Can I come with you?"

"Darian."

"Fine. Whatever. But if he fucking tries that shit again with you—"

I throw up my arms. "Darian, I wouldn't have let him kiss me that day, whether you'd showed up or not, because I didn't want to kiss him. And do you know why?"

He doesn't respond, so I supply the answer anyway, my voice louder so the dummy can hear me clearly. "Because the only one I've wanted since the minute he rescued me from an out of control kayak is *you*, you big oaf!"

Darian's eyes soften, but he continues to drive while mumbling under his breath, and I ignore him. Instead, I text Liam back, telling him I'll meet him tomorrow at the park with Arman. I took Arman on our regular walks last week too, though I purposely avoided going to the park.

When we pull into the *Truckee Sports* parking lot, Darian turns to me, dragging my hand to his mouth. He lays a kiss on the back of my fingers. "I'm sorry."

I squint at him, pretending to still be mad. "You've racked up quite a few sorries over the past few weeks."

"And I'll probably rack up more because I say and do dumb things when I can't think clearly, and I can't think clearly when I'm around you."

The corners of my mouth lift into a smile. *This man . . ..* He is so ridiculously charming, even when he's frustrating, and I know I won't ever be able to stay angry with him.

His eyes smolder. "But I'll pay for my mistakes in kind with orgasms."

Even though a blush climbs up my neck, I lean over the console and place a kiss on his downturned lips. "I'm counting on it."

~

I SPEND the entire morning taking photographs along the river and the *Truckee Sports* property. By the time lunch comes around, I've scrolled through and picked out at least fifty good pictures I can use for the newsletter series I have in mind and to update the website. I even took a few short videos on my phone to get the school's TikTok account started.

I'm giddy as I walk into the building, scrolling through the pictures on my camera. I lift my head when the cool air conditioning treks over my warm skin, and I notice Felix talking to a small group–similar to the way he did when I came here with Melody and Bella. He lifts his arm to wave at me.

I'm about to knock on Darian's office door when the receptionist from the front desk stops me. "Hi! Do you need something? Darian is busy right now."

I peek through the glass panel inside, and while Darian is facing his computer, I don't think he's in a meeting. "Oh, okay. Well, I'll come back later."

"He's in meetings all day, I'm afraid."

That's interesting because Darian told me yesterday that coming here today would be fine. I assumed he meant he didn't have any meetings.

I get closer to the woman—Olivia, based on her name tag. She seemed rather nice the day I was here for my lesson, but I'm not getting the same welcoming vibe from her today.

"Okay, well, I'll grab something to eat," I say, fixing the strap of my SLR on my shoulder and pulling out my phone.

She gives me a tight smile and goes back to whatever she was doing on the computer.

Walking toward the kitchenette, I decide to just text Darian, instead.

Me: Hi. You busy?

A reply comes back immediately.

Darian: Never for you.

Me: Oh, okay. I'm done with taking pictures, and I wanted to show you the site mockups . . . if you have time.

Darian: Why are you texting me? You should have knocked. I would have let you in.

Me: The receptionist at the front told me you were in meetings all day.

A few seconds pass before I get a response.

Darian: Did she? Interesting.

Darian: Just come in. Don't worry about her.

Me: What if she yells at me again? I don't think she likes me very much.

Darian: I just opened my office door and I'm waiting for you. Get your ass in here.

My smile broadens as I make my way back toward his office. Darian stands in the doorway with his hands in his pockets, his eyes tracking me. He gives Olivia a disparaging look—one she responds to with a withering smile.

He shuts the door behind me and pulls me to the wall adjacent so anyone peeking in won't be able to see us.

My back lands with a soft *thud* while he cages me in, his hands roaming over my waist and torso. He quickly takes my camera from my shoulder, placing it on the shelf nearby, before grasping the back of my neck.

My body arches into him while my hands fist his shirt, and I pull him to my lips. For a few minutes we devour each other—lips, tongues, groans filling the room with our heat. My body temperature spikes, along with my heart rate, as his thickening erection pushes into the top of my thigh. His lips travel from my mouth to my neck as I dig my fingernails into his shoulders.

"I want you so fucking bad, Rani," Darian growls into my ear but a knock on the door has us jumping off each other. I run my hands through my hair and shirt, reining in my heavy breaths.

Darian, as calm as if he was just changing channels on the TV on a casual weekday evening, rounds over to his desk. "Come in."

The door opens and a man with thinning hair and a sleeve of tattoos pops his head in.

"Greg. What's up?" Darian says nonchalantly.

Greg peeks further inside, noticing me fiddling with my camera before speaking to Darian. "Hey, Olivia wanted me to ask if you wanted something from the burger place down the street. I was just heading over there to get me and her something to eat."

Darian's lips are stiff when he responds, "I'm good. Thank you."

Greg lifts his hand, his eyes bouncing from me to Darian again. "No worries. Sorry to interrupt."

When the door closes, I make my way to the chair in front of Darian. I notice that while he has the picture of him and Arman still on his desk, the one of him and my sister is no longer there. "What was that about?"

He shakes his head before putting his elbows on the table and pressing his fingertips into his temples. "Nothing you need to worry about." He tilts his head in my direction. "Want to show me the mockup?"

I point at his computer. "Mind if I use that to log into my portfolio online. I can show you everything I have."

Forty-five minutes later, I've walked Darian through all the changes I plan to make. He has some questions but to my surprise, he doesn't disagree with anything I've proposed and gives me the go-ahead to get things updated. We decide to implement the changes in phases so we can limit the site maintenance banner from showing up too often.

I also discuss the series of newsletters I'd like to send out on a bi-weekly basis and the daily TikTok videos I'll post. He doesn't like that I'm signing up for all this work for him, but he agrees to it if I take a small payment in return. He tells me he'll vouch for this being an internship when I submit it to my school for fieldwork credits.

"I can't thank you enough for all of this," he says sincerely.

I get up from my chair. "You're helping me as much as I'm helping you. I needed an internship, anyway." I walk to the door before turning around. "I'm going to eat my leftovers from my dinner last night in the kitchenette and see if I can get hold of Melody or Bella. Do you want me to bring you that salad you packed?"

Darian gets up from his chair, coming up behind me. His hand lands on the base of my spine. "No, I'll grab it later. I'll see you when we're on our way out?"

He opens the door, his hand still on my lower back.

"Sounds good," I reply, stepping out.

I flick a quick glance at Olivia as I'm walking away when I hear Darian's stern voice. "Olivia, please ensure Rani always has access to my office, whether I'm in a meeting or not. Also, I'd like to speak with you in private, immediately."

Chapter Twenty-Three
RANI

I push Arman on the swing, enjoying the warm breeze on my face. "Having fun, little man? Can you say *swing*?"

Arman holds on to the bucket swing with both hands as his dark curly hair lifts with the breeze. "Up!"

I giggle, pushing him again when the crunch of mulch behind me has me turning over my shoulder. Liam gives me a small smile, his hands tucked inside his pocket and his dog nowhere in sight. "Hi. You didn't bring Pepper with you?"

He shakes his head. "Nah, I can't talk to you when she's pulling me everywhere."

I laugh. "You mean, when she thinks she's walking you instead of the other way around?"

He chuckles. "I can't wait for my parents to come back so I can be rid of her."

I laugh. "Really? I bet you'll miss her when she's gone."

"I definitely won't miss the incessant barking and the constant fear of face-planting whenever I'm walking her."

I giggle again. "That's true."

We stand in silence for a few long seconds before I turn to him. I look down at my feet, trying to figure out how to say what I've been thinking about all morning. "Hey, so first of all, I want to apologize for not getting back to you last week. It wasn't cool." I glance up and Liam seems to be listening intently. "I think I just needed a chance to think about everything."

He nods. "That's understandable."

My brows furrow, trying to get the words out but there's a sadness inside my ribs that I can't deny. I'm not someone who delivers hard messages easily. I feel a lot and sometimes that comes at a detriment to myself when I feel too much. I hate having to let someone down and hurt them, but I know this is the right thing for me to do.

I take a breath. "I truly care about you, Liam. You're easy to talk to and so fun to hang out with." I clear my throat. "I haven't met many guys who have made me feel special. But with you, I feel nothing but warmth and comfortability." I pause, hoping to lighten the air. "And you're getting so much better about using your firm voice when giving commands to Pepper." I smile at him, hoping to see him smile back.

He doesn't.

I let out a breath and forge ahead. "You'll make someone feel like a queen one day . . . but I'd like to just be friends, if you'll have me."

He looks to the mountains on our right. "Does *he* make you feel like a queen, Rani?"

I blink, taken aback by his question. "What?"

"Your brother-in-law. Does he make you feel like a queen?"

I push Arman's swing but it doesn't take me long to answer. "Yes. Very much so."

Liam nods. "Then I guess I'm happy for you. It sucks for me, but I think if you decide to be someone's friend, then you sort of have to be happy for their happiness."

I turn, stepping closer and sliding my arms around Liam's waist and placing my head on his chest. "Thank you."

He hugs me back warmly before I break away and look at him. "How did you know?"

He chuckles. "That man was about to break me in half when he saw me holding you. At first I thought he was just being a jerk and acting like a protective dad, but then I saw the softness in his eyes when he looked at you. I saw how he looked at you, like there was nothing better to see in the world. And I knew."

I look down at my shoes. "Oh."

"I saw the way you looked at him, too. You might have been embarrassed but there was this heat in your eyes . . . not from anger but from something else." Liam runs a hand through his red curls. "Something I knew I'd never see from you, no matter how much I wanted it."

I bite my bottom lip. "I'm sorry."

He playfully swats my arm. "Nah, don't worry about it. But you know what they say?"

My brows crease. "What?"

"The only way to get over someone is to have that someone introduce you to her friend." He winks at me.

I laugh. "Hmm, I'm not sure I've heard that before, but okay. I'll see what I can do."

He waggles his brows. "Have anyone in mind?"

I tap my index finger on my lips pensively when an idea strikes me. "You know what? I think I just might."

∼

THE REST of the week goes by in a flash. Between taking care of Arman, working on the *Truckee Sports* website, starting a newsletter, and creating a few TikToks for their new account, I barely have a moment to think of anything else.

Except for Darian.

Because if anything occupies the sporadic spare moments, it's thoughts of him.

Throughout the week, we take every chance to make out—in the kitchen before he leaves for work, in the evenings in his study after he's put Arman down to sleep, in the laundry room when he presses me against the spinning washer and fingers me until I come, not once but twice.

But every night, we retreat to our separate rooms. I suppose it's our way of taking things slow.

The garage door opens, and I hear Darian's truck pull in. Arman bounces on his toes on the living room floor, knowing his dad is home.

"Come on, let's go see Daddy!" I grab his hand and we walk side-by-side toward the garage door. He's been doing so well with walking on his own this week. He can't do more than ten to fifteen steps, but he shows progress every day.

Lately, he's been singing the *Stay Awake* song with me when I put him down for a nap. He hums it in his own words, and I love the routines we've set. I refuse to think about the end of summer in only seven more weeks and all the unanswered questions that come with that. For now, I'm living my mantra, *live for today*.

Darian appears in the doorway just as Arman barrels into his legs, giggling. Darian hands me a bouquet of burgundy lilies—the same as the ones he'd left inside my room that night—before picking up his son and throwing him up in the air. "Hey, little man." He kisses Arman's flushed cheek.

I press my nose into the bouquet, watching the two of them over the sea of red flowers. Their love, the way Darian's eyes—his entire demeanor—softens when he looks at Arman, and the adorable way that Arman clings to his dad makes me feel out of breath. I'm mesmerized by them.

"Thank you," I whisper, taking my flowers to the kitchen

to put them in a vase. I'd just thrown out most of the flowers from last Friday.

Darian sets Arman down in the living room before coming over to me. His hands are in his pockets. "You're wearing that glittery eyeliner . . .."

I smile. "I am. It's one of my principles, remember? I welcome Friday evenings with glittery eye makeup."

"What about take-out? Would you welcome *this* Friday evening if I ordered some take-out?"

I wrinkle my nose. "Is it going to be take-out salad? If so, then that's firmly outside of my principles."

Darian laughs and the vibrato of his voice travels through my chest and down to my stomach, making me feel warm all over. "No. It's going to be whatever you want it to be."

I grin. "Really? You mean, if I say I want the cheesiest pizza, where they fill the inside of the crust with cheese, and top it with jalapeños and pineapples, you'd eat that with me?"

He grimaces. "I should have known you were one of those people who liked sweet shit on pizza."

I scoot closer to him, pressing my chest against his. "How dare you call me *people*. It's very condescending. And you, Mr. *My-Body-Is-My-Temple*, wouldn't know good pizza if it landed in your mouth."

He smiles down at me, his eyes smoldering. "I'd like to have *something* in my mouth, and while it's another five-letter word that starts with *p*, it certainly doesn't end with an *a*."

My mouth opens at his crass insinuation. It's not the first time I've heard him say filthy things, but it still catches me off guard each time, because in front of the rest of the world–his brothers, his mom, his coworkers, and friends–Darian is nothing but reserved. Restrained. Completely in control. But I get to see a different side of him that he doesn't show anyone else, the one where he's *unhinged*, and I love that.

He takes a quick peek at Arman still playing in the living

room with his cars before going to the TV and turning on Arman's favorite cartoon show. We hardly use TV as a distraction, but it keeps him still when we need a quick break. Arman immediately becomes entranced.

I furrow my brows, wondering what Darian is up to, when he comes back and pulls me to him. His mouth catches mine in a hot kiss as his hands start roaming. His tongue dives into my mouth, sending a zing of electricity to my core. It twirls with my tongue, taunting and teasing me until I lose my breath. I turn my head to catch my breath while he nuzzles my neck.

"Darian," I moan, arching into him.

He walks me backward into the walk-in pantry as his hand palms my breasts. His lips press into my neck, his warm tongue swirling against me and sending goosebumps soaring over my skin.

His mouth slowly makes its way down to the cleavage peeking out of my shirt. "I fucking love this shirt." He bites the top of my breast, making me hiss before he kisses the same spot.

My fingers are buried in his hair, my back pressed against a shelf, when he drops to his knees, eyeing my mid-thigh skirt. "What are you doing?" I can barely get the words out, I'm breathing so fast.

He studies me, waiting for me to stop him, as his hands slide up my thighs. He hooks his fingers into the band of my panties, pulling them down slowly. "Enjoying the appetizer before my meal."

I bite my lip, fighting a moan.

His hands guide both of my feet out my underwear before he presses his nose to them, inhaling my scent. He looks up at me, and I give him the faintest of nods. He lifts my skirt and I shimmy until it's over my hips, bunched up at the bottom of my torso. I should feel embarrassed at the way he stares at my bare sex in front of him, but I watch as he devours me first with just his eyes.

"Darian." I practically whimper, begging him to do something, anything.

"Shh," he replies. "Let me just look at you." His index finger slides down the center of me, around my clit, and my legs start to quake. He does it again on the other side, circling my opening and the slick sounds his finger makes as he teases me ramps up my pulse even further. My head falls back as pressure slowly builds inside my core.

Bringing his face closer to me, Darian takes a slow swipe with his tongue all the way up my slit, staying away from my clit. Lifting my leg over his shoulder, he rubs his nose up and down my center, inhaling. His voice is a rough growl against my throbbing center. "Goddamn, you smell good."

He slowly licks at my entrance again, flicking his tongue against it before circling it with the tip. I hiss, needing to do something with my hands. I place one in his hair and the other on my breast, squeezing.

With both index fingers, he spreads my labia apart and flattens his tongue against me, licking before kissing me down where I want it the most. He still hasn't licked my needy clit, and I'm about to burst at the seams in both frustration and lust because it's the one place I need him to move his mouth.

I pull on his hair, trying to vocalize my need through my hands, and he grins against my skin. "All in due time, beautiful."

I growl softly so as to not alert the toddler in the living room. "Darian!"

Darian moves over to my thigh on his shoulder, kissing and licking it before sliding his mouth back to my entrance. He pulls one of my lips into his mouth, sucking it before letting it go with a *pop*, and I mewl.

My body arches forward as my grasp on his hair tightens. "Please." I feel like I'm about to start sobbing. "Please, Darian."

As if he hasn't even heard me, the bastard maintains his slowish pace, moving to my other lip and doing the same— licking it before sucking it into his mouth. He bites down on my soft skin while he slides a finger inside me.

I grind down on his face and his finger, biting my lip so hard, I'm at risk of tasting blood. He curls his finger, massaging my inside walls and making me squirm like a fish out of water. My jaw clenches and I manage to grit out my irritation, "Darian, for God's sake, if you don't want to see my wrath, then you'd better pick up your pace!"

He laughs against me and finally, *fucking finally*, he makes his way to my throbbing and swollen clit. His tongue flattens against it, licking before flicking it. He puts one more finger inside me and then sucks my clit with the strength of a fucking vacuum.

I cry out, pressing the back of my hand against my mouth to restrain myself, as my orgasm blinds my vision. I squeeze my eyes shut as I ride his face, unabashedly. Brazenly. Darian continues to finger me as he licks my juices, as if I'm his favorite drink, before I finally gather my breath.

"Oh my God. Holy freaking shit!" I breathe, letting go of his hair and sucking in much-needed oxygen.

He pulls my skirt down before looking up at me with a smug, glistening smile.

"You asshole!" I yell, though I'm laughing at the same time.

He gets up on his feet, pressing his body against mine before cradling my face with his hands. Something vulnerable and needy passes between us. I rub my thumb over his lips, wiping myself off him.

"Put your thumb in your mouth," he demands.

I do what he asks, tasting myself. He watches me hungrily while I suck on my thumb before I pull it out and he brings his mouth to mine. His tongue laps at mine just like it did seconds before between my legs, and I moan at the memory still fluttering over my skin.

We kiss for another few minutes, moaning and groaning into each other, before I lean my head back on the shelf, completely spent but ready to eat. "Can you feed me now?"

He stamps a quick kiss on my forehead before adjusting himself inside his pants, then he leaves me inside the pantry to make a phone call for take-out.

Chapter Twenty-Four

DARIAN

Rani: Hi.

Me: Hi. Are you okay?

The text bubble pops up on my phone again and I stare at it, pulling the covers over my waist and sitting up against the headrest.

Rani: Yes.

I wait for her to say more but when she doesn't after a good three minutes, I type another response.

Me: What's wrong?

Rani: I don't know. I feel like after what happened in the pantry, we should you know . . . talk or cuddle or something.

Another text pops up from her before I have a chance to respond.

Rani: Or forget I said that. Especially the cuddling part, because yuck, who wants to cuddle? How clingy of me to even insinuate that I'm into that kind of thing.
Rani: Because I'm so not.

She actually *didn't* insinuate; she literally wrote it. But I'm not ballsy enough to tell her that, knowing she'll probably castrate me.

I'm about to type her a message when yet another one comes through from her. She's nervous babbling but instead of in person, it's on text, and I am trying so hard not to laugh. She's so fucking cute, I'm not even sure what to do with her.

Rani: Anyway, good night. I am so sleepy. You should have seen how many times I yawned just now. Like five. Five yawns.
Rani: K, bye.

Me: What happened in the pantry?

It takes a minute for her to text back, and I can almost see the look of confusion on her face. God, I love that look.

Rani: Um, you did THINGS to me!

Me: What sort of things did I do?

Rani: I can't say words like that in text. It's unbecoming.

Me: Let me guess. It doesn't align with your principles.

Rani: As a matter of fact, that's right. Are you mocking my principles?

Me: Never. Can you say them face-to-face?

Rani: Maybe.

Me: Rani?

Rani: Yes?

Me: Open your door.

I hear her feet pad through her room before her door swings open and she finds me standing there. Her hair is wilder–long, loose curls swaying down her back–and her skin is scrubbed clean. She takes in my bare chest, her eyes trailing down from my neck to my abs heatedly. She licks her lips and I latch on to the movement.

I don't know if it's because of her freshly washed face or because of the dim lighting behind her, but she looks young, like *really* young. Her youth hits me in the ribs as I stare at her, with my hands grasping the door frame.

What am I doing?
Am I doing the right thing?
Why am I here?

"Hi," she whispers.

I hesitate, throwing my hand into my hair. "Hi."

Her eyes narrow–she's figured out my tells–and before I can turn around and go back to my room, her hand comes to rest on my chest. "Please, don't go."

My eyes go back and forth between hers before I finally nod, giving in to her. I step inside, noticing a lamp lit on her bedside table and a lily stem sitting atop her bed. She closes the door behind us and I turn around to face her.

My thoughts are all over the place. Should I be here? Is this a bad idea? Christ, why can't I think straight around this woman?

She pulls me by the hand to her bed, and I take in her tiny lavender sleep shorts and the button-down top. She gets into the bed, putting the flower on the nightstand before scooting over and lifting the covers in invitation.

I stare at her. "Rani."

Her shoulders slump. "Please. I just want . . ." she chews her lip, "I just want you to be close, that's all. You don't even have to touch me. Not like that."

I grind my teeth, closing my eyes for a second, reining in my thumping heart. "I *can't* touch you." I peer at her. "I can't touch you because if I do, we aren't going to go slow. And with you, I want to go slow."

A look of disappointment crosses her face before she nods.

I slide into her bed–thankfully, I'd bought a queen-sized one for this bedroom–but as soon as I do, she pulls up, closing the space between us and lays her head on my arm with her body flush against mine. I swear she's purposely making doe eyes at me, the nymph that she is. "Is this okay?"

No.

But who's going to tell her?

I throw my other arm over my head and close my eyes. I haven't been with someone in a bed in well over a year. More, if I count the fact that Sonia and I barely slept in the same room for most of her pregnancy. Sure, there were nights here and there, but overall, we lived almost separately under the same roof.

"Are you thinking about my sister?"

The fuck? Did I say my thoughts out loud?

My eyes fly open and I turn my head toward Rani, my cheek brushing her forehead. "What?"

She trails a finger down between my ribs and my dick stirs to life. "It's just, I wonder if she was the last person . . . I mean, unless you've been with someone else over the past year." I hear her inhale a quick breath. "You know what? It's none of my business. I'm sorry."

I don't have to see her to know her cheeks are flaming. I stay silent, peering up at the shadows on the ceiling made by the dim lamp and the moonlight shining in between the little gaps in the covered window.

I move a little and she lifts her head before I twist the small knob on the lamp and turn it off. "Good night, Rani."

She doesn't respond for a long minute, settling back down in the crook between my arm and shoulder. "Good night, Darian. I'm sorry."

Fuck. This is exactly what I was worried about with her, exactly what I told myself I couldn't get wrapped up in. *Emotions.* Mine and hers. I don't have the wherewithal to go through it all again—the tailspin romance that only ends in tragedy.

What the fuck am I doing here, then? Why is it that with every passing day, I feel more and more entangled?

But how can I not? I mean, fuck, she's magnetizing. Fucking effervescent and sweet. Unlike anyone I've ever met in my entire life.

Completely unlike her sister, save for the animated facial expressions and her own brand of determination.

She's exactly like the damn moonlight seeping in through the cracks in the window, determined to illuminate the room, even if the person inside prefers the dark. She's relentless with scattering her sweet light over anything she touches, whether it's wanted or not.

My chest constricts at the thought of her leaving in less than two months. It's not enough time and it's too much all the same. And then what? Will I just go back to a version of the life I was previously living with memories of her in every square inch of my house?

A sniffle escapes her and she turns her back to me, scooting onto her own pillow, and the hollowness I feel in my chest threatens to swallow me whole. Why am I being this asshole? What did she ever do to deserve this besides fucking care about me? Besides care about my son?

I'm so stuck, undulating between the past and the present, I can't figure out which one I want to live in more.

I brush my hand over the back of her arm and she stiffens. I lay back on my pillow, starting up at the ceiling. "Sonia and I weren't good for each other anymore, Rani." She doesn't move, but I know she can hear me so I carry on. "By the time we had Arman, our relationship was way past the expiration date. We were just trying—*hoping*—to save it for the sake of the time we'd invested in it, but deep down, I think we both knew the truth.

"She stopped loving me." It's the first time I've vocalized that truth to anyone, maybe even to myself. "I don't know when or even why, really, but she did. I felt the shift in her when it happened. It was gradual at first, but by the end, when I looked back at us, all I saw was an ashen trail.

"She blamed it on me working too much, but when I took time off to spend with her, she'd tell me I was around too much. We'd get into arguments about the dumbest things—insignificant things—but she wouldn't let them go.

"And at first, I thought, maybe it was a phase. When she got pregnant, I thought maybe it was hormonal. Turns out, it was none of those things." I take a shaky breath. "I think it was just *me*. She was just over me."

Rani turns around, sitting up on her knees before grasping my face with both hands. She brings her face closer and I see tears pool in her eyes. "It wasn't you." Her voice is hoarse. "It couldn't have been you, because I *see* you, Darian. I see the way you love. I see the boy you're raising and the way you care for him so fiercely." She shakes her head, her curls falling against my chest. "It wasn't you; it was *her,* and I'm sorry on her behalf. I'm sorry that she couldn't see you for who you are."

I pull a strand of her springy hair, watching as it curls around my finger so perfectly, as if it was made to do just that. "She used to and then she didn't"

Rani nods. "I get that. I really do. Not in the same way, but I know the feeling." She sniffs. "Because she used to care about me, too . . . and then she didn't."

"She talked about you sometimes," I tell her, hoping to chase away some of her gloom. "She said you were beautiful and bright, but you just needed to realize that you were your own advocate. That you were the only one who could fight for yourself against all those people—including your mom—who would hurt you." I remember the way Sonia would smile when she thought about her sister. She missed her. "I know she tried to get in touch with you . . . but I honestly think she reconsidered because of your mom. She didn't want her finding out and for you to have that drama in your life."

Rani sighs. "Yeah, well, I lost a lot more than potential drama, didn't I? I lost a chance to get to know my sister, too."

When I have no response, she slips back under the covers, her back to me again.

"Rani?" I squeeze my eyes shut when she stays silent before turning toward her and brushing the pads of my fingers over her neck.

I see her body relax and she finally turns around. She hides her face in the crook of my neck, wrapping her arms around my waist, and I feel her wet cheek on my skin, lighting a fire inside me.

It kills me.

I pull back from her, scanning her face—her eyes shut tight—before wiping her tears. "I'm sorry."

She shakes her head as a sob emits from her throat. "No. *I'm* sorry. I'm sorry she hurt you."

I'm not sure when I fall asleep, but between the comfort of her arms around me, her face planted under my chin, and her hair tangled between my fingers, I can't recall the last time I slept so well.

Chapter Twenty-Five
RANI

The morning sunlight streams in through the gaps around the window and my eyes flicker open. For a second, I don't know where I am. I turn, seeing the lily stem on the nightstand and the memories of last night come flooding back.

There's an indentation the size of Darian on my bed, but sliding my hand on the cool sheets, I can tell he's been long gone. I disconnect my phone from the charger and bring it to my face to look at the time. Nine-thirteen. I'm supposed to be at the nursing home by ten-thirty since we're planting flowers around the property today.

I rub sleep out of my eyes using the heel of my palm before getting up on the bed. My eyes feel puffy, a crusty film caked in the corners from falling asleep crying.

Darian's confession and pain broke me last night. The melancholy in his voice, the unshed tears, the way he was there but not really. No one should have to carry that kind of burden on their own.

Even though I hadn't heard from my sister much before she died–and when I thought I'd get to meet her, she never showed up–I assumed she was happy. Because why else would anyone sacrifice their family, if not for more happiness? And from Darian's words, it seemed they found happiness for a while, at least before things changed between them.

It shouldn't surprise me that he was another casualty in whatever war Sonia had set out to win, but it does. It does because what I see in him is a man hellbent on persevering through storms. I can't imagine he wouldn't have tried to save their marriage. And maybe Arman was going to be their refuge from the upheaval they were both experiencing, but who's to say he could have saved them?

Then there was that cryptic text . . ..

Forgetting about being late, I flip my phone to the my messages app, scrolling down to find the last messages I exchanged with Sonia.

Sonia: I'm sorry I couldn't make it to see you today. Something came up and I needed to see my doctor, but hopefully, after this baby is here, we can both visit you. <heart emoji>

I scroll further up, past the messages where I asked her where she was, while I waited for her at the coffee shop we agreed to meet in, only to be disappointed. I quickly scan the selfie she sent me of her big belly, pregnant with my nephew. She's wearing some sort of bright yellow dress from what I can tell based on the cropped picture of just her chest and belly. Her left hand is holding her stomach–a few rings on her fingers, but interestingly, none on her ring finger. I never noticed it before, but I suppose I have a new perspective.

I finally find the texts I'm searching for, dated a couple of months before she died. And just like the previous time I read it, it does nothing to settle my unease.

Sonia: I've decided to tell Darian. It's not something I can keep from him any longer, and I think it's about time we face the consequences, don't you? I think you should tell Em. She'll find out soon anyway.

I'd responded to her text with a, What?

She replied a minute later, but I recall staring at the text in complete confusion.

Sonia: Sorry about that. That wasn't meant for you.

Consequences?
What consequences? I remember thinking about that word long after she sent me the text stating it wasn't meant for me. It's not like I was close enough to her to ask for an explanation, and she didn't owe me anything, so I knew I'd have to let it be, but still, it bothered me anyway.

I wonder if she told Darian whatever it was she wanted to tell him. Who was that text intended for anyway, and what were they hiding? My gut tells me I wouldn't like the answer if I ever found out.

My thoughts go back to Darian and how heartbroken he seemed last night—more vulnerable and crushed than I've ever seen him. He'd mentioned vaguely the first night I was here that all was not what it seemed between him and Sonia, but last night was the first time he'd confided in me, giving me insight into the level of his sadness about his marriage with Sonia and a fresh perspective on the text staring back at me in my hands.

Should I show it to him? I have no other information or proof that confirms my suspicions—that my sister may have been cheating on him. Would it do him any good to know that? And what if it isn't true? What if I'm falsely accusing someone who can no longer speak for themselves?

What use would it serve to show this to him but to rip him open even further? How does this text change anything for him besides shatter whatever peace he's tried to find by rebuilding his life without her?

Sonia is gone, having left behind this red herring in the form of a text that has the potential to be absolutely nothing or something that throws Darian's world off its axis. Why dig up an old grave? It would accomplish nothing.

She hurt him in life, why let her hurt him in death?

I'm working through my thoughts when my phone buzzes in my hands.

Melody: @Rani, why have you been so quiet lately? Is it because you're too busy having earth-shattering orgasms? Please tell me you've let that hot-ass brother-in-law of yours 'paddle your kayak,' if you know what I mean.

Bella: I just snort-laughed out loud. Seriously, almost spit my coffee.

Melody: LOL! But seriously, what's happening over there? How are Darian and that Liam guy? Quite the love triangle you've got going on, and you're not doing a good job keeping us abreast!

I roll my eyes, padding over to the bathroom to brush my teeth and wash my crusty eyes. I wipe my mouth after rinsing before picking up my phone again.

Me: There's no love triangle <eye roll emoji>. Liam and I are just friends. He's one of the nicest people I've met, but I can't see him as anything but a friend. But . . .

I leave the text to go change, knowing it's going to drive my friends crazy that I haven't finished that last thought.

As suspected, when I pick up my phone again, having put on some lipgloss and mascara, I see a stream of irate messages. I giggle while reading them.

Melody: But? But what??

Bella: Hello? Rani!

Melody: Is she seriously leaving us hanging like that?

I make sure I have everything I need in my purse before I respond.

Me: Sorry. I figured I'd get changed and keep you guys in suspense.

Melody: Asshole.

Me: Hehe! So, Liam and I decided to be friends, but I did tell him I'd introduce him to a friend of mine. I was thinking of you, @Melody. I don't know, I really think you'd like him.

Melody: Would we make cute babies?

Me: You know I'd already thought about that, and the answer is a solid yes. A little version of you with curly red hair!

Bella: Oh, you know she's sold.

Melody: Well, what are you waiting for? When are you introducing us?

I giggle again, going down the stairs and pulling on my sneakers. Both Darian and Arman don't seem to be home, so I decide to grab coffee from the nursing home kitchenette.

Me: Let me talk to Darian and see what he thinks about having you guys over here one weekend.

Melody: Don't think I missed the fact that you conveniently left out any mention of Darian paddling your kayak.

~

I'm rolling a cart of flowers into the garden at the nursing home when my phone buzzes inside my pocket.

Karine: You are coming to my house for dinner tonight. Six p.m.

I stop the cart and smile before responding to the text. I don't think I've ever read a text from Karine that hasn't made me smile.

Me: I am?

Karine: `Yes. Darian and Arman are joining, too.`

A small pang of hurt hits me between the ribs when I read her response. I hate that I expected Darian's text or call all day today. I hate that I looked at my phone five times an hour, just to see if maybe I'd missed a message from him. Even Fred called me out for being distracted by 'the handsome brother-in-law.'

I suppose after the heavy conversation we shared last night, I thought we'd crossed a bridge. I thought maybe we'd progressed in our relationship or whatever this is. But maybe he didn't feel the same way?

Maybe I came across as nothing more than a clingy, insecure, inexperienced girl, and he wanted to distance himself from me.

The feeling of embarrassment at the way I acted last night has increased all day. The fact that he hasn't even acknowledged our conversation has me cringing inside, humiliated by the memory of sending him a text to come cuddle—seriously, why couldn't lightning have struck me down before I messaged him that? And then I clung to him in my bed like I couldn't breathe without his skin plastered to my face! How could I have acted like such a ten-year-old?

I'd hoped that maybe seeing him in the morning would have given me an indication as to how he was feeling, but the house was empty when I came downstairs. And since then, it's been nothing but radio-silence from him—a suffocating silence I can't seem to rise above.

I look back at Karine's text. Darian's clearly spoken to her about dinner so I know he's alive, but I can't deny that it doesn't pinch to find out from her that he'll be there. Maybe I'm a fool for expecting him to have messaged me himself to tell me.

Maybe I'm just a fool, period.
With my heart in my throat, I message her back.

Me: Okay. I'll be there.

A link to Karine's home address comes through next.

Karine: Here's the address.
Karine: <middle finger emoji>

And even as tears prick the corners of my eyes, I can't help but giggle, knowing she meant to use the index finger emoji instead.

∼

I RING THE DOORBELL, feeling my nerves fire away inside my body. I'm not sure why I'm nervous, but I suppose the fact that Darian or Arman weren't home when I went back to take a shower and change this evening has me feeling on edge.

After the nursing home, I told myself I'd talk to Darian at home and maybe we'd go to Karine's together, but the house was as empty as I'd left it this morning. Wow, he's working really hard to stay out of my way.

I swallow my anxiety and square my shoulders as the door opens, and I see Darian's dad for the first time since I moved here.

"Rani!" His voice booms as he opens the door with the brightest blue eyes and smile I've ever seen.

Clearly, one of his sons fell far from that tree.

"Come in, come in!" He takes the flowers I brought before leaning over to plant a kiss on my cheek. "I'm Marvin. I have heard so much about you."

"Thank you for having me," I say softly as a squeal erupts inside what seems to be their family room.

Arman comes wobbling to my legs with his arms outstretched and a smile very much as bright as his grandfather's. "*Mas!*"

I bend down to pick him up and give him a huge kiss before he's had enough and wiggles out of my arms.

Darian's dad studies our interaction with interest. "He is quite attached to you."

I watch Arman waddle back to the living room when my eyes collide with Darian. My heart squeezes inside my chest as the dull ache that's been there all day increases. He gets up from the couch with his brothers before the twins come toward me. Darian gives me a small wave but I shift my gaze, pretending not to have noticed it.

"Hey, Rani!" Garrett greets me with a hug before Dean chimes in.

"My turn. God, don't hog her all to yourself." Dean's arms wrap me in an embrace before letting me go. "Glad we could all hang out today."

"Thanks for having me. Where's Karine?"

Dean points me to the kitchen where Karine is getting something out of the oven. I rush to help her with Dean's voice at my back. "Good luck trying to help. She'll smack you with a kitchen towel."

"I only smack *you* with a kitchen towel because you're the only one who deserves it." Karine's prompt reply has me giggling.

I give her a quick hug, and when I lean away from her, I catch Darian's eyes on me again. Ignoring him, I focus on Karine and what looks like two large casserole dishes full of lasagna, salad, bruschetta, and a variety of dips and breads. "You didn't have to cook all this! Aren't you supposed to be relaxing and taking things easy?"

"Oh hush." She waves a hand at me. "I'm tired of everyone making me feel like a patient. I'm not one. Just because the doctors increased my meds does not mean something is so wrong with me that I can't do the things I love, like feeding my family."

I wash my hands, drying them on the kitchen towel hanging from the fridge. "What can I do?"

Ten minutes later, I've helped set the table and Arman's high chair. Karine calls out to the guys, who have been busy discussing a big fire in Southern California. Apparently, Dean is being called in to help and will be leaving tomorrow morning.

"I don't like it at all, this job of yours," Karine scolds him as he makes his way to the table. It's kind of funny to see a woman more than a foot shorter than him admonish him as if he were a kid. "It's too dangerous. I can't sleep some nights because I think about the worst situations."

Dean wraps his large arm around her and for a second, I forget that she's not even his mother. I wonder if Darian has a similar relationship with Marvin's ex-wife, though I know she lives somewhere else now. I recall Karine telling me, but I don't remember where. "Then stop thinking about the worst situations."

She smacks Dean's arm as everyone starts taking their seats. Marvin puts Arman inside his high chair before handing him a plate Karine set out to cool for him. "You don't understand how mothers think."

Dean laughs. "Well, I don't quite have the equipment to do that, so you're right!"

Garrett and Marvin laugh while Karine mumbles something under her breath, going back to the kitchen to look for something. I take a seat across the table from the twins, and I almost jump out of my chair when I feel the brush of Darian's arm against mine.

I still haven't looked at him. Instead, I focus on the food set out in front of me, hoping to drown out the scent of pine and citrus currently engulfing me with the mouthwatering scent of lasagna. Oh, who am I kidding? The only mouthwatering scent is coming from the man next to me.

Marvin and Dean continue their conversation about the fire until Karine sits down at the other end of the table, and we all dig in, serving ourselves.

Throughout the meal, I feel Darian's gaze on me, making my skin tingle. He's coaxing me to face him. Instead, I occupy myself with my meal or my water, and occasionally ask the rest of the family questions.

"So, Rani, how much longer do we have you here?" Dean asks from across the table, though I see him scanning Darian's face instead.

I clear my throat. "Til mid-August. I'll need to head back to start my next year of journalism school."

"Darian and Karine said you'll be helping with his school's website," Garrett adds, finishing up the last of the lasagna on his plate.

"I'm hoping to get as much done as I can before the tournament."

The conversation shifts at the mention of the tournament, and Marvin and Garrett ask Darian for more details about how many participants he expects and whether he'll need their help.

He seems to be cool, answering every question as it's being asked, but I feel his fingers along the edge of my thigh. I rub my lips together, hoping to keep my face impassive. His fingers follow a path across my thigh to where my legs meet, and I gently flick his fingers off.

I take in a deep breath, noticing everyone wrapping up their dinner. "Karine, can I help you load the dishes into the dishwasher and clean the kitchen?"

She wipes her mouth with her napkin. "No, no. These hooligans have promised to help in the kitchen today." She points to Dean and Garrett. "I'm taking the rest of the night off to eat dessert and put my feet up on the couch."

"As you should." I smile, picking up my plate when suddenly, I feel the grate of sandpaper in my throat and a throb pounds inside my temples. "I'm not feeling so well. If it's okay with you, I'd like to go home before I feel worse."

"Oh no! Are you alright, dear?" Karine starts scooting her chair back. "Why don't you let Darian take you home? Don't drive back on your own."

I can feel Darian's eyes—along with everyone else's at the table—on me again, but I dare not to look. I offer a feeble smile. "It's probably just dehydration from being out in the sun today. I'll be fine to drive, it's a short distance anyway."

"Rani." Darian's low voice sends goosebumps down my arms.

I flick a glance his way, avoiding his questioning eyes, before getting up. "I'll be fine, Darian. Really."

Rinsing off my dishes in the sink, I place them in the dishwasher before wiping my hands on the towel. I feel his nearness before he even gets close enough to touch me, and my body goes on high lusty alert. I swear, my body is the most traitorous thing I own.

He leans in, his hands inside his pockets. "What's wrong?"

I pretend to iron a wrinkle on my wrinkle-free dress with my hand. "Like I said, I'm not feeling well."

His gaze singes my skin. "Look at me."

I take a deep inhale, turning to him, keeping my face devoid of any emotion. I suppose I'm learning from the master.

He scrutinizes my face with his intense cappuccinos. "Why are you avoiding me?"

I blink, barely holding back from jabbing my index finger

into his chest and laying into him. How dare he ask why I'm avoiding him, when all I've done all fucking day is wait for him to say a single word. How dare he act like I'm the one being different when he snuck out of my room this morning, only to disappear all day? How fucking dare he pretend that he cares about how I feel when I've all but begged him to feel with me. To *be* with me.

I clamp my jaw tight before moving past him. "Good night, Darian."

Chapter Twenty-Six
DARIAN

"You know, this isn't necessary every single year," Dad says to the three of us—Dean, Garrett, and me—as we give him another round of hugs in the foyer. "You guys make too much of a fuss."

"It's a big day for all of us, not just you, Dad." Garrett pats Dad on the back before opening the door and stepping out.

Dad waves to my brothers, pointing to Dean. "You be careful out there tomorrow, son. Understand?"

Dean does a two-finger salute, following Garrett out. "I'll call you soon."

Mom lifts up on her toes to press a kiss on Arman's cheek. He's babbling and rubbing his eyes incessantly. After an active day in the sun, I know he's exhausted. I won't be surprised if he passes out before we even get home.

"Is Rani alright?" Mom eyes me as if I should have an answer. "She seemed quiet today at dinner. Poor thing. I felt terrible that she wasn't feeling well."

"I'm going to check on her." I lean in to place a kiss on Mom's cheek. "I'll let you know."

Rani left twenty minutes ago, so she should be home by

now, and if she thinks she fooled me with her exaggeration of an illness, then she needs to take more acting classes.

"She's a sweet girl." Mom gives me an accusatory perusal. "Is she upset with you about something?"

I grab Arman's diaper bag and the plastic bag with his wet trunks. "I won't know until I talk to her."

If it wasn't for raising suspicion with my family that something was going on between us, I'd have been rushing out after her, but with the way it currently stands, I keep my tone casual.

God knows what her deal was today. She wouldn't look at me, no matter how much I tried to get her attention, and short of calling her out on it and making things awkward in front of everyone, I couldn't do anything but stay silent. She looked at everyone else, threw them her pouty smiles for free, and giggled when Dean cracked his stupid jokes. But she never, not even once, looked at me with the same softness. Even when I tried to touch her, she shirked my hand away as if it burned her skin.

I swear, I can't get anything right when it comes to the woman.

It drives me nuts when I think about the promises I made to myself—promises I tried my fucking hardest to keep as soon as I knew she'd be trouble for the long-abandoned organ in my chest. To not let her affect me. To not get attached. To not fucking fall . . ..

And look where I am now.

She made it impossible. It's like she was born to test my resilience and my restraint, and I was born to learn that I had none, not when it came to her.

I slam the door to my driver's side with more force than I'd intended, starting the ignition. I barely register the street lights as my mind buzzes with anticipation. Mixed in are feelings of irritation and chaos. What does she want from me?

Do I just not understand women? First Sonia and now her. Even when I think I've done everything right, I seem to have it all wrong.

I get home ten minutes later, noticing Rani's car parked at the curb. After unbuckling a sleeping Arman from his car seat, I take a quick peek in the kitchen, noticing it untouched from this morning.

I take Arman up the stairs and into his bedroom. He sighs sleepily as I put him in his crib and tiptoe over to the sound machine to turn it on. Finally, after closing his window blinds, I slowly creep out of his room.

I can feel the blood inside my veins pumping as my heart rate spikes, looking at Rani's closed door and it strikes me.

She has no clue. She didn't read it.

It's the reason she gave me the cold-shoulder all evening and flinched at my touch. Because she thought—no, she *believed*—I'd be a jackass to her on purpose, even after we broke down all the walls between us last night.

It confirms the little faith she has in me, but even more so, in herself. In her ability to affect me. In her ability to have me at her fucking mercy.

I knock on her door as conflicting thoughts about whether I'm doing the right thing or not battle with my need to see her. To touch her, to hold her, and to fucking kiss her. To tell her that she's an idiot if she doesn't realize that she's not the only one at risk of getting hurt in this.

Because she has the power to undo me completely.

I hear her footsteps behind the door before she lingers at the doorknob. A few seconds later, her door swings partially open. She's wearing another pair of sleep shorts with a black tank top. My eyes skim over the gold lettering that says, *I wear glitter because I was born to sparkle*. Her wild hair is secured in a knot on top of her head with a few stray curls framing her face. And even though she looks wounded and irate—

much the same as I feel—I have to physically hold myself back from ravishing her with my hands and mouth.

"Yes." Her eyes stay on my chest, not meeting mine.

"Is there a reason you're avoiding me?"

"I'm not. Good night, again." She goes to close the door, but I put my palm against it, stopping her.

I grit my teeth, feeling the ends of my rope unravel. "Rani, I swear to God, if you don't tell me what the hell I did to deserve you acting like a brat, I'll—"

"You'll *what*, Darian?" She crosses her arms over her heaving chest. "You'll ignore me all day again? You'll not have the decency to call me to tell me you'll be at your mother's for dinner? You'll sneak out of the house everyday before you have to see me again? Is that what you were going to say? Well, save it. I've had front-row seats to that show, and it sucked."

I shake my head, chuckling incredulously. "You're really something."

"No." She purses her lips, her eyes glassy. "I'm clearly *nothing*, Darian. I thought I was something; I thought *we* were something—especially after last night—but I was wrong."

My pulse pounds inside my ears as I stare at her. "Let me ask you something. Did you have coffee today?"

She squints at me as if I've grown horns on my head. "What? What is wrong with you? Are you attributing my irritation with you to my lack of coffee? I get that you don't drink caffeine—which is crazy in itself—but that is *not* how it works. I am not angry because I didn't have my daily coffee; I'm pissed because you're an asshole!"

I take in a deep breath, not knowing how much longer I can hang on to the tiniest shred of my patience. A part of me wants to laugh, while the other wants to slam her against the wall and kiss her into submission. "Rani, for the love of God,

I'm asking you a simple fucking question. *Did you* go downstairs to have your coffee today?"

She throws her shoulders back, giving up on arguing. "No. I had a cup at the nursing home."

"Then why don't you fucking strut your sweet ass downstairs now and find the coffee I brewed for you this morning. Perhaps you'll find whatever else it is you're looking for."

With that, I stalk out of the hallway and to my room, barely holding myself from ramming my fist into the wall.

∽

THE STREAMS of warm water massage my back and trickle down my shoulder and chest. I probably have it running hotter than I should, but fuck, *I've* been running hotter than I should. The burn against my skin, creating red patches on my shoulders, feels better than the burning inside my chest. I take *that* as a win. I'm scalding from the inside out, the scorching water my only reprieve.

The glass shower fogs up with thoughts about the woman who has overthrown my self-control and ousted my sanity. Her words ring around my head. *I'm clearly nothing, Darian.*

If she only knew.

Her fucking insolent mouth and the defiant tone she flung at me, like a scared and hurt kitten, ready to scratch the hand of anyone who tried to get close, has me raging. But it also has me wanting to see her on her knees with that luscious mouth wrapped around me.

My length hardens at the thought of her pouty, thick lips pursing as she glared at me from head to toe, her arms wrapped across her heaving chest. I've thought about her tits so much over the course of the past few weeks, I've wondered if I'm possessed.

I take my dick in my hand and stroke it from base to tip,

and it thickens almost painfully as memories of my mouth devouring her heat come streaming back. She was so responsive, so perfect, so delicious. Within seconds, I'd had her warring against herself, teetering between maintaining composure and surrendering control. Even when I knew all she wanted to do was cry out and just ride my face with abandon, she held on as long as she physically could.

But I reveled in the moment she let go.

Fuck, she tasted sweet, just like I knew she would. Even just the thought of her coming on my tongue has me pulling on my erection harder.

And then, a movement past the bathroom door I've left ajar has my eyes shifting. They lock on to the voluptuous woman who's just entered my room.

She's holding the note I scrawled tightly in one hand, her eyes wild as she looks from my empty bed to the bathroom, realizing I've left the door open. I watch as she takes a step forward, leaning her body to get a closer look through the gap in the open door, before her eyes finally land on me. And I hold her stare.

Lifting my other hand, I slowly wipe the fog off the glass, giving her an uninhibited view of what she's clearly here to see.

You want a show, sweetheart? Here's one dedicated only to you.

I leave my hand on the glass, keeping my gaze locked with hers as I stroke myself again and again. The thick vein on the back of my wrist protrudes as I work myself into a frenzy—a frenzy spoken through the way I release a hard breath and the way my body stiffens. My abs pull tight and my cock throbs in my hand.

"Fuck," I mumble as heat builds up underneath my spine and my balls beg for release.

The water sloshes around me, dripping from my hair down over my thighs. A sheen of sweat peppers over my brows and my jaw locks. Rubbing my thumb over my mushroom head, I coat the smooth skin of my tip with precum while squeezing my length. Blood rushes up through my shaft, making the head look purple and engorged.

Rani's eyes widen as she watches me, transfixed. Her sight moves from my eyes to the fist I have around my shaft before slowly going back over my chest to my face again. Can she see the filthy things I want to do to her, the obscene thoughts written all over my face? Does she know how fucking badly I want to have her bent over my sink while I thrust into her from behind, sullying her for anyone else?

Does she still think she means nothing?

She takes another step before halting momentarily. A wave of something—determination, perhaps—crosses her face, and to my surprise, she starts toward me again, pushing the door open further before stepping inside.

This isn't the first time she's surprised me—had me baffled by her boldness—and I fucking hope it won't be the last.

Her fiery eyes never leave mine as she walks all the way to the shower. She puts both her hands on the glass, one of them against my palm while she regards my every movement with interest. Her tongue runs over her lips, and I don't miss the rise and fall of her chest as lust rises up inside her. It has me tugging faster, harder.

A grunt leaves my throat, and I fight the instinct to squeeze my eyes shut. God, I want her. Her mouth, her tongue, her taste on my lips. I want it all.

"You still think you're nothing to me?"

Her chest heaves as my words pierce through the drone of the shower and hum inside our ears.

My heart jackhammers inside my chest as the thrill of an impending release has me fixated on my goal. "Tell me," I grit out. "You think this is fucking nothing?"

She watches intently, fixated on the muscles twitching in

my torso and forearm, as white-hot lust shoots through me like electricity. It charges through my body as my cum sprays over my closed fist.

"Rani," I groan as my orgasm commences—thick, milky streams of my release washing off with the spray of water.

Rani's eyes never leave my body as I soap myself off before shampooing my hair. Our gazes war, colliding despite the fog and streaming water.

Finally having regulated my heart rate, I turn off the water and step out of the shower. I grab my towel, drying myself off before running it through my hair. Breaking away from her gaze, I exit the bathroom, not bothering to wrap the towel around my torso.

She hesitates momentarily but follows me. Her breath is shaky, and I have no doubt her panties are drenched. "Darian."

I turn, eyeing the paper in her fist again. "Did you get the answers you were looking for?" And I'm not just referring to the note.

She steps forward, taking her bottom lip in her mouth. "Yes. I . . . I didn't know you'd gone to spend the day with your dad and brothers. I had no idea it was something you did every year."

My fingers tighten around the towel. "There's no cell service on that part of the lake."

She looks down at her feet. "I know that now, and I came to apologize. But then . . .." A flush rises over her tanned skin as she recalls what she saw just minutes ago.

"But then you saw me fuck my fist with your name on my lips. Did that answer all your questions, all your fucking doubts?"

She nods slowly.

My eyes darken on her "Then get on my bed and show me how fucking sorry you are."

Chapter Twenty-Seven
RANI

I'D GONE DOWNSTAIRS IN A HUFF AFTER HE'D SHOWN UP TO my room. What the hell was he on about with me finding the answer I was looking for there? But then my eyes landed on the single crimson lily atop the folded piece of paper and the pot of stale coffee, and I cringed at the way I'd acted with him through dinner tonight. I was unfair to him.

Hey beautiful,
I didn't want to wake you, but hopefully you'll find your
precious coffee ready. I'm taking Arman to hang out with my
dad and brothers. It's the seventh anniversary of my dad
being in remission, and we've sort of made it a tradition to be
out on the water. Just know that you'll be on my mind. My
mom said she'll be inviting you for dinner, so I hope to see you
there.
- Dar

I didn't like the idea of entering his room without his permission, but my need to apologize for my behavior overshadowed my thoughts of breaching his privacy. Before I knew it, my feet had taken me inside. And what I saw there changed the course of my entire night.

A vision I'll recall for as long as I live.

And now, as he looms over me, gloriously naked from head to toe, I consider pinching myself to make sure I'm not dreaming. His abs flex, and I have an overwhelming need to count each one—slowly, and one at a time. That need, though, is less powerful than my need to lick each one, slowly, and one at a time.

I reach out, my breathing ragged, running my hand over his rock-hard torso. "Darian."

His fingers press into my waist, pulling me toward him, and I feel his bulge come back to life. Though it never seemed to have died in the first place.

His mouth captures mine in a heady kiss, and I gently nudge my tongue in, finding his. His fingers lift the hem of my tank top, taking it completely off me before he pulls down my shorts. His warm hand palms my ass as I deepen our kiss, my fingernails biting into his skin. I step over my shorts pooled at my feet, wearing only my underwear.

My nipples harden under Darian's perusal of my body and I fight the urge to hide. He's this perfect example of all-man, all-muscle, and I feel completely out of my depth. And even though I've worked hard at taming my insecurities, my mind swirls with them incessantly.

Why does he want me? What could I ever offer him? Why is he looking at me like I'm a coveted prize when he could get anyone he wanted?

As if reading my thoughts, his large hands palm my breasts. "You're perfect," he murmurs as he tweaks my nipple, making ripples of want course through my body. "Absolutely perfect."

Lowering himself, he takes my nipple into his mouth, sucking it so deep and so long, I moan brazenly, my voice echoing inside the room. My hands find the back of his head, pulling him closer, as his other hand palms my other breast. I feel the scrape of his teeth around my nipple before he bites down on it, making me mewl.

My panties are soaking, and I'm positive my thighs will soon be covered in my juices. "Please, Darian." I practically sob as my legs clench, trying to give myself some relief. "I need your fingers. I need *something*."

His mouth lets my nipple go in a *pop* before he lays his claim on my other breast. He moans his satisfaction into my skin as he teases my puckered tip with his tongue, circling it before sucking on it in the same way.

His hand ripples down to my panties, finding my wet core, and he groans in earnest. "Fuck, you're sopping wet, baby. You're drenching my fingers even through the material."

I can feel my knees buckle under me, and my legs are on the cusp of deciding to stop supporting my weight. They've had enough. I'm shaking with need as Darian pulls my panties aside and pushes two fingers inside me, sliding right in. When he glides in deeper, so far up that the feeling of fullness starts taking over, I feel like I'm going to catch fire.

"I need you," I pant. "Please. I want you."

He pops off my nipple, his fingers still sliding in and out of my dripping heat, before pushing me back onto his bed. His fingers pull out as my back hits the mattress.

He stalks over me before moving down my body. "Open your legs for me."

I shake my head. "No. I need you." I search his stormy eyes as I make my decision. "I don't want to go slow. I can't wait anymore, Darian. I want you inside me."

He swallows, studying my face. "You want me to fuck you?"

I nod. "Yes. Please, yes."

"Rani—"

"Please, Darian. I've never begged anyone for anything my entire life, but I'm begging you. I want this. I want you."

He hesitates. "You're sure? You're not going to like it the first time around."

"I'm sure," I say so fast that I barely let him finish. "I want my first time to be with you."

He watches me squirm under him before giving in to his own barely controlled agony. "Scoot to the edge of the bed. I need to get you ready."

Oh God. Why do those words have me pooling inside my panties again? The thrill of finally doing what I've wanted to for so long–especially with a man I'm crazy about–has me so impatient, I can't even think.

I eagerly comply, scooting my ass to the edge, fisting his sheets in my hands.

Darian gets on his knees, regarding me with utmost interest. He pulls on my panties and I help him by lifting my hips off the bed. As soon as my panties are discarded, he licks his lips. His voice is low, as if he's talking to himself. "Put your heels on the bed and open up for me. Let me look at you."

I do as he asks, and he rewards me with a finger down my center. I jump at his touch, mewling in response. Darian grabs hold of my thighs before his mouth is on my skin. He licks the side of my thighs, keeping his pace leisurely before progressing to my middle.

I wiggle and squirm as my need escalates, chanting inside my head, *Please, please*.

He chuckles and I realize perhaps I'd begged him out loud again. His mouth finally makes it to my center, and just like he did last time, he avoids my clit, licking and sucking below it. He takes my lower lips into his mouth, sucking them thoroughly before lapping at my entrance. I'm practically feral, arching my hips into his warm mouth while fisting his hair in my hand.

God, why won't he just suck my clit?

He presses his tongue into my entrance and my head turns from side to side. "Darian!" I cry out, frustrated.

He chuckles again, and I swear, I consider kicking him in the face. This is *not* a laughing matter.

He buries his mouth and nose inside my sex, eating me like an untamed animal. His moans have me climbing as I try to push his head to where I really want him. He continues, unperturbed, washing me in his spit. I can hear my juices against his lips and I continue to buck up against him.

It's when I can't take any more that he finally places his tongue on my clit. His fingers drive into me again, and he's only started sucking me when I detonate, convulsing on his tongue and groaning my satisfaction. Fucking finally!

I fly through wormholes and portals as my body enters some state of oblivion, bursting with the power of a nuclear explosion.

"You're heaven," he mumbles as I come back down to earth. He doesn't let up, lapping at me until I flinch from the oversensitivity.

He stands, his taut body imposing over me, and I notice his erection bounce against his abs, practically reaching his belly button. I don't have much to compare it to since I've only ever seen my ex completely naked, but this one right here . . . . *Yeah, wow.* This one might be one of those that tops charts and wins awards.

I reach for him as I slide back on the bed. Darian takes my hand in his before pulling himself over me. Hovering above me with his weight on his elbows, his eyes silently bombard me with a million questions. Some I'm too afraid to answer, and some I have no doubts about.

Like this moment.

His lips glisten with my want and he sees me eyeing them. His mouth descends on mine hungrily, his tongue exploring inside, making me taste everything he just tasted. Before long I'm breathless again, writhing under him.

He pulls his face away. "You're sure?"

"Darian," I huff.

His mouth twitches again. I know he pretends not to like it when I say his name in reprimand, but I think he secretly loves it, too.

"Okay," he whispers against my ear, making my heart soar. He gets up on his knees, reaching for his nightstand drawer when I stop him. "I'm on the pill."

His eyes capture mine in question.

"I had to get on them to regulate my . . . never mind." The last thing I want is to kill the mood by talking about my period. "I just want you," I reach for his thick length, my hand barely wrapping around it, making him grunt, "bare, like this."

I tug at the velvet iron in my hands with a firm grasp as he watches me with hooded lids. His jaw clenches sexily and I know he's loving my touch. I may not have experience with sex, but I know my way around an erection just fine.

His head rolls back as he kneels over me, his hand wrapping around mine. We stroke him from base to tip as he squeezes my fingers around him again. His dark eyes find mine as he lets go. "I won't make it if you keep doing that."

I pull my bottom lip into my mouth, relaxing my hold on him. He bends down to give my swollen nub another thorough lick and I moan, knotting my fingers in his hair. Once he's satisfied that I'm ready, he gets back over me and lines up his arousal at my entrance.

His hand comes to my face as my breath hitches. He rubs the top of my cheek with his thumb before gazing deep inside me. Using his hand to lift my thigh, he enters me slowly.

Oh yeah, this hurts.

I arch as my body constricts at the invasion. He is so big

that I almost want to throw in the towel and call it a day, but I breathe through my nose, squeezing my eyes shut.

"Baby, look at me." Darian's soft voice pulls me back. "Relax for me, sweetheart."

He pushes in some more and I buck under him, the pressure so intense that it feels like I'm going to rip apart. A surge of dread and uncertainty weave around my thoughts as I see myself from his eyes. What if this is the absolute worst sex he's ever had? What if I suck at this? What if he regrets this?

What if he regrets *me*?

Maybe my vulnerability is written all over my face, or maybe he's a mind-reader. Whatever the case, he kisses me gently. "Get out of your own head, beautiful. You're exactly what I want." When he sees me relax a little, he continues speaking in a soft murmur that has my skin tingling. "Hold your knees back for me. Open up."

I do as he says and he pushes in a little deeper, making me hiss. He looks down at our connection with a frown. "I need you wetter, baby." He pulls out and I arch up from the feeling of emptiness.

God, is this how it's supposed to be or am I just awful at this?

My mind buzzes before I feel his lips on my fragile, aching skin again. He sucks at my entrance, laying open-mouthed kisses on my folds before lapping at me again. My body relaxes under his tongue as lust surges through me again. He hums his pleasure, licking me a few more times before coming back up to my face.

I pull my knees back as he lines us up once more. And this time when he penetrates me, I'm lost to a perfect mix of pain and pleasure. I mewl as he pushes deep inside, to the hilt, while my stomach contracts and my core pulses.

He lays a kiss on my lips, watching my face. "Are you okay?"

I nod, panting. "Yes. Darian?"

"Yes, baby?"

"Please move."

He smiles as his hips start rocking inside me. He takes over with one hand grabbing the back of my knee before driving inside me and my fingernails bite into his shoulder. His lips find mine as we groan into each other, breathing, feeling, needing.

Finally in sync.

I moan as his tip brushes over my G-spot, arching into him again. He feels so good that it overpowers the pain, pushing it to the back of my mind. His thrusts become rhythmic before his hand curls under my ass. He pulls me forward, my sex flush against his hip.

I begin where he ends.

A sheen of sweat covers our bodies as Darian pummels me, grunting and panting. "Fuck, you feel so good. So fucking tight. I've never . . . never felt anything like it in my fucking life."

His words have me unraveling, my head pushing back into the mattress. He leans in to kiss my collarbone, biting and sucking but never letting up his blitz inside me. My body quivers as my senses heighten and his pace quickens.

I feel everything, from the delicious scrape of his scruff on my neck to his hefty erection stretching me exquisitely. From his fingers digging painfully into the back of my knee to the power of his drive inside me. My heart races like it's going to speed out of my body while his heart thumps just as fast against mine.

My breasts bounce as he continues and he observes their movement with barely held hunger. I can feel his control wearing thin. He leans in to capture my nipple in his mouth again, and I cry out at the slight change in the angle. "Yes!"

I can feel the pressure building in my core as my instincts take over. My body follows the call as all other thoughts fade, and I focus on the irresistible man above me. A drop of his sweat lands on my shoulder, immeasurable pleasure swirling in his eyes. He's close. So close.

"Let go, baby," he coaxes as his thumb presses on my clit, making me climb so high, I'm destined to do nothing but fall. "I've got you. I've always got you."

His words ignite something deep inside me, like embered coal, and I relax further into him. How can a man be both sweet and demanding? Gentle and merciless? I succumb to his claim on my body and he pummels me harder, hitting that sweet spot inside me over and over again until I let go.

Until I fall, knowing he'll be there to catch me.

My body constricts around him before I'm moaning my release, whimpering as my orgasm takes full control. "Oh God!"

Darian continues to plunge into me, coaxing out every tremor and every quake. "That's it, baby. I've got you," he murmurs as I lift to meet his hips.

God, his murmurs drive me insane—the way he whispers against my skin, the way his words tremble inside my ribs— and I know I'll never have enough.

I can barely catch my breath as he continues to undulate over me. He grabs my breast, his eyes wild and his hair wet, grunting as he comes to an abrupt stop inside me. Seconds later, I feel his release coat my womb, warm and endless. If I wasn't so exhausted and sore, I'd have come all over again, because watching Darian orgasm might be the single most erotic thing I've ever experienced.

His length is still twitching inside me as he pulls himself to hover over me again. I cradle his face with both hands, kissing him for so long, my lips swell against his.

"Thank you," he whispers.

My eyes widen. "I'm pretty sure you did all the work."

He shakes his head before pulling out and falling on the

bed next to me. We face each other, leaving less than a few inches between us. My head lays on his bicep while we breathe hard into each other. He lifts his hand to tuck my hair behind my ear. "Rani?"

I wait for him to continue but he's silent, studying me. "Hmm?"

"I'm . . .." I see his throat bob, but I don't miss his whisper—I'll never miss his whispers. "I'm falling for you."

I take in a shaky breath, my heart swooping over the clouds in the sky. "Darian?"

His eyes connect with mine, like electricity to water.

I whisper back, "I fell a long time ago."

He's quiet again, lost inside his head, as he absorbs my admission. His fingers play with my curls distractedly, like he's not even present.

I run my fingers over his scruff, bringing him back. "Talk to me. I'm right here."

His gaze bounces between mine. "Thank you for trusting me with your body, Rani. I mean that. But I feel like I took something that wasn't meant for me."

"You can't take something that was *always* meant for you, Darian."

He tugs me closer. "When I'm with you, I feel like I'm on vacation. Somewhere I never want to come back from." His frown deepens as his desire battles with his self-control. "Somewhere I want to stay forever."

I play with the curls on his nape. "I don't want to be a vacation you take, Darian. I want to be the home you always come back to."

Chapter Twenty-Eight
DARIAN

SHE STIRS INSIDE MY ARMS BEFORE HER EYES BLINK OPEN. Even in the dark, I can see the whites of her eyes.

She's been asleep for a little over two hours. I'd fallen asleep with her as we stared into each other's eyes, but my thoughts were all over the place. I knew what she'd asked of me. *I want to be the home you always come back to.* And I knew the answer. It wasn't even a question. But I couldn't just file away my concerns at the time, either.

Was I too old for her? Was she too young for me? What would my parents think? What would her mom do?

What would my dead wife think?

All my fears seemed to creep in inside the dark before I succumbed to a restless sleep, only to see the faces of my past in my dreams—of Jude and Sonia. I'd kayaked down the river to find not one, but both of their bodies lying near the rocks.

I woke with a start about twenty minutes ago, and the only thing that centered me was her—a woman I might have helped bring to shore when her kayak toppled over, but she's the woman who stopped me from going adrift.

It's a wonder what twenty minutes next to the one you're

falling in love with can do to clear up the confusion. To give you perspective.

It can make you selfish and greedy.

Resolute in your decision.

Because it was within those twenty minutes that I made mine. A decision that never really was one in the first place. A decision that's only fortified with every moment we've spent together.

A decision to choose her.

Over all the rights and wrongs. Over all the concerns about the past and the future. Over every other person I've allowed to keep her away from me, including my late wife. . . including myself.

I choose her because she isn't even a choice when she's a necessity. Like the air that fills my lungs, the water that quenches my thirst, and my shelter from the storm.

Her fingers trail over the side of my neck and she smiles. I can't see it, but I can feel it. Her voice is a raspy whisper, reminding me of the way she sings to my son. "I can hear you thinking, Mr. Meyer. Your thoughts are incredibly loud."

"They can't seem to stay silent when it comes to you."

We're whispering to each other, so softly, you'd think we were worried about someone listening in.

She nuzzles closer. She'd put her pajamas back on after cleaning up, but I'm hoping she has no intention of keeping them on. "And what are your thoughts saying?"

Things my heart has already conceded but my mouth isn't ready to speak.

I press a kiss on her forehead. "I'm wondering if you're sore."

She hums. "A little, but it's nothing I can't handle."

I tangle our fingers in front of us, bringing our hands to my mouth. "Not that I want to talk about any men in your past, but I'm a little curious . . .."

"Curious about why I was still a virgin until last night?"

I nod and I think she can feel the movement.

She's silent for a few moments. "There was this guy named Patrick I met through the school journalism club during eleventh grade. At first we were just friends, but we ended up hanging out as the year progressed and eventually, we dated but . . . not publicly. He wanted to keep things quiet about us."

A twinge of pain and guilt pinches me between my ribs. Isn't that what I'm doing?

"After a little over a year of messing around, he was insistent that we have sex." After a pause, she continues, "But something in my gut just didn't let me take that step. My best friend Melody, and my cousin Bella, were the only ones who knew about us and they hated that he wouldn't acknowledge me in front of other people, but I don't know . . .."

I squeeze her hand, urging her to continue.

She takes in a breath. "It wasn't easy for me to get attention from men, Darian. I didn't fit the perfect model-sized mold. I still don't, clearly, and I've had plenty of people remind me of that. There was an especially cruel girl named Ruby Mallory, who took every chance she could to call me shitty names." I feel her raise her chin. "I've eliminated a fair amount of negative people from my life since high school," she chuckles without any humor, "save for my mom."

I interject before she can move on. "Rani?"

"Yeah?" she whispers.

"You haven't just had my full attention since the day you showed up in my life; you've had me fucking bewitched."

I know she's pleased, though she doesn't acknowledge my words. "I guess I just wanted to feel special, to *be* with someone, even if it meant being his dirty little secret. So, I made peace with it, whether my friends approved or not." I see the whites of her eyes again as her breath fans my face. "I promised Patrick we'd have sex on prom night, and he booked a hotel room."

"So you went to prom with him?"

She huffs out another mirthless laugh. "Not technically, no. He told me he wasn't taking anyone, that he and his friends had decided to go stag. So I assumed we'd just find a chance to dance there, and then we'd meet each other at the hotel afterward."

"I'm not going to like the rest of this, am I?"

She clears her throat. "It was a strange evening . . .. We hadn't danced together, not once, and I noticed he was gone for a while, though his friends were still around. So, I went looking for him."

My chest aches with that foreboding feeling. I already know what she's going to tell me before she says it. This guy seems like the biggest asshole known to man and if I ever fucking have the misfortune of meeting him, I hope to show him what his face looks like with a few teeth knocked out.

"And I found him." Another pause, like she's reliving the moment. "In the ladies bathroom, with his dick inside Ruby Mallory."

I pull her to me, wrapping my arms around her. "I'm sorry."

She shakes her head under my chin. "Don't be. I'm not. Not anymore, at least. That, along with Sonia's death, were catalysts for my change in perspective."

I pull back from her, still running my hand through her curls. "How so with Sonia?"

She lifts her shoulder. "It taught me not to wait for tomorrow; that I need to find my happiness today."

I lean in to kiss her. "You asked me what I was thinking about earlier." I feel her nod. "It was along the same lines."

She waits for me to finish.

"I want to be all-in."

"What does that mean?"

I pull her bottom lip into my mouth again. It's so plump, I want to suck on it for hours. "I don't want to hide from this. I don't care to keep us hidden."

"What made you change your mind? My prowess in bed?" She giggles, making light of the question I know she's genuinely curious about.

"You, Rani. *You* changed everything."

Her hands find their way into my hair, tugging. "I don't want to hide things either, not from my friends and not from my parents."

Fuck, I'd forgotten about her mom. "Your mom is going to find a way to murder me in my sleep."

"That, she will. But let's not worry about her right now. She's for my future-self to deal with." She writhes against me, her hand trailing down my bare torso. She wraps her hand around my hardening shaft, stroking me until my breathing becomes ragged. "Let's worry about the fact that I'm up for round two."

I exhale slowly, trying not to think about how she got so good with her hands. It'll just reignite my desire to kill her ex. "You're sore."

"I am." She presses her thumb against the tip of my dick, rolling the precum around it. I grit out a, *fuuuck,* squeezing my eyes shut. The way she moves against me, the way she squeezes my erection, and her whispers against my mouth, I'm past ready to go. "But you know what they say? You can't reach your goals without working through the pain."

I groan. "And what's your goal?"

"You."

"You have me," I whisper.

"Good, then show me."

∽

My hand slides down her back as I line myself up between her open legs. I'm behind her with the most exquisite view of her ass pressed to my hip. The side of her head lays on the pillow below her, while her long curls rest at her side, exposing her neck. Her arms are laying above her head, her fingers intertwined so tightly, I worry she's losing blood circulation.

She's a vision.

My beautiful nymph who's made her home under my skin.

I slide my length to her front to gather her juices before trailing it all the way back to the crack of her ass. I slap it in between her ass, making her whimper. I know she's ready for me, impatient even. I slide my hand over her ass cheek before squeezing one in my hand. Goddamn, she's hot.

"Please, Darian."

She pulls a hand down, directing it toward her pleading core when I stop her, my voice firm. "Hands together over your head. If you want something, you tell me."

"I want you inside me. I want your fingers playing with me."

I do exactly what she asks. Pressing my wet and swollen head into her entrance, I push in deep and stretch her as wide as she can go. She whimpers and I watch my entire length disappear inside her. I'm completely encased.

We both moan before she wiggles, adjusting to my size. She's so fucking tight, I feel like I'm wearing her like a glove.

I place both hands on her hips before pulling out almost all the way. She makes an *ooh* sound before I slam back into her, making her mewl again. I do it again and again, making the mattress creak underneath us, until she's mumbling unintelligibly under her breath.

"Oh fuck, that feels so good, Darian. Oh God, yes."

I increase my pace, feeling her get wetter around me. Sliding my hand down her back, I wrap it around the nape of her neck, keeping her pressed against the pillow. My balls slap against the bottom of her mound and the sound drives my pulse higher. "I love this ass," I grit. "So fucking much."

"What else?" she whispers shakily.

I pummel into her, my arm wrapping around to her front before my fingers slide down her stomach to find her swollen clit. I move around it, sliding my two fingers into her folds. I won't let her come until she's chanting my name. "Your fucking easy smiles. Your raspy songs." I can feel her core tighten around me as she moans. "The way you smell, the damn Friday glitter on your lids," I slam into her again, "your fucking principles."

"Mmm, God, I love that you love my principles. It's so hot," she pants, her hands fisting the sheet above her. "Darian, I'm close."

"Tell me what you love."

"Besides coffee?"

I tweak her clit in punishment and she bucks against me, moaning, but I don't give her the satisfaction of a second time.

"I love your non-smiles, the way you keep your face expressionless, but the way I can still read it. I love the way your nostrils flare when you're angry or turned-on." She cries out as I give her an example of how turned-on I really am when I slam into her, feeling her deep inside. "The way you watch me."

"I can't stop watching you."

"Darian?"

I slow down, wondering if I'm going too hard on her. "What's wrong? Does it hurt?"

She shakes her head. "No, please. Please don't stop. I just," she breathes, "I just wanted to know if it feels good for you, too. I don't feel like I'm doing much here."

I fight a smile. "You're fucking heaven, Rani. I could come in an instant."

"Okay, good," she muses, softly. "Because this is something I could get addicted to."

My balls ache to pour into her, my abs dancing as I plunge inside. *She's already someone I'm addicted to.* "Is this better than coffee?"

"It's a close call."

At that, I press my thumb against her clit, laying over her to place my mouth on her shoulder. I increase my pace, rotating my hips when she convulses. I feel her pulsating around me as she milks my dick and moans out her release. Her hips push into me as her body takes over, giving in to the building need inside her. She comes so long, it elicits my own orgasm.

I groan, pumping inside her, seeing flashes of light behind my lids. "How about now?" I growl into her ear, panting. "Still think it's a fucking close call?"

I collapse before rolling off. She's heaving into the pillow, trying to catch her breath, her back glistening over my sheets and her arms splayed out over the pillow. I'm sure there are famous paintings of such beauty displayed in museums around the world.

"Definitely on par with an expensive whipped mocha."

Chapter Twenty-Nine
RANI

"You need to go," I mumble against Darian's mouth. "You're going to be late."

"You're right." He slides down to my neck, kissing it. "I need to go. You're making me late."

I giggle, attempting to push him off with my hands on his chest but fisting his shirt, instead. His hands splay over my ass as he presses his growing erection into me.

I hear the pitter-patter of Arman's feet get closer. He's making his way into the kitchen. "Darian."

Darian must hear him too because he grumbles, disconnecting from me, "Fine."

I've been in Tahoe for close to six weeks, and it's been a little more than a week since Darian and I made things 'official.' While we decided that we didn't mind letting our families know, the opportunity just hasn't really presented itself. I did tell Melody and Bella, however.

God, if anyone wants to know what it feels like to have their eardrum punctured from high-pitched squealing, they should have been there the day I revealed my relationship with Darian to my friends. I could barely understand them for a good five minutes because I don't think they even took a breath.

To say they were ecstatic would be like calling the Empire State Building a little hut. They were over the moon.

What was it like? How was he in bed? Did you love taking a ride on Poseidon's trident? Did he churn your waters? Oh, my God! We are so happy!

Arman comes into the kitchen, holding his toy airplane in the air. "*Mas!* Plane!"

He's been walking almost on his own and has even started running—well, more like speed-walking. It's been a little crazy to watch him make such progress, and so quickly. It's almost like something out of the *Matrix*—he goes to sleep and then wakes up with new skills and a newfound confidence.

I kneel down to him, splaying out my palm. "Ooh, let me see. Is that the new airplane Uncle Garrett got for you?"

Arman smiles at it, zooming it over my palm and grinning up at his dad.

"I think he's going to be a pilot like his uncle Garrett," I state, winking at Darian. He's finishing up his smoothie, watching my interaction with Arman.

"As long as he can be a pilot and manage *Truckee Sports*, I'm fine with that."

I whisper in Arman's ear, knowing Darian can hear me, "Your daddy has some big dreams for you, little man."

Darian rinses out his glass before he comes over and gives Arman a kiss. Over the past week, I've noticed he hasn't been as prompt about leaving for work. He'll stall as long as possible until I make him leave, usually pulling me into the garage to kiss me until I'm breathless before finally getting into his car.

We've been spending every night together in his room, where he'll spend the beginning of the night inside me and the early hours of the morning with his face between my legs.

He says I'm insatiable, but I'm pretty sure he hasn't looked at himself in the mirror.

Arman and I follow Darian to the garage door to say bye when Darian turns and pulls my face toward him. The rest of his face is still as impassive as ever, but his coffee-colored eyes always seem to do the talking. "Come visit me at work today."

"Are you sure you'll get any work done with us there?"

"No."

I giggle. "Okay, then. Well, maybe that's not such a good idea."

I look down at Arman. He's happily rolling his airplane on the ground, making *whooshing* sounds. I tiptoe up and lock my hands behind Darian's head. He's wearing his *Truckee Sports* cap, along with a navy blue shirt that stretches perfectly over his chest and shoulders, showing off all the hard lines and corners of his body deliciously.

I reach his lips, tangling them with mine and closing my eyes. His hands span the sides of my waist, holding me in a way that makes me feel secure and safe. He opens his mouth and I breach it with my tongue, weaving my fingers through the curls at the nape of his neck again. *Oh, how I love being able to do this whenever I want.*

He pulls me flush against him, sighing into my mouth, and I realize it's another one of my favorite things about him—especially when they're done during a lip-lock with me. I've started living for his contented sighs almost as much as I live for his non-smiles, intense stares, and sexy groans.

I pull my head back from him and he grunts in frustration, trying to tug me back. By the size of the bulge he's sporting, he has no intention of stopping, but it seems I'm the only one with a clear head. "Darian."

He palms my ass, staring into my eyes. "I want you."

"Later."

"Call my mom to keep Arman today for a couple of hours.

Have lunch with me at the office. I wanted to discuss more updates to the website."

I giggle, knowing he's bluffing. I walked him through most of the updates a couple of nights ago, and he thanked me for all my hard work by pulling me on top of him and giving me two orgasms. "Oh, do you? Okay, I'll see what Karine is up to."

He finally graces me with a smile before leaving a chaste kiss on my lips and one on the top of his son's head.

For the next hour, I play cars and planes with Arman before changing his diaper and taking him to the backyard. We point at the fish in the koi pond, giving them names, though we're not sure which name belongs to which fish. But Arman decides most of them will be called Poppy.

I text Karine as soon as we get back inside, asking her if she can come take care of Arman for a couple of hours during lunch. She replies that she's free until the evening today so it will be no problem.

Afterward, I change Arman's diaper again, wondering if I should be worried that he's dirtied it more than his usual number of times this morning. I'm not sure it's anything to be concerned about since he doesn't feel warm and is still pretty active, but I decide to text Darian, anyway.

Me: Hi.

Darian: I was just thinking about you.

Darian: Wait, what's wrong?

Me: Nothing, I don't think, but I wanted to run it past you. Arman's pooped three times this morning. It's definitely not very solid but other than that, he looks and feels fine. I checked and he doesn't have a temp, either.

Darian: He probably just ate something that was harder on his stomach. I don't think we need to worry.

Me: Okay.

Darian: Did you text my mom?

Me: Yes. I'll be there for lunch.

When I don't get a response from him after a minute, I type another message.

Me: Darian?

Darian: Yes?

Me: Are you non-smiling right now?

Darian: No.

Me: Rude. Well, in that case, I'm considering rescinding my decision to come.

Darian: Oh, you'll fucking come alright. On my desk and against every fucking surface in my office.

∼

I KNOCK before slipping into Darian's office, closing the door behind me before eyeing it curiously. "Did you get a new door? This looks different from last time."

He scoots his chair back, taking me in from head to toe as if he didn't just see me a few hours ago. "No, I just had them install an opaque glass insert as part of the renovations we're doing."

"Interesting." I bite my bottom lip, wondering if he's really planning what he said in his text. My body is already starting to tingle in anticipation. I lift up the bag of food I bought for us. I'd stopped at one of those healthy restaurants that serve cardboard for food. I've seen him eat stuff from there. "Hungry?"

He gets up and meets me against the adjacent wall. Taking my face in his hand, he tucks my curl behind my ear. "Maybe after I work up an appetite."

I look at him mischievously. "Yeah? I think I can help you with that."

Placing the food bag on the floor, I turn him so his back is against the wall. I'm sure no one can see inside with the bubbled glass, but my heart still bounces around in my chest from the thrill of knowing I'm about to do something more salacious than I've ever done before.

Darian focuses on my movements, but my hand on his chest lets me know his heart is beating just as fast. He watches me drop to my knees in front of him. "Rani."

"Shh." I look up at him as I pull on his belt buckle. "Please. I want to."

Over the past week and a half, Darian and I have had a lot of sex, and he's made it a point to tell me how much he loves to pleasure me, so I want to give a little back.

After unbuttoning his pants, I slide them down his thighs and lift his shirt. His thick, veiny erection bobs out, so hard and long, it's intimidating. I wrap my hand around it and

Darian hisses. His eyes turn hooded as his hips protrude further out. I can feel the tightness of his body as his abs flex between the V-shape of his torso. Jesus, the man is truly magnificent.

I lick my lips before flattening my tongue under his shaft, sampling him from base to tip. His smooth skin slides in my mouth like velvet, and I taste the precum on his tip from just the little I've done.

Darian grunts, his hand jutting out to catch behind my head. "Fuck."

Titling his erection a little toward me, I slide my lips down his shaft, putting him into my mouth as far as I can go. I feel his hand tighten over my head, his thighs flexing, as he tries to yield his control. Wetness collects inside my panties as my nipples pucker to the heightening of his breathing. I suck on him, feeling the weight of him on my tongue. He's so large, my entire mouth stretches over his girth. I continue to use my hand, rubbing my spit all around him with my hand, my head still bobbing over him.

Darian groans again when I pull up almost to his throbbing head before going back down and swirling him around in my mouth. "Jesus, Rani."

I suck and lap at him, with both my hands wrapped around him, before my own need has me sliding my hand into my shorts. I rub my clit, moaning, before pressing my two fingers into my heat.

Darian's eyes fly between my mouth and my other hand. "Fuck, yes. You gonna come on your fingers to the taste of me, baby?"

I nod, pulling him further into my mouth and I almost gag around him. My fingers reach my G-spot, and I hum around his length. I'm so close, my thighs quiver from need. My rhythm feels off as I try to please him while I pleasure myself, but fuck, I want both!

Darian seems to understand my silent request, guiding my head so he's pumping into my mouth, hitting the back of my throat. "I'm going to come, Rani."

I moan in approval, circling my G-spot, before erupting on my fingers. My moans get louder as Darian pumps faster into my wet mouth. Within seconds, he growls and I taste the hot streams of his release on my tongue.

We're both breathing so hard we can barely speak as he lifts me by my hand to meet him at his place against the wall. I wouldn't be surprised if there was a Darian-shaped inclusion on it now.

"Oh God. Christ." Darian pulls me against him by my waist. "Where the fuck did you learn how to do *that*?" I start to speak and his jaw clenches. "Don't answer that."

I smile against a kiss to his mouth, still trying to catch my breath. "How's that appetite of yours now? Hungrier?"

"Starving."

∽

I STIR awake with the sound of my nephew's voice on the monitor, and then I look over at Darian. His bare arm is loosely around my waist as he breathes softly into my neck. It's rare to see him sleeping so peacefully between the stress and nightmares that always seem to keep him up.

Glancing at the clock, I see that it's a little past four. Arman whines again, and my gut says something is wrong. He's not crying—he's not even that loud—but whatever it is, I need to be with him.

I slip out of the bed, trying not to stir Darian awake before walking over to the monitor to turn it off. I don't want to wake Darian up unless I need him.

Turning the knob, I enter Arman's room. He's sitting up

in his crib but doesn't stand like he usually does to greet me, even in the middle of the night.

"Oh, baby boy, what's wrong?" I whisper, traipsing over to him. I pick him up, already knowing he needs a diaper change, but it's his heated skin that has me jerking back to look at him. He's flushed, and I'm sure he has a high temperature.

He wraps his arms around me loosely as I take him to his diaper changing station. After cleaning him up, I put a thermometer in his ear. *One-hundred-two point six.*

"Oh, sweetheart. You're burning up." I hand him his sippy-cup of water, which he takes a few listless sips of before letting it drop to his changing mat.

I debate waking Darian up to tell him, but we've talked about what I need to do if Arman is ever sick, and I'm confident he'd do the same thing—give Arman meds and a cold compress. Plus, I've read enough to know that if the fever isn't too high, it needs to be reduced by meds before alerting his doctor.

After taking off Arman's shirt and leaving him in only his diaper, I pull him into my arms and carry him to his bathroom. I set him down on the counter before finding the fever reducing medicine. After giving him his dosage through the syringe in his medicine cabinet, I wet and wring out a towel.

Pulling him into my arms on his chair, I lay him over my lap and elbow and place the wet towel on his head. Arman whines, trying to take it off of him, but he settles down when I sing him his favorite song.

About twenty minutes later, he's asleep, his eyes twitching as he breathes deep. My tired eyes trail over his sweet face and the nose he shares with my sister and me. He's so perfect, my lids pool thinking about him . . . us.

Everything.

There's a quote by Buddha hanging in my mom's closet

that says, *The root of suffering is attachment.* It intensifies in my vision as my thoughts carry me from one place to another.

How will I be able to live without seeing this little boy after I move? Will he miss me? How often will I be able to see him? How often will I be able to see his dad?

Will everything change?

Can we even make this work once I'm not physically here?

My heart aches as I think about the eventuality that both Darian and I have avoided talking about. Sometimes I think we're too new in our relationship to talk about the what-ifs, but I can't help assess the depth of my feelings, either. Never in my entire life have I felt so completely in love, so *attached*, to anyone as I do to these two men in my life. They've become ingrained in all my thoughts and the reason for all my smiles.

Will they also be the reason for my heart break?

The sun peeks through the blinds in Arman's room as the birds wake up outside. I haven't slept a wink, deliberating the realities I know I'm going to face soon enough.

Arman takes a deep breath, settling further into my arms, and I press the back of my hand over his forehead. Given how sweaty he is, I'm not surprised that his fever seems to have broken. I pull him closer, hugging him to me.

"Rani?" Darian's whispered concern pulls me to his form lingering in the doorway, and I give him a soft smile. He regards his son in my embrace before his expression softens. "What's wrong? Why are you in here?"

A little uncertainty pierces my mind. What if he gets upset that I didn't wake him up? Arman is *his* son, after all. "Arman had a fever last night, so I gave him some meds and a cold compress. I didn't want to leave him alone, so I decided to rock him back to sleep." My anxiety builds and I keep babbling. "You said you have a vendor meeting this morning so I decided I'd let you sleep. I hope you're not upset. I would have woken you up if I didn't think I could handle it."

Darian's soft steps close the gap between us. He lifts a sleeping Arman into his arms before gently putting him in his crib. He presses the back of his hand over Arman's head, likely noticing what I did—that his fever has broken.

Weaving our fingers together, he pulls me out into the hallway before closing Arman's bedroom door. He drags me to his room before closing the door behind us. He considers me intently, as if he's trying to figure out what to say, and the fact that he *hasn't* spoken so far does nothing to ease my growing uncertainty.

What if he thinks I'm unfit to take care of Arman? What if he thinks I made the wrong call by administering the meds on my own?

"Darian—"

But before I can finish, Darian's mouth slams into mine. His tongue sweeps over my lips and I'm momentarily so struck that I don't even respond. I regain my senses quickly, opening my mouth, allowing our tongues to commence in a delicious battle. He grasps my face in his hands, as if he's afraid I'll slip away if he doesn't hold on.

He pulls his lips from mine. "Whenever I think you couldn't surprise me more, you go and do just that."

I search his gaze. "You're not mad? I'm sorry if I should have woken you up."

"No, baby, I'm not mad. I'm . . . I'm bewildered. I'm amazed, but I'm not mad. You're something else, Rani."

I smile, trying to gather my thoughts. I'm feeling like they're all swimming inside my head and I can't capture anything. "Darian . . . I want this to work. I want *us* to work."

He focuses on me, not quite understanding where my words are coming from. "I want us to work too, baby."

The corners of my eyes prick. I don't know if it's because of the moment between us or the lack of sleep or even the fact that there are words I'm physically holding myself back from saying to him about how I feel. For some reason, this moment–out of all the moments–feels monumental, but my mind still feels like it's spinning.

How are we going to make this work? Does he really mean it when he says he wants this? What does that mean to him? What does he expect will happen in a few weeks when I'm no longer here? How will we continue to see each other with everything we have going on in our lives?

If someone were to ask me why I chose this moment to bare my soul, to show him exactly what runs through my blood, I wouldn't be able to answer them. I don't really know myself. But it's as if the moments spent holding my nephew today, along with the countless moments I've shared with the man in front of me, have me feeling like I'm suffocating. Like I need to lift the weight off my chest to be able to breathe again.

Because I can't fucking breathe.

Darian studies my face and his frown deepens. "Talk to me. What's wrong?"

"Nothing. I just . . .." I inhale fast, as if I won't be able to again if I don't take a breath now. "I'm in love with you, Darian, and I'm just overwhelmed by it."

Shit.

My chest heaves as I watch my words strike him. It heaves again as they bounce off him and back to me. His eyes widen as the shock of what I've said registers on his face.

I'm about to tell him to forget it, that it was a slip based on my lack of sleep and my strange emotional state, when his entire face morphs with the biggest smile I've ever seen. And even though I want to hide my face behind my hands because my cheeks are on fire, I can't look away.

"You love me?"

My phone buzzes on my nightstand and I ignore it. I lift

my hand to Darian's mouth, shaking my head, holding myself back from smiling. "Shut up."

Darian removes my hand from his mouth and laughs. "You love me. Rani–"

My phone buzzes again and Darian growls under his breath.

What perfect timing.

And also, holy shit! I just told Darian I loved him!

How are my legs not giving way under me?

I turn toward the nightstand, and Darian reluctantly lets my hand go. "I should get it. I don't get calls this early . . .. It might be important."

He comes up behind me as we read the name on my screen together: Mom.

"Hello?" I pick up, wondering why she would call me this early in the morning.

"Your dad had a heart attack this morning. I'm in the emergency room." I hear her sniffle and my heart falls to my stomach. "It doesn't look good, Rani."

Chapter Thirty
RANI

I try to focus on the circular blue shapes on the beige carpet. They're linked together in a psychedelic design, and if I squint, it looks like the circles are jumping off the floor.

I've been rubbing my bottom lip almost incessantly with my thumb since the moment I sat down in this waiting room chair next to my mom. I'm positive I've scratched it with my nail, but I can't stop, even when my skin screams in pain.

"I always cook healthy food; I avoid using too much oil and salt. How could this have happened?" My mom rubs the bottom of her eyes with the heel of her palm as a sob bubbles out of her. "Why do we keep getting punished? What did I do in my last life to deserve so much pain in this one?"

I sigh, closing my eyes momentarily to gather my thoughts and patience. Because if I've ever been tested thoroughly with anything in my life, it's having patience with my mom. She's repeated the same thing at least fifteen times in the past half hour that I've been here.

I didn't even think this morning. I just threw some clothes and toiletries into my overnight bag and rushed to my car after I got Mom's phone call. She said they were just getting my dad prepped for his emergency angioplasty. Apparently, two of his major arteries were almost eighty percent blocked. The procedure usually doesn't take more than a couple of hours, but the nurse said with the extent of his blockages, it could take a little longer.

Still, I'm hopeful.

Dad's interventional cardiologist said he was extremely lucky. It was a severe heart attack—and thankfully, he was able to wake Mom in time—but his blockages could be alleviated with stents. He's going to have to change his lifestyle and it will take him a week or two to recover, but at least my dad is alive. At least he will have another lease on life.

"He's going to be alright, Mom. The doctor said they have a solid plan in place, and while this is an emergency angioplasty, at least it's not open-heart surgery. Look at the silver lining here."

She swivels her head so hard, I'm surprised it doesn't roll off her neck. "Silver lining? You want me to look at the *silver lining* when my husband is fighting for his life? You want me to look at the *silver lining* when I've lost more than anyone should in a lifetime?"

I watch two other people in the waiting room, who had been speaking softly until now, shift on their seats. *Yeah, welcome to the show, folks. She's just winding up.*

"That's not what I meant," I hedge, trying to calm my mother down. It's no use repeating history and telling her that she 'lost' Sonia a decade ago and that she had that same decade to make amends with her—they both did. It's no use telling her that she's not the only one who lost; we all did.

"And what do you even care about silver linings? Huh? All you've cared about for the past month and a half is yourself—selfishly frolicking off to Tahoe to 'take care of Arman.'" She puts air quotes around the last words, as if insinuating I had any other reason to go to Tahoe, and it pisses me off.

I sharpen my gaze on her, having had enough of her derision. "What does that mean? I *have* been taking care of Arman. And I've been doing a damn good job of it!"

She huffs out a high-pitched laugh. "You've also been doing a damn good job of having an affair with your brother-in-law."

The two people in the seats near us get up and leave the waiting room, probably cringing at even having heard a part of our conversation.

I can't decide whether I should laugh or cry. We're sitting here, on a day when we should be reflecting on the fact that everything could have been worse—a lot worse—but instead, all my mother can seem to do is find a way to goad me into a fight.

I'm done.

I'm done mincing my words, done thinking about her feelings and respecting her views.

Just done.

"Alright, Mom. You want to do this here? Then let's do it." My lips tremble the way they always do when my temper starts rising. I can tell I'm seconds from losing control, and I need to rein it in. It doesn't happen often, but my mother has a way of bringing it out. "First, it's not called an *affair* when the wife is deceased—"

My mom gasps.

"Second, I didn't frolic off to take care of Arman. Unlike you, I *stepped up* to the plate. I've always stepped up, whether it was to take care of myself when you and Dad barely remembered you still had a pre-teen daughter to take care of when Sonia left the house or when I needed to take care of my nephew because you know what? That's what I do. I move forward. I keep going, and I try to help others keep going.

And, yes, I look at the silver linings. So don't talk to me about being selfish, because that is the one thing I can unequivocally say I'm not, and the one thing I can decisively say *you* are."

She tries to speak but I bulldoze over her. "From the way you treated Sonia—constantly trying to mold her into someone she wasn't—to the way you shut down Dad's every attempt to speak, treating him like an invalid rather than a person, to the times you've made fun of my weight, my outfits, my hair! You've compared me to Sonia or Bella or basically anyone else, just to make me feel awful about myself when I've done nothing to you but be born as your daughter."

My mother's mouth quivers as my words pierce her heart, but I'm well past the point of caring. I'm well past the point of tiptoeing around her feelings. It's my damn turn to speak and it's about damn time I did.

"You think it's been easy for Dad, having been caught in the middle of you and Sonia? Having lost his daughter because both your egos were too big to fit in one room together? Do you think it's been easy for me to grow up without the sister I used to have? Do you know how many times I've wondered if you lost the wrong daughter, because of the poisonous words you've hurled at me? It's sad how many times I've wondered if it would have been better if I was the one who died instead of her. Wondered whether you would have been happier."

"Rani!" my mother sobs, placing her hands over her mouth. Tears—streams of sincere and painful tears—rush down her face as her sob turns into a heave. "Please."

But I continue, unperturbed, taking in a shaky breath as my eyes pool. "Do you have any idea how hard I've worked to not let your words sink deep into my soul? Do you know how tiring it has been to not let all those people who have hurt me chip away at my core? Time and time again, your words have cut me open, and time and time again, I've stitched up my wounds. Do you have any idea how many scars you've left?"

I clutch the sob waiting inside my chest. "So, no. You don't get to tell me I'm selfish or fat or any of the awful things you think you should say because it's your fucked-up version of reverse psychology and you think it'll somehow mold me into the version of me you want. Because I won't let you." My mother cries, sobbing into her hand as I wipe the tears streaming down my face. "And I say this with only love for you, but also with love for myself . . .. If you can't mold yourself into being a better mother to me, then you'll lose me, too. Because I'm done, Mom."

My mother cries without holding back as I sob into my hand.

When we've both managed to regain a tiny bit of composure, she tries to speak again. "I might have done all those things you've mentioned . . .." She looks at my face and takes back her words. "I know I've hurt you, and it's clear to me how much I didn't consider from your perspective. But Rani, I have *never*, in my entire life, wished for you to have died in place of Sonia. I wouldn't wish the loss of even one child on my greatest enemy. But I see now maybe I haven't been very fair to you."

I glance at her, my body still reeling from the monumental unpacking and discarding of pain it had been holding on to. "No, you haven't."

Her frown etches into her face while her lips tremble and she looks down at the armrest between us. "I'm sorry, Rani. I'm truly sorry."

I don't respond, wiping my nose with the back of my hand, and my mother wordlessly takes out a few tissues from her purse. She hands me one as we both sit, silently absorbing all that's been said between us.

I sniffle, turning to her and dropping another bomb that

I'm ready to explode between us, because if it's not now, then it's never . "I'm in love with Darian."

Mom's eyes shut for a moment before she puts a crushed tissue to her mouth, staring straight ahead. "I knew this was coming."

"I'm sorry if you disagree, Mom. But if you knew him, if you ever *cared* to get to know him, you'd understand why." I pause. "Sonia didn't make a mistake when she chose to follow her heart for him. He's hard-working, sincere, and so incredibly devoted, and I know exactly why she fell for him." I lick my chapped lips. "It's the same reason I've fallen for him, and I'll never regret following my heart."

My mother finally turns to me, nodding. I see a reluctant surrender in her eyes, but it's the most I can hope for given the circumstances. She's trying—whether she wants to or not, at least she's trying. "I don't want to lose you. I don't want to lose another daughter." Her eyes swim inside tears again. "I almost lost my husband, too. I . . . I don't want to be alone."

My heart feels heavy in my chest. "Then don't be." I grab her hand. "I don't want you to be alone, but we can't live like this, either."

She squeezes mine back, and I realize it's been ages—years, at least—since I've felt her hand in mine. She takes a deep breath, seemingly coming to a decision, though her lips still quiver. "Then we won't."

I smile, seeing the transformation happening before me. I'm young but not naive. I know these things don't happen overnight, but if this unfortunate event—my dad's heart attack—had to be the catalyst for change, then I'm going to grab on to it and hope to hell that it'll carve a road to a happier future for all of us.

"Will you forgive me, Rani? I've said things that have hurt you and I'm . . ." her chin trembles, "I'm ashamed."

My eyes dart between hers. "Will you give Darian a chance?"

She raises her chin almost defiantly before her shoulders slump. "Yes. I'm not thrilled about the idea of my nineteen-year-old daughter in love with her much older brother-in-law, but I won't lose her over it, either."

I pull my mother into my arms and she squeezes me like I'm her life raft. "Then yes, Mom. Let's start over."

∼

THE SOUNDS of machines beeping intermingle with my dad's heavy breathing. He looks at peace, though his skin is still pale and there are deeper dark circles around his eyes than I recalled from a month ago.

Mom, Bella, and I sit on either side of his hospital bed, lost in our own thoughts. My aunt had briefly dropped by to check on us and Dad during her shift, but when Mom forced her to go back to her patients, my aunt promised to come visit tonight when she got off work. Bella's been at my side since the moment she arrived a little while ago.

The doctors told us the angioplasty was a success, but Dad will be in the hospital for another day so they can monitor him.

My phone vibrates with another text inside my purse. It's been buzzing non-stop with messages from Melody, Karine, and Darian, whom I've kept abreast of the situation. Letting my dad's hand go, I pull it out.

Darian: I miss you. Badly. I wish your dad a speedy recovery, but I couldn't help not sending you this message to tell you how much I miss you.

My lips quirk as I read his message a couple of times. Everything happened so fast this morning—from my admission of my feelings for him to my mom's phone call—and we haven't had a chance to talk.

I thought a lot about my admission to him on my drive here—second-guessing my unplanned decision. Should I have revealed what I feel so early? Will this change things between us? He never said it back, and though that doesn't change how I feel for him, can I assume that his smile meant he was genuinely happy about it? Because I'd never seen him smile like that before.

Another thing to add to my list of things I'm in love with—Darian's smiles.

Dad stirs on his bed, and all three of us sit up straight to watch him. The doctors said he'd wake up on his own, so we've been waiting, ready to talk to him again.

"Ramesh?" my mom says, getting up with his hand in hers. She stares down at him as his eyes start to flutter open. My dad squints at her and for the first time, I see my mother run her hand over his forehead in affection. "Hi."

My dad manages a tiny but exhausted smile before finding me and then Bella. We both get up, looking at him with smiles.

"Hi, Dad." I squeeze his hand. "You gave us a scare there."

He smiles again. "I'm sorry."

I shake my head. "You have nothing to be sorry about." My throat is tight, but I give him a smile back. "It looks like you'll be off all the good stuff, like barbecue chicken wings and *samosas*. You can't take on any more stress, either."

Bella puts her hand on top of mine and his, giving it a squeeze. "How are you feeling, Uncle Ramesh?"

"A little stiff, but the pain medication seems to be working." He takes a breath and I can tell he's struggling to talk much. "How long have I been here?"

"Almost five hours," I answer. "I got here not too long ago."

He studies me wearily. "How's my grandson?"

I smile, recalling the message Darian sent me earlier this morning telling me Arman was feeling much better. "He's good. He's so incredibly sweet and smart."

"I want to see him." Dad looks at my mom almost in approval. His expression tells me he's worried about her reaction, but then it changes to confusion when she smiles at him.

"Why don't you get healthy first, then we can figure out a time for us to see him in person," my mom supplies.

My dad's frown deepens. I'm sure he's thinking he's woken up in a parallel universe where his wife is kind and freely gives him smiles and affection.

I decide to clarify to minimize his confusion. The man just woke up from surgery, and the last thing he needs is something else to be stressed about. "Dad, Mom and I had a long chat while you were in surgery." I regard my mom across my dad's bed. "I think we're both ready to move forward together and leave some of our past hurts behind."

Dad seems to process what I've said for a few long seconds before I visibly see him relax. He nods, slowly. "I'm glad to hear that."

I swallow, looking at Mom and then back at my dad. "And Dad . . .." I glance at Bella and she smiles back at me, likely knowing what I'm about to say. I suppose when someone has known you for so long, they start to read your mind even before your thoughts have fully formed. "I'm with Darian now."

My dad's brows lift. "With him?"

I nod. "Yeah. I'm in love with him. I want to be with him."

My dad regards my mom, but when he sees that she does

nothing but stare back at him with her version of a small smile, he turns back to me. He seems to think about how he's going to respond. "Some say love is blind, but I say our heart always has a way of finding the one it was made for." His mouth tightens, and I can see he's holding back his emotions. "I'm proud of you, Rani. I'm proud of the woman you've become."

My nose tingles as tears linger inside my lids. "Thank you, Dad," I whisper, leaning in to give him a kiss on his temple.

∽

THE DOORBELL RINGS, and I leave the cucumber I was slicing on the chopping board. "I'll go see who it is."

"Okay." My mom stirs some seasoning into the soup she's making.

Dad was discharged from the hospital this afternoon, and since then, there have been a few deliveries for him of flowers and care baskets. I've been taking all of them to the guest room downstairs where he's been resting.

I tuck my hair behind my ear and open the door, seeing a man holding a huge bouquet of burgundy lilies and blush-colored roses.

"Delivery for a Rani Shah?" The man peeks at me from behind the massive vase in his arms.

I press my lips together, fighting my urge to squeal like a little kid. It's Friday, and there's only one man who remembers to give me flowers on Fridays—even if I'm three-hours away. "That's me."

The delivery man hands me the flowers and I close the door, trying to make my way up the stairs to read the note sticking out above the bouquet.

"Rani? Who was it?" My mom comes out of the kitchen,

examining the flowers in my arms. "Oh, wow, those are beautiful. Who sent those for Dad?"

I clear my throat. "They're not for Dad . . . they're for me."

She stares at me for a moment before she turns back to the kitchen. I could swear I saw a smile on her face. "Well, go on then. I know you'll want to call him."

I dash up to my room as fast as I can, holding the behemoth of all vases and praying I don't drop it. I set the vase on my nightstand and my room immediately fills with the delicious scent from the fragrant lilies. I pull out the card from its perch inside the bouquet, my lips already turning up, not even having read what it says.

But I'm pretty sure they'll be set in a permanent smile after this.

These flowers have become the couriers of my most important messages.
I love you, too, my Rani. So fucking much.
-Dar

Chapter Thirty-One

DARIAN

Garrett: Good morning, shitheads. Poker night tonight?

Me: Can't.

Garrett: Why the fuck not? You waxing your pubes or some shit?

Dean: His sister-nanny is coming back today. He's getting all dolled-up for her.

SUCH ASSHOLES. I ROLL MY EYES, REFUSING TO RESPOND. So what if I am a little preoccupied with the fact that my girl comes back to me tonight? Three days without her has felt like a fucking era.

We've only been able to chat here and there over the past couple of nights, and I'm fucking dying to kiss her, hold her, and have her come on my lips.

She called me Friday night to thank me for the flowers and the note, and just hearing the smile in her voice had me rock-solid inside my pants. Then, at the end of the conversation, I heard her breathe out a soft *bye*. I could tell she was feeling unsure about how to end the conversation, and I wanted to eliminate her doubts as fast as I possibly could, so I said the words to set her at ease—words I never thought were possible for me to say or feel again. *"I love you, my Rani."*

My phone buzzes again, and I realize I've been lost in thought for the past five minutes.

Garrett: Wait, why isn't he denying it? Holy shit! Is there something going on with you and Rani, @Darian?

Dean: Dude, were you not present during dinner at Dad and Karine's house where these two looked like they couldn't decide if they wanted to kill or fuck each other?

Dean: Btw, @Darian, I'm assuming by the fact that both of you are still alive, you chose the latter.

Garrett: Mind blown. <brain exploding emoji> I must have been on another planet.

Dean: Or back on your last flight, initiating another flight attendant into the mile-high club.

Garrett: It's quite possible. But seriously, @Darian, congratu-fucking-lations! Rani is a total sweetheart and hella-cute. Do Karine and Dad know?

Me: Thanks. Not yet. I plan to talk to Mom today, so keep your piehole shut. Now can you guys stop blowing up my phone so I can get work done?

Dean: Yeah, congratulations, bro. I mean, you could have fathered her but hey, we don't need to bring that up.

I don't respond because it's exactly what my asshole brother wants me to do.

Dean: What? Did that one cross the line?

Garrett: Shit. You probably made him cry, bro. Remember the time when he was eight, and he cried because we tickled him too much?

Dean: God, he was such a pussy. So glad he grew out of that.

I turn off my screen and flip my phone over. They'll continue going back and forth like this for the next hour, but some of us have shit to do and beautiful nymphs to pleasure.

A half hour later, I'm scrolling back and forth, comparing some statements and setting some financial targets for the next month when Olivia knocks on my open door. It's been a little tense between us over the past two weeks—ever since I found out she was rude to Rani and told her to cut it the fuck out.

At first, she denied saying anything, but then she straightened her shoulders, as if she was taking the high road, and left my office. Since then, we've kept things professional and ice-cold.

"Come in." I close my laptop.

Olivia twists her hands, walking toward my desk. "Hey. Actually, I wanted to clear the air between us."

I sit back in my chair. "Olivia, you and Greg are like family to me. Honestly, I couldn't run this place without you, but I feel like the whole thing with your sister–"

Olivia juts out her hands, silently telling me to not say anything more. "I actually had a longer conversation with Violet, and she's extremely embarrassed about her behavior at Greg's party. She said she sent you a text message saying so."

"She did." I just never responded.

Olivia sighs. "After speaking more to her, it was clear to me that she's not in the right headspace to have a man in her life right now. I don't know if she told you, but she went through a pretty nasty divorce a few years ago after she caught her husband cheating on her. She's never been the same since."

"I wasn't aware of that, but I can only imagine how that kind of betrayal could mess with a person's head."

We stare at each other for a minute before she speaks again. "Anyway, I'm about to head home. Felix and Greg will be here. I just wanted to apologize for being rude to your sister-in-law. I felt a little threatened on behalf of Violet, even though I had no right and you and my sister have nothing going on. I've just always thought you were an amazing guy, and I wanted someone like you for Violet."

"I appreciate your words, Olivia, but I'm not interested in Violet."

She winces. "I hear you loud and clear, and I think Violet did, too." She turns around to leave but seems to hesitate at the door. She's always been on the wordier side. Turning over her shoulder, she looks at me again. "I really did mean what I said about you, Darian. Any woman would be lucky to have you. And, not that it's any of my business, but if that lucky woman is your sister-in-law, then I'm happy for the both of you."

I stop her before she walks out the door. "Hey, Olivia?"

"Yeah?"

"How did you know?"

Olivia chuckles, raising her glasses on her nose. "I actually saw it the day you brought her back from the river after her kayak toppled over. The way you buzzed around, trying to find an ice pack and the first-aid kit, the way you looked at her when she left with her friends. There was a sense of longing on your face that I hadn't seen in a long time." She winks at me. "There's a lot one can observe from their view behind the reception desk."

∼

"DADDY!" Arman comes wobbling on his little legs as fast as he can toward me when I step inside from the garage. He has his arms stretched out and a smile that's a mile wide, singularly focused on me.

I lift him up before he can barrel into me. "My man. How are you?" I kiss him on his cheek, pushing my fingers through his hair to tame it as best as I can. "You need a haircut."

"He does. And he has a checkup with his pediatrician tomorrow." My mom walks toward me, reaching up to give me a kiss on my cheek.

I tilt my head in confusion. "How did you know about his appointment?"

She laughs. "Rani. She messaged me yesterday to tell me that if she couldn't come back by Monday, I would need to take him to his doctor's visit."

As if it wasn't already twice its size, my heart swells, threatening to bust out of my ribs as I think about my girl messaging my mom, concerned about my son, even though she had more than enough on her plate. Who the fuck is she and what the fuck did I do to deserve her?

I put Arman down and he zooms off in a hurry to do something in the living room. "Hey Ma . . .."

"Uh-oh." My mom eyes me suspiciously.

I raise a brow. "What?"

"Darian *jan*, you have not called me *Ma* in a very long time."

"So?"

She laughs, wrapping her arms around her chest. "So, a mother knows her son's tells. You call me Ma either when you need something or you're about to tell me something you don't think I'll approve of."

Clearly, the women in my life have me all figured out.

I take off my cap and hang it on the hook inside the mudroom, walking past my mother to the living room. Rani is supposed to be here in the next fifteen minutes, so I'd better hurry up with my confession, admission, or whatever I'm about to do.

I'm a thirty-two-year-old, grown-ass man. I don't have to tell my mother any of this, nor can she do much about it since I already have my heart set. But my mother has been in my corner, having given me nothing but her support and love. I've seen what it's like for those like Sonia and Rani, who don't have the kind of advocate I do, and I don't take that lightly, which is why I owe her this consideration out of sheer respect.

Though there is no rush to tell Mom any of this today, after the text conversation with my brothers and the one with Olivia, I'd feel guilty if Mom found out through someone other than me.

I take a seat on the couch, putting my elbows on my knees. It's not that I'm worried my mom won't like Rani—I already know she does—but my mother is still more traditional and conservative than I am. It's hard for me to guess how she'll react to the fact that I want to be with my late wife's nineteen-year-old sister.

"Ma, Rani and I are together."

My mom gives me a blank stare, like she's not sure what I've just said. "Together . . . ?"

"We're dating." I've yet to take her on an official date, but that's neither here nor there. This was meant to be a 'for all intents and purposes' sort of conversation.

Mom breathes out a small, "Ah," before finding a seat next to me. Arman brings us each one of his toy cars before swapping the ones in our hands with two others he deems more appropriate. Mom uses the distraction to think, I presume.

"I'm not surprised. She's a beautiful girl and so very sweet." She regards me with a mixture of both hope and concern. "Though, she's young. Very young."

Here it comes . . . . I brace myself to hear Mom's disapproval.

"I assume you've already gotten past the fact that she's your sister-in-law."

It's not a question, but I answer it as such. "It wasn't easy, but yes, I have. But, Ma, Rani is so much *more* than her title or her age. When I'm with her, I forget how hard the past year has been. I forget that I'd made a resolution to never be with someone again.

"She makes me laugh. God, she makes me laugh like no one ever has. But even more than that, she holds me accountable, doesn't take my crap, and pushes me right back if I'm irritating her." I huff out a laugh. "I can't stop looking at her. Seriously, I feel like a creep sometimes around her because I just can't take my eyes off her. I want to know what she's thinking. I want to see how her mouth purses and her nose scrunches when she reacts to something I've said."

My mom smiles at me knowingly. "You're in love with her."

I don't respond, and she doesn't need me to because it's written all over my face. "The walls in this house resonate with her raspy songs. I swear, I heard her echoes in every room this weekend." I watch my son, happily playing with his cars. "Ever since she came into mine and Arman's life, it's like she brought in the goddamn sun."

I run a hand through my hair, finding my mom's soft gaze pinned to me. "I know she's young, Ma. I get that. But she's a hell of a lot more mature than I was at her age. There's nothing I can do about her being the age she is or the fact that she was related to Sonia. All I know is that I'm crazy about her."

Mom bobs her head, still smiling. "And she's crazy about you."

I shrug. "I hope so. I think so."

Mom rubs my back. "I know so, Darian *jan*."

"You do?"

She nods, chuckling again. "I wouldn't be surprised to find out that you two were the last ones to know you were crazy about each other. I think everyone around you has already suspected it."

I hear a car door slam shut outside and watch my son freeze on his spot in the living room. He examines me, questioningly.

"It's *Masee*," I confirm and he lets out a squeal, rushing to the window to see if he can find his aunt. He's missed her presence all weekend.

"*Mas*!" His sweet little baby voice squeezes my lungs. He spots her in the window and waves. "*Mas*! Hi *Mas*!"

Both Mom and I get up when we hear Rani's key in the lock. The door opens and I set my eyes on the woman I've been thinking about incessantly for the past three days. *Has it really only been three days?*

She looks at my mom before hitting me with a beaming smile, practically knocking me off my feet. "Hi!"

Arman gets to her before either me or my mom, and she kneels to shower him with hugs and kisses, making him laugh and squeal. "I missed you, my little monster."

"How's your dad, Rani?" my mom asks, getting Rani's attention.

"Recovering." She sighs. "It'll be another week until he's moving around more, but he was in good spirits earlier this afternoon when I left."

"Good." My mom closes the distance between her and Rani before grasping her face between both hands and bringing it down to kiss her forehead. "You're a treasure, my sweet girl, a rare gem. And whoever has you," she looks back at me pointedly, "should know you're not just precious, you're priceless."

Mom pats Rani's cheek—with a confused Rani staring back at her—before picking up her purse from the table near the front door. "I'll leave you two to it." She turns as if remembering something. "I managed to make dinner for the two of you when Arman was napping. It's sitting in the fridge."

"Thanks, Ma."

Mom laughs, opening the front door. "You can go back to calling me *Mom*, Darian. You already have my approval."

Chapter Thirty-Two
DARIAN

Her arms are wrapped around my neck and she's gazing into my eyes. Or am I the one gazing into hers?

"Do you want to put Arman down for bed tonight? I know he missed you." I trail the tip of my nose against the side of her neck as I mumble into her skin.

She shivers inside my arms. "I can do that. Though, I'm surprised you're letting me, considering the evening routine with him is at the top of the list of things you love."

I place soft kisses over her neck, feeling her writhe against me. I don't have to see it to know she's getting worked up. "That list has grown since you came into my life. Now I'm up to two."

I can hear the smile in her voice. "Mmm. I think something else is growing, too."

I press my erection against her. "Yeah? What should we do about that?"

She pinches my side, making me bite her neck. She's positively squealing inside my arms. "Nothing, because we have a baby to put to bed."

We have a baby . . ..

My mind locks on to that little part of her sentence. *We have a baby* . . ..

What if we had a baby?

One thing at a time, cowboy. She's fucking nineteen and in school. Plus, you still don't know how this is going to work long-term. Kinda hard to raise a baby when she's living in another city and you only see each other when her schedule allows it.

She pulls away from me, giving me one of her sweet smiles. Instead of returning her smile, I stare at it like I always do, making her giggle. "I live for your non-smiles, Mr. Meyer."

I watch her, awestruck, as she lifts my son into her arms before dashing up the stairs with him. Her wheezy voice permeates the kitchen through the monitor, and I listen as Rani tells him how much she loves him, how she'll always be there for him. My throat constricts, knowing that even though he doesn't understand her words, they have a profound power over my heart. A power she's likely not even aware of.

Her melodic rasp fills the room as she sings his favorite song, and I quickly go to my car to get the items I'd picked up on my way home today, then hurry upstairs to my bathroom, tiptoeing past Rani and Arman in his room.

Fifteen minutes later, I've gotten everything ready when I hear her knock on my open door. I peek my head out of the bathroom. "Come in."

She slowly steps toward me, assessing me curiously since I'm looking out of a dark bathroom. "What are you doing in there?

I watch her come closer. "You don't ever have to knock, you know. You're free to come into my room whenever you want." I pull her by her hand into the bathroom.

She's in a daze as she drinks in the display of lit candles and flowers. Her mouth opens then closes. "Darian." She searches my gaze before admiring the room again. "When did you . . .?"

I reach for her, pulling her hair out of the bun on the top of her head, letting her wild curls hang over her back. I kiss her soft lips, wrapping my hands around her face. "Rani?"

"Mmm." She hums with her eyes closed.

"I love you."

"Darian?" She reaches for my lips again with a smile on her own.

"Yes."

"Show me."

I curl my fingers around the spaghetti straps of her dress and pull them off her shoulder, peering into her eyes. Sliding the material down her arms, I pull it over her chest and her waist. She's in nothing but a strapless, powder-blue bra and panties.

I grab the back of her neck and pull her in for another kiss, tasting her sweet breath and tongue against my own. Using my other hand, I unhook her bra, letting it fall to the ground in the heap of her dress. "I need you to do something for me," I whisper against her mouth.

"Anything."

This girl.

"I want you to stay silent until we're finished. Not a word, not a moan, not even a whimper. The second I hear you, I'll stop whatever we're doing."

Her hand wraps around my wrist. "You're asking for the impossible, Darian."

I put my lips over her ear, caressing her skin with my breath. "I'll make it worth your while, my Rani."

I find her eyes and she gives me a quick nod, though I can tell she's already worried about how she's going to stay so quiet when she's rather expressive in bed and otherwise.

Kissing down her neck and over the top of her chest, I

wrap my hand around her breast. I love that it's such a perfect size for my hands. I squeeze gently, massaging her and running my thumb over her nipple. I hear her swallow and it makes me smile into her skin, knowing how much I'm affecting her.

I make my way down to her other awaiting breast, sucking her pert tip into my mouth hard, making her buck. Her hands grasp my hair and she pulls to let me know how affected she is. I bite down on her nipple and she lets out an almost inaudible breath.

I continue to flick her nipple with my tongue, alternating between sucking and teasing as she starts to wiggle and writhe in my hands. Her legs clench and release, her hands moving to grasp my shoulder with an iron grip. I can tell she's working hard to stay upright.

Moving to the other breast, I slide my hand down her stomach and into her panties. She's positively drenched. I circle her clit before rubbing between her folds, up and down. Rani throws her head back as her fingernails dig into my shoulders. Her chest heaves as I continue my ministrations with both my mouth on her breast and my fingers massaging her center.

I press two fingers inside her and she takes in a quick breath. I release her nipple from my mouth, standing to find her eyes. "Do not come." I raise an eyebrow, keeping my mouth set. "Do you hear me? I'm going to fuck you with my fingers until you can't take another second, and then you're going to sit on the edge of that tub and I'm going to fuck you with my tongue."

She shudders, biting down on her lip. Her eyes close as I continue to pump in and out of her, her juices dripping down my fingers. I pull my fingers out completely and add one more, and Rani practically jumps.

I stop abruptly, gauging her expression. The last thing I

want is for her to be in pain and not tell me. "Did I hurt you?"

I think she sees the fear on my face when she shakes her head, grinding down on my fingers, silently telling me to keep going. My lips quirk at her insistence, and I finally start moving again. Within seconds, her body starts flexing, and I can feel how swollen her clit is with my thumb. I gently rub her clit with my thumb and she rocks into me.

One more press against her swollen nub and I know she'll be coming all over my hands. I shake my head and we watch each other through hooded eyes. Her's beg me to let her have her release, while mine tell her there's so much more to come.

I take my hand out of her panties before pulling them down her thighs. She steps out of them, and I coax her onto the edge of the bathtub I'd filled with warm water and rose petals. Her eyes glaze over the candles illuminating the bathroom before they widen when she sees that I've picked one up.

"Do you trust me, sweetheart?"

She hesitates for a second on the candle in my hand before nodding.

"This isn't a regular candle. It heats up the oil in here, and I want to massage your skin as I devour you. If you say no, we won't use the candle."

She bites her lip, but nods. And then, I get to work.

"Put your hands on the edge of the tub and open your legs." She does but not enough. "More, Rani. I need you to widen up for me."

She does as I ask, and I drop to my knees in front of her. Bringing the candle closer, I blow out the wick and look at Rani with raised brows one more time for confirmation. She nods again, both thrill and hesitation entangled in her expression.

I slowly drop the heated liquid on her thigh and she

tenses, blowing out a breath. I massage it into her skin, using the pad of my thumb to move it up her thigh. "Lean back for me, baby."

When she does, I press my nose and lips into her center. I hear the softest of moans, but I'll forgive her just this once. Using the tip of my tongue, I roll up and down her core, laving her, tasting her. Her thigh quivers under my palms as I continue to massage the side that has the oil on it. My tongue finds her entrance and I ravish her, using my lips to suck on her in earnest.

I can see her hands clench the edge of the tub as if they'll break it and her toes curl, begging for relief. I flatten my tongue and devour her like she'll be my only meal for the next century. It's when I hear her gasp and moan that I pull back from her.

She shakes her head, her eyes begging me not to stop, taking in my glistening lips. "Please," she hisses. "Please, Darian."

"Not a sound." I lift a brow. "I don't care how close you are, I'll stop it right there."

Her nostrils flare as her jaw clenches. She's so pissed and aroused, she barely knows what day it is. She nods vigorously, tilting her head toward her center to encourage me back again.

I almost lose my battle with the laugh I'm holding back, but I know what's good for me and keeping my balls intact is one of them.

Dripping more of the hot oil on her other thigh, I watch her chew on her lip, tracking it down her thigh. She's so turned-on, she can't decide if she likes the experience or not, but if I had to take a guess, she wouldn't mind doing it again. Her skin turns pink from the contact of the oil but I quickly work my fingers into it, massaging her thighs with an upward movement toward her center. Keeping that movement going,

I shove my face back into her dripping center. Her hips rock into me as I impale her with my tongue.

Once my hands are close to where I want them, I move my mouth to her clit and put my middle two fingers inside her. Sucking her swollen nub, I pump my fingers in and out, feeling her body contract around me.

With nothing to go by but her heavy breathing and her trembling body, I know she's close. So fucking close. I continue thrusting my fingers inside her before I curl them, finding the spot that will have her going over the edge. And just like magic, she does, pulsating around me while rocking into my mouth. I taste everything she has to offer, loving the scent of her enveloping me.

As she comes off her high, her fingers glide into my hair softly, letting me know to come up and I do. I straighten up on my knees, regarding her from head to toe. She's a sight like no other—her hair wild, her skin glistening, her chest heaving. I could make staring at her my full-time job.

My voice echoes inside the bathroom. "That was just the beginning . . .."

Chapter Thirty-Three
RANI

To say I'm exploring my sexuality and learning a whole hell of a lot about myself is an understatement. I'm not only learning a lot, but I'm learning it at the speed of light, and my body is singing with contentment.

Darian stands in front of me as I continue to rein in my racing heart. His heavy and hard erection presses against his black boxer-briefs like it's trying to carve its way out. I can barely move from the violent release my body just had, leaving me feeling boneless, but my mouth waters at the sight before me.

He takes off his boxers, and I immediately go to grab his hard length inside my palm. Looking up at him, I stroke it, making him grunt. Straightening up, I lean forward, trying to get my mouth around his angry purple tip when he stops me.

"I'm getting in the tub and when I do, you're going to sit on my lap, your back to my chest."

I'm a little concerned about the mechanics of this—whatever this is he's suggesting—but I get up and let him enter the tub anyway. I don't think I'm allowed to speak or ask questions yet—dare I risk another orgasm—so I'm going to assume he knows what he's talking about. Though, with my body still reeling from the after effects of the climax to shame all climaxes, I am positive I've got nothing left. If he thinks he can get one more out of me, he's smoking something–and it's not chicken.

By all accounts, I'd say this tub is on the massive side. It's not quite a two-person tub, but it's definitely large enough, so that paired with some maneuvering and my limited flexibility, I think I can manage what he's asking. It won't be easy, though.

The water splashes, moving the flower petals in disarray, as he settles back into the tub. He grabs my hand as I place one foot in after the other.

"Turn around." He catalogs every inch of my skin as I stand over him, his nostrils flaring. I don't have to touch him to know how desperate he is for me, and it makes me feel powerful and admired.

I do as he asks, and I turn before sitting on my knees with my legs spread apart over his thighs. His erection slides against my ass and I feel myself get wet again.

The water comes up to my mid-thigh and the contradiction between its warmth with the cool air on my chest rouses every sensory cell inside my body, spurring goosebumps along the entire surface of my skin.

Darian reaches behind him, grabbing a couple of hand towels. "Here, place these under your knees." His hands slide up and down my thighs as I put the towels under my knees before he pulls me back into him.

His hand comes around my waist to my front and he massages my thigh, near the crease between my leg and my once-again throbbing center. His movements send little pulses of sensation deep into my core, and I grind down on him helplessly.

Seriously, how is this even possible already?

His fingers tease me between my folds and I lift up, my body instinctively knowing what it needs. Darian straightens his shaft under me and I slide down on it, reverse cowgirl style, fitting around him exquisitely. We both moan at the same time before I abruptly press my fingers to my mouth.

Darian chuckles behind me. His hands wrap around my waist, and I grab hold of the edges of the tub, lifting my bottom up before sitting back down on him. He guides me up and down his shaft, making my head roll back so my hair touches the water over his chest. "That's it, baby. Take me all the way in."

I whimper as my core starts to tingle, riding him with his guidance.

Darian turns on the faucet and at first, I think he's just adding more hot water to the tub but instead, his hand wraps around the flat, handheld shower attachment. He turns it on, the water from the faucet switching to the handheld shower. Using his thumb, he changes the intensity with a button so the water is focused in a strong stream coming out through the middle. He aims it at my swollen nub, sticking out above the water and my body kindles with a new understanding and need.

Oh, God.

"Lean back for me, sweetheart." His words are mumbled into my shoulder as he rubs his lips all the way to the nape of my neck, pressing kisses over the top of my spine.

I lean back as he starts to pummel me from below. He's intentional and slow at first, letting me get used to his thickness before he increases his speed. When we find a good rhythm, he adds the intensity of the water stream again, stimulating my clit. His hand moves in small circles, aiming the water exactly where I need it most. The prick of the steady stream vibrating at my center, along with his erection impaling my body, has my eyes rolling into the back of my head. I feel heady and delirious, like I'm having an out-of-body experience.

"Oh, my God, Darian! Oh, yes," I wail as the pressure builds inside me, making me feel like I'm rocking somewhere between reality and fantasy.

Darian brings the shower head closer, letting the stream pellet me in such a way that it sends electricity coursing through every vein in my body. I feel charged, as if I could power an entire city, as my orgasm speeds out of me. I cry out, not giving a shit about his rules to stay quiet, because if he quits on me now, I will fucking kill him.

Darian continues to thrust into me, holding my waist with one hand in a grip that will leave the most memorable of bruises. His other hand trembles but stays with the shower head directed at my pulsing center.

"Rani," he grunts, pummeling me from below. He speeds up, taking his fill until he can't take any more. Pressing against my ass, he growls into my neck, thickening inside me before flooding my womb with his seed.

Gasping for breaths, we both collapse backward.

"Oh, God," I wheeze. "I don't think I'll ever catch my breath."

Darian kisses my temple. "With you, I never want to."

∽

I STIR AWAKE, feeling the bed shake next to me. Squinting my eyes open, I notice Darian's body is rigid again and he's in yet another nightmare beside me. I don't know what time it is, but with the faintest amount of light coming in through the window, I'd guess it's sometime right before sunrise.

"Dar," I whisper, cupping his cheek with my hand. "Baby?" I lay a kiss on his temple, feeling his damp skin under my lips. God, I hate this for him. How long will he keep reliving the same thing?

It's been two weeks since I came back from visiting my parents, and while Darian has slept soundly for the most part, with us curled into each other, I've noticed he's been restless over the past couple of nights.

He gasps as his eyes flip wide open. "Fuck." His chest rises and falls as he finds his bearings, turning toward me when he realizes he was just dreaming. "Sorry if I woke you."

I pull him into my arms and we hold each other. I wish I could do something to help him. "Same dream with Jude?"

He nods.

"Darian, I think you should see a therapist. You need to talk to someone. Maybe they'll help you realize that none of it was your fault."

"I've tried to schedule some time with a therapist before, but with everything going on, I've had to cancel."

"But I'm here. If you need to make an appointment during the day and stay a little later at work, I can take care of Arman during that time. I'm here to help you."

He's silent for a minute. I know he hasn't fallen asleep because his lips move at the edge of my forehead. "It'll take weeks, maybe months, to make progress and . . ."

He trails off, but I know what he's not saying. We don't have months; I'm leaving in less than four weeks.

So, what do we have?

I nuzzle into his neck, not knowing what else to say as I listen to his breathing get steadier. But as he finds sleep again, I stay awake, battling my thoughts.

I looked into transferring to a small college here in Tahoe. I'd have to take two more credits but overall, it wouldn't delay my graduation. And I suppose this is where my lack of experience with relationships and my age works as a disadvantage. I don't know *how* to say what I want, what I expect. Wouldn't it put him in a predicament to have to figure out what we mean long-term if I ask him to tell me now?

What if he hasn't thought about the long-term this whole time? And if he had, wouldn't he have brought it up by now?

He told me he wanted to be 'all-in' but what does that really mean? Did that mean *all-in* for the summer or *all-in* forever?

Am I too naive to expect forever?

Am I too naive to expect anything more than this?

~

"I LOOK BETTER FROM THIS ANGLE." Fred turns to his left slowly, holding on to his walker and lifting his chest. He puts his hand inside his suit pocket. "Take my picture from this angle."

I fight a giggle, watching Lynn give her husband the biggest scowl from my viewfinder. "Well, now I look like I'm just an accessory, standing all the way over here."

Fred shakes his head, scooting up closer to her. "Well, alright, we can do it your way . . . even though I'm technically the star of Rani's article." When he gets a raised brow from her, he explains further, "Sweetheart, you read the same thing I did. The article talks about how sweet I was and what a risk-taker I was to go after my high school teacher, and then how hard I worked to finally sweep you off your feet."

Lynn turns Fred in another angle with her hands wrapped around his biceps, coming up in front of him to pose with a smile. "Goodness me. It's *extraordinary* how you don't just float away with that big ol' head of yours, Fred."

Fred frowns at me where I crouch with the camera in front of them. "Do you hear the sort of hurtful comments I have to live with, Rani? I wake up every day telling myself that my head is perfectly in proportion to the rest of my body."

My arms shake because I'm laughing so much. I have never met a cuter couple than this one. Even their bickering is cloaked in such deep and profound love and respect, I can't imagine the standard they've set for their children and the type of partner they should be with.

Once they've situated themselves, they both look over at the camera and smile. I take a few pictures like that, but it's one of the few I take of them smiling at each other—where Lynn looks up at him towering almost a foot over her, even when he's hunched a bit on his walker—that I know will be the one I post on the blog. I make a note to get it printed and framed for them after I do a little bit of post-editing to it.

We're sitting in Fred and Lynn's apartment, playing Uno and drinking some sweetened iced tea Lynn had made. Fred examines the cards in his hand as if the next one he puts down will change the course of history when Lynn turns to me. "So, how much longer are you here in Tahoe with us, dear?"

I groan internally, wishing to have avoided thinking about this question a little longer. It's not that I haven't thought about it—it's been swimming in the back of my mind. No, I'll rephrase. It's infested the back of my mind like a virus multiplying. "Three weeks."

Lynn raises her brows. "We're going to miss you, Rani. I hope you come to visit every now and then."

"You know I will."

A silence settles between us as we drop our cards with questions hanging in the air. As if Fred can't stand it anymore, he clears his throat. "So, have you and Darian spoken about the future? It seems you've had a very adventurous summer, but with three weeks left, have you talked about how you'll manage a semi long-distance relationship?"

I put down a yellow reverse card, not necessarily even thinking about what I'm doing. "Not really. I guess I don't want to put him on the spot, you know? I'm pretty sure I could transfer to a college nearby–I'd have to get that process started really soon to be able to be admitted in time for fall semester–but I don't know if that's something he'd want. Committing to live with someone for a summer is so different than living with them indefinitely. What if I put too much pressure on him?"

"You have your own pressures too, dear. You have a life to live and a career you want to build. One day you might even want to start a family of your own. If that's not with Darian, then you should know that up front." She puts down a card on the stack. "I understand that youngsters these days have what are called short, meaningless flings, but has what you have with Darian ever felt meaningless to you?"

I look at the cards in my hand but can barely tell one color from the other. "No. Never."

"Then just talk to him," Fred chimes in. "Ask him how he thinks you both will continue once you leave."

I nod but don't respond, lost in my thoughts through the rest of the game. Asking Darian about our future should seem easy enough, but a part of me is worried that maybe we're on different wavelengths, along with different phases in our lives. While I know neither of us thought of this as a summer fling–given we didn't even plan to start a relationship in the first place–I can't help but wonder why he hasn't brought up anything about what we'll do after the summer is over.

My doubts and uncertainty are getting the best of me. I can almost taste the acid curdling in my stomach at the thought of saying bye to both Arman and Darian with no sense of a future with either of them–besides going back to seeing Arman on a monthly basis when Karine brings him for visits.

Isn't this what I was always afraid of from the beginning, though? Getting attached. And with nothing to show for it at the end of summer, won't I be the cause of my own suffering?

I suppose it's been the story of my life when it comes to men. I'm the temporary reprieve—an interim shelter until they find a better-suited home, like Patrick did with Ruby Mallory.

I'm the one allowed to go adrift, knowing something better will wash up on shore.

Chapter Thirty-Four
DARIAN

I hear the front door open and shut, knowing it's Rani. After washing Arman's sippy-cups, I dry my hands on the towel and turn expectantly toward the foyer.

She's been out almost all weekend at either the nursing home or at a coffee shop, working on my website and her blog. But I can't relinquish the doubt that churns my gut, making me feel like she's avoiding me. She came home late last night–well past when I was asleep–and slept in her own room. I thought we had an unspoken understanding ever since that first night we were together that we'd always sleep in the same room.

And then she was gone this morning before I woke up. I texted her earlier this afternoon, and she messaged me back saying she's working from the coffee shop.

Is it just me or does history seem to be repeating itself? She did the same thing when she first moved in with me– avoided me for an entire weekend, and then again when we were at Mom and Dad's house for dinner.

Oh, hell no, we're not going backward!

She puts her keys in the bowl on the table in the foyer and

glances at me with a forced smile, her face the mood ring she's always admitted it to be. She twists her mouth this way and that before she takes a step toward the stairs. "I'm going to head to bed. I've just had a long weekend."

"Rani." I stop her before she takes the first step. "What's wrong?"

She looks down, her forehead creasing between her brows. "Nothing. I'm just tired."

I clench my jaw. "I get that this is your thing—avoiding me when you're pissed or unsettled about something—but I'm not a mind-reader, Rani. I need you to verbalize what I've done because I won't know what I did wrong until you tell me. I know all too well what it's like when lack of communication tears up a relationship, and I don't want a repeat of that again." I watch her shoulders slump and I soften my voice. "We aren't going to make it very far in a long-distance relationship if you don't talk to me, sweetheart."

Her eyes snap up. "Are we even going to make it past this summer, Darian?" She lifts her arms, letting them fall back to her sides. "Because all I can see is *today*. I can't see into tomorrow. I can't see into next week or even next month. So I don't know; I'm just not sure what to say to you when I don't know where your head is and I'm about to leave in three weeks."

I throw the towel on the counter and take a step toward her. I'm so confused, I can't tell if we're even in the *same* relationship—which, to me, is a relationship full of love and admiration. Because those are the only things I feel for her. I'm fucking crazy—no, insane—about her. I've said as much, haven't I? I told her I was all-in with this. So the question is, where did we go amiss?

"What do you mean, you don't know where my head is? What do you mean, *are we going to make it past this summer*?"

She crosses her arms over her chest defiantly, but it's not

her stance I'm observing, it's her hurt expression and that look of fear and uncertainty in her eyes. It punches me in the gut. "I don't know. We haven't talked about anything, like what happens when my time here ends? I have an option to transfer credits to the college nearby and–"

"You have an option to move here?" I reel back in complete shock. A–I didn't even know there was an option for her to study journalism nearby, and B–I didn't think she'd want to upend her life for me with two years left in college. I wholeheartedly expected that we'd continue to meet as often as we could until she graduated.

And that's the crux of the problem. That's where I fucking messed up.

I told her I wasn't a mind-reader and here I was, expecting her to be one.

"Yes. I'd have to submit my transfer request soon, but–"

I suck in a sharp breath but it does nothing to appease the constriction in my chest. "You'd do that for me?"

She lets her arms back down to her sides and closes the distance between us. Taking both my hands in hers, she peers into my eyes. "Dar, I would do anything for you. Haven't you figured that out by now?"

I stare at her, baffled. *How in God's name is she mine?* "I guess sometimes I just don't believe it."

Her lips tug up. "Well, believe it, Mr. Meyer, because I love you."

I lean down to kiss her, pulling her closer by her waist and taking a whiff of her delicious lily scent. "I love you so fucking much, my Rani," I mumble over her mouth. "I'm sorry I was such a dumbass. But I need you to promise me something."

"Anything."

"When you get pissed at me–because let's face it, I'm going to mess up again–don't ghost me. I can't fucking deal with it. Talk to me, tell me I'm being a jackass, throw something at me, but don't avoid me. Don't make it look like it's easy to be without me, because I can't stand a second without you."

Her eyes glisten and she tightens her hold over my neck. "I hurt you."

I stare at her, watching her lashes get wet. "You have no idea of the power you have."

"I do now, and I promise to be better about talking to you when I'm upset." She swallows. "I'll be here until you don't want me to be."

"Then I guess you're stuck with me forever, sweetheart, because I'll always want you." I grind the guy that's been twitching in my pants over the course of this conversation against her. "Like right now."

~

I'M FINISHING up my conversation with the contractors working on last-minute touches to the school's bathrooms and locker areas when my phone buzzes inside my pocket.

Rani: Check this link out. She seems really qualified—a degree in early childhood development and five years working for a family as a live-in nanny. What do you think?

Rani's been reviewing the applicants who have applied for the permanent nanny position we'd created together online a couple of weeks ago after we had the chat about her moving here. With her being in school for the next couple of years, I want her to focus solely on her school work, so we need full-time help at home with Arman. Even after she graduates, I want her to pursue her career in journalism. I've been stalking her blog ever since she told me about it, and I've read the newsletters she's sent on behalf of my school. The woman was born to write!

Fuck, my body is buzzing in anticipation of an upcoming future that seems a hell of a lot more exciting than having to figure out maintaining a long-distance relationship, along with everything else I've got going on. I would have done it–I would have done anything to make it work–but it helps tremendously that she'll be able to move here. My girl is going to be living with me, permanently! From what she told me last night, she submitted her transfer application, too.

Finally, with both our families supporting us, things seem like they're going in the right direction with both of us on the same path.

I was shocked when Rani FaceTimed with her mom yesterday, and her mom asked me how I was doing. I honestly got tongue-tied for a minute because I couldn't believe she was showing interest in my well-being. Then she legitimately sat and watched Arman play instead of commenting on whether he was walking faster or talking more. Even Rani's dad came on to say hello.

At one point, her dad put his arm around her mom's shoulders, and I heard Rani gasp. I couldn't understand why, but then I remembered from my conversations with Sonia that her parents didn't have the most loving relationship. I didn't ask, but I guess that maybe it was the first time in a long time that Rani saw her parents be affectionate to each other.

Rani told me she had a heart-to-heart with her mom–she put those words in air quotes, so I got the feeling it wasn't quite so much a heart-to-heart as it was an ultimatum–and that her mom promised to make more of an effort to see Rani's point of view. A tiger can't change its stripes, but perhaps a mother who's been shaken to her core with a dose of reality could try.

I head to my office, glancing up at both Greg and Olivia directing some handymen to put up banners and vendor advertisements on the wall. We're almost completely ready. I can't believe the tournament is this weekend. The time has just flown by, but I'm ready to get it done with and start a new chapter of my life with my queen.

She invited her friend Melody and her cousin Bella for the weekend. I was more than happy to have them stay at my house, but Rani insisted that we'll all be more comfortable if they stayed in a hotel. That way, if the girls want to go out to the bars or casinos nearby and get in late, they don't have to worry about waking up the baby. Apparently, she invited the lanky pipsqueak Liam, too. She claims he might be a good match for Melody, though she didn't seem too impressed when I told her he'd be a better match for the end of my fist.

It's a moment in time I'm working really hard to erase from my memory—with him wrapping his grubby paws around her arms to pull her in for a kiss—but clearly failing. It still has the power to have me seeing red.

All in all, we have almost sixty people signed up for the tournament, a backup safety team who will be patrolling the river, a couple of food trucks, and a few of our vendors, who'll be displaying apparel and water accessories. Both of my brothers will be there, along with Mala, my brother Dean's so-called best friend.

I click on the profile of the woman Rani has sent me, reading her credentials and noting down the phone number of the family she referenced in her bio.

Me: She looks like she'd be a good fit. I'll call her reference.

Her response comes back seconds later.

Rani: I already called them and left a message. I've got this under control. Just tell me if you don't like someone I shortlist, otherwise, I'm thinking we interview the three I've sent you so far to get the ball rolling. What do you think?

Me: How long has it been since I told you I loved you?

Rani: We're going on about fourteen minutes.

Me: I'll wait another fifteen minutes to say it again, then. I don't want to come off as excessive and needy.

Rani: LOL! No, you definitely don't want to do that. You're already walking a thin line.

Rani: BTW, I hope you don't mind, but I sent you the names of a couple of therapists to look into in your email. They specialize in post traumatic stress disorder, which is what I think is causing your frequent nightmares.

I read her message again. How long has it been since someone has taken care of me and my needs? Even when I was with Sonia, she never went out of her way to do things for me, especially unsolicited. She cared about me, sure, but she didn't *think* about me. There's a difference in that, and I never realized it until Rani came into my life. A difference I can't be without again.

Me: My Rani?

Rani: Yes.

Me: I don't give a shit about being excessive or needy. I love you.

Chapter Thirty-Five
RANI

"*Queenie*! I'm so glad to see you!" Melody wraps me in one of her tight hugs that's more like a chokehold before placing a kiss on my temple. "I missed you."

Melody and Bella drove in late last night before checking into a hotel nearby.

I hug her before pulling back and admiring her hair. She's changed her box braids for dark micro braids with blonde highlights, which she put up in a ponytail. "You look beautiful."

"You do too, boo. Not being single suits you." She giggles, elbowing me.

"Where's Bella?" I look around the beach. There are so many participants arriving already, dressed in similar attire, it's hard to find anyone without searching. I lean to see if maybe Bella is near one of the vendor booths.

Melody squeezes my forearm, bringing my gaze back on her. "I think she went to the restroom but, *queenie,* I think you need to talk to her. Something is up with her."

I can feel the wrinkle between my forehead. "What do

you mean? I just FaceTimed her a week ago, and she seemed fine. Did something happen recently?"

"She wouldn't say. I asked her several times last night on our drive here, but I've never seen her act so distant. I honestly felt like I drove alone because of how quiet she was through the entire drive."

"That's really strange." An apprehensive knot twists inside my stomach. While I've always thought my cousin tried too hard to solve her own problems and not share her burdens, I wouldn't say she's ever been reserved. She doesn't necessarily volunteer information about her life, but she's always been honest with me and Melody whenever we've asked her.

I see Bella walking back from the *Truckee Sports* building and just from her stiff gait, I can tell something is wrong, like *really* wrong. She passes by a couple of women rubbing sunscreen on each other, watching them, but I can tell she's not even paying attention. I run to meet her in the middle. "Hey, Bells."

"Hey!" She forces a smile, letting me pull her into a hug. "I just chatted with Darian in there." She throws a thumb over her shoulder, indicating the building behind her. "He was talking to Felix and a few other people, but he was very sweet to break away from them and come say hello to me."

That makes me smile. Darian and I got here at five AM this morning. He wanted me to stay in bed and come in later, but knowing what a big day it would be for him, I just couldn't. We left Arman at Karine and Marvin's place. Thankfully, he only jostled awake for a few minutes but was able to go back to sleep during the drive there.

I also brought my camera along to document the entire event for my photojournalism project. I only have a week left to turn it in, so I need to make sure I get as many good shots as possible, but with the overcast weather we have today, I'll likely have to do some post-editing to the pictures.

"He was excited to formally meet both you and Mel," I respond. "Hey, you look really tired. Is everything okay? Melody said you didn't talk much on the drive here."

Bella waits until Melody joins us in the middle of all the commotion. We really ought to find a quieter spot, but my stomach is still churning uneasily and I'm having a hard time moving from the spot. Her bottom lip trembles, but she quickly pulls it into her mouth. "I fucked up . . .."

Both Melody and I reel back at the same time. Bella isn't the type to curse, but more than that, she's also not the type to fuck up. She's always been intentional and focused about her goals and decisions—having graduated from high school early and knowing exactly what she was going to major in. She'll be graduating with honors soon.

"What do you mean, you fucked up?" I ask, wrapping my hands around her arms instinctively when I see her tremble. My eyes pool, seeing the tears in my cousin's eyes. "Oh, sweetheart. What's wrong?"

"Bella, tell us. We're always here for you, boo," Melody urges. "Always."

Bella's face drops and she looks at the sand at our feet. "I'm pregnant."

Cue the music screeching to an abrupt halt.

"What?" I don't know if it was me or Melody who said it, but I feel the wind leave my lungs.

A tear runs down Bella's cheek and she quickly dabs at it. "I fucked up, Rani. I didn't know." At the look of confusion on both mine and Melody's face, she continues, "I met this guy at a conference I went to in Boston a few weeks ago—"

"The hardware engineering summit or whatever it was called?" I don't know why I interrupt. I think it's my mind's way of trying to get a few extra seconds to process what I'm hearing—that my straight-laced cousin, who's been more like a sister to me than my own sister was, made a decision without thinking through the consequences.

She nods. "We were there for four days, and I don't know . . . it was instant-lust I guess. The night before we were leaving, he showed up at my hotel room and . . . I let him in." She puts her fingers on her trembling mouth. "He wore a condom but . . .."

"Oh, shit." Melody gawks at Bella. "Did you get his number? Have you told him?"

Bella blubbers out a sob. "Well, you'd think me being pregnant, less than two months into my first internship was bad enough, but that's not even the worst part. I called him last week to tell him—I had to go through all these hoops to find his number since he came there on behalf of another company."

"And?" I blurt out. My heart is beating so fast, I feel like I need to sit down. "What did he say?"

She shakes her head, closing her eyes as if in shame. "He's married."

Both Melody and I gasp. "What?"

"I had no idea, of course. I was just a dumb girl wanting to do something off the cuff, without really thinking too much about it, you know. I just wanted to have fun for a night without all the pressure to be perfect." She laughs without mirth. "But look where that got me. He said he didn't care what I did with it, but he wanted no part in it."

"You *are* perfect," I assert. "You're beautiful, generous, and the kindest person I've ever met." I pull her into a hug, and Melody wraps her arms around both of us so we're huddled together. "Have you thought about what you're going to do?"

She sniffles. "I'm keeping it. I know I'm young and it's not ideal, but I'm graduating at the end of the year so at least I'll be done with school. Beam Systems offered me a permanent job after graduation, so I'll work until the baby is born and then go back after maternity leave. I still have to figure out childcare afterward, but I can't think about all that right now."

"Wow. Honey, we're here for you, no matter what," Melody assures her. "Have you told your mom?"

"Oh, God no. Not yet. I just needed time to think about what I wanted. I haven't told anyone besides you two." Her eyes move past me, and we all turn to see Darian walking toward us. "Rani, can you keep this between us? I don't even want you to tell Darian yet."

I nod. "Whatever you need; I won't say a word. But," I risk a smile, "can I at least say congratulations to you? I know this really complicates your life, but it might also be a blessing in disguise."

Bella breaks into a small smile for the first time since I've seen her. "Thank you. I'm going to need both of you through this entire experience."

We hold each other in a hug, and as I break away from them, I lean back and feel Darian's broad chest at my back.

"Hi," I say, turning and smiling up at him.

He kisses my forehead. "Hi. Did you guys catch up?"

I give him a hesitant smile. "We did. Let me formally introduce you to my best friend, Melody. I think you already met my cousin Bella inside."

Melody waves. "Great to meet you, Mr. Poseidon, sir."

I purse my lips, fighting a smile at Darian's confused face. "Uh, good to meet you, too. I've heard a lot about you both." He turns toward the crowd assembling in front of the beach, though the tournament will start in less than a half hour. "Let me introduce you guys to my brothers. They're both helping out with various things I have them doing."

We follow Darian to where Dean is hauling paddles, finding Garrett right behind him, carrying life jackets. They set them down in a heap on the sand when they see us approach.

"Well, it's not every day that our little brother walks around with not one, but three beautiful ladies in tow," Dean announces with a smirk. A few strands of his long hair that aren't secured at the top of his head fly in the wind. He reaches out a hand to shake both Bella and Melody's. "I'm Dean, Darian's older, more mature brother."

I giggle, exchanging a look with Garrett before I notice his eyes sweep over Bella.

Darian turns to my friends. "Don't worry, only one of the three of us is cocky." He indicates to his brothers. "And this is Garrett. Garrett, this is Rani's cousin Bella, and her best friend Melody."

The four of them chat, exchanging pleasantries about the tournament and weather, while Darian pulls me to a quieter area away from them.

His fingers tuck some of my hair behind my ear. "Are you ready to take pictures and notes?"

I nod. "Yup, all good to go. I'm going to be putting some short videos on TikTok, too."

His cappuccino eyes gleam under his hat. "I noticed we already have quite a following."

"We do. Hopefully we can get some real interest and new customers through that." I turn to look at my friends, who are giggling about something one of Darian's brothers must have said. My heart aches as it lands on my cousin, who is smiling but I can tell she's distracted and worried. I school my features when I turn back to Darian. "Did you see the newsletter I sent out yesterday?"

He pulls me closer. I love that he doesn't care about how publicly he gives me affection. "I did. It was perfect. Are you sure you can work on all this while you're in school next semester?"

I wrap my arms around his waist. "I'm sure. You stressed about this?"

He watches the participants grab life jackets from where Garrett had dropped them. "Nah. We're ready for it. I'm just ready to have it ove—"

Darian's eyes sharpen on something behind me and he doesn't finish his sentence. I look back and for a second, I don't see what's distracted him, but then I see Ryan, dressed in a *Truckee Sports* tournament shirt with a number on the back. It's the same attire all the participants have received. He's laughing with a woman standing next to Olivia. She looks a lot like Olivia, so I assume perhaps she's her sister.

"What's wrong?" I ask, turning back to Darian.

He brings his eyes back to me, but they have none of the warmth that was there only a minute ago. "Nothing. I just didn't realize he had signed up to compete."

"I noticed he hasn't been coming to your poker nights lately."

Darian caresses my jaw with his thumb. "I didn't like the way he talked to you that one time. Sonia and his ex-wife Emily were friends so I tolerated him, but he was always a bit of a tool. Now that they're both not in the picture, I have no reason to stay friends with him. He rubs me the wrong way."

"He seems like an ass, but don't worry about me. I'm way over allowing douche-canoes like him to get under my skin."

"Hey, Rani." I hear a familiar voice behind me when Darian stiffens in my arms. "Hey, Darian."

I turn around to see Liam standing nearby with his hands in his pockets. He has a hat on and with his red curls peeking through the sides, it makes him look even more boyish than usual. "Hey, Liam!" I reach out to give Liam a hug, feeling Darian's arms tighten around me before he lets me go. "Thanks for coming!"

Darian reluctantly shakes Liam's hand, but neither of

them say anything further to each other. *Progress*, I think to myself. It's better than the outright animosity my guy would prefer to show if it were up to him.

The whistle blows somewhere in the distance near the water, and the participants all line up with their kayaks. Felix starts speaking into the bullhorn in his hand.

Darian rests his hand on the small of my back. "I've gotta get on safety patrol duty, sweetheart. You go do your thing, and we'll meet back here in a few hours when the tournament finishes."

"Sounds good. I'll take Liam to meet my friends before I do that."

I wave to Darian, whom I notice gives Liam a leery look, before gesturing to Liam to follow me.

Melody immediately locks her eyes on Liam when we get closer. Before I even know it, they're wrapped up in a conversation. I hug Bella—she's going to be on my mind all day, I know it—before telling her we'll talk more about everything later. She nods, and I again notice the way Garrett's eyes linger on her, as if he can't peel them away.

As much as I wish for more between them—given how much I would love Garrett for her—my cousin is probably overwhelmed with her upcoming future. Even if she were interested, I doubt Bella will give Garrett any indication that she's available.

I take the lens cap off my camera and stride toward where the kayakers are starting the race—completely unaware that the next time I'm back here, I'll be horrifically regarding Ryan as he squirms, lying in a pool of his own blood.

Chapter Thirty-Six
DARIAN

I stay close behind the competitors. For the most part, they're all experienced kayakers, but there are parts of the river where the currents can be unpredictable, so I like to hover around there until everyone is past it. Thankfully, I'm not the only patrol in the water—we have several keeping a close eye on the participants.

I was a little worried throughout the week since we had unusually high winds in this area. If it had been as bad as it was a couple of days ago, I would have had to push the tournament to another weekend, and what a mess that would have been. But thankfully, while today is more overcast and cooler than a typical August day, the wind seems manageable and safe for all the kayakers.

A few kayakers pass by me, trying to find their place in the race. I don't recognize them from my short glance at their profiles, but they seem to know what they're doing, adeptly maneuvering through the choppy water.

I look at the low cliffs nearby, hoping to find Rani, but I don't see her. I shouldn't be surprised. We're quite a ways down the river at this point, but I find myself always being disappointed when she's not nearby. Her presence, her laugh, and her closeness has become such a familiar part of my day that if I don't see her for a few hours, I can feel myself get antsy. I'm looking forward to finishing up today and coaxing her into a nice warm bath at the end of the night.

Perhaps I can entice her to enjoy the hand shower again, like she did the night she came back from her parents'.

And now I'm kayaking with a hard-on. *Just perfect.* Hopefully a few splashes of the cold water will have my dick relaxing.

Holding my paddle up to wave at Felix, who is a few yards ahead of me, I keep paddling through the rushing water, coming to an area where the water isn't as turbulent. I look around to make sure everyone still seems comfortable, specifically around the areas where I know there are some unpredictable currents behind me.

"How's it going, Darian? Or should I call you 'King' like all your minions around here?" The voice has my head snapping to my left. Ryan smirks. "Long time, no see, buddy. Are you guys no longer playing poker or am I just no longer invited?"

I look ahead, trying not to get wrapped up in whatever it is he's trying to goad me into. "I need to focus, Ryan. You should, too."

"Can you even focus anymore, man? I mean, if I was ramming that ass every night, I'd probably be unfocused by daybreak, too."

My eyes lock on him, and I barely hear the rush of water around me—the surge of my blood against my eardrums is deafening. "What'd you say?"

He paddles ahead, jeering over his shoulder. "Fuck, I thought lightning only struck once, but you lucky bastard, you've had two times the luck. Picking apples from the same tree, I see. Good for you, man." He chuckles, and I swear the thought of closing the distance between our kayaks so I'm close enough to shove him off spins through my mind. "I mean, Sonia had a nice ass, but Rani . . .? Now that ass is what the phrase 'cushion for the pushin' was made for.

"You motherfucker." I paddle past him, but my blood is speeding through my veins faster than any white water rapid. My heart is pumping so hard, it's fogging up my brain.

Every cell in my body screams to unleash on this asshole.

I fly down the river, keeping a steady gaze on the participants near me. Who the fuck let this douchebag into this tournament? I must have missed his name on the signups. Though, I wasn't really paying attention to who signed up.

∽

About forty-five minutes later, we have five participants coming up to the finish line with the rest following behind them.

My mood is shot to hell, and I can't see straight. Worse, I can barely think straight. I knew Ryan was an obnoxious piece of shit, but to bring my late wife up as if she was nothing more than an object for him to ogle, and then having the fucking audacity to talk about Rani! How dare he even *look* at Rani, let alone say her name or speak of her using his filthy mouth. I'm ready to pull his fucking tongue out and throw it into the river as fish food.

I get out of my kayak, watching as Felix and Greg call the first, second, and third place winners. While everyone else high-fives each other, I pretend to be focused on my kayak, begging the buzzing inside my head to stop. It feels like it's a hive for angry bees.

"King!" Felix calls from where he's shaking hands with the winners. They look exhausted but thrilled. They'll be getting trophies, free kayak rentals, and a ton of complimentary items from our vendors. "Get over here. You're handing out the trophies."

I straighten and walk over to the area where many of the participants are standing, breathing hard and completely drenched. Schooling my features the best I can, I shake hands with many of them, including the winners. Thankfully, I don't see the asshole Ryan anywhere in sight. Good. Maybe he's decided to stay the fuck away from me, knowing what's good for him.

I'm in the middle of exchanging more pleasantries when I spot Rani's long curly hair waving behind her. She's wearing a simple outfit—a *Truckee Sports* T-shirt and black leggings—but she's as radiant as ever. With the way her tan skin glows, presumably from her being slightly sweaty from her hike to get good pictures, and the way her dark brown eyes sparkle, hitting the light just right, she's absolutely stunning.

She gives me a knowing smile, like she's caught me ogling her, but as usual, I do nothing but keep my eyes pinned on her. Giving her a smile back just seems so insignificant in comparison to my fucking feelings for her—a smile will never encompass how much I feel. But what my smile can't say, my eyes do—that my fucking soul lights up whenever she's around.

I hand the winners their trophies, with Rani's instructions to pose this way and that for the camera. Once we're done, she tells me she's going to take some other shots of the winners alone, and I tell her I'll meet her inside the school.

I'm just picking up a few stray life jackets on the beach when the hair on my neck rises and I stand straighter, searching for the threat I feel around me. I find it—*him*, next to my girl. He must have just gotten out of the water, and he's grinning at her like he's the fucking cat who got the cream, leaning in to say something into her ear as she examines her camera. Whatever he's said has her reeling back, surprised at his presence next to her.

"Get the fuck away from her," I growl, stalking closer, my voice low and deadly.

Ryan lifts his hands in surrender before running one hand through his wet hair. "Chill the fuck out, bro. I didn't say anything to her that she doesn't know already."

My jaw clamps so tight, I'm sure I'm going to break my fucking molars. I wrap my arm around Rani's waist. "Let's go inside."

Because if I don't get the fuck out of here with my girl in the next minute, I'm going to turn into the raging beast I feel inside and most likely create a PR mess that a small company like mine doesn't need.

She's still gawking at Ryan, pain caused by his words swirling in her eyes—pain she tries to hide under a look of incredulity, but the emotion can't be veiled. Whatever the fucker said to her, he doesn't deserve another second of her time or energy. I squeeze her waist again and she nods in understanding.

I'm just walking with her hand-in-hand, back to the school building, as my staff and most of the participants watch in shock when Ryan makes the mistake of speaking again.

"Yo! I told her she's hot for a fat chick, though completely different from your usual type." He shrugs. "Just complimenting the lady. You know, in case you slipped back into your old ways and stopped giving her enough attention."

I don't even realize I've moved forward. I don't know when I get close enough to him that my fist is able to make contact with his nose. To be honest, I don't even feel my knuckles against his cartilage, nor do I hear the crunch of his bone breaking. Not then, at least.

I feel it, hear it, and see it all much later, though. Much later than I should have. Much later than I could have done anything about it.

Because by the time I've stepped away from his splayed-out figure on the sand, he's already inflicted deeper damage–much more than I could ever have–crushing way more than he could have if he'd broken my bones.

Shaking the earth under my feet with his mumbled, but perfectly audible words before he slipped into unconsciousness, making my world go into a frenzy. And I stood there, rooted to my spot in the shifting sand, hearing his words spin inside my head as if they were stuck on rewind and replay, praying there was another translation for the language he spoke.

Because it couldn't have been what I was hearing. It couldn't have–

"Ever wonder why your son looks nothing like you, Darian?" He chuckled, gurgling on his own blood, spitting it out on the sand as every onlooker watched on in disbelief. My fucking ears rang like I had fire alarms for ear drums. "I fucked your wife. I fucked the king's wife because she practically begged me to." He gasped, moaning from the pain, his eyes rolling to the back of his head as a few people rushed to his aid.

He coughed. "Don't worry, though; I don't want the kid, big guy. I used to feel guilty." He lifts his hand feebly from where he lays on the ground, pinching his index and thumb together. "Not too guilty, but a little because you were such a nice guy. A nice guy, but a dumbass who had no idea how miserable your wife was those last couple of years. Miserable enough to confide in another man."

He tried to laugh again. "But now? After this? Fuck that guilt. I like the idea of you seeing your failures written all over the face of the son I gave you."

Chapter Thirty-Seven
DARIAN

He's lying.

He's fucking lying.

There's no other explanation for this.

I stare at the floor in my office with my fingers at my temples. My cap is still lying on the ground where I threw it, and my heart is still sprinting inside my chest as if it's nearing the finish line.

Ryan's words echo in my head over and over again. *I like the idea of you seeing your failures written all over the face of the son I gave you . . .. Of the son I gave you . . .. I gave you . . ..*

No.

I refuse to fucking believe it. How could that be true? It's not. Not when I feel the truth in every single fiber of my being—that Arman is my son. *My son!* Not the son of a sleazeball who has nothing better to do than run his mouth.

Arman is mine. The way he smiles, the way he stares, the way he recognizes me deep inside his soul, same as I do. He's one-fucking-hundred percent mine. And no one, not even the asshole who was taken to the hospital for his superficial wounds—which he deserved when he inflicted catastrophic damage to my soul—can take my son away from me.

My stomach turns and I feel like I'm back inside the hospital delivery room with Sonia's body lying next to me. My eyes skate over her cold skin and expressionless face, and I question everything I thought I knew about us.

Did she really do what that piece of shit claimed? Did she really cheat on me with Ryan? Did she really hide the fact that he was Arman's father? Was she so miserable with our life together that she would hurt me so callously?

No.

No way.

We were working on it. We were taking the right steps to improve our marriage—therapy, communication . . . sex. We'd had sex before she told me she was pregnant with Arman. I know we did. It was part of the intimacy conversations our therapist made us discuss, and we worked on making our sex life a priority. Didn't we? *I know I did.*

But was she also fucking Ryan?

Bile rises up through my stomach, and I suck in a lungful of air to tamp it down.

I'm just scrolling through my contacts list on my phone when my office door opens and Rani hurries in, holding an ice pack. She's been by my side since the minute we came back in.

"Here." She kneels in front of me, reminding me a lot of the first time we met in this office when she offered to help take care of Arman. Pulling my hand toward her, she places the ice pack on my knuckles. "Your hand is swollen."

I throw my phone on the desk and lay my head back, pinching the bridge of my nose with my other hand. I can't believe this day. I can't believe my life.

"Darian?" Rani squeezes the hand she's icing. "Will you look at me? Please?"

I swallow, feeling my eyes prick—something they haven't done since the day I cremated Sonia, but my tears aren't for her this time. If what Ryan said is true, they'll never be for her again.

I lean forward as a tear slips from the corner of my eye, and Rani catches me inside her arms. She cups the back of my head on her shoulder and I let out a sob. I don't know what I'd do without her right now. She's been my anchor, keeping me from floating away completely. "Shh, baby." Her hand runs up the back of my head and through my hair. "It's going to be okay. I know it is. We're going to figure this out together."

"He's mine, Rani," I sob again. "I know he's my son."

I feel her resolve crack inside my arms and her chest shakes. "He's yours, baby. He's always been yours. Nobody can take him away from you." She sniffles. "You're his dad and nothing can change that."

I lift off her and we gaze into each other's watery eyes. I rub the tears off her cheeks. "I can't believe she would do that to me . . .. Our marriage had issues, but I never thought she'd betray me like that."

Rani's face falls and she nods, her eyes fixed on the ground. A crease forms between her brows, like she's struggling to suppress an ache. "Darian, I need to tell you—"

A knock on the door interrupts her, and we both look up to see Garrett and Dean peek their heads inside.

"Hey, man. We just heard about what happened from Olivia." Dean's face looks more stoic than I've ever seen. His blue eyes have a chill inside them that I've only witnessed a couple of times before, and I've always wished I'd never see it again. "I would have done a lot more than just broke the motherfucker's nose."

I swallow again. My throat feels like a nest of red ants have made a home inside it. "He'll press charges, I'm sure."

"Let him," Garrett chimes in with a shrug. "Fuck that asshole. We'll worry about all that when it happens. We just came to see how you were handling everything."

Rani's hands squeeze mine again. She's still in the same spot in front of me. I squeeze hers back and shake my head, looking at the picture of Arman on my desk. I'd already removed Sonia's pictures from my office and my bedroom since Rani and I became more. "I can't fucking believe I missed the signs of her cheating."

"You don't know if she was for sure." Dean steps inside, giving Garrett more room behind him. "That asshole could be lying."

"I can't believe what an shitbag Ryan turned out to be," Garrett laments. "I always just thought he was loud and annoying, but I never thought he'd turn out to be such a dick. And Dean's right; you never know, he could totally be lying to get under your skin."

"Or maybe he isn't."

All three of us—my brothers and I—turn to look at Rani. She gets up, standing in front of me with her face downturned, a frown pulling her lips. She slowly lifts her eyes to meet mine and a shudder ghosts down my spine with what I find in them.

"What do you mean, maybe he isn't?" I ask her. My gut tightens like it's preparing to be punched.

She regards my brothers before turning back to me, her face a little paler than earlier. "A couple of months before Sonia died, she sent me a text . . . but it wasn't meant for me." Rani pulls out her phone and scrolls through her messages while we wait.

My breaths feel heavy inside my lungs, but I reach out to grab her phone when she juts it in my direction. I ignore the way my hand shakes when I bring the phone to me. I read

Sonia's text several times, but it feels like I'm reading fiction—something that happens in movies, not in real life.

I read it out loud for my brothers to hear.

Sonia: I've decided to tell Darian. It's not something I can keep from him any longer, and I think it's about time we face the consequences, don't you? I think you should tell Em. She'll find out soon, anyway.

But the more I stare at it, the more I realize that my wishful thinking was just that—*wishful*. This text, Ryan's searing words, and Rani's decision to withhold something so crucial is not fiction at all. It's all real life. My *real* life.

Dean runs a hand over his mouth, processing everything as Garrett gives me a look I can only decipher as empathy. They realize, as I do, that the text is not just a confirmation of Sonia's sins, but Ryan's as well. Sonia was one of the few who called Emily, *Em*.

My hands tremble again with the weight of Rani's phone, and I look to my brothers as a chill settles into my bones. "Can you give Rani and me some privacy? I'll talk to you both a little later."

They both nod somberly. "We'll be outside, helping clean up."

Rani takes a step forward to comfort me as soon as my office door closes, but I lift my hand, halting her. I put her phone on my desk but can't take my eyes off it. I don't even know how my life just went from smelling like lilies to reeking of betrayal. I ball my hand in a fist to keep from screaming or crying or throwing something.

First Sonia and now Rani?

"You've had that text from her since before you came here." I don't even recognize the ice in my voice. I refuse to meet her gaze, preferring the image on the corner of my desk. I refuse to be sucked into her shallow promise to be by my side, to 'figure it out together.' Because if we *were* together in this, she would have told me about the text a long fucking time ago. Way before my life imploded on me.

"Darian."

"No." My eyes snap to hers. "You don't get to use my name to stop me from speaking or to tell me I'm being ridiculous, because I'm not, Rani. I just need to know why? Why didn't you tell me about the text before?"

Her eyes sharpen at the same time as they pool. The frown on her face ascends to settle between her brows. "If you think for even a second that I hid the text from you to hurt you or betray you, then you don't know me at all. You're—"

"You're right. It looks like I *don't* know you. Just like I didn't know your sister. God knows I spent ten years with the woman and didn't know her, so how can I trust myself to know *you* after just a summer? I can't."

She scoffs as the dam in her eyes bursts and two identical tears run down her face, setting her cheeks aflame. "Wow. Well, clearly, you think you have me all figured out. At least the version of me that makes sense in all this. The version of me you can blame for the mess my sister and her dirty little secret left in your life. And if that's what gives you peace—for me to be a convenient scapegoat—then I'll let you have it." She wipes at her cheek angrily. "But you're a selfish bastard for thinking you're the only one hurt today, because newsflash, Darian, you're not. Because, ultimately, your lack of faith in me means we're done, doesn't it? And if that's the case, then that means I don't just lose once, I lose *twice*. I lose two people I've fallen in love with."

"You'll always have your relationship with Arman; I would

never take that away," I state curtly, though the constriction inside my chest threatens to bowl me over.

She gives me a single nod, her chest heaving. "And what about you? What will I have with you?"

I want to respond but the pain inside my chest is too much to bear. I'm so fucking confused, I can't breathe. I can't think. I can't move.

My heart tells me to rush to her, to grab hold of her and tell her that I'm being irrational. To tell her to forgive me because I'm a fucking idiot who doesn't know what's good for him, even when she's standing right in front of him. But my head keeps my body locked. It tells me I've trusted too easily and have been burned too badly. *So fucking badly*. It tells me I can't possibly trust someone I've only known for a summer when the person I loved for a decade betrayed me so viscerally.

Can I?

Rani waits another minute before she seemingly comes to a resolution at my silence. Her nostrils flare as she picks up her phone and camera off my desk before heading to the door. She looks at me over her shoulder. "If you stopped thinking about yourself for just one second, you'd know why I did it, Darian. Because of love, loyalty, and a sense of protection so deep, I'd throw myself in the line of fire for you. *That's why* I chose not to tell you. But if you can't see that, then you've purposely blinded yourself."

She pulls the door open, stepping out.

"Rani, wait." My heart screams, overriding my head, but my legs won't let me go after her.

It doesn't matter anyway, because my voice is cut off with the bang of the door as she whisks out of my office. And, for the first time in a long time, not only do I feel truly alone, but I feel like a complete and utter failure.

Chapter Thirty-Eight
RANI

You're right. It looks like I don't know you.

I wipe my face furiously with the back of my hand but it does nothing to cease the flow of fresh tears that replace them. I rush toward the exit, completely oblivious to the staff and volunteers around me. My heart feels like a defunct appendage inside my chest, doing nothing but encumbering my strides.

You're right. It looks like I don't know you.

He doesn't know me? He doesn't know the person who has done nothing but be there for him in every way possible from the moment she met him? He doesn't know the woman who has loved his son like her very own—who would do anything for him, come hell or high water? He doesn't know this fucking heartbroken girl who gave him not only her body but her heart and soul?

He doesn't know me?

Then what the fuck *does* he know?

"Rani!" a familiar voice calls out behind me—either Dean or Garrett—but I keep moving. It's against my principles to cry in public. Even as a kid, I'd cry silently in the comfort of a bathroom stall or under the covers in my room.

I'm not entirely sure where I'm going or how I'm going to get there–given that I came here in Darian's car–but I also have nothing to say to anyone. I have nothing left to give.

Is this what a heart shattering feels like? Like shards of glass pressing themselves from the inside, trying to get out? Like the type of pain that even though it's targeted in the middle of your chest, you feel it on every inch of your body?

I hear one of the brothers say something that sounds suspiciously like, "Fuck, whatever he did, he messed up, didn't he?" before their voices fade like they're no longer nearby. Either that or my ears are still ringing with Darian's words and I can no longer hear anything else.

I turn a corner on my way to the exit, spotting Olivia. Unlike the usual glower she always has ready for me, she offers me a sincere smile. I must look like a hot mess if even she can't help but give me an empathetic smile.

Exiting the building, I gulp in a big breath of air when I hear someone else call out my name. I don't have the energy to even turn around. I keep walking aimlessly until I'm somewhere in between the cars in the parking lot. And when I finally have a second alone, I plant my face inside my open palms and allow the sob I'd swallowed to release into them.

I sob for my first love and for the last time I'll know something like it. I sob for the man who reigns unconditionally in my heart and for the tremendous weight he now has to carry on his own. And I sob for the fear that's been burning a hole in my stomach ever since Ryan declared that Arman was his son.

What will happen if he's right? He said he didn't want Arman, but after the way things went down between him and Darian, will he exact more revenge than just pressing charges?

Darian couldn't go on without his baby boy.

And I can't go on without the both of them.

My shoulders shake from my intense cries as two pairs of warm arms wrap around me. My best friend and my cousin hold me in their embrace, letting me cry. "It's going to be okay, hon. I promise."

I pull away from them. "I need to get out of here. Can you please just take me to Darian's. I need to leave."

They exchange a look but Melody nods, taking her keys out. A minute later, I'm slumped in her backseat, gazing out the window but not seeing a damn thing.

I spy Melody eyeing me from the rearview mirror. "Do you want to talk about it?"

I go back to inattentively watching the cars next to us through the window. "It turns out Sonia was cheating on Darian."

Bella turns around to look at me from the front passenger seat, the purple tips of her hair brushing against the center console. "So, what that Ryan guy said is true? We weren't there to hear it, but Garrett had mentioned it."

I nod, my thoughts faintly recalling the way Bella and Garrett kept glancing at each other when the other wasn't. It was fucking cute, but love sucks and I should warn her, even though no one warned me.

"So what does that have to do with you, though?" Melody asks. "I can't believe your sister would ever think to have an affair with anyone when she had that fine ass piece of man meat at home, but she always struck me as someone who was a bit off, based on everything I've heard about her." She examines me in the rearview again. "No offense, and may she rest in peace."

"She sent me a text months before she died, but it wasn't meant for me." I pull out my phone and read them the message Sonia had sent me. "I told Darian about it today because it all made more sense after Ryan said what he did."

"Oh, gosh. And I'm guessing Darian felt betrayed that you didn't tell him right in the beginning?" Melody infers.

"He said he didn't think he knew me at all–" My throat feels like it's closing up again. "I told him in not so many words that if he couldn't trust me, then that meant we were done. And when I went to leave . . . he didn't stop me."

"Wow." Bella sighs. "I mean, I don't blame you for not showing him the text earlier. What would it have done, anyway? Sonia's gone and seeing something like that–finding out the wife you spent so many years with was sleeping with someone else behind your back–would bring nothing but needless pain. Pain he couldn't really have done anything about. Not to mention, at the time you read it, it probably just felt like a suspicious text, not something that confirmed she was cheating. So, to jump to telling Darian based on a suspicion–even if your gut said Sonia was doing something nefarious–seems irrational."

Melody seems to be quiet, focused on the road, which means she's trying to weigh her response against her loyalty to me and our friendship. I know my best friend well enough to know she wouldn't be quiet otherwise.

"Mel, I know you disagree, so spit it out." I wrap my arms around myself protectively. I still don't think I would have chosen to tell Darian about the text, even knowing what I know now. In my heart, the text is a confirmation of Sonia's infidelity, but not worth the pain in Darian's eyes today. Like Bella said, to have shown him the text would have been to inflict needless pain on him, and if there's one thing I've never been able to see, it's him suffering in any way.

Melody wiggles in her seat, both her hands on the steering wheel. "*Queenie*, I'm not here to tell you if your decision to keep the text from him was right or wrong. I can personally see it both ways. Had Ryan not been in the picture, and had the question of Arman's paternity never come up, I would have agreed that the text would have been like putting a new cut on an already wounded man. But I guess I am trying to see it from Darian's perspective, too."

She flips the blinker on to turn left. "With everything he found out today, I think the text was just the last straw to push him over the edge. He'd just found out he was betrayed by someone he loved and that his son might not even be his. Then, you told him you'd been keeping a text from your sister. Had he known about the text from the beginning, perhaps he could have made peace with it or been more prepared for what that jerk Ryan said to him. I think it just had Darian second-guessing everything in his life, and I don't blame him for feeling so confused."

My chin trembles, and I hate that in the process of saving Darian from more grief, I've become a part of hurling him further into it.

Maybe I *am* too young and too immature to be in a real relationship. Maybe it's better that I leave now and let him find the peace he wholeheartedly deserves. If all he sees is my sister's betrayal when he looks at me, then I can't imagine being a source of comfort for him at all.

But nothing quells the feeling that I'm breaking inside at the thought of leaving.

We all sit quietly, consumed in our own thoughts for a few minutes, and I think about my next steps. I can't stay here, not when Darian made it clear he doesn't want me to. I blink back the fresh set of tears. I was so excited to move here permanently to start my life with Darian. I'd get to see my boys everyday and be with the two people I'd come to consider as my own little family. But now, I'll be returning empty-handed—worse off than when I arrived because at least then, I had no notion of what I'd lose. No understanding that I'd be changed forever.

At least then, I had no idea that I'd be forsaking my heart forever.

"At the end of this, we'll all be bankrupt." Mom's words circle around my head, and I can't help but wonder if she foreshadowed the complete barrenness in my chest at this very moment.

"What are you going to do, boo?" Melody pulls me out of my thoughts.

"What can I do?" I shrug sadly. "I have to leave. I can't stay here, not after everything that's happened."

Bella offers me her hand over the seat and I take it. "Do you want us to help you pack?"

"No, I didn't bring much, anyway. It'll just take me a few minutes, and whatever I leave here, I'll figure out a time to meet with Karine to get it back."

"I'm sorry, hon." Melody pulls into Darian's driveway. "I wish you guys didn't have to end it this way."

Me, too.

I force a smile, trying to lighten the mood and pretending I'm still whole inside. "It was my fault. I broke one of my guiding principles and fell in love with a good-looking man who turned my brain into mush."

Bella gives me a knowing smile that says I can't fool her. "Do you think you can try talking to him again? Maybe you both just needed a little space to think."

I wipe my nose with the back of my hand. "He didn't seem like he wanted to speak, but his last words to me made it clear we were over."

Both Melody and Bella stay quiet, absorbing my decision.

"I'm sorry about today." I pull my camera strap on my shoulder, getting ready to get out of the car. "I know you guys wanted me to go out with you tonight, but I think I'm just going to drive back home."

"Don't worry about it." Melody gives me an understanding smile.

I stop on my way out of her car, remembering. "God, I've been such a shitty friend. I didn't even ask how things went with Liam." I lean around the seat to look at Bella. "And we didn't even talk more about everything you're going through. Bells, I'm so sorry. You've got so much you're dealing with right now, and I just completely took over with my sob story."

Bella shakes her head. "We have time to talk about my stuff later. Don't worry. I'm actually good with my decision. My mom's going to be so disappointed that I'm even in this position, but she'll have to get over it."

"She's a lot more level-headed than my mom," I supply, knowing that while my aunt won't be thrilled with the fact that her twenty-one-year-old daughter is pregnant, she'll be supportive. I lift a brow. "By the way, did I see something between you and Garrett?"

Bella tries to fight a smile, but Melody reaches over and tickles her. "Yes! Yes, you did see something between our Bells and that fine-ass pilot friend of yours. If it's not too on-the-nose, I'd say she was on cloud nine today!"

"Shut up." Bella bats Melody's arm playfully before her expression becomes forlorn. "With everything going on with me, I don't plan on taking this past friendship. No guy wants my kind of complication in his life."

"Don't say that, Bells." I squeeze Bella's shoulder. "I promise you'll find someone who'll make you happy one day." Bella doesn't respond, and I try to lighten the mood by changing the subject to Melody. "And what about you? Did you like Liam?"

"Like him?" she repeats, as if it's the dumbest thing I've ever asked. "He is the cutest thing I've ever seen and so flippin' sweet! We're all going out tonight—the twins, Liam, Bella, and me. I wish you and Darian could have come too, but . . .."

My shoulders sag. "I better go and get everything done. I don't want to be too late driving back today." I fake a smile. "Have fun tonight. I'll call you guys later."

The girls lean back to give me a hug, and I make my way into the house. It's quiet, with nothing but the echoes of Arman's laughter and Darian's murmured words bouncing off the walls.

The same echoes that'll fill my ears and heart from here on out.

Chapter Thirty-Nine
DARIAN

"Are you a fucking idiot?" Garrett storms into my office with Dean tagging behind him just as I'm heading out.

"I get that you've had a lot thrown at you today, man, but what in the actual fuck? Why did you take it out of Rani? She didn't deserve that shit," Dean adds.

I scrub my hands down my face, the back of my hand still throbbing. "Can you assholes give me a fucking minute? Can everyone just give me *one fucking minute*?"

"Why? So you can overthink this and find a way to fuck up your relationship even more?" Garrett seethes.

I reel back. "*Find a way to fuck up my relationship?* In case you missed what happened today, I was just told that my late wife of ten fucking years cheated on me and that my son may not be mine. To put icing on that shitcake, my girlfriend–my late wife's sister, no less–told me she has been holding on to a text from her that could have revealed all this fucking information sooner." I huff out a mirthless laugh. "So, no, I'm not the one who fucked-up a relationship. I'm pretty sure that blame lays solely on the hands of the Shah sisters."

Dean is the one to reel back this time, his eyes widening

before they narrow in on me. "Are you seriously comparing Rani to Sonia right now?"

"She hid a text from you—a text that had the potential to spin you off your axis unnecessarily when your wife was already dead." Garrett's tone is serious and low. "It was another way for Sonia to hurt you from the grave, and Rani made the decision to save you from that pain."

"I would have done the same fucking thing," Dean presses. "That text was vague as fuck and didn't mean a whole lot until douchebag Ryan spewed off his venom today. But let's just say for shits and giggles that Rani *did* put it together that her sister had cheated on you. What would you have gained if she told you?"

An emptiness constricts my chest and I feel a burn rise up my esophagus. I press my hand to it, hoping to squelch what surely must be a riptide threatening to tow me under.

My head and my heart are still in battle, but I can feel my mind's surrender as it answers Dean's question. I can feel it giving in, knowing it's hanging on to a falsity. Knowing it's connecting dots that aren't there. Knowing my girl would never intentionally try to hurt me.

"Where—" I choke on my next question, my throat closing up. I already know I'm not going to like the answer. "Where is she?"

"She left," Dean says, throwing a thumb over his shoulder. "I saw her getting into the car with her friends, and by the tears streaming down her face, I'd say you'd be hard-pressed to find her back at your house."

I grab the hair at the back of my head. "Fuck!"

Garrett bobs his head up and down. "'Fuck' is right, brother. If you're at all convinced of the reasons Rani chose not to tell you, I'd say you should leave right the fuck now and try to get her back."

I grab my wallet and keys, rushing toward the door. "I need to get out of here."

"Fix this, Dar!" Dean yells at my back. "Don't lose the best thing that's happened to you since Arman. Because you'll never find someone like her again."

I know. I fucking know.

~

I'm running late.

I can feel it in my bones. I'm running late, and I'm going to regret not getting off my ass the minute she left my office.

I've called her four times already, and unsurprisingly, she's sent me to voicemail each time. Jesus, I fucking messed up, and based on the five-alarm resounding incessantly in my head, I can tell I'm too late to fix it.

I speed down my street, my heart bouncing around in my chest as a foreboding feeling weighs down my stomach like an anchor pulling me deeper into a pit of despair.

Her car's gone.

"Fuck!" Parking my car in the driveway, I open my car door before zooming up the patio stairs. I already know she's gone, but my heart doesn't want to believe it. *Maybe, just maybe, she's still here.*

"Rani!" I yell as I get in the house, my panic setting my teeth on edge. I run up the stairs to her bedroom, throwing the door open and noticing nothing but a perfectly made bed, empty drawers, and the scent of lilies in the air. The fresh burgundy lilies I got her last night sit atop the dresser like a beacon for my internal turmoil.

The same lilies she didn't take with her.

I pull my phone out again and call her once more, getting the same response I've gotten the last several times–her voicemail, a sweet message that does nothing to douse the acid inside my stomach. "Rani, please. Please pick up the phone. I'm so sorry. I'm so fucking sorry, baby. I messed up. I fucking messed up—"

I run my hand through my hair before collapsing to the floor against her bed rail, my sorry excuse for a heart threatening to stop completely.

I messed up. I blamed the one person who has done nothing but help me every step of the way from the moment I met her. I'll never forget the look on her face when I hurled my calloused words at her, comparing her to her sister. I'd gutted her with little regard for anything but my own situation, my own personal chaos.

She threw her shoulders back but there was no denying the way her face wilted. There was no denying the way her chin wobbled and her eyes swam inside a pool of disappointment.

I hurt her when she'd done nothing but provide me her own form of protection every step of the way. And now, I don't know that I'll ever get it back.

Do I even deserve to get her back?

I don't know how long I sit there, my mind a puddle of incoherent thoughts wading between memories of Sonia—from our ski trips together to our arguments over my failure as a husband—to Ryan's vicious words. My life feels like it's mid-ride and harness-free on a roller coaster in hell, and I'm the lone occupant.

I didn't need to be lonely. I could have still had her with me, my Rani. My fucking queen. I didn't need to go through this alone when I knew she would have shouldered my pain right along with me.

Perhaps Sonia's words had some truth to them after all. Perhaps I wasn't ever meant to make someone else happy.

My eyes flip open inside the empty dark room when a buzzing resounds next to me. It's when I pick up my phone that I notice the time. Seven-forty-two. I'd dozed off for two hours at least and missed a dozen phone calls and messages.

Seeing three missed calls from my mom—probably wondering when I'll pick Arman up—and a couple more from my brothers, I scroll past their respective texts to find the one I was hoping for. The one I was waiting for.

> **Rani:** Hey. I just got home. I didn't want to talk while I was driving and I think we both needed the time to think. Plus, I promised you I'd never avoid you, so I wanted to make sure I responded to your voicemail and messages.
>
> **Rani:** I get why you jumped to the conclusion that I'd betrayed you just like my sister did. I can't begin to understand the pain you must have felt today when you found out. But I guess I believed you'd know I was different . . .. I believed you'd know I would never do anything to jeopardize your happiness.

I read the message and type out my response with so much speed, I'm surprised my thumbs aren't battery-powered. I try not to linger on the word *home*. Where she is now is no longer her home in my opinion. *This* is the only home she belongs in.

> **Me:** I do know that, sweetheart. Believe me, I know that. I just needed to wrap my head around everything.

Rani: I understand.

My heart lifts in my chest and I finally take in a steadying breath. She understands.
She understands!

Me: Will you please talk to me? Will you please come back?

Minutes stroll by as I wait for her response, the same foreboding feeling pulling me back into a familiar abyss. If she wanted to come back *home*, wouldn't she have answered by now? I'm just about to call her when my phone buzzes again.

Rani: We'll talk one day when we're both ready. Thank you for everything, Darian. Thank you for letting me spend the summer with my nephew and for showing me the strong woman who was hiding inside me. The one I've always wanted to be. I owe that all to you.

No!
My eyes cloud and the phone shakes in my hand as I type another message. I can't tell if the floor is wobbling or if that's just the way my heart is hammering, sending my entire body into a tremble.

Me: Please, baby . . .. Please don't do this.

But of course, my texts go unanswered after that.

Chapter Forty
DARIAN

Me: I know we haven't spoken in quite some time, but you should know that I'm unapologetically in love with your daughter. My son and I love her with every fiber in our being, and if you care for her happiness even a little bit, you'll have her answer the door when we ring the bell in the next ten minutes.

I SEND OUT THE MESSAGE AS I WAIT AT THE GAS STATION for the tank to fill. I don't expect a response. In fact, I wouldn't be surprised if she responded with a middle finger emoji or worse, a lie in the form of "she's not home."

I know Rani's home. I know it because I got her best friend Melody's number from our school database—unethical, I know, but I don't care—and texted her to do some sleuthing for me. She wrote back saying Rani hasn't left her house since she got back yesterday.

There was no way I was going to spend more than a night without my girl by my side. No fucking way. I don't care that her text said we'll talk when we're both ready, because I know in her heart that isn't what she wants. In her heart, she can't live without me . . . just like I can't live without her.

So, after getting Arman ready this morning, I put him in his car seat and drove straight to find her and bring her back where she belongs—to *our* home.

Arman's asleep in his car seat when I get back in, but he stirs awake when I close the car door. I catch him gazing out of the car window in a daze before he yawns with a little squeak at the end.

"You ready to bring your *masee* back home, little man?"

Arman smiles at me, his recognition for my words catching my eyes in the rearview mirror. "*Mas*."

Pulling into the address I've only been to once, many years ago when Sonia brought me to meet her parents, I swallow my nerves. That first meeting didn't go as well as we'd hoped—Sonia's mom practically threw us out, calling me a 'good for nothing junkie' and an 'uneducated piece of trash'—so I'm praying this one ends on a better note. I don't give two shits about what her mother thinks of me, though. The only woman I'm here for is the woman who's every opinion matters to me.

I'm just pulling Arman out of the car when my phone vibrates with a text.

Rani's Batshit-Crazy Mom: Okay.

Well, isn't she the chatterbox!

Maybe seeing me again will trigger another bout of verbal diarrhea. Still don't give a shit, though.

I hand Arman what I need him to hold, hoping he doesn't try to put it in his mouth before taking out the extra large bundle from the back of the car.

Holding his hand in mine, we make our way up the driveway. I ring the doorbell and move over to the side so Rani doesn't see me when she opens the door. My son regards the lily in his hand curiously, then bounces on his feet as if the flower has just somehow played him his favorite song. Kids are fascinating little things.

The lock slides and Rani opens the door, finding my son standing near her feet. "Arman!"

Her startled voice, along with her gasp, have my lips twitching. I step up behind my son and Rani eyes me with a mixture of shock and elation before she schools her features. "What are you doing here?"

I bend down to Arman, whispering in his ear, "Can you give it to her, buddy?"

Rani studies the flower in Arman's hand before she gulps a soft but quick breath. Her eyes soften. "What—"

Arman looks at the flower once more before lifting his arm and the flower toward his aunt with a semi-toothless grin. She bends down to take it from his hand, pursing her lips to stop them from quivering.

It should be known that I feel absolutely *zero* guilt in using my adorable son to help us get our girl back.

Getting back up, I search her eyes, gesturing to the flower with a tilt of my chin. "Read it."

Rani swallows before finding the note attached to it. I'd scribbled it as fast as I could, but it's clear enough that she can read it. At least, I hope that's what the tears rolling down her cheek indicate.

My dad is an idiot. Please come back home, Masee.

Rani pulls her bottom lip into her mouth before her body slumps. She bends down to give Arman a hug and a kiss before wiping her cheek. She still hasn't said a word. I have no idea what's going through her mind, so I know I have to move to phase two.

With my pulse feeling erratic and out of control, I hold the bouquet up in one hand while I hold Arman's hand in the other. Her stance is back to being stiff, and she turns her head to look anywhere but at me, but not before I see the pain swimming in her eyes. I yearn to reach out and cradle her face like I've done so many times before. I yearn to kiss her and bring her back to me, but I know she won't let me get off the hook that easily.

"Remember when I told you that you were like a vacation I never wanted to come back from, and you told me you didn't want to be that? That you wanted to be the home I always came back to?" She glances at me briefly before going back to looking at something past me. "So, here I am, Rani, standing in front of you and asking you to let me in.

"My house in Tahoe . . ." I shake my head, "it's just a structure. I thought it was my home; I thought it was all Arman and I needed, but it's not. It's empty without you because *you* make it a home. *You* give us a home, and I can't fucking live," I suck in a sharp breath. "I can't fucking *breathe* without you in it."

She studies me. "You hurt me, Darian. You hurt me when you said you didn't know who I was, that you didn't know if you could trust me."

I put the bouquet of flowers on the ground before lifting my son up in my arms. With my other hand, I reach around Rani's neck, pulling her face toward us. "I fucked up, sweetheart. I was so wrapped up in everything that had happened yesterday that I didn't think about every fucking sacrifice you've made for me and Arman. I was just focused on that one specific moment, not seeing the reasons why you did what you did."

Her eyes water and a tear runs down her cheek, dripping

from her jaw. I brush it away with my thumb and she sniffles. "I would never intentionally do anything to hurt you or Arman."

"I know."

"I kept that text from you because I thought I was protecting you. And while my gut disagreed, somewhere inside I hoped I was wrong about Sonia–that perhaps my uncertainty was unfounded and that I was misinterpreting her text."

"I know, baby." I rub her cheek. "After I had a chance to think about it, I realized that I might have done the exact same thing in your position."

She drops her gaze, grimacing.

"I tried so fucking hard to resist you, Rani. I told myself you were too young, that I was too damaged. I told myself it was too soon to feel anything for anyone–let alone my sister-in-law. I told myself that this was all temporary, that you'd leave at the end of the summer so it was better to not let my heart get involved. I told myself all of that."

Her brows pinch and she continues to look at my feet. "I'm waiting for the part where you tell me you were an utter and complete oaf, Darian. When will you get to *that* part?"

This girl . . ..

My lips twitch but I dare not smile. This would *definitely* be the wrong time to smile. "I couldn't resist you. You were a fucking magnet to my soul, sweetheart. No matter how much I tried to wrestle my feelings, every fiber of my being needed you." I lean in, placing a kiss on her lips while Arman grabs a strand of her hair, giggling. "I trust you with my fucking life. I trust you more than I trust myself. I was lost before you came into my life, but you found me. You gave me a home."

Rani gasps against my lips when she notices my unshed tears. "Darian."

I swallow, forcing myself to not blink, to keep the tears

from slipping. "Come back to me, baby. I know I fucked up. I shouldn't have said what I said, and I should have chased after you as soon as you left. But, please, come back to me. Don't leave my son because his dad is a dumbass."

Rani sucks in her bottom lip, trying to hide her smile. "How dare you use my adorable nephew to manipulate my decision."

"I never said I was above it."

Rani smiles, placing a hand over my cheek while holding the lily Arman gave her in the other. "Well, you did call yourself a dumbass. You're an oaf *and* a dumbass."

I rest my forehead on hers. "Agreed. An oaf and a dumbass. But a handsome dumbass, who loves you more than he knows how to put into words."

"A handsome dumbass who's all mine," she whispers.

"Just yours. Always yours." I find her lips again, sucking them in between mine, pulling her to me with my hand at her waist. "I missed you."

She giggles. "Eighteen-hour breakups are the *worst*."

"Worse than eighteen-hour stomach bugs. Let's never do that again," I murmur.

"No. We were foolish. Let's never be foolish again."

I stare at her, taking in her beautiful face and her perfect lips. "Forgive me?"

She hums, pretending to think about it. "Can you think of a good way to earn my forgiveness?"

"I can think of a few good ways . . ." I bring my mouth close to her ear, feeling her shiver in my arms, "but they all involve me being balls-deep inside you."

She leans back, her cheeks slightly flushed. "How about you take me back home and show me? I'll make my final decision after that."

Chapter Forty-One
DARIAN

"Thanks for meeting with me. I know it was last minute." I enter Emily's office, and she ushers me to a chair in front of her desk.

"When I saw your text, I knew we needed to talk." Emily seats herself, her petite frame looking almost childlike inside her oversized office chair.

I haven't spoken to her since Sonia's funeral and on that day, I could barely decipher night from day, so I don't quite recall if Emily and I even spoke more than a few words. I look around at her neatly kept office at the local university where she teaches, the shelves full of physics books.

"You didn't seem surprised when I texted you yesterday to tell you about mine and Ryan's altercation or when I sent you the text Sonia mistakenly sent to her sister." I clear my throat. "Were you . . . were you aware that Ryan and Sonia . . .?"

She nods, understanding the reason I've trailed off. "Was I aware that Ryan and Sonia were having an affair?" She chuckles mirthlessly. "No. Not until after her funeral. I actually found the same text you found on his phone one day, except he'd written back to it." She sighs. "I've had some time to make peace with it, but to be honest, you can never really get over your husband cheating with one of your best friends."

I run a hand over my scruff. "I'm guessing it was the reason you divorced him."

She smiles tightly. "I was distraught over Sonia's death—she was so young and healthy. She had so many dreams of raising Arman. It wrecked me when I found out I'd never see her again. But something about the way Ryan was agonizing over her death—not eating, not sleeping, crying—for weeks set off an alarm bell inside me. I'd never really had a reason to not trust Ryan before. I mean, he was always flirty with women, but I never thought he'd cheat on me."

Emily plays with a pen on her desk. "So, I searched his phone one night and found the text exchanges between them." She shakes her head, her straight brown hair brushing her shoulders. "I couldn't believe it. Apparently, it had been going on for over a year. I couldn't be with him after that." She scrutinizes me over her table. "I didn't want to tell you, Darian. I'm sorry if you thought it was wrong of me not to, but you'd just lost Sonia and had a newborn you were taking care of. I just . . . I didn't have the heart to tell you."

My jaw tightens. "Do you mind me asking what their texts said? I'm just trying to put the pieces together, and I never found anything more on Sonia's phone when I tried going into it recently."

"Ryan told Sonia he didn't want to tell me yet. I was mourning the loss of my father, and Ryan replied to that text from Sonia saying he needed more time and that he would appreciate it if she held off until after the baby was born. She wrote him back, saying she'd give him until Arman was born and that at that time, they'd tell us together. Apparently, they were in love."

The pit in my stomach deepens, and I take in a couple of deep breaths to keep myself from feeling nauseous again. How could I have been oblivious to all of this? How could I not have known my wife was having an affair . . . and sleeping with me as well? How fucking clueless was I?

"Darian, I'm so sorry." Emily regards me warmly. "I'm sorry you had to find out that way and for what it's worth, I'm glad you punched him. I wish I'd done it myself."

I sit back on the chair and pinch the bridge of my nose. "I guess I don't understand what he gets out of it now. I'm Arman's legal guardian. I signed his birth certificate, I'm the one he's been staying with. I did a lot of research over the past couple of days and even called up a friend of my dad's who's in family law. Even if Ryan was Arman's biological father, he would have to petition in court to try to get custody, but the chances of him winning are low."

"Ryan never wanted kids, Darian. Believe me, I know because it was something we argued over. He never wanted to be a dad because he felt like he'd be a lot like his own dad, who was never there. I frankly think he didn't want the responsibility of having children, either." She scoots up, placing her elbows on the table. "I don't think you have to worry about him petitioning for custody."

"So then why tell me? What did he get out of that?"

"After I left Ryan, I think he fell into depression. He'd lost his wife and the woman he was apparently set to run off with–"

"If they were going to run off, they would have taken Arman. Whether he wanted children or not, he had to have known that he would be in Arman's life if he wanted to be with Sonia. Sonia loved Arman since the day we found out she was pregnant. There was no way she would have given him up to be with Ryan."

Emily shrugs. "Perhaps he'd made peace with that. He

didn't care as long as he had Sonia. But after she died, he didn't have anyone. And I think when he saw you again, that bothered him. Maybe it annoyed him that you were once again finding happiness but he wasn't."

"So he decided to explode my life up in my face?"

"I'm not defending him. Ryan is a complete asshole, and I haven't spoken to him since our divorce was finalized, but people do crazy things when they're in pain, Darian. They act irrationally out of jealousy, and they think that you're the cause of their unhappiness when you're not."

I press my fingers together over my lap. "I still can't believe she did something like this." I look at Emily. "I still can't believe it."

"I was shocked when I found out, too. I honestly never saw any signs of a relationship between them."

We're quiet for a moment when Emily licks her lips, seemingly contemplating something.

"What?" I ask, urging her.

She takes a breath. "I wasn't going to tell you more because I don't believe it will help you now that Sonia is gone—she'd sworn me to secrecy when she was alive—but Sonia had been unhappy for a long time." Emily closes her eyes for a moment before continuing, "She complained that you were obsessed with your school and that the two of you no longer had similar interests."

Her words hurl me into my memories of having the same arguments with Sonia over and over again. When we first met, we loved to do the same things—skiing, kayaking, hiking, basically anything outdoorsy. But as time passed, Sonia became bored of those activities—she preferred to stay indoors and watch mindless television. In an effort to spend time with her, I'd watch her shows with her but even that wasn't enough.

We'd grown apart, and we didn't know how to grow together anymore.

"She'd considered leaving you several times but didn't know what to do with her life if she actually did. She was so reliant on you. She had no connection with her family, her career was tied to your company, and she'd basically only had one serious relationship—with you. So, every time she'd think about leaving, she'd convince herself to stay for a little longer." Emily clicks the pen in her hand a couple of times. "Looking back, I saw the signs of her depression, but I didn't know how to help."

"We tried marriage counseling, therapy . . .. I'd come home earlier from work to spend time with her. I even tried to get her help for her depression, but she refused to believe she had anything to worry about."

"Oh, Darian, I know you did whatever you could. I don't think her mental state or misery was your fault. I think one has to do a lot of soul searching to find the root of unhappiness before he or she can get on the path to happiness. But if you constantly expect happiness to be provided to you by someone else, you'll be sorely disappointed because your definitions of happiness may be vastly different."

I nod as my thoughts take me to my bottle of sunshine—the woman who gave away free smiles and kept a pocket full of fairy dust with her at all times. She was so different from her sister, forging her own path to happiness and living for her todays.

Even with the way I'd treated her, even after hearing my insensitive words, she didn't lose herself to her anger. She gave me an earful back—hell, she left me for a day—but she also let me speak. She heard me. She saw me. She gave me a home. A home I didn't deserve, but a home I'd cherish for the rest of my days.

I get up from my seat, taking my leave from Emily.

"So, did Ryan end up pressing charges?" she asks when I'm almost at the door.

"Not yet, but it wouldn't surprise me if he does."

She taps her lip with her index finger and her green eyes seem to twinkle. "He's been begging me to talk to him just once. I don't know that we'll ever make amends, but perhaps I can make a deal with him . . .." She smiles. "I'll give him one conversation if he refrains from pressing charges."

I exhale a short breath. "You'd do that for me?"

She shrugs. "What are friends for?"

∾

Rani snuggles into the crook of my arm, pulling the sheets up over her bare chest. "You're frowning."

"I like to see your beautiful body, especially when you're in my bed."

She smiles. "You've seen my body plenty tonight."

I stare at her face—the way her lips move when she speaks, the way her lashes almost reach her brow line when her eyes are open, the way her nose wrinkles when she laughs. I can't stop staring because she's the only one worth looking at. "I'll never get enough of you, my Rani."

She tilts her face to kiss my jaw while her hand scratches the other side of my face. She loves rubbing my scruff with the tips of her fingers and I love her touch. "Arman was fussy tonight. I think he's teething."

I tangle my fingers in her hair. "Yeah, or just growing pains."

She's lost in thought, probably thinking about my son and what she can do to make him more comfortable.

My thoughts haven't stopped spinning since the minute that bastard brought up my son using his filthy mouth.

Rani lifts off of me on her elbow, eyeing me curiously. "What's wrong?"

I should have known she'd figure out I was in my head. I give her a quick shake of my head, staying quiet and trying to gather my thoughts.

"Are you thinking about what Ryan said again?"

I wrap a curl around my finger like I love to do. "How did you know?"

"Because your jaw was clenching and your body was all stiff. I knew something was bothering you. Plus, I'm smart." She smirks.

"That you are." I clear my throat. "I'm going to take the paternity test."

She searches my eyes. "Are you ready to?"

"I'll never be ready to, but it doesn't matter to me. Arman's mine. He'll always be mine."

She nods and her chin wobbles. "He'll always be yours. There's no one he loves more."

"The family lawyer I talked to recommended I know for sure just to get ahead of anything in case Ryan does change his mind." My throat feels dry. "I'm just . . .."

"Nervous?"

I look at her. "Does that make sense? He's mine, no matter what, but I'm terrified the DNA test will come back negative. It's this weird contradiction."

Rani runs her hand through my hair. She seems to love my curls as much as I love hers. "It's completely understandable. I'm scared, too. I just want him to be yours biologically."

"Me, too," I whisper. "I just want to move past this nightmare."

"I'll be right by your side through the whole thing." Her lips tip up.

"How did I get so lucky?" I murmur.

"Hmm." She purses her lips. "By saving a girl from a kayak gone astray."

I squint at her. "Hey, wasn't I supposed to get you back on a kayak again?"

Rani quickly turns off the lamp on her side of the bed, yawning dramatically before falling into her pillow with her eyes shut. "Boy, I'm super tired. Sweet dreams, Darian."

I roll my eyes, smiling in the dark.

"I can hear you rolling your eyes at me."

Chapter Forty-Two
RANI

Everyday I learn something new about the beautiful man I'm now sharing a home with. For example, I recently learned that his favorite season is winter because his favorite sport is cross-country skiing. I've also learned that he's broken at least six different bones in his body—a couple more than once—he sneezes every time he eats something minty, and he and I have birthdays one day apart.

The last fact was the reason I found myself back on a kayak yesterday. It was his answer to my question when I asked him what he wanted for his birthday. *A day with you, a part of it on a kayak and the rest with you naked in my bed.*

I had to relent but I suppose he's never played fair.

It's been three weeks since I moved into Darian's house—having finished up my summer photojournalism project, transferred my credits to the nearby university, and moved the rest of my living essentials here. We haven't spent more than the absolute minimum number of minutes apart, mostly when he's at work or I'm in class.

Thankfully, we also found a really incredible caretaker for Arman. She's a middle-aged lady who stays at home with him throughout the day. She even takes him to the baby gym sometimes and has become someone Arman feels really comfortable with.

I peel my eyes open at the sound of squeaky baby babbling. Arman's warm smile greets me along with the sunshine on my bed–mine and Darian's bed. "*Mas!*"

I sit up after adjusting my tank top underneath the bed sheet. "Hey, sweet boy! What are you doing here? Where's your daddy?"

I pull him into my lap, showering him with kisses when I smell the unmistakable aroma of syrup and eggs.

Darian comes into the room moments later, holding a tray but it's not the breakfast he's carrying that makes my mouth water. He's wearing low-slung pajama pants without a shirt. His biceps flex as he moves closer and when he bends over me to place the tray over my lap, my eyes lock onto his absurdly muscular abdomen.

I lick my lips as my gaze trails up his body, caressing the soft hair on his chest, moving up to his shoulders, and past the smooth skin around his thick neck. I want to latch my lips on the side of his neck like a sucker fish or a vampire and mark him as mine. He's so unearthly beautiful, he makes me feel like a savage.

His knowing smile finds me when I finally make my way to it. "Happy birthday."

Darian leans over to kiss my lips, and I pull him in to make it deeper. Our eyes lock when I pull back from him but we continue to breathe each other in. I've spent every night in his bed–save for the weekend I left to get my stuff from my parents' home in the East Bay–but every morning feels like a wrapped gift I yearn to wake up to. Like Christmas morning . . . or in this case, my birthday.

He's been sleeping a lot better as well–definitely an improvement from the constant nightmares that used to keep him awake—ever since he started therapy. It's only been a couple of weeks, but I'm hopeful that with time, he's going to be able to manage his PTSD even better.

His smiles, his smoldering eyes, his whispers along my heated skin—they're the gifts I cherish, the secrets I'll never part with because they're mine and mine alone. Everyday I learn something new about this man, and every day I fall deeper, climb higher.

I look down at the tray over my lap, noticing two plates—one for me and a smaller one for Arman—with waffles, eggs, bacon, and fruit. Along with my favorite cup of coffee that Darian has perfected, there's also a small vase with what's now my favorite flower—a burgundy lily. "Thank you."

Five minutes later, we're sitting side-by-side, with Arman in the middle, splitting our attention between our respective breakfasts and the movie Darian put on the TV, *Mary Poppins*.

I can't think of a better way to spend my birthday.

We're half-way into the movie when Darian's phone pings with a message. His frown follows subsequently.

"What's wrong?" I ask, mid-chew, watching his jaw tighten.

He worries his bottom lip.

"Dar, tell me," I repeat, my concern climbing.

"The test results."

I swallow down the last bite of my waffle. "Oh."

After deliberating with his nerves for another few days, Darian went to take the paternity test last week. He hasn't mentioned much about it since then, but I know he's distressed about it. I have absolutely no doubt that even if Arman is not his, Darian will remain the same loving father to him no matter what, but for the sake of his already battered heart, I pray that the results are in Darian's favor.

We discussed the news of Sonia's betrayal with mine and Darian's parents a couple of weeks ago. Both our moms were in tears–my mother even apologized to Darian on behalf of Sonia, looking ashamed–but it was the less than surprised look on Karine's face that caught my attention. She never said as much–I'm sure out of respect for me–but I felt that her shock was subdued.

We received a written statement from Ryan last week saying he wanted nothing to do with Arman, whether he was his biological father or not. And whatever magic his ex wife Emily did, Ryan never ended up pressing charges on Darian, either.

After all the damage he's caused, it was the smallest kindness he could have shown us.

"What does it say?" My pulse pounds inside my veins.

Darian grips his phone tighter. "I haven't opened the link in the email. I . . . I can't."

I scoot Arman up on the bed and move in next to Darian, our shoulders touching. Placing a hand on his thigh, I look at his profile. "Do you want me to open it?"

He gives me a slight nod and even though there's a musical score playing on the TV, I can hear Darian's heart pounding in the air between us.

I pull his phone from his grasp before putting it on the bed and straddling his lap. I cradle his jaw in my hands, bringing his eyes to mine. "I'm right here, right by your side." I look over at the little boy near us, completely engrossed in the movie and chewing his fingers. "Your son," I emphasize it again, "*your son* is right here by your side. Nothing changes, sweetheart. Nothing."

Darian takes a shaky breath, swaying his head up and down. "Nothing changes."

I lay a kiss on his lips and he tightens his grip around my hips. "You ready?"

Another nod.

Staying on his lap, I bring the phone to me and click on

the link in the email that's already open on his phone screen. My heart pounds in my chest, mimicking the scared feet of wildebeest in a stampede as I read the results.

"Probability of paternity . . . ninety-nine point nine-nine-nine-eight percent," I mumble. My breath catches in my throat as I look up at Darian's unreadable expression. "Darian! Ninety-nine point nine-nine-nine-eight!"

My body feels like I'm floating as chills run down my arms and legs, my eyes pricking at the corners. Darian is motionless under me, almost like he's forgotten how to breathe. "Darian!"

As if he's been hauled out of a dream—or a nightmare—Darian finally takes a breath, his mouth falling open. "I'm . . ." He clears his throat but not before his eyes cloud with tears and his chin quivers. "I'm his biological father?"

"Yes!" I toss the phone to the side, throwing my arms around his neck. "Yes, baby, you're his father!"

Darian holds me, his face tucked into my neck as a sob escapes from his throat. His body shakes in my arms as he finally allows himself to let go. Weeks and months of sadness and confusion. Months of asking, "Why us? Why me?" that turned into weeks of more bitter questions like, "How could she?" He releases them all just like he releases each tear on my shoulder.

"He's mine," he whispers resolutely, finally. "He's mine."

I pull away from him, finding his red-rimmed eyes. "He's yours."

I wrap my arm around Arman's tummy, pulling him to us and both Darian and I kiss him incessantly, making him giggle. When he squirms out of our hold to get back to the song Mary Poppins is singing, Darian brings my attention back to him with a squeeze on my waist.

"You're mine, too."

I sigh, pressing my lips to his. "I'm yours, always."

∼

Cappuccino eyes study my every expression, moving from the way my bottom lip is pulled under my teeth to the way my cheeks pick up a tinge of color. He moderates his every thrust, plunging into me almost sluggishly. Between the way his eyes smolder and the way his erection sheaths itself inside my heat, he creates a concoction of the most powerful aphrodisiac inside me. *Him*.

I widen my legs, letting him find purchase deep within my body, feeling the throb inside my core magnify. It thrums against the walls of my sex, creating a headier, more potent wetness. We're slick from head to toe as he slides inside me after pulling almost completely out.

A groan leaves his chest but his gaze never falters. "I love you, my Rani."

I lick my lips, arching up to meet his onslaught as my thighs start to shake. An electric charge builds under my spine, buzzing unbearably in my center. "I love you."

He swivels his hand down my stomach, rolling the pad of his finger around my clit. "You're stunning. Made for me." His thunderous plunges have my eyes rolling back in my head. "I want all of you. I need all of you—"

"You have all of me," I pant.

He continues his ministrations over my clit with his thumb, never letting up his blitz inside me before taking my nipple into his mouth. He sucks hard. So hard, I buck under him in the best of ways, mewling.

"I love all of you." He finishes his previous thought in a mumble around me. "Fucking delicious from head to toe."

My toes curl as his words sprinkle over me like ethereal morning mist. "Darian!"

He increases his pace. "I need you to come, baby. I need you with me. Come with me."

His girth impales me over and over before he groans one last time. I feel his ejaculation inside me, thick and warm, hurling me into my own ecstasy. I shatter with a scream, squeezing every last drop of him into me. "God, yes! Yes!"

Darian slows his thrusts but doesn't break our connection until he's sure I've stopped pulsing around him.

Pulling out of me, he lays down next to me. We're both trying to fill our lungs with oxygen. "Well, it's a good thing Arman's with my mom. Pretty sure you woke the neighbors."

I laugh and pant at the same time, holding a hand over my chest. My heart thumps against my palm. "Yes, it is. God, you're good at that."

He pulls me closer so we're face to face, lying on our side. "Feel free to say that as much as you want."

I giggle. "I'll think about it. Can't stroke your ego too much."

His lips twitch. "You could stroke something else though . . .."

I huff. "Pretty sure that's how I got into this position today."

We're staring at each other in a comfortable silence, his hand over my cheek when I remember something I've been meaning to ask him for a while. It slips my mind even though he gifts me a new bouquet every Friday. "You told me one time that each color of lilies has a meaning."

He nods, his lip lifting on each corner ever so slightly.

"What do they all mean?"

He holds my gaze. "The white ones mean purity, but they also mean the start of something new."

"You had those sitting in my room the first day I came to live with you. I thought they were there from when your mom used to stay over once in a while."

"They were always for you."

The warmth I always feel inside his arms spreads throughout my chest. "And the pink ones?"

He tucks a strand of my wayward curl behind my ear. "It means admiration, but it also can be used to say, 'I'm sorry I was an ass.'"

I chortle. "That you were." Burrowing myself further into his arms, I recall the next color. "What about the orange ones?"

"Passion, devotion." He looks like he travels somewhere in his thoughts for a moment. "It wasn't just the way I was starting to feel about you, it was also the representation of . . . *you*. The way you loved Arman, the way you sang to him and cared for him. I was enamored with you, the passion you showed for everything from your blog to the way you tackled new challenges . . . including me. You broke my walls before I even knew there was a breach."

My eyes shine with unshed tears and I'm left speechless.

"And while the orange lilies expressed *your* passion and *your* devotion, the burgundy ones express mine. They represent my devotion to you. You unarm me, Rani. You make me powerless, and I can do nothing but concede my heart to you. And you own it so completely, I really can't call it my own any longer. It beats only for you."

I pull in a breath, releasing it with a whisper, "Darian."

"It'll always beat only for you."

EPILOGUE

Rani – Three Years Later

"Rani," she takes a short breath, saying my name on the inhale, "you look absolutely beautiful. Perfect."

I look down at my white bridal *lehenga* with the burgundy trims, the maroon henna on my palms holding the tightly packed stems of my burgundy lilies, and the long gold necklace and clinky bangles Mom gave me this morning to adorn my outfit.

Perfect.

It's a word I've never really cared for; one I stopped worrying about—or tried my best to—when I realized it was just an illusion, a forever-moving target.

But today, on the most important day in my life, I don't mind it from the mouth of the woman who's used it in her life almost as sparingly as she uses saffron in her rice dish because in her words, "No one is worth spending that kind of money on."

Despite the two decades my mother and I spent disliking each other's company, I can't deny the work she's put in over the last three years since Dad's heart attack. But because I'm a firm adversary of the word *perfect*, I have to remind myself that I can't expect from her what I don't require from myself. She's working on herself, taking feedback and trying to be there for me *now*. And right now, that's enough.

"Thanks, Mom."

I thought I'd be a nervous wreck today. It always seemed to me like brides were required to be so worried–about the weather or the food, about the photographer or the guests, or just plain and simple worried. But worry is the last emotion I feel on the ever-growing list of emotions I'm feeling today.

I'm marrying the man of my dreams. Someone I've come to call my best friend and confidant. I'm not only marrying him, but I'm promising my love and devotion to his son, my nephew. So while my mind feels calm, prepared for this next stage in my life and unconcerned with the various things that could go wrong on this day, my heart pounds at the prospect of seeing my two favorite boys in the next few minutes.

They're the todays I want to live. They're the tomorrows I know I'll cherish.

Dad squeezes my bicep, and I look up at his lean frame. His watery smile pierces my resolve and I feel the prick of tears against the corners of my eyes. He's silent, but his quiet encouragement and tenderness speaks volumes for the love I know he's always had for me–for both of his daughters.

Mom shifts on my other side and when I look at her, she also gives me a smile. She's wearing one of her expensive silk *saris* and her diamond earrings, appearing more like the mother I'd always yearned for–proud . . . satisfied.

With affection gushing from her gaze, she pulls my hand to her mouth and places a quick kiss on the back. Her chin wobbles before she presses her lips together to control her emotions. "I haven't been the mother you deserved, but you've always been a daughter only the luckiest few receive. I've made a million mistakes, Rani, and I'm sorry for all the

EPILOGUE

past hurt I've caused you, but I promise to never be the cause of any more in the future."

I pull my mother into my arms, placing a kiss on her forehead and feeling my heart lift even further. "I forgive you, Mom."

The doors open and she wipes the corners of her eyes. I know she wants to say more but with time running short and us wanting to stay on schedule, she leaves it with, "Now, let's go. My daughter is getting married, and I don't want to be late!"

The music starts as the breeze catches my long gown, lifting it slightly behind me. We chose the instrumental version of a song that was significant in forging our happy little family–*Stay Awake*–and even just hearing it stream through the sound system with the rustling sound of the calm river behind us, my emotions are threatening to engulf me completely.

My eyes lock on to the man I've been waiting to see all morning as I walk down the aisle and the world fades away. I don't hear the not-so-whispered chatter from my friend Fred sitting next to Lynn on the bridal side of the aisle. I don't see the sheer burgundy drapes tied to the corner pillars of our make-shift altar or the lily petals spread over the aisle. I don't even recognize the familiar faces of my beautiful best friend and cousin, who are both crying happy tears as they wait in their spots to be my bridesmaids and my lifelong support systems.

All I see is him.

I'd never thought I'd hunger for someone's love and affection. I never thought I'd crave someone's desire. But then I tasted his and I knew I'd become an addict.

Darian's coffee-colored gaze sweeps down the length of me before coming back to rest on my eyes. His lips that usually lay in an unmoving line on his face are turned up in a smile that's dedicated only to me, his eyes blazing as I approach closer.

It was almost exactly a year ago today that Darian surprised me with a graduation gift during dinner–one that my nephew opened the box to reveal and Darian slipped onto my left hand ring finger–and I haven't stopped smiling since.

I know he can see the adoration in my eyes as I scan him from head to toe, fitted in a suit that clings to his broad shoulders and muscular frame, his burgundy tie matching the highlights in every corner today. His hair is slightly gelled back and the curls I love so much rest over the collar at his neck, beckoning me to tangle my fingers inside them.

I slip my hand into his awaiting warm palm as he helps me over the steps. Pulling me into him, he lays a kiss on my lips, making the audience swoon. My eyes close on their own accord as Darian's lips pull mine further into him, gifting me with not just his love but his total devotion. His hands cradle my neck, his thumbs caressing my jaw, as his tongue makes a quick sweep over my lips. I find his tongue with mine when his kiss turns into a smile against my lips. Our guests cheer– the loudest of them being my two brother-in-laws and Darian's groomsmen, Garrett and Dean–before the officiant clears his throat.

Darian and I finally pull back from each other, and my heart skips a beat at the way he continues to look at me like I'm the most precious thing he's ever seen.

Garrett leans over to say something in Darian's ear, but I don't catch any of it. What I do catch is Garrett's eyes trailing past my shoulder to someone behind me as he moves back into his spot behind Darian.

It doesn't take me more than a second to realize he's looking at one of my bridesmaids. Specifically, the bridesmaid who also happens to be my cousin.

If the past two years haven't been a testament to the

EPILOGUE

strength and courage my cousin exudes, I don't know what has. Between raising her two-year-old daughter almost entirely on her own and working a full-time job, Bella has been nothing short of an inspiration. She's a living example of what it means to pick yourself up, dust yourself off, and rise again after a serious fall. But that tumble over the past two years didn't come without leaving some scars.

Gone is the girl who trusted easily and smiled definitively. Gone is the girl who cared about what others thought or how they perceived her. In her place is a more determined, albeit more guarded, woman who no longer believes in happily ever afters—at least, not when it comes to her own story.

So while she's been nothing but polite to my brother-in-law every time she's run into him, she's quick to dismiss his advances. Her argument is always the same. *"I refuse to watch another sunset with someone, not knowing if they'll be there for the sunrise. Because it's within the daylight that I need them the most, not when the lights are all turned off."*

My eyes wander back to the man I love more than any sunrise or sunset. The man who might think I'm his sunshine but who is nothing less than the sun himself.

We wanted a quick ceremony, but because my parents requested seeing some parts of the Hindu ceremony incorporated, both Darian and I agreed to extend it a little bit. So, after a small prayer and the seven rounds around a holy flame—each round symbolizing a vow taken by the both of us to love, cherish, protect, and honor one another—Darian turns toward the audience, finding the other most precious love of our lives, sitting on the first corner seat, patiently waiting for his turn.

Darian lifts his hand toward my four-year-old nephew, who walks over to stand next to his father, holding his hand. He's wearing a matching suit and tie, with his jet-black hair slicked back. I'd gotten him ready earlier this morning before my own hair and makeup started because my little guy refused to get ready with anyone else.

With the bouquet between us, I bend down at eye level. "Are you ready to marry your dad off to me, little man?"

Arman bobs his head enthusiastically, his eyes gleaming at the prospect. "You look so beautiful, *Masee*."

My nose tickles as tears spring to my eyes again. "And you look so handsome, my sweetheart. Will you and your dad put the wedding band on me together?"

After another excited nod, he peers up at Darian, who smiles at our exchange before taking the box from his pocket. Arman opens the box and allows Darian to pull out the band.

Before Darian puts the ring on my finger, he looks at his son and winks. "What do you say, little man? Are you ready to capture our sunshine inside this golden band?"

I'm not sure that Arman understands what Darian means, but he seems to know that the answer should be yes, because he nods again. "Yes, Daddy! Let's do it! Let's capture her!"

With that, both my men scoot the band over my finger, capturing not only my heart and soul, but all my smiles forever.

BONUS EPILOGUE

Darian - One Year Post Wedding

Mom: The cake is very cute. He'll love it. <cake emoji, heart emoji>

Me: Thanks for picking it up for us, Mom.

Rani: Yes, thank you so much, Karine. I can't wait until Arman sees it.

Mom: <changed the group name to 'Call For A Good Time'>

Mom: Heading to your place now. Are the guests already arriving?

Rani: The lovebirds, Liam and Melody, are going to be here any minute. With her being eight months pregnant, she's moving a little slower. Bella and her daughter Meera came in last night, and Garrett just got here.

Me: @Mom, why did you change the group name to that? It sounds inappropriate.

Mom: Those two are WTF. How long will they circle around each other?

Mom: Oh, I didn't know you could see the group name, too.

Me: WTF? Mom, I don't think you're using that correctly.

Mom: Of course, I am. I use it all the time.

Me: What does it mean?

Mom: Way Too Funny.

Me: Yup, let's go with your version.

∿

"Happy fifth birthday, buddy!" My brother Dean ruffles Arman's dark hair as he enters the house before handing him a gift bag.

"Thanks, Uncle Dean!" Arman immediately discards the wrapping paper inside before pulling out what looks like a red and black fireman costume with suspenders and a black helmet. "This is awesome!"

Rani approaches us, and I track her like I always do. No matter where she is, my eyes only feel truly content when they're on her. She gives my brother a hug before addressing

Arman. "Little man, I know it's your birthday, but I'm going to need you to pick up the mess on the floor. We're almost ready for cake."

Arman does as he's asked, skipping toward the living room to build a Lego fort with three-year-old Meera and his uncle Garrett.

Dean peeks at the sleeping bundle in my arm. "And how is this little nugget?"

I yawn. "She's fine. It's her mom and me who aren't sleeping all night."

Avya Karine Meyer was born almost exactly a month ago—a year after Rani and I got married—weighing in at a whopping nine-pounds, two ounces. I won't deny that I wasn't nervous after the last time I was in the delivery room, but my wife persevered like a champ.

While we planned to wait on having a baby, a couple of months into our marriage, Rani found out she was pregnant. Thankfully, since she owns her own content writing business and works from home, she was able to set her own hours.

Just months after graduating, Rani created an incredible consulting business managing digital marketing for several companies—including *Truckee Sports*. This year, she was even able to hire another person to help her since she was getting so much business that she was having to turn away prospective clients.

It's another quality I'm absolutely crazy about when it comes to my wife—her work ethic and dedication to whatever she does. She dives in and puts her all into every challenge.

Dean rubs a thumb over the back of Avya's tiny hand. "She's worth it, though." He peers into the living room and both Rani and I follow his gaze. "How are things with the lesser good-looking twin and Bella now? Any progress?"

Rani huffs out a breath. "Nope. My cousin is just as

adamant today. She truly just doesn't trust that any man would want to share more than a few days with her. She likes Garrett, I know she does, but she clams up around him."

"I've never seen him work so hard to get a woman's attention. I mean, Darian here wouldn't know what it's like to be born with such stellar looks, and even Garrett is lacking some, but it's a blessing and curse, I tell ya."

I roll my eyes. "And on that note, I think we need to get on with cutting the cake."

Arman smiles from ear to ear as everyone sings for him before he blows out the candles.

"Did you make a wish, buddy?" Rani asks him, squeezing his shoulder gently. She bends down to place a kiss on his cheek.

"I wished for the same thing from last year," Arman responds, regarding the blown out candles sheepishly.

"Yeah? Can you share it?" Rani's eyebrows waggle, making some of our guests chuckle listening to their exchange.

"I'm not supposed to share it, but since it came true last year—even after I told Uncle Dean about it—I think I can tell you."

Rani regards my brother, who leans back on his heels, giving us both a sheepish smile. "What was it?"

"I asked for a baby sister . . . and I got her." Arman faces me, admiring Avya inside my arms. "Can we feed her some cake, Daddy?"

Rani covers Arman's face with kisses. If there's one person who owns her heart completely, it's my son. He can do nothing wrong in her eyes.

"Unfortunately, not yet, son," I answer. "Give your sister a little bit of time to grow up before you can share a cake with her."

He seems content with my answer as Rani helps him cut his cake.

"Wait a minute, little man," Rani says with a look of fear as realization dawns on her. "Did you say you wished for the same thing . . .? As in, you want another sister?"

Arman bobs his head. "I want four!"

Both Rani and I reel back. *"Four!"*

After passing out pieces of Arman's birthday cake to our parents, my brothers, her cousin, her best friend Melody and–I still cringe at the acknowledgement–Melody's fiancé, Liam, Rani comes to stand next to me, putting her nose on our baby girl's soft head.

"Let's never get him candles to blow out again," I murmur.

Rani nods with a grave look on her face. "No more candles. He can make wishes when I'm no longer fertile."

I lean down to press a kiss on her lips. Everyone seems to be wrapped up in their own conversations, eating cake, or hugging my son.

I find her ear. "I love when you say *fertile*. It does things to me."

She gives me a look of mock incredulity. "You're a heathen, you know that? I only popped out this monster-sized baby of yours a month ago. My vagina will never be the same."

My eyes smolder. "You're not helping your case when you say *vagina*."

Rani bats my arm playfully. "Based on the fact that your son just made another wish for one more of these little things, I'm pretty sure you're going to be staying away from my vagina for a while, Mr. Meyer."

I laugh, tilting my head back. The woman is a real comedian. "Nothing on this earth has the power to keep me away from your sweet pus–"

The baby wails in my arms, effectively cutting me off. I

bounce and shush her when Rani leans over. "Seems like your daughter disagrees."

The End

Your reviews matter! Please consider taking a few minutes to write a review for Adrift on Amazon.

ABOUT THE AUTHOR

Swati M.H. prefers to call herself a storyteller rather than an author. She lives in the Bay Area with her incredibly patient husband, two beautiful daughters, and her pitbull, Sadie Sapphire. Her days start with caffeine and sometimes end with a glass (or three) of wine.

Swati's goal as a storyteller is to distract her readers from their daily grind with stories about everyday couples finding and fighting for incredible love with the help of a little luck.

Swati loves staying in touch with her readers. Find her at www.swatimh.com or through Facebook and Instagram. Be sure to join her Sweeties reader group for daily fun.

ACKNOWLEDGMENTS

If you've gotten this far then I'd like to first and foremost thank YOU. Thank you for reading my words and for allowing me to show you a little piece of my heart. You've not only made publishing Adrift worth it but you've also encouraged me to continue writing.

There are countless people I want to thank for supporting me through the journey of publishing my sixth book but I'd like to start by thanking the guy who owns my heart—my husband. I'm truly the luckiest girl on the planet to have married my own book boyfriend and there is no way I could be doing what I do now—my dream job as a romance author—without his love, support, and constant encouragement.

A huge thank you to my parents and my in-laws for being such cheerleaders for me. They may not read my books (and I'd like to keep it that way ;-)) but I love being able to talk about the plot and premise with them.

For an author, the team of people who help bring a book to market are just as important as the story inside the book and there is no way I could have done it without the best editor on earth. I barely feel confident writing a grocery list without her help :) So, thank you Silvia Curry for not only being my editor but for being a friend and someone I can talk to about so much more than just books.

Stephanie Rash—thank you from the bottom of my heart for the support and encouragement you always provide me. You are not only my PA but also someone I can rely on in a pinch. Thank you also for the constant laughs, straight-talk, and the strange TikTok video forwards that have made me question my own sanity. You have no idea how much your daily dose of humor and fun is appreciated.

A huge thank you to my Alpha Reader team. Your enthusiasm after I've written only a chapter (sometimes only a few words) is the reason I even finish a book!:

- Rachel Childers—boy, I really hit the jackpot when you decided to take a chance on this newbie writer almost 2 years ago! Since day 1, you've been in my corner and I can't thank you enough for that. Thank you also for being such a valuable member of my alpha team, for listening to my ramblings, and for always steering me in the right direction. I truly appreciate your insights and opinions.

- Rachael Poxon—oh my goodness, I can wholeheartedly say I struck gold when you agreed to be a part of my team! And now that I have you, you can be sure I'm not letting you go! Thank you so much for your perspective and thoughts. They were invaluable to me through the writing process. Thank you also for listening to my long voice memos and for responding with such smart advice. I am so glad to have found you!

- Amy Crull—It's rare to find people you can count on without having met them in person. It's even rarer to be able to call them friends. You're both. Thank you so much for being such an avid cheerleader of my work—telling anyone and everyone about my cinnamon roll heroes—and for being so easy to talk to. Your enthusiasm and kind words have brightened up so many of my days and I am grateful for having you on my team.

- Melissa Schmidt—I have yet to begin writing a new book without your thoughts. Most of the time that entails a phone/FaceTime conversation but I think it's just my excuse to chitchat. Thank you so much for your honesty, opinion, and encouragement but also, thank you for checking in on me and for being such a wonderful friend. I appreciate you.

My beta readers—Marla Knobb, Jerrica Martin, and Anita Arora. Thank you all for making me feel confident enough to release another book into the wild. Your opinion and support mean so much to me and I appreciate you taking the time to read the book and provide me with your insights. Above all, thank you for making me giggle and squeal while I read your comments in the document. They always bring a huge smile to my face.

A special thanks to my author friends Jenni Bara, Brittanee Nicole, and Garry Michael for giving me such good feedback during the writing process. You are all incredible authors and I feel grateful to call you friends. Jenni—thank you so much for beta-reading and talking to me about some of my concerns. Your insights were crucial to getting Darian's story right. For all those readers who haven't picked up books by these talented authors, you're missing out! Run to their Amazon profiles and read their books today!

Another special thanks to Melanie Harlow. Your insights and feedback on everything I've ever needed have been beyond anything I could ever expect. You're not only an incredible author but an inspiration to the indie author community.

Ara Abrahamian—A huge thank you to you and your family for being my sensitivity readers and making sure my representation of Darian and his background were correct. I so appreciate your feedback and patience. Thank you also for helping me expand my own knowledge about the Armenian culture and I hope I have done it justice with this book.

To the members in Swati's Street Team—THANK YOU! Thank you so much for all that you do for me by promoting my work. You do it with so much heart and enthusiasm and I can't thank you enough for that.

Lastly, thank you to each and every reader. I hope you enjoyed Darian and Rani's story. It was my foray into the world of the forbidden and I'm extremely proud of it. I pride myself in writing strong and successful female MCs and while Rani is at just the beginning of her life in this book, she has all the grit and wisdom for becoming a full on badass one day. I've hopefully shown a glimpse of her badassery in the bonus epilogue that you can get through the links at the end of the book. And Darian—oh my wonderful, sweet, charming, dirty-talking, Darian. How he captured my heart through the writing of this book and now he refuses to give it back. I hope he captured yours too.

Printed by Amazon Italia Logistica S.r.l.
Torrazza Piemonte (TO), Italy